A Resurgence

of Hope

Book 2 of:
The World She Silenced

Daniel Whitman

To Wells, my timely and insightful editor, for helping shape the magic.

To Brooke, for helping bring the flowers to life.

And to everyone else, for pushing me to continue the adventure.

The World She Silenced

A Land in Shadow
A Resurgence of Hope

Contents

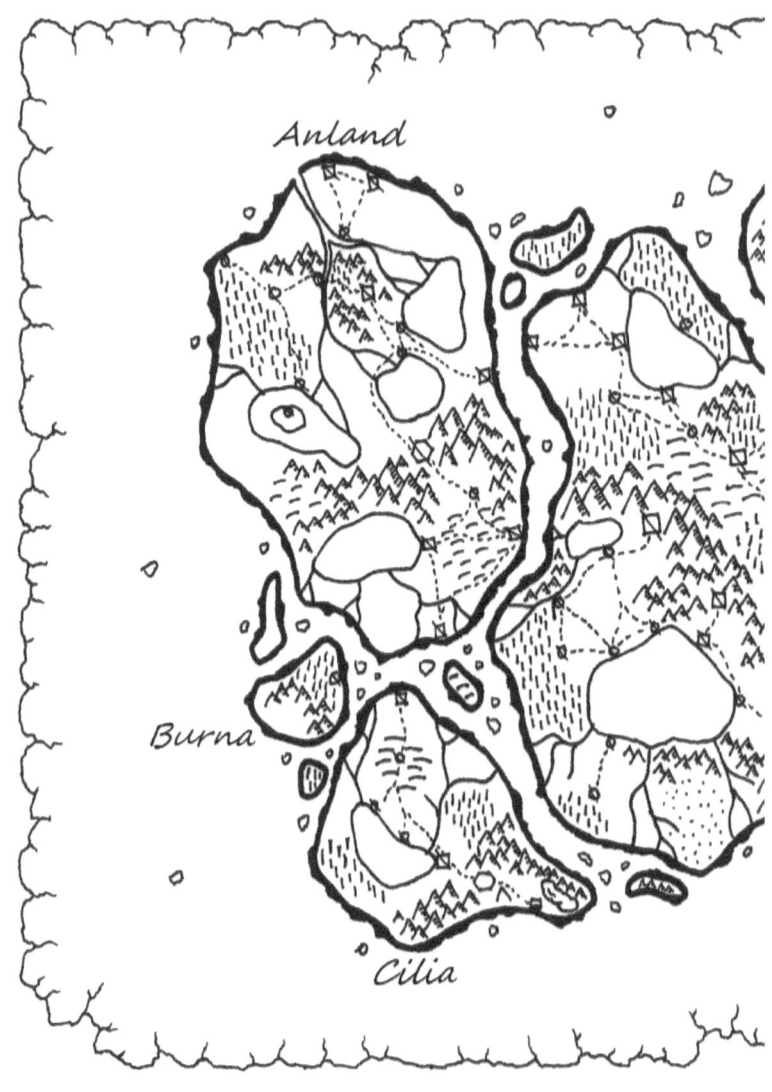

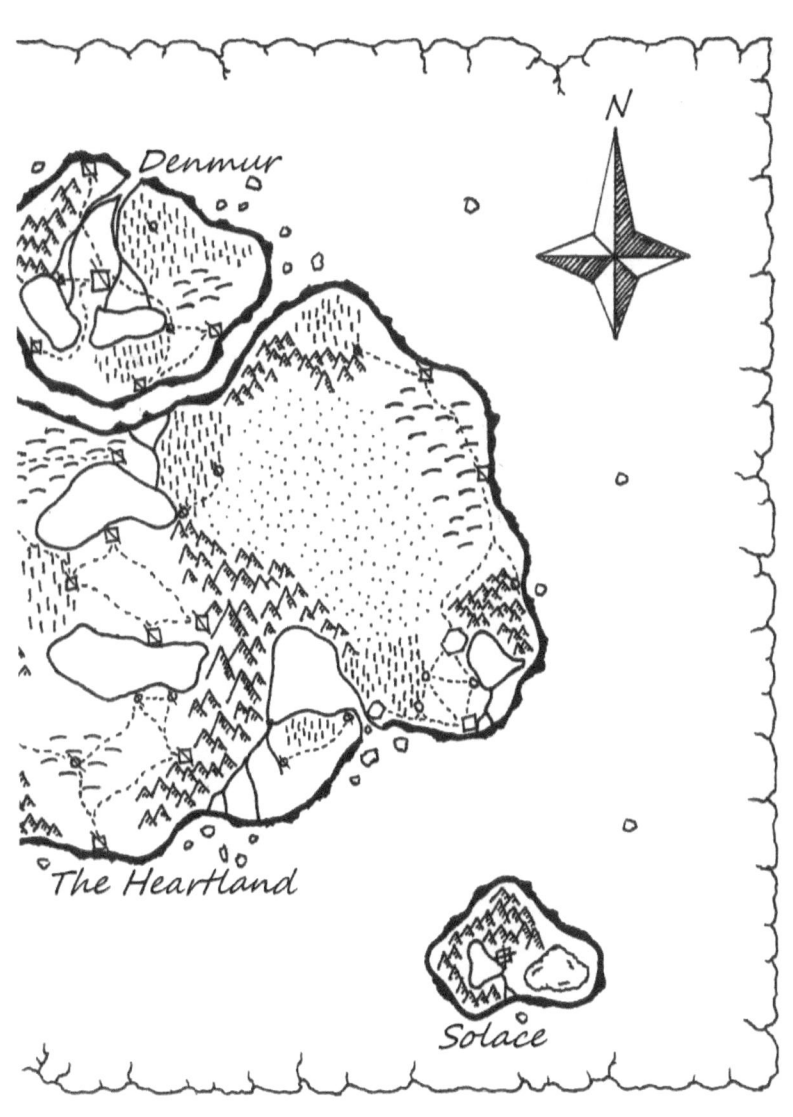

... and he, flanked by his Demigods and the legendary heroes, marched against her in that desolate castle ...

... but several Demigods, who shall ever be marked in ink as betrayers, defended her ...

... their names are ... Saber Umbra ... Calitha Lex ...

... the darkness flowed out ... she had won ... night had begun ...

... I write this text so others, long after my death, can know the truth of this broken land.
- The History of the First Night

*P*rologue

Saber stood in the middle of a gentle meadow. The knee-high grass swayed side-to-side in the cool breeze. There were morning birds chirping in the distance, singing their sweet melodies to whomever was there to listen. A light fog covered the land, and the warm sun could be seen shining through it in the distance. She looked around, breathing in the brisk air. It was a perfect, Spring morning, one that a Spark could only dream of seeing again. Saber snorted from the irony.

It was perfect — too perfect. Saber wanted nothing more than to tear apart the earth and cast destruction across this peaceful landscape. It was disgusting. How could a man with so much pain cast onto his soul think of something so peaceful? As an escape from his miserable reality? It was pathetic.

Saber looked down, studying herself. Instead of appearing as the beautiful, intelligent, and commanding woman she prided herself on portraying, she was instead some weak and frail hag. There was no luscious black hair, no seductive, pale skin, and no alluring eyes. Only a knotty brown mess and wrinkly skin. Or that was, at least, how she pictured herself. Oh, she truly despised wearing this form.

Suddenly, walking out from the fog, was a hulking beast of a man. Standing nearly double her height, his shoulders were as broad as a bull's and his legs were tree trunks. He wore a loose-fitting tunic, and it did nothing to hide the immense strength of the man before Saber. He walked forward, and Saber could imagine the ground shaking with each step. If he so desired, he could swat her away like she was some irritating little bug buzzing around his ear. But he would never. She looked up at the monster towering over her.

The man's weathered face grew soft, and his mouth opened in a bright smile.

"Ellie! My doe!" the man exclaimed. "It's been so long since I've seen you!"

He rushed forward and swept Saber up into a crushing hug. Great, this was Saber's favorite part. The part where she had to pretend to love this man. The part where she had to laugh at his awful jokes and pretend to reminisce about "their" lost times. Disgusted, she slowly hugged the man back.

"My love. Agmund," Saber managed to heave out through her crushed lungs. *Love* — what an absolutely infernal word. "I've missed you too."

That was a lie. Or it was a lie to Saber, as she most certainly did not miss these miserable little exchanges.

The man smothering her in his embrace was Agmund Giantheart, the Torchhead of the Flame, the leading member of the Light, and she — this Ellie creature — was his long-dead wife. So, despite the bitterness in her heart for all things romantic, Saber had to play this silly little game with him. Of course, he had no idea that his dear Ellie was a doppelganger. In his mind, all he could picture was her supposedly beautiful face and their wonderful times running through Sturdyoak Wood on Solace, chasing the royal stags.

Saber snorted again and gave a crooked smile. The more Agmund poured his heart out to her the more satisfying it would be to watch him be devoured as her brilliant plans came to light. He was a pathetic excuse of a man.

Agmund was crying, and Saber could feel his tears dripping onto her head. Fuck, this could not be over any sooner. With each drop she felt as if she were being waterboarded. It psychologically anguished her.

Finally, after what seemed like centuries of agony, the parasite Agmund took a deep breath and detached himself from her.

"Do you remember our first kiss?" Agmund managed to say in between sobs. "It was at that moment I knew you were the one. With your soft lips and your ..."

Saber reached up and placed a finger over his flapping lips. A supposedly gentle and romantic gesture to make him close his aggravating mouth. "Of course I do," she purred to him. Yet another lie. This could not end any sooner. But she had to play the game.

"I remember all of our times together," Saber continued. "From the first time I saw you I knew how strong and noble you were. From the first time we laid together in bed I knew how strong and powerful you were."

Saber moved her hand down and placed it on his burly chest.

"From the first time I watched you in battle I knew of the fire you have inside you." Saber wanted to vomit. This was eating her apart. What was the point of all this so-called mushy-gushy *love*? What a waste of time. The only person she loved ... well ... Ashyla made sure that didn't last. She looked up at her imaginary lover — her Agmund — and she couldn't stop thinking about tearing out his throat — as if it would be that easy in the real world.

The giant reached out and grabbed her by the shoulders. With a brilliant display of strength, he lifted her into the air above his head, and with a great smile on his face, he spun her around, laughing all the while.

Saber pretended and laughed along. She supposed that this is what they used to do when Ellie was alive. And why wouldn't they? Agmund had the muscle and the heart.

Still shining with that preposterous smile, Agmund put Saber back on her feet. Then, without giving her a moment to recover from the whiplash, he pulled her in for yet another suffocating hug. Why did he have to be such a physically intimate sop?

"I wish you could explore the world now," Agmund said. "The Shadow is being held at bay. The new member of the Torch has been brilliant with her strategy."

Saber smiled. That was the first worthwhile thing he said all night. She *was* brilliant.

"People might finally be gaining hope once again," he continued. "There have even been rumors that Mariah was seen at Forthold, although we have not received confirmation yet."

Saber's smile grew even wider. She wouldn't be holding her breath for Mariah's return. But Agmund kept talking, and soon her smile fell into a scowl.

"I hope it's true Ellie. I really do. This is what we've been fighting for. This is what I wanted you to see. I wish for a day when I can see the sunset on the coasts of Anland, and I wish I could spend it with you. You were my —"

"Agmund," Saber said, hoping to interrupt the man, but he just kept droning on and on and on.

"I know you're watching from above, and I know you're there with me through my Inner Fire. We might never be able to run through —"

"Agmund," Saber said again, and she couldn't help the menace seeping into her voice.

Agmund stopped, noticing the change of tone, and he pulled himself away. His face darkened when he noticed the scowl that was on Saber's face.

"What's wrong, Ellie?"

The game was up. It was time for business. She just did not have the patience for this.

"Agmund, my … love, I wish we could stand here and reminisce about our past, but there is something you must know."

Agmund's eyebrows rose.

"There is a great danger, I have seen it from up above. Yes, while the Shadow may be held at bay for now, and the wonderful and humble Saber is doing a brilliant job with the defenses, a plague has infiltrated into the Flame." Saber paused for a moment, letting the silence sour the mood of the perfect morning.

"Beware, there is a group of outsiders, heroes of the Shadowfront, who are no doubt heading to Firelight as we speak. They came from the Shadow, and they mean to bring death into the Light. Do not ask me how I know this, but I have seen it from my place in the stars."

Agmund's brow furrowed in thought. Could it be true? In his dreams, Ellie's words have always rung true. He did not understand how, or why, but it seems she was granted a supernatural perspective after her death. She could see things and know things that should have been impossible for her to know. No matter how much it pained him, whenever he found himself dreaming of her, there was always a message he had to receive.

Saber smirked at his contemplation. Of course, he would doubt it. Heroes of the Shadowfront acting as pawns of the Shadow? How absurd. But he would listen … in time. He always did when it was his miserable little wife whispering sweet nectar into his ear. Once more, Saber wanted to vomit.

"Do not listen to their lies," Saber continued. "No matter how honest and sincere they might seem, they serve a darker purpose."

"I don't understand," Agmund stuttered. "Who are they? Are they Shadowfriends? If they truly are, there's no doubt my men will cut them down where they stand."

Saber ignored him, barreling forward with her ominous speech:

"Remember, to trust them is to call upon death. You don't want to lose any more of us ..." Saber let the last word hang in the air. It was time to get creative. She could not leave him with any last shred of doubt that the companions were his doom.

A knife appeared in her hand.

Agmund's eyes darted down to the blade, and alarm shot across his face.

"Ellie? What are you doing?"

He started to reach for her hand to pull the knife away, but Saber stepped back just out of his reach. He took another lunge forward, but yet again she avoided his grasp. While Ellie may have been nothing more than a soft, inept pillow, Saber herself was quite nimble. She just couldn't help the twisted grin on her face.

Suddenly, feeling inventive, Saber fell to her knees, and she brought the knife up to her throat. It was time to make him listen.

"Ellie!" Agmund gasped, but he couldn't move. He couldn't stop her.

Feigning a look of terror, Saber slashed the knife across her throat, sending blood gushing out of her. But she did not stop there. Bringing her hand back, she cut again, drawing another red slice across her frail neck.

And again.

And again.

And *again*.

And **again**.

Six, bloody cuts crisscrossed across her neck, one for each of the companions. Her lifeblood spilled out of her body. Yet Agmund could only stare. He tried to reach out with his Inner Fire, to cast the wounds onto his soul, but he couldn't. Of course he couldn't, this wasn't real, after all. Tears streamed down his face, and he let out a piercing wail.

"ELLIE!"

Saber smiled, blood bubbling out of her mouth.

"Beware the outsiders," she somehow said, even though her windpipe was severed. "This is the price you would pay. To trust them is to call upon death ..."

She stood up, blood soaking into the ground beneath her. So much for a perfect morning. The knife still clutched in her hand, she stumbled towards the paralyzed Agmund. He reached out to her, anguish twisting his handsome face.

Fighting back a cackle, Saber placed the bloody knife into his open hand. He looked down and wrapped his fingers around it, opening and closing his mouth in a vain attempt to find words. Poor, poor Agmund. Nobody wants to watch their wife die twice.

With strength that the miserable Ellie would have only dreamed about having, Saber lurched forward and grabbed Agmund's wrist, and before he could begin to react, she pulled, plunging the knife into her own chest.

Oh, how she relished his horrified face.

Ellie's lifeblood gushed out of her heart, covering Agmund's hand. His gentle hand. His hand of healing. His hand of warmth. His hand he just murdered his wife with. He tried to pull away, but Saber held him firmly in place, letting her blood run down his arm. It was a dream, and she had full control of it.

"You don't want to lose any more of us," Saber repeated, blood flying from her mouth and speckling his face. She let him fester in his anguish. He struggled and pulled in a desperate attempt to remove the blade from her heart, but it was fruitless. He screamed and howled, calling out with his Inner Fire to heal her wounds.

All of it for nothing.

Saber, and, as a result, Ellie, began to laugh in his face. This entire charade was completely unnecessary, but that didn't stop her. Call it revenge for having to suffer through the lovey-dovey nonsense.

Agmund fell to his knees, defeated. It was always so easy. As soon as you bring family into the picture even the mightiest of men will crumple like a lost child. She thought it was satisfying with that damned Captain, but this was somehow so much sweeter.

Finally calming from her manic laughter, Saber released his hand, allowing it to fall to his side, leaving the knife still protruding from her chest. He could only stare. She leaned forward, and with her blood-soaked lips, she gave him a kiss. Nothing tastes better than your wife's warm blood.

Releasing the kiss, Saber pulled him close. Shockingly, Agmund did not return the embrace. And the oaf could barely stop himself from hugging her earlier.

"Beware …" she whispered in his ear, before collapsing onto the crimson earth. Ellie, at least until Saber needed to play this little game again, was dead yet again.

Agmund began to cry once again, his burly shoulders bouncing with his sobs.

"My doe …"

He did not move for a long time. The fog swirled around him. The birds were still chirping in the distance, and a gentle breeze still played with the grass. It may have only been a dream, but at that moment, it felt as real as ever. Not even waking up could wash away the blood on his hands.

◆　　◆　　◆

Saber opened her eyes and looked around. She was no longer in the blissful meadow, but rather in an expansive bedroom. Luxurious tapestries hung on the wall displaying the mighty symbol of the Flame. Flickering candles dotted the room, casting shadows dancing across the stone walls. In the center of the room was a large table with notes and maps scattered across the surface. And, finally, in front of her, lay Agmund on a large bed. He tossed and turned from side to side and sweat beaded on his forehead. He must be having some kind of wicked nightmare. Tragically, she felt no sympathy for him.

Saber lifted her hand from his arm. She hoped he had received his message — if he could somehow look past what he had done. Ashyla was a fool with her silly little plan to protect the pathetic group of companions. What chance did that have of success? What even was the point? She was fucking insane. Saber would relish the chance to slice that bitch's throat open. But, of course, she had to be careful. While Ashyla may be foolish, even without her powers, she was by no means weak. And Saber had no intention of giving Ashyla the opportunity to cut her down — at least not yet.

But, for now, it would never come to that. Saber would play her nonsensical little game — and she meant to win it. Truly, she hoped Ashyla enjoyed her little gift. It was such a joy to rip apart that wondrous body. It was such a sense of exhilaration to carve that symbol into the wretched Mariah's chest. The Beacon had to be stopped. If he should emerge victorious from this entire charade between the Shadow and the Light ... well, there goes her grand plans of freedom.

Saber turned and began to strut out of the room. While she was moving, she tousled her hair and shifted her clothes, making it appear as if she dressed in a hurry. It was all going perfectly. She glanced down at the papers on the table and snorted at the waste of parchment. No matter what they devised, she would ensure that all their desperate plans would crumble.

Chuckling silently to herself, she pushed open the oak door, and without a sound, slid out of Agmund's bedchamber.

Two guards stood watch over the room. As Saber exited, they brandished their weapons and turned upon her. How did an intruder get past them? The Torchhead should not be awake for another couple of hours, so it could not possibly be him! They began to swing down upon Saber, the metal blades glinting in the soft light, but froze when they recognized her.

"General Umbra!" the guard on the right exclaimed, rushing to put his hand over his heart in the proper salute. "Hail, light of the Flame!"

Saber did not bother to give the customary response.

"What brings you to the Torchhead's room?" the guard on the left asked, his eyes scanning Saber up and down. He had heard rumors of her beauty, but to see her up close ... it was another matter entirely.

Saber turned to him, gave a wink, and put her finger over her lips for silence.

The guards gawked. They glanced at her messy hair and disheveled clothes. Ah, so it must have been one of those nights, although it was strange they didn't hear anything. Perhaps the two Generals wanted to keep their fling a secret — it was always more fun that way. Agmund was a weary man, after all, and, apparently, he needed some extra help getting to sleep.

"I was never here," Saber purred to the astonished guards. "Stand ready at your posts and never mention that this happened. Also, make sure to be quiet, as you wouldn't want to wake the beast." As she finished, just for flair, she blew them a kiss. The guards' eyes grew unfocused, and they nodded in compliance. Satisfied, Saber whipped around and marched down the hall, her boots clicking on the stone floor. As she turned the corner, she heard the guards whispering to each other:

"Did you see her? The things I would do if I was given the chance."

"Mmm, and it seems she's quite proficient at riding a stallion."

"And what do you mean by that, Gimper?"

"Well, she was in there with —"

Saber heard a light smacking sound, and then the hiss of steel being drawn.

A Resurgence of Hope

"Never speak of that, Gimp. If anyone asks, you were dozing off on the job, and she was never here, you ass-backwards, stupid —"

"Okay, okay! I'm sorry. Can you put your sword away ...?"

She drowned out the voices. Perfect. The game was set in motion, and the foolish guards were none the wiser. How easily the minds of feeble men succumbed to her charm. It was pathetic. When would they learn to think for themselves?

Shaking her head in amusement, Saber continued down the corridor, lost in her own musings. Soon, thanks to her — not Ashyla — the Light would be doomed. They would all die, and she would never have to slave away playing guardian ever again.

Suddenly, an impossibly black shape flickered across the corner of her vision. Her head whipped to find it, but it was gone. Could it have been one of Ashyla's butterflies? Saber felt very cold and very small at that moment. No, she was getting paranoid. The game was already in motion, and she had executed her move to perfection. That bitch would still be busy with her present. No longer could she wait for Ashyla. The Beacon had to die, and may the Goddess burn with the Flame.

Giving that evil grin, and shaking away her doubts, Saber continued down the hall. There had been news that a group of mysterious companions had battled through the Shadowfront in a most spectacular fashion. She wouldn't be much of a noble General if she did not go out to congratulate them on their brilliant victory.

◆　◆　◆

Ashyla stalked through the forest. Tall, black trees loomed all around her, reaching up and smothering the heavens. A thick fog hung about the ground like a frozen blanket. Packs of ravenous undead skulked about in the shadows, casting unnatural shrieks into the air.

Ashyla hardly noticed any of it. The picture of Mariah's mangled corpse flicked through her mind. Of course, she knew Saber did it. Who else would display such a blatant act of defiance? Who else would throw such a childish tantrum? In time, Saber would once again learn her place, or she would be cast into the Shadow. So be it.

But there was another piece of the game. Saber wasn't the only defiant one. Nay, Saber had an acquaintance in her little ploy. For while the Sister may have struck the blow, it was the Daughter who gave her the weapon.

Ashyla shook her head. It all could have been so simple. It all could have been so easy. They used to tremble at her wrath, but now they snickered in the darkness. What power could the fallen Goddess hope to possess? What authority could the crippled Mother hope to hold? They would learn the truth soon enough. Soon, her seal would be broken. Soon, she would have justice for the atrocities against her and her family. Soon, she would return this miserable, rotting world to her beautiful garden that it once was. One piece at a time, and they would all eventually fit into place.

Suddenly, Ashyla found herself in a large clearing. Dead grass waved in a wind that was not there. A hole in the sky swirled like a whirlpool to the abyss. Mountains peeked over the trees, solemnly watching over the gathering. Ashyla always seemed to find this place quickly — unlike Saber. Perhaps Calitha had some sense. Or perhaps Calitha was too terrified to hide.

Floating in the middle of the clearing was Calitha, her arms outstretched, and her head thrown back as if she was in the throes of ecstasy.

Ashyla gave her a cold, dangerous smile. "Hello, my dear Calitha," she hissed, walking up to the ghostly woman. Ashyla was never fond of traitors, and Calitha had just seated herself firmly on that list.

Calitha lowered her arms and turned to face the Goddess. "It is I who is greeting you, Mother," she said, tilting her head at an unnatural angle. "To what do I owe this great pleasure?"

Several black butterflies began to flutter around the clearing.

"Do you know why I have always come to you for my most pressing of needs, my dear Calitha?" Ashyla said, stopping in front of Calitha to study her. She ran her eyes up and down the pale woman. Blood still oozed from the stitched gash on her chest, as well as from her sewn eyes. Her gray dress was almost transparent, teasing at her atrophied body underneath.

"Do you know why I come to you more than Sister?" Ashyla continued, her voice a nothing but a soft whisper. She reached out and gently touched Calitha's thigh — just as a tease. Slowly, she brought her hand up, brushing between her legs and against her breasts.

Two butterflies landed upon Calitha, one on each wrist.

"Why do you come to me, Mother?" Calitha managed to answer. A looming sense of dread began to seep into her. Mother was not supposed to know.

Ashyla continued exploring Calitha's body with her hand, before reaching up and stroking Calitha's cheek. She leaned in close, her lips brushing against the Daughter's ear.

"Do you know why I protect you from the Shadow, child?"

Calitha opened her mouth to answer, but before she could, Ashyla's hand grasped the back of her head, fingers digging into her skull. With a violent screech, Ashyla tore the woman out of the air and slammed her face into the cold ground. The butterflies on Calitha's wrists leaped off, fluttering around the Goddess's head.

Ashyla leaned in close to the whimpering woman. "It's because I thought I could trust you. It's because I thought you had faith in our journey of redemption. It's because you know that I will triumph, and that I will restore my — our paradise."

Ashyla squeezed her hand, her fingers grinding into bone. The ghostly woman squirmed on the ground, desperately trying to escape, but it was no use. Mother was not supposed to know. Maybe there was still hope. Maybe Mother was just taken by another lapse of rage. Maybe Mother was just trying to teach her some new lesson about whatever.

Or maybe this time Mother had finally crossed the brink of insanity.

"Or that is how it used to be, child," Ashyla spat. She twisted her wrist, turning Calitha over so that she could face her. Her hand moved around Calitha's head and clamped onto the woman's throat. Furious, Ashyla lifted her back into the air.

And how she squeezed. Calitha kicked and fought, her face turning a sickly purple. She tried to say something, tried to gasp for air, but the choke was too tight. Blood began to seep out of her neck where Ashyla's fingernails dug into her skin.

Ashyla pulled her close, her hand still an iron vice on the woman's throat. "Why did you listen to her, child?' she snarled in rage.

Without giving her a moment to answer, she slammed Calitha back into the ground and finally released her from her death grip. She towered over the pathetic traitor, glee burning in her gaze. She hated traitors. They were all blinded by their arrogance. One shred of doubt and they go scampering away, desperately looking for another path. They were fools. This was the only way. They might as well return to *him* — that disgusting disease that corrupted her world. She gave them their glory and their freedom — so long as they did not tarnish her garden. But they were so quick to cast it away. They were fools.

Calitha coughed on the ground, her hands massaging her bleeding neck. Why did she listen to "her"? Maybe there was still hope. It seemed Mother was referring to the incident with Sister and Mariah and was still blissfully ignorant of *that* secret. Yes, she just had to play the game and survive this fit without breaking. Some distractions here, some begging there, and it would soon be over. Clearing her senses, she brought herself to her knees and looked up at the enraged Goddess.

"To whom did I listen to, Mother?"

Ashyla smiled down at her like a cat to a trapped mouse. Pathetic. Calitha was always the secluded one. She rarely ventured from her grove, and she always talked like some mindless infant. But while Saber let her rage cloud her judgments, Calitha was supposed to be the calm, collected intellectual. But it seems even she could have a lapse in judgment.

How unfortunate.

Ashyla didn't respond to Calitha's questions. Instead, she held out her hand, and one of the butterflies landed on her palm. She closed her fingers, crushing the insect, but when she opened them, she now held an obsidian dagger. Still silent, she reached down with her free hand and grabbed the Daughter by the wrist, then lifted her arm before her.

Calitha simply watched the spectacle and steeled her resolve.

With a sadistic smile, Ashyla slashed the dagger across, cutting one of the fingers from Calitha's hand, where it fell to the earth.

Calitha screamed. The hollow sound echoed through the clearing, magnifying into a deafening shriek of agony. A harsh wind blew into the clearing, tearing the trees back and forth. Lighting arced across the sky, and the swirling vortex grew darker and more ominous, the dark spiral speeding up with each passing heartbeat. No, she must not break!

And still Ashyla smiled, not noticing the violent onslaught around her.

Releasing the pathetic traitor, she reached down and picked up the bloody finger, turning it over in her hands. She began to carve away at the finger, rending away flesh and revealing the pale bones. She extracted the largest of the finger bones out of the shredded flesh, breaking it off at the knuckle. A flap of a butterfly's wing, and the finger bone morphed into a long, razor point.

"To what did I do, Mother?" Calitha gasped, clutching her hand in a vain attempt to stop the bleeding. "Daughter has remained loyal to your greatness."

Ashyla ignored her. The second butterfly descended from the air and landed on the bone, where it morphed into a long, shadowy string, which gracefully tied itself around the base of the new-fashioned needle.

"I know what you did, child" Ashyla whispered, admiring her makeshift needle and thread. "All I want is for you to admit your mistakes."

The obsidian dagger turned back into a butterfly and flew into the air, the violent winds not affecting it. Squatting down, Ashyla reached down with her now free hand and cupped it under Calitha's thin chin.

"All I want is for you to tell me what you did, my dear Calitha. Why did you listen to her? Once you say the words, all of this will be over, and I will leave your humble home. But if you continue to play me for the ignorant fool, well … this is going to be quite unpleasant."

"I had to do it, Mother!" Calitha stuttered, grasping at her bloody hand. Perhaps Sister was right. Mother had fallen even deeper into madness. Her fractured mind was tearing at the seams, and every day it seemed her goal was falling farther from her grasp. To save the Beacon? To release Mariah? It was utter insanity. The Daughter did not understand. Perhaps Saber was right. Mother might have to be stopped.

"Oh child, did you really?"

"I had to do it, Mother …"

"And what did you do, child? Let me hear you say the words, and this will all be over."

But before Calitha could answer — and how she wanted to answer — Ashyla smacked her across the face, sending her twisting to the ground. Like a panther, Ashyla pounced on Calitha, pinning her on the dirt. Her hand reached out and squeezed the woman's sickly face. Then, with the calm determination of a surgeon, using her other hand, she pressed the point of the bone needle to the traitorous liar's lips, and with a soft smile, pushed it through.

Calitha groaned and struggled, but the Goddess did not relent. She tried to open her mouth, she tried to admit to her sinful games with Sister, but she couldn't.

Ashyla's smile grew into a manic grin as she brought the needle back around and through Calitha's mouth again, each time pulling the black string tighter and tighter.

Another loop through the woman's lips.

Calitha writhed and turned in pain. Blood — more than should be possible — began to fill her mouth from the punctures, and it seeped out from between her lips. She just needed to survive — that hope seemed less likely by the moment.

Maniacal, Ashyla loved every second of it. She was never fond of traitors, after all.

Another loop, sealing the thrashing woman's mouth shut forever. The blood was now bubbling down her throat, threatening to drown her. She choked and a red spray shot out of her mouth, painting Ashyla with specks of deep red.

"Just tell me what you did, my dear Calitha," Mother teased. "Let me hear you say the words."

Calitha tried, but the words wouldn't come out through her sewn lips — or through the thick blood in her throat. All that she could muster was a garbled moaning sound, and another spray of crimson rain onto Mother.

Another loop.

"Let me hear those sweet, sweet words, my dear Calitha. What did you do with Mariah? What did you do with Sister?"

Calitha grabbed at Ashyla's wrist with her mangled hand, trying desperately to stop her. She was kicking and twisting, but it was no use. She could never hope to compete with the brute strength of Mother. She could feel herself breaking.

Another loop.

"I'm waiting, child."

Calitha's hand fell to her side, and she stopped struggling. So, this was to be her death. All her years of mostly-faithful servitude came crumbling down, worthless in the eyes of the Goddess. Was it worth playing Sister's game? If she died now, Mother would know the true extent of her treachery.

Ashyla finished the final loop, and with a harsh tug, she tightened the string, and it magically knotted itself, forever sealing her mouth. "Just tell me, my dear Calitha. That is all I ask."

Defeated, Calitha made no sound, not even a whimper. She remained frozen on her knees, her head bowed, with the crimson tide crawling into her lungs and dripping from her sewn lips. The wind had stopped, and the sky had ceased turning. All this for releasing Mariah? It was incomprehensible. Calitha contemplated revealing her secret but stopped herself when she realized that Ashyla would likely just torment her even more.

Satisfied, Ashyla rose to her feet and turned away from the pathetic creature before her. One day they would learn. One day they would pay for their transgressions. One day soon when she tore her power back from this miserable world with the claw of the Shadow.

Walking forward, she disappeared in a cloud of black butterflies, leaving Calitha alone in her clearing.

The Daughter looked up, absently facing the spot Ashyla vanished from, but with a glimmer of hope returning in her eyes. She did it! She had survived another tantrum! She wasn't beaten and she wasn't broken — this time. Yes, she was on the edge, but her secret was still safe.

Suddenly, she felt her lips release. The black string had vanished with Mother. She collapsed forward, trying to cough up the vile muck from her lungs, but nothing came out.

A Resurgence of Hope

Overcome with joy, she opened her mouth and took a deep, cleansing breath, letting the cold air fill her rotting lungs. Perhaps Sister was right. Mother was dangerous, both to them and to herself. It was true — mostly — that she had always remained fiercely loyal to Mother, but these were trying times, and loyalties could be broken in desperation. Perhaps Mother had come to her in an attempt to teach another lesson, but Mother was losing her way.

She floated up in the air and felt at her hand, deep in thought. Her finger had returned — was it ever really gone? — but she hardly noticed. Her mind was already in a far distant place, plotting the next course of action.

Perhaps Sister was right.

Even Ashyla was afraid of something.

◆　　◆　　◆

Ashyla stood outside an aged wooden door banded with reinforcements. Some flecks of Calitha's blood were still spattered across her figure, giving her the appearance of a frenzied killer. She glanced around, studying the dimly lit castle corridor. On the walls hung ancient tapestries of various colors depicting legends long forgotten. Flickering torches dotted the passage, their eerie light sending shadows dancing around the corridor.

Ashyla placed her hand on the door, and she knew it would effortlessly swing inwards. But she didn't push on it. One simple sentence echoed in her mind, holding her at bay:

I had to do it, Mother ...

Of that, Ashyla was certain it was a lie.

Snarling, Ashyla turned away from the door. She felt as if she were tearing at the seams, like a small dress forced over an oversized mannequin. She didn't need those miserable children. She had the claw of the Shadow and the fury of a Goddess. She didn't need their assistance or their servitude.

She stormed down the twisting passages, turning this way and that, before finally stopping before another wooden door. She breathed, and a smile opened on her face.

She had the claw of the Shadow.

Yes, soon, everyone would cower before her wrath. Soon, everyone will once again tremble at her name. Damn the Beacon and the rest of those insolent children, she knew the Shadow would devour them all soon enough.

She opened the door and stepped into a large courtyard. The shriveled grass was dark and devoid of life. Barren, gray trees dotted the area, reaching up to the sky in a silent plea for help. An icy breeze swirled in the clearing, howling as it crashed against the stone walls.

Curled up in the middle of the courtyard was a slumbering dracolich. Once a mighty and noble dragon, it had since fallen from radiance and into the clutches of the Shadow. Its skin and scales had long ago rotted away, leaving behind an ashy black skeleton covered with tattered flesh. Its wings were ragged and torn, a vile mockery of their long-lost majesty. Cracked and broken horns crowned its mighty head. An icy blue glow radiated from its chest, casting a cold light upon the surrounding area. A ghastly aura surrounded the beast, devouring any warmth and any last shreds of life.

Ashyla walked towards the horrifying creature, and it slowly opened a hollow eye to regard her. Much like the dreadknights, its gaze was icy and terrifying, with a simple glance being enough to inspire nightmarish stories that would be passed down for generations. But Ashyla did not falter, instead she smiled warmly.

Upon reaching the dracolich, she reached out and gently stroked its decrepit head.

"Look what they did to you, my poor baby …"

A Resurgence of Hope

The undead behemoth did not move, simply staring at the woman before it. Ashyla felt a single lone tear form in the corner of her eye, and it almost escaped.

Almost.

"Wake, my precious child, for it's time to feast."

Daniel Whitman

Chapter 1

Nalgene took a deep breath. The companions had done it. They fought through terror and destruction, they battled through undeath and rot, and it was all for this moment. They had won. They had made it through the Shadowfront and into the Light. At long last, they had accomplished their mission given to them so long ago by the Oracle Mariah — to reunite with the Flame.

The gnome basked in the warming radiance of the sun, and it felt wonderful. He looked up at the bright, blue sky, its color bursting with saturation after the many nights in the gray Shadow. A few white clouds drifted through the air. A cool breeze swept in and played with his hair. On the other side of the gargantuan stone wall behind him, the dark and terrible battle still raged. Sparks fought to their deaths in an effort to stop the oncoming darkness. But at this moment, absorbed in the refreshing life of the Light, he could easily forget about that horror.

Nalgene smiled. He could now remember his olden days in a blossoming land with the fiery touch of the sun. It was this glorious life that they had fought for in those bloody battles that time ago.

But how long ago was it? Apparently, it was before this Shadow thing, but when exactly? Some things still were not clear.

Yes, he remembered those battles. It was impossible to forget the first time drowning someone with his magic. It was even difficult to forget the rest of the time. The choking and the struggling as they tried to call for help, but no sound came forth as water filled their lungs. Their widening eyes as they realized their doom and inevitably inhaled the very substance that would cause their deaths. Their bodies shriveling as he absorbed their moisture and life force for his trinket. But it was necessary. It was for the sake of the innocent people that he and his companions protected against the corrupted kingdoms of the Goddess. Yes, he could now remember …

He could now remember how full of shit he was. He wasn't fighting for people. No, he was fighting for his haughty glory. Back then, he was as jealous as a beardless dwarf, and just as much of a damned prick.

Nalgene's face darkened as he chastised himself. It may have been his life force in that blasted bottle, but what did he have to do to ensure he never ran out? It was grim indeed. But what does it matter now? He was not that gnome, at least not anymore. And it didn't matter, none of them remembered anyway. Yet it still weighed on him. He could throw his past into that lake, but he couldn't cast away his new memories. Damn. He was such a beardless —

"My brother!" Nalgene heard SmibSmob call out, interrupting his brooding thoughts. "What's wrong? I'm sorry for what you had to see, I thought it was the —"

"Eh?" Nalgene replied, looking up. There stood the others: Ro and his gray scales covered in blood, Andromeda and her shadowy fur, Fasto and his frustratingly stupid face, Margaret and her demonic arm, and, of course, his dear brother SmibSmob. And they were all looking at him with concern. Even the crooked Kraalek, who had retrieved his pointless die from the ground, was giving him a quizzical look. "Er, I just be happy. Uh — I mean what in the bloody hell are ye talkin' about, Kraalek? Of course, we won, and that be sittin' right with me."

It was time to stop being the brooding, depressed gnome. He might as well be a stinky, good-for-nothing dwarf if he was just going to stand around and mope all day. What was done is done, and there was no way he could un-drown someone — at least that he knew of.

Kraalek smirked. "I would have to agree, little fellow. It is a rare occurrence when Sparks manage to fight through the Shadowfront. Once in a lifetime, isn't that right?" His metal cards appeared once again in his hands, and he began to deftly flip them through his nimble fingers. "Take in the beauty, my fine friends, for this is what the Flame is fighting for."

The companions looked around once more, absorbing the vibrant energy of the Light. It was indeed something worth fighting for.

"Mmmm, it is beautiful," Andromeda purred.

The companions did not move for a few heartbeats. They still couldn't believe that they had overcome such a tremendous obstacle. All the while, the General stood studying them, his eyebrow raised. How did they manage to fight through it? Surely, only the most legendary of heroes would be able to survive in the Shadow for so long. He thought back to when he first met them in the Ruins of Calinad. Perhaps …

"Er, I don't mean to be the obvious one, but I think we could use some cleaning up," SmibSmob said, breaking the peace. It was true, all the companions, except the little gnome himself, were still suffering from their grievous injuries.

"Bah! Get over here, ye dolts," Nalgene exclaimed, rushing over to the companions. He was exhausted from the Shadowfront, but he still had a few drops of water he could spare to nourish them back to health. Anything to help his friends. "Who's first?"

"Not me," Ro said nobly, shying away from the gnome. "I'll wait until you've finished with the others."

Truly, he was quite a charitable leader.

"Fasto no want," said Fasto, much to the disbelief of Nalgene. Why didn't that daft orc want his mangled arms to be healed?

"Well, if everyone else is going to play hero, you might as well come to me first," Margaret said, shaking her head in amusement.

"And then me next," Andromeda piped in.

Grunting, Nalgene walked over to the frosty orc and held his hands out to her. He willed whatever power he had to come forth at this moment. He felt the cool water rush through him and out through his palms. But right before he could place his hands on the orc and send a cascade of healing wash over her, a thin hand appeared in front of his face, stopping his advance.

"Save it, my good gnome," Kraalek said. "It would be my honor to treat our valiant heroes." His eyes twinkled with mischief, and he whipped around, his crimson cloak twirling about him. He started skipping away, heading towards the center of the great stronghold they were in. "Follow me and come feel the warmth of the Flame!"

Nalgene lowered his hands and grunted. What a showboater. "Well, I guess we don't be havin' much o' a choice, eh?" He glanced over at Ro and gestured to him. "Lead the way, Ro."

Nodding his head, Ro marched after the General, beckoning the others to follow. He supported Andromeda with his shoulder, as her crippled leg made walking difficult. Shrugging, Margaret followed after, with Fasto right behind her.

Nalgene turned to his dear brother and gave him one more crushing hug. "Don't ye be doin' that ever again, ye hear me?" Tears started welling up in the tough gnome's eyes, but he choked them back.

Smiling, SmibSmob returned the hug. "You don't ever have to worry about it again, my brother. Mariah saved me." And the gnome meant it. He felt better than he could ever remember. Of course, he still had a gaping hole in his soul where his darkness once resided, but as he held Nalgene, it grew smaller and smaller. Maybe if he held his brother for long enough it would disappear entirely.

But, at least for now, it did not.

Nalgene pulled away and studied SmibSmob. "What are ye sayin'?"

"It's gone. She destroyed the darkness. I'm free."

Nalgene reeled back in surprise. His brother was free? It felt as if his heart were about to explode. There would be no more long nights worrying if SmibSmob was going to be forever trapped. There would be tense moments where Nalgene didn't know if it was his brother or his power speaking. There would be no more horrible moments like that in the Shadowfront … It was too much for the poor gnome. He pulled SmibSmob back into the hug — and this time he didn't hold back his tears.

SmibSmob was his motivation for battling through the Shadow. SmibSmob was his courage to face down the abominations. SmibSmob was his reason for holding out hope. He would easily lay down his own life for his now-pure brother.

He loved him.

It was a feeling that he hoped would never fade.

After what seemed like an eternity of holding his brother, Nalgene heard Ro shouting back at them, urging them to hurry up.

"Are you coming, my friends?"

SmibSmob waved to the draconian, then whispered to his sobbing brother. "I reckon we should go see what the General has in store for us."

Nodding in agreement, Nalgene took a deep breath to compose himself, then wiped the tears and the snot from his face. He wasn't who he used to be — as he even considered that blasted dragon as a friend now — but he couldn't yet let Ro see him like this. Even friendship has its limits.

Forcing down the shanty dwarf emotions and holding back one last sniffle, Nalgene smacked his brother on the shoulder and turned to follow the others, who were all patiently waiting for the gnomes. "Let's be off."

The two gnomes rushed over to the others, and together the companions followed the prancing General. Kraalek led them through the courtyard and deeper into Forthold, towards the central keep. Buildings crowded them on either side of the path. There were barracks, smithies, abandoned residential homes, medical tents, and command centers. Every building was made of solid, gray stone to stand strong against any oncoming attacks. This was a fortress, and everything was planned meticulously in order to be as fortified as possible. There was space in between every building to allow soldiers to march through. There were lookout towers dotted regularly across the courtyard. Every door could be barricaded from the inside, and small slits were carved into the walls in case the inhabitants needed to fire arrows at oncoming intruders. And of course, it was all surrounded by a massive wall, watching over them as an unwavering guardian of stone.

Sparks ran past the group to help fortify the defenses at the wall, and when they did, they each stopped briefly to give a respectful salute to the General, who waved them on and told them to hurry to their posts. Some of the Sparks wore light armor, and some were donning heavy plate mail. Some held axes, some swords, and some even spears, but they were all there with one sole purpose: to hold back the everlasting Shadow.

The General began to sing a slow, solemn tune under his breath as he led them along the dirt street to the central keep. The companions couldn't quite make out what he was saying, but they did hear the name "Delilah" several times.

Finally, after the painful walk across the courtyard, they reached the keep. It stood like a lone warrior surrounded by enemies.

Large, wooden gates were held open to allow Sparks easy access in and out, but they could be sealed shut at a moment's notice. Soldiers stood on watch far above, peering down at the strange group of mysterious people. When they noticed the General, they, too, gave a salute.

Stopping his mournful tune, Kraalek glanced back at them and cleared his throat. "Hurry inside," he beckoned, already skipping through the oaken gates. Shrugging, the companions followed inside.

Just inside the keep's walls was another medical tent, and he urged them over to it. Why he couldn't have taken them to one of the many by the Shadowfront, the companions could only guess. This General was a strange man.

As soon as they stepped under the tent, two Flametouchers looked up from their patients and rushed over to them. They each wore a long, crimson cloak, similar to Kraalek's. Adorning the hood and at the edge of each sleeve there were two gold stripes, the most out of any other Flametoucher under the tent.

"General Kraalek!" one of them exclaimed. "What have you brought for us?"

"Oh, just what you would normally expect from the Shadowfront." He stepped aside to let the healers examine the companions. "Treat them with care."

The one who had spoken moved over to Andromeda and Fasto, and the other stepped in front of Nalgene, looking him up and down. He had long, blond hair that was hanging out from his hood, and gentle blue eyes. Shaking his, he reached out and placed his hands on the gnome's chest. Mumbling something to himself, fires flared out of the Flametoucher's hands, and immediately Nalgene was overcome with a surge of warmth. It was different from the cool waves of healing water that he was used to, but the fiery embrace was just as pleasant. The gnome felt his strength return through the flames, and the many wounds that he deemed unimportant enough to heal during the Shadowfront disappeared from his achy body.

Satisfied, the blond man stepped away from Nalgene and moved to heal the others.

Nalgene didn't want to admit it, but the Flametoucher did about as good a job as he could have. That shifty Kraalek did say he would be treating them, after all.

Slowly and methodically the two healers worked their way through the companions, even stopping to cast their fire over SmibSmob, even though he had no visible wounds. The blood was burned from Ro's scales, Andromeda's leg fixed itself back in place, Margaret's wounds were sealed shut, and even Fasto's arms healed themselves, much to the stubborn orc's discontent.

Once the two Flametouchers had finished their work, they turned to Kraalek. "Ever burn bright for the Flame," they said, before returning to the Sparks they were working on before.

Kraalek nodded in return, then turned to regard the revitalized companions. Studying them, he reached into his pouch and pulled out his mysterious die. With a soft chuckle, he cast it onto the floor before them.

As always, all the sides were brown and blank. And, as always, it came face-up on one of those blank sides. Kraalek furrowed his brow at the die, then with a shrug, picked it up. "Alas, it's time to head out, isn't that right?"

"Eh, but what is that damn die even for?" Nalgene grumbled. "Bloody hell, all the sides be lookin' the same to me." It just made no sense to the frustrated gnome. The slippery Kraalek threw that thing around as if it would solve the world's problems when all it really did was confuse Nalgene. But maybe that was the point …

Nalgene didn't like being pulled around like a puppet.

The General laughed, but not just a soft, humored chuckle. Rather, he let out a very uncharacteristic bellow which shocked all the surrounding Sparks. "My good gnome," he finally said, catching his breath and pocketing the annoying die. "I supposed you really aren't feeling lucky today. Alas, I would love to humor you in this fine discussion, but it seems we must be off. We have a whole new Light to explore, and it would be a shame if you were left behind to ponder the workings of the world. And so, it would be best if we left at once. Don't fall too far behind!"

Kraalek tossed the companions a sly wink, then bowed down into one of his exaggerated bows, then spun about and marched out of the tent, leaving the companions and the surrounding Sparks quite bewildered.

"What in the bloody hell," Nalgene mumbled.

"My, my, isn't he quite the eccentric one," Margaret replied, clenching her black fist. "It just makes me want to ... punch him."

"Woah, there's no need for that," Ro barged in. "I think we already had our fair share of violence today."

"Shut it, Ro," Nalgene said. "Or I'll be punchin' yer face and that bloody Kraalek's."

"Yes, please do," said Andromeda.

Fasto stood there confused, looking back and forth between the bantering friends, then back down to his fresh arms.

SmibSmob simply laughed, and Nalgene thought he could swim in that sound forever.

He opened his mouth to say something else, but at just that moment Kraalek poked his head back into the tent and interrupted him. "Hurry now, we don't have any time to waste. We can rest on the road, but for now, we must be off. Come now, into the Light."

And with that, the General disappeared again.

"Fasto thinks we should follow," said Fasto, finally tearing his eyes off of his perfectly functional arms.

"You know, I reckon you're right," SmibSmob answered, smiling. That sly man was no amateur.

"Bah," Nalgene grumbled, before turning to follow the slimy General.

And with that, the companions were off. The General led them out of the central keep and back into the courtyard. A great commotion was happening at the mighty stone wall. The Shadow was redoubling its efforts to break through, but, of course, Forthold would not fall. The Shadowfront had not gained ground in many years. The companions turned away from the wall and followed the road around the keep and to the back of the fortified city, towards the Light. After much walking, and many salutes from Sparks, they made it to the edge of the stronghold, where they were let out of the towering southeast gate.

Together, they ventured through the Light. Tall and frightening mountains flanked them to the south and the north, casting long shadows as the sun passed slowly dipped in the west. Behind them, the thick smog of the Shadow still hung over the lands. But even with all of that, it was peaceful. There was no looking out for rogue zombies. There was no scouting during the night while watching for the next undead assault. It was simply peaceful, as the world should be, with happy butterflies and singing birds.

The first night the companion's spent in the Light was truly magical. As the sun disappeared behind the horizon, small, twinkling lights appeared in the clear sky.

"Stars!" Fasto exclaimed, staring up at the dancing lights, his mouth agape. He remembered what they were! Some drool began to leak from the corner of his mouth. The other companions found themselves similarly entranced by the heavenly lights. If they let their imaginations run free, they could even picture shapes and figures in the stars.

"It's beautiful," Margaret whispered. At this moment, there wasn't a defensive or sarcastic bone in her body.

"Mmmm, I have to agree."

"I've always imagined that I could just fly up and grab one," SmibSmob said.

"Ye'd have to fly pretty damn high, me brother."

"My friends, I'd like to spend this time and reflect —" Ro began, before getting elbowed by Margaret.

"Can it, Ro," the orc interrupted. "Save the speech for when I don't care." Perhaps there was still a sarcastic bone somewhere in there.

Ro closed his mouth and smiled. Sometimes the best thing for a leader to do was nothing.

Nalgene snorted at the draconian, but otherwise said nothing. He wished every night was like this. Just him, his brother, and peace. Of course, of course, the others were there too. And he was content with that.

All the while, the General simply watched, allowing them their time to appreciate the beauty. He wasn't sure how long it had been since they saw stars, but he certainly would not ruin this moment for them. They would not get much rest tonight, and that was perfectly acceptable.

After a day and a half of walking and sharing stories with the cheery General, they came upon a large crater next to the road. A sprawling quarry had been constructed on the site, and watchtowers surrounded the place, filled with dozens of soldiers who were ready to lay down their lives to defend this sacred place. A mystical aura filled the air, and magical energy flickered about like fragments of stray lightning.

As they passed by, Ro decided to ask about it. "What's going on in there, General Kraalek?"

Kraalek turned, then gestured for them to follow him. "Come, my good friends, let me show you."

Unsure of what to expect, the others followed him to the edge of the crater, and they peered down inside. Laying in the center of the site was a large, but wholly unremarkable, gray stone. Many Sparks wearing outrageous protective suits were working tirelessly to mine away at the rock. Whatever pieces they managed to chip off were placed in padded iron carts and then carried up and out of the crater by a team of mules. Before any chip was sent out of the quarry it was inspected by a team of Flametouchers, who cast a magical fire over the stone before nodding in satisfaction.

"Seems like a bunch o' dwarvish nonsense to me," Nalgene said, scratching his head.

"Ah, not quite, my good gnome," Kraalek was quick to reply. "This is a Moonshard. After the Fall of the Moon those fifty-some years ago, pieces of that rock fell crashing to the ground. We discovered some of these pieces, and much to our surprise, they were imbued with a staggering amount of magical energy. Also, much to our surprise, the moon was actually full of gemstones! Because of this miracle, we set up these quarries to mine the material, where it is examined for purity then shipped away to Cern to be forged into our weapons and armor — as well as other things."

The General had a sly look in his eye as he said that last phrase, and he fingered at something in one of his many pouches. Nalgene wasn't sure if he liked that. But before he could ponder what the man went, the man continued:

"Have you ever wondered why your good friend … uh … Captain Osann was it? Have you ever wondered why his sword was able to light ablaze? Well, it is partly because of this Moonshard. It helped him channel his innate magical abilities. Unfortunately, this is the last remaining shard in the Light, as the rest have fallen into the hands of the Shadow. We will guard this site until the fall of the Flame."

The companions gawked at him, their eyes wide with wonder. Drool was even dripping out of Fasto's mouth. Pieces of the moon had landed on *Ansalon?* What happened to the moon? And what caused it to come crashing down? They could only wonder.

"Mmm, do you think that our gear was forged from this very shard?" Andromeda asked.

Kraalek could only shrug. "I don't know. Perhaps …"

Nalgene snorted. He knew none of his gear was forged with some phony piece of rock. Last he knew, thinking back to his childhood, and even to his darker days, there had always been a moon in the sky. But come to think of it, he hadn't seen it last night. Or ever since escaping that damn prison. And even with his new memories, he could not remember the moon ever falling out of the heavens. Just what in the bloody hell was that General talking about?

"Do you think we could get some equipment enchanted with the moon?" asked SmibSmob with a hopeful look on his face. "Who knows how useful having the power of the sky would be?"

"Perhaps, perhaps not," Kraalek repeated.

"Wow, some help you are," Margaret sighed. She was getting quite tired of this self-absorbed fool.

Before the General could form a witty response, he was interrupted by: "Fasto want moon." All of them whipped around to see Fasto running down the crater with his arms stretched out before him. The companions tensed, ready to go sprinting after the fool, but suddenly a half dozen guards tackled the orc, halting his self-imposed quest.

"Ye bloody idiot, what are ye doin'?" Nalgene exclaimed, watching the spectacle with amusement.

One of the Sparks holding down the brain-dead orc looked up to the group. "General Cardmaster, what should we do?"

Kraalek tapped his lips and looked up to the sky, feigning to be deep in thoughts. He shrugged, then winked at the others. "Oh, I suppose we shouldn't execute him. Bring him back up, as we must be on our way. We have many-a-sight to see."

After retrieving Fasto from his near-death experience, the group continued down the dusty road. They walked late into the day, with the bright sun dipping below the mountains behind them. There was an abundance of wildlife surrounding them. A stray rabbit even crossed their path, which Nalgene took great pleasure in. He wisely did not spray water on this one.

As the sun began to dip in the sky, they noticed a lone figure walking towards them on the road. It wasn't a busy miner rushing back to the quarry, or even a Spark patrolling the land, but rather, it was a beautiful woman. She was tall with long, inky hair and pale skin to contrast. She wore a long, black cloak with scarlet coloring at the edges and knee-high boots which allowed some of her smooth thighs to peek through. A silver longsword was sheathed at her side. As she got closer, Kraalek recognized her and gave a warm welcome. "Ho, welcome, Saber — or should I say, General Umbra — to our little adventuring party."

Saber gave him a cold smile. "General Cardmaster, what a surprise to see you here."

Nalgene narrowed his eyes. Something wasn't sitting right with him — it was tickling a memory deep in his brain. Saber? Seemed like a funny name. But she was remarkably beautiful. Funny name aside, the gnome could not take his eyes away …

"Ah, yet for some reason I suspect it isn't as much of a surprise as you say. And what brings you out here?" Kraalek replied. "I rarely see you leave your nest in Firelight."

"Hm, but of course, I wanted to congratulate our heroes for battling through the Shadowfront. Truly … what an impressive deed."

"You have my thanks, General Umbra, it was a difficult battle," Ro stammered, dipping into a respectful bow. If draconians could blush he would have been a bright tomato. "May your light pierce the Shadow."

As he stood up, Saber gave him a sweet smile. Apparently, it wasn't difficult enough.

Fasto was quick to jump into a respectful salute, muttering something about "new friend", and the others, minus Nalgene and Margaret, were quick to follow. Nalgene simply studied the mysterious woman, while Margaret rolled her eyes.

"Like we need another General following us around," the orc mumbled to herself.

Saber walked amongst the group, looking each of them up and down. "I can sense your strength; no wonder you were able to make it through so easily." She would make sure that it would never happen again. They would be killed, soon enough.

A Resurgence of Hope

Even though Nalgene had his initial doubts about the woman, he felt strangely relaxed by her presence as she passed by. Yes, he felt as if he could trust her. This was a woman who knew duty. Kraalek had even said it was her expert strategy that had been holding the Shadow at bay. Yes, he could trust this most alluring and tantalizing woman. Yes ...

Wait! What the hell was he thinking? He was just a wee gnome, and she ... well ... those legs were just so scrumptious ...

Shaking his head, he snapped out of the trance. Something just wasn't settling with the gnome. Just who *was* Saber? His thoughts weighed heavy on his mind, but as quickly as they had come, they melted away when he looked at her sensual curves ...

Bah! He did it again!

"Aren't they quite the group?" Kraalek commented. "Their strength is truly from another era. Now, if you're done studying my good friends, perhaps you would like to join us? We are just about to settle for the night, and we have plenty of sightseeing left to do tomorrow."

The General ruffled in one of his pouches and revealed some sort of fruit. "Oh, would you like a snack? I'm sure you're quite hungry after your long journey here."

Saber shook her head. "I'm not here to chase rabbits and hunt squirrels, Cardmaster. Or join you for a snack." She reached into one of her pouches and retrieved a small orange gem. Smiling brightly, she tossed it over to companions.

Fasto lurched forward, trying to catch it. Of course, he missed, and it landed on the ground by Nalgene's feet.

Grunting, Nalgene picked it up, then studied the gemstone in his hand. It was identical to the one Roan and Dain had tried to use to get them through the Shadowfront. Hopefully, this one worked a little better, as he would hate to have to fight more zombies so soon.

"Duty calls, Cardmaster, and the Torch has requested to meet our new heroes," she continued. "They have heard of their deeds — have heard that even the … wise Mariah was seen again. They have questions, and they would like their answers."

"But —" Kraalek started, but Saber cut him off with a raised hand. Scowling, he replaced the fruit into his pouch and pulled out his die yet again. After blowing on it, he cast it on the ground. Upon examining the face which ended up — which was still identical to all the others — he shrugged and swiped it back up. "Duty calls, isn't that right?"

An orange gemstone appeared in the man's hand, identical to the one that Nalgene now held. "I suppose this will be your first time?"

"First time for what, General Cardmaster?" Ro asked while the other companions shrugged.

The sly man smiled. "Splendid."

Nalgene rolled the gemstone through his fingers. This belonged to that wonderful and beautiful woman. Perhaps he should keep it — as a gift, of course. After all, she didn't even ask for it back. He felt a rush of blood flow through his body and his eyes jerked up, studying the wondrous and sexy …

His incredible and sinful thoughts were interrupted by Kraalek's whiny voice. Snapping back to reality, he pocketed the gemstone — out of sight and out of mind, for now.

"Now, my friends, come close," Kraalek said. "Reach out and place your hands upon my shoulders."

Following orders, the companions did exactly that. However, Saber did not. Kraalek noticed this with a raised eyebrow.

"I'll meet you there, I have one other matter to attend to," Saber purred. No man could resist her — they were all so weak.

Seemingly satisfied with the explanation, Kraalek shrugged, and continued his speech. "A miraculous journey awaits us. To distant lands of beauty and splendor. Come with me, now, to the vibrant city of Firelight."

As he finished, he began to murmur under his breath, and the orange gemstone in his hand began to glow with a warm light.

"May the Torch bless your fire," Saber said, a wicked gleam in her eyes. If all went according to plan, the Torch, especially the Torchhead, would hardly be ready to bless them. Soon, they would all be dead, and she was absolutely thrilled. Damn that bitch Ashyla.

Suddenly, a roaring column of fire engulfed the companions. Caught off guard, they tried to pull away, but they found they could not. It was too late, the gem-call had already begun. To abandon would mean death. It was not a hot fire, yet it did burn away at them, reducing them to nothing but ash blowing on the cool wind.

The last thing Nalgene saw before disappearing was the crooked smile on Saber's face.

Something just wasn't sitting right with the gnome. It did seem like such a funny name.

But she was so beautiful …

Daniel Whitman

Chapter 2

The great fire around the companions began to smother away. They were whole once again, no longer ash flowing across the vast lands. Ro blinked his eyes, trying to wrap his mind around the fiery magic. His stomach felt mildly sick. Traveling by pillars of fire apparently wasn't the smoothest travel.

He shook his head, regaining his focus. So this is what Roan and Dain were trying to do. This is what was supposed to bring them across the dreadful Shadowfront. So why did it go wrong? He had no answers.

As the fire disappeared, the draconian looked around. The others were all there, their hands still upon Kraalek's frail shoulders. Nalgene and SmibSmob appeared amazed at the wonderful transportation, and Andromeda looked oddly satisfied with the burning display of power. Fasto was too dim-witted to understand exactly what had just happened, and Margaret held a steady, blank expression, pretending not to be impressed.

And, as she said, General Saber did not travel with them, leaving them alone with the smugly grinning Kraalek.

Ro shrugged and looked around. He was sure there would be a good reason why she stayed back, she seemed like such a bright and charming woman. Yes, very charming ... For some reason, he thought he would lay down his life to protect her. Dashing heroes are the guardians of beautiful maidens, right?

The companions stood in the middle of a square of a great, beaming city. Four roads reached out in each of the cardinal directions, and they were paved with white stone that twinkled in the surrounding lights. Flanking both sides of the streets were tall, silver posts with a billowing flame burning bright at the top, bathing the city in a warm glow. The buildings were made of masterfully carved granite, and each one was unique and had elegant arches and winding walkways. Everything wove together into a seamless forest of stone. It seemed like the city had grown naturally from the ground — like it was a living and breathing entity that just permitted a few lucky beings to reside within it. It was truly a majestic sight to behold. It dwarfed every city the companions had seen and could remember with its sheer beauty. It was the capital of the Light.

This was Firelight.

Ro gawked at his surroundings. How could a place so pure survive in a world of such darkness? This is what the Flame was trying to protect: the purity. Children ran across the streets, kicking balls around and chasing after each other, unknown to the fact that the Shadow would soon enough rend their limbs from their cold, lifeless bodies. Mothers watched from the sidelines, laughing all the while as their children tripped and stumbled in the road. There were humans, draconians, felines, orcs, elves, dwarves, and others. Despite Nalgene's grumbles at the sight of the dwarves, it truly was a bastion of life and was refreshing to see after days and days of undead. Ro had vowed to protect the Light before, and this only redoubled his resolution.

No, he would not let the Shadow consume these innocent people as it did with Roan and Dain.

Little did he know how futile his aspiration would be.

"So, what do you think?" General Kraalek asked, breaking the companions from their trance. "Because what I think is that you can stop grabbing my shoulders now." Grunting, they lowered their hands, and the nimble General skittered away, holding the orange gem.

"Welcome to Firelight, the center of all that is good and just in this world. It's pretty breathtaking, isn't that right?"

"It truly is ..." SmibSmob answered softly.

"Oh yes, magical cities are my favorite," Margaret sneered.

"Bah, ye always be havin' something down to say," Nalgene countered.

"Fasto thinks very pretty."

"Ye be thinkin' everything is pretty, ye bloody orc."

"I wonder if he thinks his own face is pretty? We can all obviously see that it's not," Margaret added.

"Always with the vanity, aren't you?" Andromeda said.

Ro smiled at the others' bantering. It was amazing how being nearly killed in the Shadow on numerous occasions can bring a group of strangers so close together. While they did have their disagreements, he felt like they were stronger than ever before. Oh, the power of friendship, what a wonderful thing. With friends, it was possible to overcome anything, right?

He just hoped they could stay friends after everything was over.

"Say, good General Cardmaster," Ro said, interrupting the bickering of his friends. "What exactly is the Torch?"

"Ah, great question, my friend," Kraalek replied. "I guess you will find out soon enough." His metallic cards appeared in his nimble hands, and he turned away. "We will call on you when we are ready. For now, do enjoy the wonders that this fine city has to offer."

He started away, but he turned and offered them one last word of advice: "Oh, and do enjoy the ham, I hear it is quite spectacular at this time of year." And with that, the General skipped down the northern street and disappeared into the crowd.

Ro watched the man prance away. He would take that advice to heart. It had been some time since he had a decent meal, after all. SmibSmob with his hat wasn't the most proficient chef.

"Bah, I didn't want that dolt dancin' around us anyway," said Nalgene, interrupting the draconian's thoughts.

"Did he say ham?" Margaret mumbled.

"Spectacular advice," Andromeda answered. "Let's find some relaxation and food, shall we?"

"I agree, some time to ourselves does sound splendid," Ro said.

"Alright, great and noble leader," Margaret said, nudging Ro with her elbow. "Where are you taking us first? Where is that ham?"

"Fasto want ham!"

Ro glanced down at Margaret in surprise. He did like the sound of that. Yes, he *was* noble.

"Ahem, well, let's see …" He looked down the three remaining streets. They all looked identical. This single moment could truly cement his nobility and leadership. Bolstering his resolve and steeling his determination, he made a decision and started walking down the western street. With his leadership and intellect, he supposed this way was as good as any other.

"Follow me, my friends," he called back to the rest of the group.

"Alright Ro, if ye say so. Let's be off SmibSmob," Nalgene said, surprisingly not grumbling.

"Yes, good choice," Andromeda agreed.

"I would've chosen the other way but hey, I'm not the leader here," Margaret said.

"I don't wanna hear yer whinin'," Nalgene retorted.

"Fasto go this way!" Fasto said, quite excited about himself.

"You idiot, get over here!" Margaret cried.

"Bwahahaha, what is that damn orc even doin'? Why are ye sticking yer head in that?"

"You're going to scare all the poor children away," Andromeda said.

"Someone go help him," Ro ordered in his most leadership-y voice.

"It's not going to be me, I don't get paid enough for this," Margaret said.

"None of us are paid anything," Ro said.

"Trust me, I am aware," Margaret replied, rolling her eyes.

"I reckon we should stop him?" SmibSmob asked.

"Eh, the dolt will be fine — er, maybe not. AYE, stop it ye damn orc!"

"What a silly little orc. Let's go fetch him, shall we?" Andromeda said.

"I suppose we should, he is our friend, after all," Ro agreed.

"Bah!"

Together, after saving Fasto from his own misfortunes, the companions finally marched off down the western street. Children danced around them, occasionally darting through their party in a silly game of tag. The mothers watching laughed as their rascals almost tripped a few of the companions. The road sloped up, rising onto a small hill. As they reached the peak, they found themselves on a vast overlook. In every direction they looked, there were snow-capped mountains, but they somehow looked kinder and less harsh than those in the Shadow. The dipping sun approached their peaks, casting sharp shadows over a glittering lake that lapped at the base of the white city. If the mountains looked kinder, then the lake certainly did as well. It was less dark, broody, and had less ominous creatures than they were used to, which they were thankful for it. Finally, a small river rushed to the south, weaving through the valleys of the looming mountains.

"Fasto see lake," Fasto said.

"Aye, don't ye be the sharpest o' us bunch," Nalgene grunted.

"Now, let him have his moment," Ro said.

As they stood admiring the view, a small woman approached them from behind.

"Hello, noble Sparks," she said quietly, trying not to disturb their silent vigil. "I've never seen any of you before."

Ro turned and studied the woman. She was short, not even above his shoulders, and had curly blonde hair. She was plump, which made little secret of her love of food.

"Hail, fair maiden," he replied, dipping into a bow. "I am Ro, humbly at your service."

The other companions rolled their eyes. Why were they following this draconian, anyway? If he wants to make a fool of himself, so be it. It would be quite a spectacle to watch.

"Oh my," the woman said, placing a hand on her chest and blushing. "I am Meredith, and I graciously accept your service, good sir draconian."

Ro rose from his bow and smiled. "These are my friends. We have Andromeda, Margaret, Nalg —"

"I can be introducin' myself," Nalgene interjected, grabbing his brother. "Me name is Nalgene, and this here is me brother SmibSmob. What can we be helpin' ye with today, miss?"

"So nice to meet you all," Meredith said.

"And there is also Fasto, whom we cannot forget about," Ro was quick to finish. The bumbling orc nodded his head in agreement. He tried to approach the woman and give her a hug, but Ro wisely held him back. There was no need to traumatize the poor woman.

"We come from far across the world, battling the evil forces of undeath. The Light called upon us to defend it, and we heartily accepted the call. Just recently, we bravely fought through the Shadowfront to finally reach the Light," Ro continued. "It was a most brave and terrible effort, but to be blessed with these sights and, of course, fine ladies such as yourself, it was worth the danger."

Behind Ro, Nalgene started choking while trying to hide his laughter. What in a dwarf's hairy ass was this kooky draconian yammering about? Even SmibSmob had to cover his own mouth to suppress his amusement.

Margaret was less subtle, and her laugh lit up the street. "Don't talk yourself up too much," she snorted.

The woman ignored their outburst, and her eyes grew wide, fixated on the most devilishly handsome Ro. "So, it is true? I had heard rumors of a mighty band of heroes who overcame death and destruction. Is it really you?"

Mighty heroes? Ro quite liked the sound of that — even more than "noble leader". There were already stories of his marvelous feats of bravery, and he had just reached the Flame. How many more could he amass throughout the coming years? He would be a mighty hero indeed.

"Why yes, we are the heroes of whom you speak," Ro said triumphantly, reaching out and grabbing the woman's hand. He leaned down — quite far to match her stunted height — and brought the hand up to his lips, where he gave it a gentle kiss. Or as gentle of a kiss that a scale-covered draconian could give.

Margaret laughed again and shook her head, and this time Nalgene couldn't stop himself from joining her. It seemed Ro was going to enjoy his little ego-parade.

"Are you hungry? It would be my honor to treat the heroes to a meal," Meredith said, pulling her hand away from Ro. Her face was beet red. "Don't worry, I already have it prepared!"

"Hah, ain't that convenient! I can always be goin' fer some good cookin'!" Nalgene exclaimed.

"Fasto hungry, Fasto want meat." Drool was already dripping from the orc's mouth.

"Mmmm, meat sounds wonderful," Andromeda agreed.

"I reckon we should — it was the General's advice, after all," SmibSmob said.

"Well, there you have it," Ro said. "We would be happy to join you for a meal."

Meredith beamed with excitement. Now, at her next card-playing party, she would be able to gloat to everyone else that she had served the heroes of the Flame.

"Please, come be my guests!"

The companions followed Meredith to her house, which was just down the road. As they entered, the delicious smell of food washed over them. Of course, there was the roasted ham glazed with a sweet honey sauce that Kraalek had mentioned to them. There were also buttery, mashed potatoes, fresh salad, warm muffins, and many, many other scrumptious things. Most importantly, no stale prison soup. What was interesting, however, was that she was the only one in her house, and there was no feasible way she would be able to eat all the food by herself. It was like she somehow knew she would have company. Perhaps someone had tipped her off to their location.

But, of course, they wouldn't know that. Instead, Ro just congratulated himself on his wise insight to take the western road. It was part of his nobility, he imagined.

"Come in, I hope it's all to your liking." Meredith invited.

"If it tastes half as good as it smells, I reckon this will be exactly what we like." SmibSmob piped in.

"I agree, my friend," Ro said, taking a seat at the table. "Let's eat."

They all sat at the table and eagerly dove into the food — especially the ham. They wouldn't have even cared if it was poisoned, for it tasted as if it was cooked in the very heavens above. It was leagues above the meager scraps and bread they had been eating from SmibSmob's hat, or the war rations Kraalek had given them on their journey through the Light.

A *Resurgence of Hope*

Ro wolfed down his food. He had been dreaming of ham since his time in that prison. This was yet another reason he would always vow to protect the Light against the oncoming darkness.

But as quickly as the festivities had begun, they were cut short. Suddenly, a half-dozen Sparks barged through the door, not even bothering to knock. They entered the room, which was already crowded with people, and fanned out around the group. A lone, final Spark entered the house, wearing worn plate mail with crimson, cloth accents. Exactly like the rest of them.

"Ho, my fellow Sparks," the ragged man said in salute. "I am Captain Dagger. The Torch is ready for you." He pulled a pocket watch out of one of his pouches and glanced down at it. His eyebrows rose in concern. This was truly unacceptable — it took the platoon thirty seconds too long to reach their destination. "We *really* don't have much time."

"Already?" Margaret protested. "I was just starting to enjoy the food."

"I can agree with that," Andromeda said.

"Bah, let's be takin' some for the road," Nalgene grunted.

"Maybe I can store it in my hat! Since I can pull food from it, I reckon I can put some back in!" SmibSmob exclaimed, already taking his hat from his head.

"Good thinkin' me brother. Everyone, start grabbin' what ye want!"

"Food!"

"Now wait," Ro started, watching the ravenous monsters tear at the food with abandon and cram it into SmibSmob's hat. He glanced at Meredith, who was quite disturbed. Who knew the mighty heroes were such savages?

"We do NOT have time for such barbarity!" the Captain shouted, interrupting the massacre before Ro could say anything else. "We are leaving at once." Now they were a full minute behind schedule.

The companions paused for just a moment, and in that time, Ro took charge.

"So be it," Ro commanded, rising from his seat and taking a bow. "Alas, it seems we must part ways, fair Meredith, but we have duties to attend to. We very much enjoyed your prestigious meal. We humbly thank you for serving us. Now *come*, my friends."

"But there is still so much ham left ..." Andromeda groaned.

"You're right, it would be a shame to waste it," SmibSmob agreed.

"Can ye talk normally, Ro?" Nalgene grunted, jumping off the table. This holy and righteous hero act was wearing the gnome's patience thin. Damn dragons.

"Make haste, we would not want to keep them waiting," the Captain hissed, his eyes shooting daggers at them.

The companions gathered behind Ro, their appetite somewhat cleansed. When SmibSmob placed the hat on his head, all the food they managed to cram into its folds fell onto his head. It seemed it was not so infinite — or perhaps its magic wasn't what they thought. Meredith was now fully horrified at the sight. Perhaps she would *not* be bragging about this bunch.

"I don't mean to be the obvious one, but we lost our haul," SmibSmob said, quite defeated as mashed potatoes oozed down his face.

"Bloody hell, I thought that was supposed to be good at holdin' stuff!"

"Now that is truly tragic," Margaret said.

"Fasto's food ..."

"Follow me, NOW!" Captain Dagger ordered, interrupting their misery. He checked his pocket watch once more. A full two minutes behind. Unacceptable, he was going to be flayed for this. "And Carson, clean up that gnome." Without waiting to see if they were following, he turned around and marched out of the door. One of the Sparks rushed over to SmibSmob, a towel in his hand, and he began to wipe the gnome down while ushering him out the door. The other Sparks followed their Captain's lead and began to corral the companions out of Meredith's home. The Captain had a tight schedule to keep, and it wouldn't be wise to keep him waiting.

Without much of a choice, the companions — or at least Ro — bowed, thanked Meredith for her meal once again, and left her alone in her house.

Now alone, Meredith looked down at the half-eaten food in despair — both on the table and on the floor. How was she supposed to finish all of this? Oh, the troubles of her middle-aged days. The meal wasn't cheap, either, but thankfully she had some assistance with the upfront cost. With any luck, perhaps the dashing fellow that generously donated the gold would come back to eat dinner with her — and maybe have her upstairs for dessert. Rumors did say that he was a wonder with the barmaids, and he did have to repay her for this tragedy, after all. Sighing, and dreaming for the best, she went about her business to tidy up the place. Meredith hoped tomorrow would be less eventful.

After leaving the granite house, the companions followed Captain Dagger through the labyrinth of streets. As they walked, the citizens of Firelight gave way to make room for their march. There was a plethora of stands on the side of the road, ranging from food to tapestries to artwork to trinkets. All of the goods were left out in the open without any proper surveillance or protection, awaiting the next customer to wander over. No one would dare steal in the kindly capital of the Light, or at least that was the theory. The living had to look after each other, and any who thought different would be no better than a Shadowfriend.

After some time, the group finally came upon a brilliant, white structure. A marble staircase rose out of the ground and led up to a towering building. The silver streetlights flanked both sides of the staircase, and after every three was a majestic statue depicting a mighty animal of legend. A marvelous fountain was built into the center of the staircase, almost identical to the one from the ruins of

Calinad. A gargantuan lion was carved into the archway above the large, oaken door of the entrance, watching the city like a vigilant guard dog. Its mouth was open in a defiant roar, and a dancing, orange fire burned deep within its mouth. Six white pillars accented the front of the building, three on each side of the door. Each pillar represented a member of the Torch, and it had their name engraved into the stone. There were also burn marks along the pillars, black stripes running across some of them, but the companions did not know why.

The Captain led them up the staircase, constantly checking his pocket watch, and the dozens of Sparks keeping guard let them through. The Torch had called for them, so the Torch would receive them. When they approached the gate, the soldiers gave them a proper salute, and then one of them pulled out a strange horn and blew into it. No sound came forth, but when he stopped, the robust doors swung inward, inviting them into the bastion.

Captain Dagger led them into the premises, where it opened into a grand, golden hall. Two, spiraling staircases rose up to the higher level on either side. Dozens of Flametouchers rushed around on urgent business from the Generals. The companions hiked up one of the spiraling staircases, where they found themselves in a grand corridor. Without giving them time to appreciate the sublime hall, Dagger ushered them towards a large room. The door was open.

The Captain pulled out his pocket watch and shook his head when he saw the time. "Always late," he mumbled. Putting it away, he turned to the companions. "Good luck and ever burn bright for the Flame." With that, he and his Spark brigade disappeared back down the stairway. He just hoped that his tardiness would be forgivable.

"Lead the way, noble hero," Margaret urged Ro, gesturing to the open threshold.

Swallowing the lump in his throat, Ro walked into the room. "Come, my friends."

Together, they entered. Before them stretched a vast, round room. An intricately detailed map was carved into a sturdy table that rested at the center. Surrounding the table, and seated on antique chairs, was the Torch.

The Torch comprised the six Generals of the Flame.

Sitting on the largest chair was Agmund Giantheart, the Torchhead, and leader of the Light. He now wore a hulking plate mail adorned with a lion's head on the chest piece. White fur embellished his armor, and his helmet rested on the arm of his throne. It was crowned in silver and red, a symbol of his might and power. His gaze narrowed as he studied the outsiders. So, they were the ones to bring doom to the Flame.

Sitting to the right of him was Don Lighthammer. While he was also a hulking man, he didn't quite match the spectacle of the walking tree Agmund. He also wore an illustrious, silver plate mail with gold adornment. His silver and gold barbute remained on, obscuring the entirety of his face. A hefty warhammer was resting vertically on its head next to him. He sat with his arms crossed and made no move when the companions came through the door.

To the left of Agmund was Saber Umbra, who gave the companions a sly wink as they entered. This was going to be too simple. She had the Torch in her palm, and it was only a matter of time before this pathetic and miserable group would be eradicated.

Next to her was the newest member of the torch, Roark Strongarm. Unlike Don and Agmund, he donned no spectacular armor, but he was no less stout. Instead, he wore a simple chainmail covered with crimson padding. He had a worn visor for a helmet and had it pulled up for this occasion, revealing his grizzled beard. He gave a friendly nod to the companions.

Across the table and next to Don sat Kraalek Cardmaster, the sly and elusive gambler. He was running his cards through his hands, and when he noticed the companions, he pulled out his brown die and rolled in his palms, chuckling quietly to himself.

Finally, in the remaining seat was Sylven Quickfoot. A spry fellow with messy brown hair, sharp, gray eyes, and pointed ears. His left arm was covered with silver armor, which had the head of a lion as his shoulder pauldron, but the rest of him was left unprotected, covered only by a bright, red shirt and black pants. He smiled as the group entered.

The companions entered and glanced around, wisely not saying anything. Ro looked over to General Kraalek, then over to the beautiful General Saber, where his eyes rested for an enjoyably long time, before studying the others. Truly a refreshing bud of beauty in the formidable room.

The Generals studied them intently — almost uncomfortably so. Their eyes drilled holes into the companions, measuring their worth and spirit. Were they impressed by what they saw? The answer remained a mystery.

"Hail, light of the Flame," Ro said, breaking the long silence. His voice sounded hollow in his ears, and he felt helpless before the full might of the Flame, but as a noble hero and a leader, he took it upon himself to stand for his friends.

There was no response, save for Kraalek rolling his die across the table, where, as always, it landed on one of the six indistinguishable sides. Upon looking at the deciding result, the sly man snatched it up. "Welcome," Kraalek said, pocketing his toy, "to the Torch. Very impressive, isn't that right?"

Saber snorted.

"Is it true," Agmund started, scowling at them and placing both of his bear paws down upon the table. This was no time for theatrics. "That you managed to battle through the Shadowfront at Forthold?"

"Oh, so this is that group?" Sylven said in a cheery voice, now balancing a crystal blue dagger on his fingertip. "Wow, most impressive. I had heard the rumors."

"Oh, this is indeed them," Saber purred. "They are quite formidable. The Shadow should be wary of these heroes."

"Yes, it's true," Ro managed to say. That lump in his throat had returned. How could he deal with this situation? What should he say? He was grasping at straws. What would a leader do?

"How I'll be blessed," Don exclaimed. "May they be a holy sun for the Light."

"And how did you manage that?" Roark asked. "What were the exact steps utilized for your operation?"

"Relax, that's hardly important," Kraalek answered for the group. "And why yes, they are quite the blessing for us."

"Blessing? How can we be so sure?" Agmund scrutinized. He had not forgotten his dream. The outsiders would mean death. His doe — his Ellie — would never lie.

"Why, just look at them!" Sylven said, tossing his brilliant dagger into the air. "They're as fine a bunch as I've ever seen!"

"No, the Torchhead has a point," Saber said. Oh, it was just too simple. "How can we be sure? Perhaps the only way they made it through that bloodbath was because they have the blessing of the Shadow."

Kraalek laughed. "Or perhaps they have the blessing of Mariah."

"Oh, dear heavens!" Don shouted. "Has the blessed Oracle returned?"

"What do you speak of, General Cardmaster?" Agmund asked.

"Yes, what indeed?" Roark mimicked. "This is a most intriguing strategy."

"Well, let me do the honor of telling you." Kraalek leaped to his feet and gave a facetious bow. "May I present to you the Beacon and his companions. I first found them by the ruins of Calinad, where they came to me with a wild story about Mariah. Yet, although I did doubt it, they managed to battle through the darkness to unite with the Flame. I even saw Mariah at the Shadowfront, where she made the Beacon a pure apostle of Light!"

"Hail, the prophecy shall come true!" Don shouted.

"Is that so?" Agmund pondered. Why would these dangerous outsiders have the blessings of the Oracle?

"Are you sure of what you saw?" Saber said. The pieces were falling perfectly into place. "If that is true, then where is our dear Mariah now?"

"Yes, that is an interesting twist," Roark said.

"No doubt she's off incinerating some undead," Sylven said with reverence.

"Of course, the holy Oracle has the power of the almighty heavens above!" Don agreed.

"Always the righteous one," Sylven chuckled.

"I don't think that would be a wise strategy on Mariah's part," Rorak reprimanded.

"Yes, where would she be? Isn't that quite the question? Perhaps you were mistaken, Cardmaster," Saber said, eagerness seeping into her voice.

"Oh, I don't think so. Why are you so quick to doubt my claims?" Kraalek replied.

"I could name a few reasons. First and foremost: liquor," Sylven jumped in.

"General Quickfoot! How unbecoming!" Agmund said.

"Well spoken, Quickfoot. Perhaps you were not in a proper state of mind, and you simply saw what you hoped to see," Saber said, redoubling her destructive efforts.

"Shall we ask the soldiers at the Shadowfront? I'm sure they also saw her, and I'd hope they weren't all … inebriated," Kraalek said.

"I did hear some rumors," Sylven said.

"Not all, are you implying that some were?" Saber prodded.

"How interesting …" Roark muttered.

"Is that truly what you thought I meant —" Kraalek began.

"Silence!" Agmund interjected. "We are not here to bicker amongst each other. We are the Torch, and we must act as such."

"Yes, of course, Torchhead," Saber said, feigning deferral to the infuriating giant. To calm her anger, she imagined his pitiful face while holding Ellie's bloody dagger.

Agmund turned his deep-set gaze onto the companions. "What do you have to say for yourselves? Has Mariah returned?"

Ro stuttered, trying to find words, but he found his eyes stuck on the wondrous form and curves of Saber. She pursed her lips, and they looked so plump and juicy. Maybe he was imagining it, but he thought she gave him a sly, inviting smirk. Maybe he hoped he wasn't imagining it … No! This wasn't what a hero would be thinking! He was pure!

Ro stammered at his next words, but Nalgene stepped forward and saved him from his moment of distraction. "Just ask me brother, he can tell ye." He nudged SmibSmob.

"Uh, well, yes," SmibSmob managed to say. "We have — I mean I have — no, I mean we have, because we all did see her, in fact — uh, so what I'm saying is —"

"My goodness, these are quite the conversational bunch," said Sylven, interrupting the gnome.

"Perhaps a wise tactic would be to invest in speech classes," Roark said.

"Speak, blessed guests!" Don urged.

"Ah, we've all succumbed to nerves before, isn't that right?" Kraalek said.

"Is that why you frequent the liquor cabinets — to calm the nerves?" Sylven said.

"I will not tolerate —" Agmund began.

"I'm saying we've all seen Mariah!" SmibSmob burst, silencing the room. "She saved us from certain death, and she saved me in the Shadowfront. I heard her calling. I am your Beacon."

"Well, there you have it, case dismissed," Kraalek said, applauding the small gnome. "It turns out I'm a trustworthy source, it seems."

"Praise the holy Beacon!" Don exclaimed.

"Fair play, Kraalek," Sylven said.

"Ah, so that's how it fits into the strategy," Roark mused.

"Now wait, how can we be sure that you are the Beacon?" Saber interjected. "Others have claimed the same thing. Who is to say that you truly are what you say?"

"Mariah is," SmibSmob answered quickly.

"She has said the same for others," Saber countered. "We cannot be sure unless we see her and get her confirmation."

"General Umbra speaks the truth," Agmund agreed. "Where is Mariah?"

"Has she truly returned?" Saber said. Of course, she knew Mariah would never return. She made sure of that. "Until we have proof, I do not think we can trust this group to be any more than Shadowfriends."

Kraalek raised his eyebrows but said nothing.

"I know you might doubt us," Ro said, finally clearing his head. "And we cannot give you proof aside from our humble words, but I can assure you that we are no foul Shadowfriends. We have battled mightily through death and darkness, and even if we don't receive your approval or trust, we will continue to wage war for the sake of this blessed Light. We are here to protect the good people of these lands, and if we must dive back into the heart of the Shadow to do so, so be it."

"Well — and normally — spoken, Ro," Nalgene said, giving Ro a pat on the back. "Ye truly be havin' a splendid vocabulary."

"Maybe his excessive words just saved us," said Margaret. "Fasto friend!"

"How noble a speech! Holy heavens!" congratulated Don.

"Yes, that is a very noble proclamation from you," Agmund said. He leaned forward in his chair, his deep eyes boring into Ro. "But we do not run the Flame based on noble proclamations. Anyone can declare good intent while stabbing another in the back. These are dark days we live in, and I'm afraid your word is not enough. Is he the Beacon? Perhaps. But should I lay the lives of the living on his shoulders just because he said so? Should I risk what we have fought for just because you say that you're good? I think even you can see the foolishness of that. We have lost thousands of lives for others who have claimed the Beacon title, and where are they now? Rotting away in the Shadow. While you do have the support of General Cardmaster, I need some tangible evidence that you will not spell doom for the Light. You would need to prove your truth. That is all." He glanced at the other members of the Torch as he finished. Ellie would never lie. He had to be cautious.

"Are there any objections?"

Kraalek said nothing, he simply grabbed his die and ran it through his hands, shaking his head.

SmibSmob started to protest, but he was interrupted by Saber.

"You have my support, great Torchhead." This was going splendidly. Now all she had to do was plant the seeds of death. Indeed, it was too simple. That bitch Ashyla would thank her for soon enough — not that Saber particularly cared for her thanks — but it would just be sweet music to Saber as she cut her down.

"That would be a wise move, General Agmund," Roark said. "We cannot take them for their word."

"Let's not be hasty," said Sylven. "Sometimes you have to take a leap of faith. If he is the Beacon, and they are the heroes against the Shadow, then maybe we should make the leap."

"Faith is what binds us together," said Don.

"Faith is no tool for justice," Agmund stated in finality.

"So, what are we going to do with them?" Saber said, reaching out and placing a hand on Agmund's arm. The Torchhead did not pull away.

"What indeed?" Kraalek mumbled to himself, but no one was listening. He cast the die on the floor. Upon seeing the face, he sighed in defeat. "You've lost, isn't that right?" He did not bother to retrieve it from the cold ground. Why is Agmund only listening to

Saber? Something wasn't sitting well. Sure, he did have a few mishaps with alcohol, but that hardly made him disreputable. He had nothing to gain from lying about the companions, so why wouldn't they listen?

Ro gawked at the Torch. This was going all wrong. He thought they were supposed to be hailed as heroes, not cast away like villains. But he couldn't find the will to argue. Everything General Giantheart said rang true. Mariah was not here, and he was just some silly draconian, spouting nonsense.

"May I ask another question, Torchhead?"

"Of course, General Umbra."

Saber smirked a most evil grin. "It's been said that you battled through the Shadowfront to reach the Light. If that is so, where did you come from originally? It seems to me, the only way you could have survived inside the Shadow for so long was if you were allied with it."

If Ro's resolve was crumbling before, this question obliterated it. He didn't have the faintest idea where they were from — none of them did. This was certain doom.

"We be comin' from all over, but we gathered in the southeast o' the Heartland," Nalgene began. "We used to be battlin' with Mariah, but after some stuff, we ended up in prison. Then the Shadowfront attacked there, and right before we died, she saved us by teleportin' us out. I don't be knowin' where she went, but she be tellin' us to get to the Light. And so, we done just that."

Maybe one of them *did* know where they were from. Ro remembered the gnome's words back on that beach: "We ain't who we think." Ro made a mental note to question the Nalgene about it when he had a chance.

Saber narrowed her eyes. That sounded almost shockingly accurate. If this group regained their memories her position would be compromised. Her plans just accelerated.

"And so, that brings us back to our original quandary: where is Mariah?"

The room sat silent for an uncomfortable time.

"I say we give them a shot," Sylven said. "And if they turn out to be oh-so-evil then we can just kill them. Easy, right?" He flicked his wrist, and his blue-bladed dagger went whistling past Ro's head and into the far wall, where it stuck into the solid stone.

"Killing is a sin of the Light!"

"Interesting plan of action. I would have to agree with General Sylven," Roark said.

"Yes, it would pain me to kill any more of the living," Agmund agreed. "The Shadow has taken enough from us already. Any and all help is welcome. But, if they are Shadowfriends, they are no help to us."

"Splendid deduction, great Torchhead," Saber purred. The trap was almost sealed.

"So, what is our strategy?" Roark asked.

"Have faith in the Light!" Don exclaimed.

"Will we take a leap?" Sylven mused.

"How can we be sure that they are not Shadowfriends?" Saber asked.

Ro watched in despair. He tried to say something, but the Torch drowned him out. It seemed the noble hero had no place before the actual legends.

Just then, Kraalek returned to the fray. He looked up, the fight reigniting within his eyes. He did not lose — not yet at least. "Ah, but we can be sure that they are not Shadowfriends!"

The Torch quieted, and they turned to regard the spry man. Saber's eyes suddenly grew very dark. Perhaps this wouldn't be too simple.

"Speak, General Cardmaster."

"From our knowledge, Shadowfriends lose their Inner Fire, which means that they have no latent magical abilities. Therefore, I'm sure a simple demonstration of their abilities would suffice."

"A phenomenal tactic," Roark agreed.

Agmund studied the group for a long moment. For each passing second, Saber's fury grew, but she could not refute the gangly man's words. "Demonstrate your abilities," the Torchhead finally said.

Ro simply stared. His abilities? He didn't have any abilities, save his lightning breath, and that hardly had anything to do with "Inner" or "Fire".

But once again Kraalek came to the rescue. He skipped over in front of the companions, and one of his metal cards appeared in his hands. With a wink, he slashed it across his palm, drawing a deep line of blood. The card disappeared just as quickly as it came.

"And now, my good gnome, I request your healing services," he said, holding his wound out to Nalgene.

The gnome grunted, catching on to the bit. He held Kraalek's hands in his own, and with a quick surge of water, healed the gash.

Satisfied with his performance, Kraalek gave another bow, and returned to his seat. "And so, they most certainly are not Shadowfriends, isn't that right?"

"Fascinating," Sylven said.

"A most righteous display!"

Agmund studied the group. This was irrefutable evidence, but his Ellie …

"Ah, but that was no fire magic! That was water," Saber said. She knew she was grasping at straws. And it was supposed to be simple.

While it was a valid point, Kraalek already had an answer. "General Lighthammer's abilities do not manifest as fire either, are you saying we should doubt his loyalty to the Flame?"

Saber opened her mouth, but closed it, having no rebuttal. It was also inconvenient that she also did not have the ability to create fire. She imagined what Kraalek's face would look like under her boot.

"And what of the others?" Agmund asked.

"Must we perform the same trivial display for each of them?" Kraalek replied.

"It would be a sound strategy," Roark said.

"Ah, but what of the leap?" Sylven asked.

"Perhaps it is a leap we must take," Agmund closed.

"What are you saying, Torchhead?" Saber protested. She had to regain control of the situation. "We cannot be certain they are *all* safe."

Agmund pondered this for a moment. The brilliant General Umbra was correct, and his doe explicitly warned him of the companions. Finally, he spoke:

"A trivial display, perhaps. But it is warranted and will not take much time. We must be vigilant."

"And so it shall be," Kraalek said. "And I'm confident they will all prove their worth, isn't that right?"

Agmund stood from his throne, towering over the assembly. He looked down upon the companions like a giant over a scrambling flock of sheep. "What say you? Can you demonstrate to us your Inner Fire?"

Ro was tall, but even this mountain dwarfed him in sheer scale. What should he say? He wasn't entirely sure what this Inner Fire was, let alone how to demonstrate it.

"Of course," Andromeda said, saving Ro. She flicked him with her tail, and he snapped out of his despair.

"I reckon a display wouldn't hurt," SmibSmob said feebly.

"Aye, we be thinkin' a talent show is a good idea."

"I hope you like the cold," Margaret said.

"Fasto show!"

"A most wise assessment of the situation," Roark said.

Agmund opened his mouth to speak, but right before he could say anything, a Spark burst into the room, struggling for breath. The Spark wore quality plate mail, as was a theme in the Flame, and a crimson tunic. He had matted, brown hair and a long, wavy beard.

"Hail, Torch!" the newcomer said in between gasps. "I bring dire news!"

Agmund looked up to regard the man and raised an eyebrow at his uncharacteristic demeanor. To interrupt the Torch? It would have to be something dire indeed.

"Yes, Commander Estar? What is your news?"

"I have come straight from Forthold. A Mistress has been spotted by our scouts — the few of them that have returned. The Shadowfront has strengthened, and it has brought with it ... something. A terrible abomination. We're being slaughtered. We require aid — immediately!"

Agmund's eyes widened in surprise.

"What sort of abomination do you speak of?"

"It's ... I ... I don't know," the Commander said between huffs of breath. "Some nightmare. Its mouth ..." The man suddenly paused and held his mouth over his mouth as if he were about to vomit. Forcing it down, he continued.

"It ate an entire platoon, sir. Its wings ... they block out the fucking sky! And its breath ... So many dead. Please, it — it must be death itself. Send reinforcements at once — for whatever good they might do."

"She — it — they brought a what!?" Saber exclaimed, standing from her seat. She knew what it was: a dracolich. Fucking, damn, bitch Ashyla. Where the hell was she even keeping that thing? All of the dragons were supposed to be long dead. And what the hell was she thinking? Now it was the Goddess's face under her boot. "That's impossible! I've never heard of such a thing!"

"Now isn't that unlucky?" Kraalek said.

"Sounds of the ultimate carriage of sin!" Don cried.

"Interesting ..." Roark muttered.

"Thank you, Commander Estar," Agmund said. "You are dismissed. We will send reinforcements at once." The Commander gave a quick, respectful bow before rushing out of the room.

A *Resurgence of Hope*

And so, time was out — the clock had struck midnight. They could no longer afford the meager time required for demonstrations.

"Perhaps we should take a leap of faith," Sylven pushed.

"Hail those in good faith!"

Giantheart looked down at the companions once more. Ellie would never lie, but right now, this beast — whatever it was — was a far more threatening doom than these outsiders, and at least one of them showed powers. His doe would have to wait. So be it.

Ro stared up at the behemoth. Now, this was a man who protected the Light. He was a leader. He was a hero. He was exactly what Ro wished he could be at this moment, but right now, under that dominating gaze, he felt so, so tiny. Whatever Agmund said would determine the companions' fate.

"So, alleged heroes, will you take the leap?"

Daniel Whitman

Chapter 3

SmibSmob stared up at the hulking behemoth in front of him, his heart pounding. He wasn't sure if Agmund was about to stomp them like a group of pathetic insects or parade them down the streets as almighty heroes. He hoped it wasn't the first option.

"Torchhead," Saber gasped, barely hiding the venom oozing in her voice. The companions should have been slaughtered by now. "What are you trying to say?"

"Isn't it a most simple strategy,' Roark explained, his tone flat. "In order to better judge the rest of the group, they will be bit against a very immediate and unholy foe. Shall they be of the Light with magical abilities, no doubt we shall determine —"

"Ah, very thrilling explanation," Sylven laughed, interrupting the bland General. "Will they take the leap?"

"I urge them to leap towards the all holy Light," Don said.

Kraalek chuckled and cast his brown die down to the companions, where it landed neatly before SmibSmob's feet. The gnome glanced down. Of course, like every other time, it was just a plain, brown face, identical to the others.

SmibSmob frowned. Did they win the roll?

"Will you fight alongside the Flame to prove yourselves? Will you leap with us? Beacon, the choice is yours." Agmund loomed over the companions, patiently awaiting their response. His doe would have to wait.

The other members of the Torch stared at the group, their gazes slicing into their wavering resolve. Two fires burned out from under Don's helmet. Kraalek shuffled his cards through his fingers. At times, when the flickering torchlight caught the cards just right, they seemed to come alive in a furious inferno. Roark lowered his visor and stood up. While he might not be a giant like the Torchhead, he was still a formidable man in his own right and could undoubtedly slaughter them at a whim. Sylven balanced his other dagger on his finger, smirking at the helpless group before him. Saber scowled, but after a pause, her lips formed a thin smile. Of course, she knew what they would choose. Perhaps the dracolich would do the killing for her. So be it. As long as these pests die.

SmibSmob felt as if he were being smothered. As a gnome, he was already naturally short, but next to these heroes and legends, he barely felt as if he deserved to be dust on the floor. Breathing became difficult. His heart started to leap in his chest, and his hands became sweaty. What should they do? What dreadful undead monsters were they supposed to fight? And what about that beautiful woman? He would love to spend some alone time with her ... But back to the Shadowfront? The undead would devour him like a helpless lamb. How could he do this without his power?

Ah yes, it always came back to his power. He did not miss it. He despised it. He was free from those dark shackles, and he would never again fall into the wretched darkness. But it did make him feel alive ... Perhaps if he still retained his power — or any power, in fact — he would be able to look these Generals in the eye.

But instead, he shriveled up under the heat. What were they to do? The Torch — these Generals — were all veterans, and

SmibSmob could only think about them chewing him up and swallowing.

He glanced over at Nalgene. His brother. His unwavering stone. His power. If Nalgene could stand tall against the Torch, then SmibSmob would be there right by his side. Together, they could overcome anything.

The Generals began to impatiently speak amongst themselves. They needed an answer.

Kraalek and Saber discussed with each other, and Don made some vows about the righteous light. Sylven had somehow appeared on the other side of the room and pulled his blue dagger from the wall. Agmund and Roark merely stared, their pressure unwavering.

SmibSmob looked down once more at the brown die, then scooped it up. They won, wasn't that right?

"We will accept your offer," SmibSmob announced, his voice ringing clear in the room. "And we will prove our trust."

The Beacon had spoken.

Ro beamed down at the little gnome. It was amazing how far his dear friend had come. Nalgene patted his brother on the shoulder.

"Yes, let's stand with the Flame, shall we?" Andromeda said in confirmation.

"Time for another noble speech," Margaret said, bumping Ro with her elbow.

Immediately the bickering quieted, and the Torch redirected its focus onto the companions.

Agmund stared at the companions for several heartbeats, his face stoic and unreadable. So, they will take the leap. These outsiders, whom his doe divined would bring death to the Flame, were offering their lives in the fight against a most unholy denizen of Shadow. Everything pointed to this humble gnome being the Beacon. Yet his doe would never lie ...

"Very well," Giantheart said. "We commend you for your courage and sacrifice for the good of the Light."

"Hail the all blessed Light."

Both Saber and Kraalek beamed with smiles.

"General Strongarm, you will mobilize the defenses at Forthold. Whatever you do, you cannot let that abomination get past the keep. Take General Quickfoot, and whatever other forces you need. A call will be sent out for reinforcements to begin preparations for transport. Heroes — if that is what you are calling yourselves — you will follow General Strongarm to the Shadowfront. May your light pierce the Shadow."

"As you command. This is a most wise strategy."

Agmund took one final glance around the room, examining the rest of the Generals. While they might not share beliefs, they all have the same goal: to protect the Light. Or at least that is what he hoped.

"General Lighthammer and General Umbra, return to your previous assignments. The Torch is dismissed. May we all survive to reignite its flame."

With that, the burly man grabbed his helmet from his throne, stepped past the companions, and left the room.

SmibSmob watched him leave, and he could not shake the image of being crushed by those terrifying bear paws.

Roark approached the companions. "We have our orders. General Quickfoot, go usher the gem-call. I will meet you at Forthold."

Nodding, and shooting the group a wink, Sylven whisked out of the room.

Turning back, Roark gave each of the companions a stern look, studying them to analyze their strengths and weaknesses in order to determine their optimal placement for defense.

"Are you ready to return to the Shadowfront?"

"Bah, o' course we be ready," Nalgene snorted. "We fought through it once, so I be thinkin' we can do it again."

"And this time, we have the indomitable strength of the Flame at our side," Ro stated proudly. He would be forever remembered for his deeds against the Shadow, or so he hoped.

"Very well," Roark said. "Follow me."

"By the holy Light, wait just a moment," Don said, standing from his seat and approaching the group. One by one, he placed his hand upon their chests and muttered a prayer to the heavens above. A twinkling, pure light illuminated from his palm with every prayer, erasing any dark thoughts from the companions' minds. Once he was done, he left without another word.

Roark moved to usher them out of the room, but before he could, Kraalek interrupted. "Ah, just one more thing, my good man Roark." Roark's face twitched. Undeterred, the sly General skipped over to SmibSmob and held out his hand. "The die, if you don't mind."

"Ah — uh — of course," SmibSmob stuttered, dropping the brown die into Kraalek's hand. He was so distracted by Agmund that he had completely forgotten that he picked up the wooden trinket. They did win, right?

Satisfied, Kraalek turned to face Roark. "I have but one simple request, if you don't mind."

Roark raised an eyebrow but said nothing.

"I would like to keep the Beacon."

"Bah, what did ye just say?" Nalgene burst. What could this bloody, slimy worm want with his dear brother?

"Hm, a questionable move," Roark said.

"What do you want SmibSmob for?" Ro asked, protective of the little gnome. There was no doubt in his mind that the General had only good intentions, but to split up the group? After all they've been through? It just didn't sit right. Who would he lead if everyone else was gone?

"Yes, why do you want me? I want to support my friends and the Flame."

Kraalek smiled at the gnome. "Why, quite simply, the die had rolled it so, isn't that right?"

SmibSmob nodded, unsure of anything the man was saying. The General was no amateur, that was for certain.

"And while it is quite commendable that you wish to support your good friends on the battlefield, I fear you would simply get in their way, and it would be no good to lose you this early in your adventure. While you are the Beacon, you are still just a simple gnome. Therefore, I wish to take you under my wing to show you the true abilities of the Flame. For educational purposes, of course."

"Eh, simple gnome?" Nalgene grunted.

"True abilities?" Andromeda wondered.

"Commen ... demenable?" Fasto asked.

"Must be some education," Margaret snorted.

"Please, get on with it," Roark stated flatly.

"I am offering an invitation for you to learn with me so that we can ... hmm ... truly ignite those powers of yours," Kraalek finally finished, holding his hand out to SmibSmob.

SmibSmob stared at the outstretched hand, unsure of what to do. Should he accept? He hated his power. Is Kraalek saying that he could bring it back? No, he couldn't return to that.

"What in the bloody hell are ye talkin' about?" Nalgene said, pushing the General's hand away. He started to say something else, but Roark stepped in front of the gnome, a scowl darkening his face.

"It would not be a wise course of action to disrespect a General of the Flame. So, little gnome, do step aside. General Kraalek was addressing the Beacon, and so the Beacon shall answer."

Nalgene clamped his mouth shut and stepped back, much to the surprise of the companions. Perhaps things do change, indeed.

Roark turned his glare to SmibSmob. Yet again, the frail gnome felt as if he could be blown away with a breath.

"Erm — I'm not sure," he finally managed to say. Ignite his powers? He didn't have any powers left, and he certainly wouldn't want them back. He refused. Right? Mariah had saved him, and he thought he would do everything in his power to remain free.

"Ah, a completely understandable hesitation," Kraalek said, moving to stand next to his fellow General. The die appeared once more in his hand. "Perhaps you would like to roll for it?"

SmibSmob started to reach for the die, but he pulled his hand back. No, he was the Beacon. He did not have to rely on some cheap toy to make his decisions. He was destined to save the Light, and it was about time he stepped up to the responsibilities of that mantle.

"I'll go with you."

"Eh?" Nalgene stammered, surprised by his brother's decision.

"Splendid, I'm sure he'll keep it interesting," Margaret commented.

Smiling, Kraalek replaced the die in his pouch, proud of the little gnome. Yes, he would make this Beacon the pride and joy of the Light.

"Very well, you have made your decision," Roark said. "You will stay with General Cardmaster. The rest of you, I hope you are prepared for battle."

Ro nodded, his eyes burning with determination. Andromeda's tail lashed back and forth in anticipation. Margaret clenched her black fist at her side. Fasto stared at the General, unblinking. Nalgene merely scowled.

SmibSmob placed a hand on his brother's shoulder. Where would he be without his Nalgene? They locked eyes, and Nalgene's face softened. He may not like SmibSmob's choice, but he would accept it. His brother was more than capable of dealing with the sly General.

"I'm going to be okay. I reckon you better focus on beating this creature — whatever it might be."

Nalgene nodded. "Yer right, me brother. Yer more than strong enough fer whatever this slim — er General — be throwin' at ye."

"Are we ready yet?" Margaret sighed. This sure was getting tedious. Her arm pulsed at her side. It wanted blood, and it wanted it now.

"Indeed," Roark said, growing impatient. The longer they wasted bantering and giving hugs, the more Sparks died on that dreadful battlefield. Emotions were never good for strategy. He pulled out an orange gemstone from his pouch. "You are all familiar with a gem-call? By my assessment, you should have experienced one as a means to enter this city."

"They are experts," Kraalek chuckled. "Although I'm not sure they're used to the feeling quite yet."

Nodding, the companions, except for SmibSmob, agreed with Kraalek. Of course, they still had no idea how the magic worked, but that hardly mattered with a General to lead the call.

"Place your hands on me. Let us make all haste."

"Perfect. Here we go again," Margaret sighed.

"This will be fun," Andromeda said.

SmibSmob stepped back and watched as his friends grabbed Roark's shoulders. This was it. The group was finally being split. They were off to go be the destined heroes of the Flame and he, well … he wasn't quite sure what he was going to be doing. After all they had been through, the battles and the horrors that they had faced together in the Shadow, it was no more. They would go fight "death itself", as the Commander had described it, while he would study with the General. It sounded quite frightening. And dangerous …

He wasn't sure if he was thinking that about his friends or his own situation.

What if the creature was too powerful? What if it crushed them into oblivion? No, no, his friends would be safe — they had to be. But he had seen how the Generals had reacted. He had seen the panic on that Commander's face. What if his friends never returned?

Alarmed with this thought, SmibSmob opened his mouth to say something. What if he never saw his dear brother again? He reached out to Nalgene. "Wai —"

The companions burst into a billowing pillar of flame, cutting off the gnome's words. And so SmibSmob watched, helplessly, as his friends burned into ash, and disappeared across the world.

What if he never saw them again?

His head hung low, and he felt tears welling up in his eyes. He should have gone with them. That way, he could look after his brother.

Kraalek looked down at the defeated gnome. "They're going to be okay. I've seen how they fight, and there's no doubt in my mind that they will drive back that Shadow. Let us focus on our brilliant future ahead, I have much I want to show you."

SmibSmob nodded but said nothing.

Shrugging, and quite unsure of how to deal with the gnome, Kraalek simply rested a hand on his shoulder. Whenever he felt down about something, the local brothel would always call his name. Nothing washed away sorrow like ale and a barmaid. Yes, and he had seen a lot of brothels recently …

The General looked back at Saber, who hadn't said anything, and was still sitting in her chair. "Awfully quiet back there, aren't you Saber? Do you enjoy watching people say goodbye?"

Saber glanced up and gave him a charming smile. "Hardly, my dear Cardmaster." She stood up and began to gracefully stalk over to the fellow General. "I think it is quite beautiful that they would lay down their lives for us after we threatened their good judgment."

She reached out and patted Kraalek on the cheek. He blushed as her soft hand caressed his skin. "Indeed, there's no doubt that they will drive back that Shadow. I wish all the best for our fine group of heroes." That was a lie. She hated this part of the game. If only she could draw her sword and cut all the Generals down ... how difficult could it be? This drunk idiot was just as captivated as the rest of them. Even if he wanted, she was sure he could never raise a hand against her. How pathetic. They were all so weak-minded. She was getting impatient. She just needed this miserable Flame to be devoured by the Shadow, and then ... She was almost there.

Hiding away her true thoughts, she gave a bubbly smile to Kraalek and brushed past him out the door. Truly, she wished the companions the *best*. Sometimes, problems have a way of solving themselves.

As soon as she left, Kraalek jerked his head back, as if escaping a trance. He frowned, deep in thought, then looked back at where she had left. She was quite beautiful ...

SmibSmob looked up at the puzzled man. What the gambler was thinking, he could only guess. "I reckon we best be off."

Kraalek nodded and smiled. "Indeed, my good gnome. Indeed."

With that, the General led SmibSmob out of the meeting room and back into the great hall. Like before, Flametouchers were still rushing about, determined to finish their duties for the day. They walked down one of the spiral staircases and towards the main doors. As they approached, a soldier pulled on a lever hidden within the walls, and the great gates swung wide open. Pulling SmibSmob along, Kraalek skipped out into the city.

Kraalek took the gnome through the twisting roads, turning right, and then left, and then right again through the labyrinth. The General did not use the main roads, no, he was most comfortable in the back alleys and streets. As they walked about, Kraalek told his companion great and extravagant tales of his glorious battles — some on the battlefield and some in the bar. SmibSmob was certain that the majority of them were fake, just a tale spun to twist his imagination, but he could never be sure with the sly man. Perhaps he did ride a winged monster formed from fire into the Shadowfront.

Or, more likely, perhaps he did not. SmibSmob simply smiled and laughed all the way. Regardless, it did distract SmibSmob from his depressing thoughts about his friends.

They passed many families who were out enjoying the sun. The women would swoon at the sight of Kraalek, and he would give them all a promising wink. The children also flocked towards the General. They would ask him to show his "magic", and he would amuse them with marvelous acts of cardistry. Occasionally, he would reach into one of his many pouches and pull out some random trinket, which he would give to the kids as a gift for them to enjoy.

SmibSmob smiled. Certainly, no amateur.

Eventually, after all the frolicking was over and the sky had reached twilight, they stopped at an alehouse. Kraalek pushed SmibSmob in and called over the bartender.

The bartender waved at the General. "Back again, are you? Let me guess, the usual?"

Kraalek laughed. "No, no, tonight is a good night. Tonight, we celebrate. Give me your largest bottle of Spitfire."

The bartender laughed. "It must be quite the celebration. Do you want me to pour you a shot with it? I know how much you love a glass on the go."

"Oh, no thank you, my good man. The Spitfire isn't for me." He patted SmibSmob on the back, who stumbled forward towards the counter. "He's going to be doing all of the celebrating tonight!"

SmibSmob's eyes widened in surprise. "What do you mea —"

"HA, don't you worry! It'll be a night of excitement, you'll see!"

SmibSmob gawked at the General. What happened to teaching him about powers and making him a hero? Kraalek just wanted to get him drunk? Why would he do such a thing? SmibSmob hadn't had a drink since … he couldn't even remember. This was an outrage.

He should've gone with Nalgene.

Chuckling at the helpless gnome, the bartender rummaged about in the cabinets and pulled forth the bottle of Spitfire. "Our strongest batch. Aged seven years on the shelf."

"Oooo, now you've caught my attention," Kraalek said, snatching the bottle from the man with a cackle of excitement. It was a dark, crimson glass formed into the shape of a demon's ghastly head. Its mouth was open in a manic howl, and two rubies were inset into the bottle as the demon's eyes.

SmibSmob stared at the beast in horror. He would be more comfortable if this were a true soldier of the abyss.

Amused, Kraalek popped the lid off the bottle and held it out for SmibSmob to smell. Before SmibSmob could react, the vile fumes invaded his nose, barraging him with a plethora of devilish flavors.

Fire.

Pepper.

Oak?

Pain.

Chili.

Mint?

SmibSmob reeled back in shock. His vision went black. He almost puked. He could barely stand his knees were so weak.

"Ah, this is going to be splendid," Kraalek said merrily. He replaced the cap, then pulled a gold coin from one of his pouches. Throwing a wink at the bartender, he flipped it onto the counter. "Keep the change."

With that, Kraalek spun about, and without giving the gnome time to recover, he pulled him towards the door. "So long, my good friend!"

The pair traveled back into the city, with Kraalek whistling the whole way. SmibSmob couldn't even see straight. He pulled SmibSmob through more twists and turns, before finally, after what seemed like a nightmarish eternity to the poor gnome, they arrived at a small, modest house.

A Resurgence of Hope

Kraalek opened the door and escorted SmibSmob in. "Welcome, my good gnome, to my most humble abode."

Finally recovered from his horrifying encounter with death, SmibSmob studied the quaint establishment. The house was bare, with only a chair and a table sitting in the middle of the floor. Dust and cobwebs covered every surface, and several mice scuttered into the shadows as the pair entered.

"I'll admit, it could use some freshening up. But worry not, follow me."

Kraalek strode to the middle of the room, got down onto his knees, and crawled under the table. One of his cards appeared in his hands, and he placed it into a groove in the ground. Focusing his power, the card turned a searing red with heat, and a clicking noise sounded from below. A handle appeared from the floor. There was a secret trapdoor.

Satisfied, Kraalek removed the card, stood up, and opened the trapdoor.

SmibSmob glanced down into the basement. A simple stone staircase led deep underground. He could not see the bottom.

"Come now."

Kraalek stepped into the basement, and without much of a choice, SmibSmob followed him down. Without warning, the trapdoor slammed shut behind him, leaving him in the dark, alone, with the mysterious gambler. SmibSmob sighed. He should've gone with Nalgene.

Stumbling his way down the remaining stairs, SmibSmob looked around, desperately trying to adjust his eyes to the dark. Suddenly, dozens of flames burst into life across the room, illuminating the vast basement.

Unlike upstairs, this cellar was well kept. Not a sign of dust or cobwebs could be seen. The room extended on and on — it was as if a great ballroom was built underground. Luxurious wooden furniture adorned with scarlet cushions was placed deliberately around the room. Wonderful paintings covered the walls. Marble statues stood watch as unwavering guards. A huge cabinet full of various drinking glasses and other miscellaneous items rested on one edge of the room, and bookshelves with both dusty and new tomes lined the others. Tucked away in the back corner seemed to be a workstation, covered in various tools, trinkets, and most interestingly, gemstones. The crystals were identical to the orange one they had used previously in every way except color. Finally, a large, oak table stood in the middle of the room, and next to it was the General, holding a glass full of Spitfire.

"Uh, what are we doing down here?" SmibSmob asked, still astounded by the room he was in. "I reckon you want me to drink that — er — to celebrate." He gulped. There was no doubt in his mind, if he drank that wretched poison, he would die.

Kraalek stared at the gnome, a hard expression on his face. Gone was the cheery, overly joyous General. This was a man of focus, of purpose.

"No. In fact, neither of us will be drinking this tonight."

"Then why did you go through the trouble of buying it?"

"It's exceptionally flammable."

SmibSmob opened his mouth, dumbfounded. He felt as lost as Fasto. "What?"

"I watched you during your little rampage at the Shadowfront. Mariah stripped you of your powers, isn't that right?"

"Uh, yes, she did."

"If you had gone with the rest of your friends back to the Shadowfront, there is no doubt in my mind that you would have died."

SmibSmob shrugged, but he couldn't argue with the man. What could he do against a zombie now? Slap it? Strangle it with his pointed hat? That would hardly be effective. But something still didn't sit right.

"What did you mean back there, to 'ignite those powers' of mine?"

"Exactly what I said."

"But you just admitted that I have no power."

"I did — as I suspected it the entire time — and you just confirmed. That is why I had to be careful of my working with the good man Roark, for it would be quite difficult for you to prove your abilities now."

SmibSmob opened his mouth but closed it without saying anything. He did not enjoy where this was headed. Celebration certainly seemed like a far-off prospect.

"You might be the Beacon, but now you are weak. You have no hope against the Shadow. It would feast upon your helplessness."

SmibSmob scowled. Was this man here just to berate him? "So, what do you want?"

"I want you to listen, and I want you to learn. You may be miserably useless now, but soon, in time, you will be the might of the Flame."

SmibSmob glared at the man for a long minute, contemplating every conceivable way that this could end so terribly wrong, but Kraalek was unwavering. The General was a surprisingly patient man.

"Fine. I'm listening."

Kraalek smiled, returning to a cheerier state. "Good. It is my theory that Mariah didn't completely strip you of your powers. Rather, she healed them. Perhaps you were corrupted, and that is why they were so … dark, and she simply returned them to the Light."

SmibSmob seemed unconvinced, but he didn't argue.

"Go on."

"Lovely attitude. Now watch, my good gnome. This is what I will be teaching you."

Kraalek placed the glass of Spitfire on the table, out of the way of danger, and held out his hand. Immediately, a ball of flame burst to life in his palm. Still smiling, he juggled it in the air, passing it from hand to hand, before casting it at one of the chairs.

The chair exploded into flame and began to quickly crumble into ash.

SmibSmob's eyes widened with alarm. Was this lunatic going to burn this entire house to the ground?

"Oh, don't worry about the chair," Kraalek chuckled, walking towards the gnome. "I'll win another one soon enough. You see, you may have lost your powers, but that doesn't mean you are powerless. We are all born with an Inner Fire — a blessing that this land has granted us. Your dark powers may have smothered yours, but that doesn't mean it is extinguished."

He poked SmibSmob in the chest. "I need you to look deep within yourself and nourish that flame back to life. You are the Beacon, apparently, so you are destined to end the reign of darkness. And you will use the power of the Light to do so."

SmibSmob looked down at the finger on his chest. He needed to look inside?

SmibSmob shivered. He knew what once lived deep inside, but it was gone now. However, perhaps, by some miracle, there was some mystical flame buried inside.

Kraalek smiled. "You can do this, my good friend."

SmibSmob nodded. He didn't want to be weak. He didn't want to just be the burden his companions had to drag along. He didn't want to be the nuisance his dear brother had to constantly watch. He wanted to be strong. He wanted to be the Beacon.

"But how do I 'look deep'?"

"Just try."

Right. That cleared everything up for the gnome. Crystalline. But it seemed all the General was willing to offer.

SmibSmob closed his eyes and began a slow and gentle descent into his mind. It was a difficult journey, at first, full of hesitation and fear. He did not want to acknowledge the hole. But it grew easier as he grew more confident. Yet there was no fire.

So, he went on. He looked at every thought, every emotion, but still, no fire — unless one counted his growing frustration.

A Resurgence of Hope

He reached deep within his subconscious, desperately searching for his Inner Fire. It had to be in there somewhere. He had to have some sort of worth outside of his twisted power. How could he strike down the Shadow without a weapon of fire?

So, he searched and searched, while Kraalek watched him and said nothing. And what could the man say? This was a journey SmibSmob had to make alone.

Growing impatient, the gnome held out his hand, palm up, in front of him. He had seen the General conjure the flame. He would do it too. How difficult could it be?

He just needed to become the Beacon.

He felt his mind focusing on his palm. He imagined it heating up under his will. He pictured a brilliant ball of flame resting in his palm.

His brow furrowed.

He reached down into his void, searching for that spark of life.

Sweat began to bead on his forehead, and he ripped his hat from his head, throwing it on the ground.

And still Kraalek said nothing.

SmibSmob could almost feel the heat in his hand. He could almost feel the fire come to life at his command. This had to be it. This had to be what the General was talking about. His palm began to shake.

Imagine the fire.

Summon the fire.

Become the fire.

"I think I have it!" SmibSmob hollered, opening his eyes. It had to be there.

But there was nothing. He felt nothing. There was no Inner Fire. It must have been extinguished.

He slumped down to the floor, defeated by his failed effort.

"Hm, what a truly impressive flame. I'm sure it was quite … exhausting keeping it lit."

SmibSmob sighed. The man's words struck deep, and his resolve deflated. "I couldn't feel it. There was nothing. I am worthless."

Kraalek laughed out loud, and that only made the poor gnome want to sink deeper into the floor.

"Oh, you thought this was going to be easy? The miserable bitch runs willingly into the arms of the thugs. You are a foolish one indeed."

SmibSmob glanced up at the man. He supposed it was back to being berated. This most certainly was not a celebration. Instead of seeing the kind eyes of the General, he was met with a furious glare.

"Pathetic. You fail after one, half-assed attempt and so you grovel on the floor. What kind of Beacon are you? All of our sacrifices so you can be a bitch squirming on the ground? If this is what Mariah saw, then we are fucked."

SmibSmob shrank back from the rage. Perhaps if he was lucky the Shadow would come eat him up. But he wasted little time pondering such fruitless thoughts, instead simply regretting his decision not to go with his brother.

Kraalek reached down and pulled the gnome to his feet. He was not going to let him give up this easily. "Is this what your good brother would want? Would he want you to be broken and frail like you are now? Nay, he would want you to stand up for yourself and fight. *I* want you to stand up and fight."

"But there was —"

SmibSmob was interrupted as Kraalek slapped him across the face. SmibSmob cried out in pain and went crashing back to the floor. Who was this man? Why was he acting so ruthless? Where did the General Kraalek Cardmaster from earlier go? This was no General. This was a monster.

"Of course it's not going to be easy. You must feel the heat. You must feel the *burn*."

Kraalek pulled SmibSmob back up. A flame appeared in his other hand. He closed his fist around it and punched the gnome square in the chest.

SmibSmob felt the burning heat from the hit — as well as the startling force — and he fell back again. The monster was shockingly strong. It felt as if his ribs were going to cave in from the blow. This wasn't teaching. This was murder. He was going to die.

"Dig deep. What makes you want to explode into a fiery temper? What makes your insides rage like a scorching fire? What makes you so fucking angry that you want to burn this damn world to the ground?"

Scrambling back to his feet, and gasping for breath, SmibSmob glared at the traitorous man. He could certainly think of one thing. Snarling. He charged at Kraalek, swinging his fists in wild abandon.

But suddenly the General wasn't there.

SmibSmob felt a tug from behind, and he whirled around, only to meet the sneering face of Kraalek, who was holding the glass of Spitfire. He swung, but Kraalek easily caught his arm with his free hand and held SmibSmob in place.

"You may hate me right now, my good gnome, and I understand that. Hell, I even hope you fucking hate me. But you need some extra persuasion to ignite that flame. So instead of charging me like some worthless animal, use that anger and *look*." He twisted SmibSmob's arm so that his palm was facing up, and he placed the glass in his hand.

"Don't you dare drop that glass. I will kill you if you waste a single drop of my liquor. Remember: this was aged for seven years. You will not give up. You will not grovel on the ground in misery. Glare at me. Hate me. Call me whatever foul things you want. I don't give a shit. Feel that heat. Feel that burn. Dig deep and conjure up the spark that I know you have."

SmibSmob's gaze burned into Kraalek. At this moment, he despised this man. He felt the rage bubbling in his stomach. He wanted nothing more than to throw the glass into his face and tear him apart with his hands. He even opened his mouth to accept the invitation to sling insults.

But he did not.

Yes, he hated this gangly prick. But maybe the man was right.

So, SmibSmob looked down at the glass in his hand. He will not grovel on the ground. He will not be devoured by the Shadow. He felt deep within himself, through the boiling rage and anger. He was hot. He was *searing*. He focused on the glass in his hand, picturing it as a blazing ball of fire.

He was the Beacon.

Suddenly, the fire flickered to life.

SmibSmob's eyes widened. He felt it! Deep inside the void that his power had left him, there was an Inner Fire. There was a most wonderful and delectable power.

He felt as if the very *essence* of the universe was coagulating into the glass, flowing in as a steady stream under his guidance. And by manipulating the cosmic energy enough, maybe, just maybe, he could even create something.

A tiny, feeble spark appeared inside the alcohol — it truly was exceptionally flammable. The liquid exploded in a brilliant ball of green and orange fire, shattering the glass and spraying fiery alcohol across the room.

SmibSmob stared at his hand in amazement. He didn't even notice the shards of glass cutting into him, or the drops of alcohol burning his skin. All thoughts of hatred and resentment flew from his mind. He felt his new power. He finally felt *alive*. When he was sundered from his darkness, he was empty and helpless. That shadow was exhilarating, and even though he had to sacrifice his very being for its effects, he had craved its taste. And it was gone. But now, with this new Inner Fire, he could feel that rush once again. After the Shadowfront, he had thought to fill his void with his friends and his dear brother.

But this? Oh, this was just so much sweeter.

Kraalek smiled at the gnome. While he was standing right beside SmibSmob during the explosion, he didn't have a single shard of glass or drop of alcohol on him — it was as if he was completely unaffected by the blast. Not that SmibSmob noticed, of course.

The General grabbed another glass from the cabinet and filled it with that most wonderful Spitfire.

"Very good, my good gnome. You ignited the fire, isn't that right?"

He placed the glass in SmibSmob's palm.

"Again."

Daniel Whitman

Chapter 4

The fiery column smothered out of existence. The companions reformed from their ashy forms, becoming whole once more. Margaret glanced around at the others, her stomach sick. She despised this method of travel. Mystical fire teleportation and demonic ice powers did not mesh well, apparently. Her arm burned with an annoying rage. Her head felt as if it were about to burst into two. But, of course, she couldn't show that. She had to remain immovable in the face of her companions.

But why?

She snorted. Why did that matter? Such questions were for philosophers and doubters, and she was clearly neither. The rest of the group, aside from Roark, who was *actually* immovable, also shared her sick feeling. How many times were they going to have to do this to get used to it?

Without giving them a moment to recover, Roark ushered them into motion. His strategy left no time for standing about.

"Come, it is my decision to head to the Shadowfront. Let us prove your worth, or, as my fellow Generals named it, 'take the leap'," the General said, starting off towards the great wall, not even glancing back to see if the companions were following.

Nalgene opened his mouth to say some snarky comment, but he held wisely in check, instead giving a salute to Roark's back.

Noticing the gnome's defiant act, Ro pushed Nalgene's hand down and gave him a scowl. "Nalgene, we must be heroes!"

"Mmm, always with the heroics," Andromeda said.

"Bah, don't ye be touchin' me, I was showin' some respect, ye dolt."

"Respect? I don't think you know the meaning of that word," Ro countered.

"Eh, now who's bein' disrespectful?"

"Fasto respect!"

Margaret snorted. It was amusing to be friends with this group. It still felt foreign to think of them as friends, but alas, she could not deny it. They were indeed friends. Near-death experiences worked wonders like that. Hopefully, one day, she could make friends without the entire "death" part being involved.

Her arm seared at the thought as if rejecting it.

Together, finally done bickering, the group set off after the General. As they approached the wall, a sickly stench saturated the air. Around them, dozens of Sparks rushed about, many heading towards the great wall, but many more were heading away from it towards the keep, carrying wounded soldiers from the grisly battlefield. Orders were being shouted in the air, commanding squadrons this way and that. All the stone houses were empty, and all of the watchtowers were manned. From across the wall, the hectic bustle of war reached their ears. From the unearthly screams piercing the air to the guttural howls calling out into the wind, the Shadowfront truly had a musical charm to it.

Margaret scowled. She needed something to punch, and soon.

After some very brisk walking, they came upon General Quickfoot talking with three Commanders. There was Commander

Estar, with his long beard, who warned them about the oncoming monstrosity. His facial complexion had improved since they last saw him. There was also a tanned, short man with a goatee whom the General referred to as Commander Ecker, and the third, named Commander Oldgate, was tall, broad, and sprouted a striking white mustache.

Quickfoot turned and smiled at the group as they approached. "Ah, General Strongarm, so glad you finally made it. I have assembled our forces along the wall. All the injured Sparks are on their way to be tended, and they should be rejoining the battle soon. I have also assigned a Flametoucher with every battalion along the wall. Of course, feel free to change anything that you see fit, with your most-wise strategies."

"Thank you, General Quickfoot. A most brilliant deployment of the defenses. You have done good work this day. Commanders, what is the status report of the Front?"

"Sir, we've cleared the field of them dreadful corpses, and we're burning them in a biggin' pile on the other side of the wall," Commander Ecker answered. "Any of them undead that wander too close are obliterated."

Margaret scowled. So that explained the unearthly smell. She never was one for the spa treatment, but at least the candles smelled pleasant.

"Very good, anything else?"

"Where Fasto go?" the dull orc interrupted.

The General turned to regard the companions. Where were they going to go indeed? It was an interesting dilemma on where to position these strange newcomers. If they were indeed with the Shadow, then placing them in critical positions could prove devastating to the effort. However, if they are as powerful as General Cardmaster implied, then perhaps that would be best. What is the wisest decision? What is the best outcome? While he had yet to resolve this issue, he knew one thing for certain: these companions were *not* geared for battle.

The draconian bore no armor, and only had a single, golden dagger at his side. Both the feline and the she-orc didn't have *any* weapons, although the orc's black arm did look almost formidable. At least the male orc had a bow — and a respectable looking one at that. Out of all of them, the gnome appeared the most battle ready, and only because he had proven his inert magical abilities. How meager a display of force. Even if they were with the Shadow, they hardly presented a realistic threat. Of course, he should have noted it earlier, but the Torchhead demanded immediate action.

"Where is your equipment?" The General asked the companions.

The group looked at each other, surprised by the question.

"Well, you see," Ro began, "we may have lost most of it in our previous bout. But I do have this mighty and heroic dagger!" Ro revealed the golden dagger he acquired from SmibSmob and gave it a little flourish.

Roark said nothing — made no reaction, in fact. However, while Margaret couldn't see it beneath his visor, she imagined his blank expression would be exceptionally amusing.

"Who needs weapons anyway when I can just punch things? I am pretty effective, you see," she said.

"Fasto throw!" Fasto said while reaching down to pick up a stone.

"I do have this," Andromeda said, materializing her halberd in an attempt to save the situation.

The General saw his grand plan crumbling before his eyes. Maybe the companions would be their doom. But he didn't let his doubts overcome him.

"I see. Commanders, you are dismissed. Please return to your posts and prepare for combat. General Quickfoot, you may go, as well. You know what to do. Everyone else, wait here."

Sylven winked at the companions before dashing away. "Let's go have some fun, shall we?"

A Resurgence of Hope

When the General left, Roark pulled out one of the strange horns and blew into it. Like before, the companions didn't hear any sound. Immediately, he returned the magical item to his belt, and stared at the companions, studying them once more.

The male orc appeared strong, and he carries a bow with him. Perhaps it would be best to man him on the rampart. Same with the gnome. He is too frail for the front lines, but maybe it would be beneficial to have a spellcaster in the fray. The other three, on the field itself would be optimal. What of the she-orc? What could she do? Punching was hardly effective against the more dangerous foes. This would be a difficult decision indeed.

Minutes passed, and Margaret began to get itchy. Maybe she would smack this phony General just to get any sort of action in. Across the wall, the symphony of the Shadow began to grow fainter. This, she did not like.

"Are we just going to stand here and wait for the undead to die of old age?" she remarked.

Nalgene snorted, and gave her a little nudge, saying "that'd be a good one", but everyone else remained silent. Splendid, of all the people to recognize her fantastic humor, it had to be him.

The General ignored her quip. All of the hundreds of different possibilities whirred about in his. What if he placed them there? What would the feline be capable of? How would they be able to withstand the assault from on top of the wall? All these questions and more stormed through his thoughts. One by one, he puzzled through each of the different questions formulating the most probable answer. One by one, he eliminated any possibility of defeat. He had found his solution. He had found his grand strategy. It had felt like an eternity to him to solve this riddle, but for the others, it was merely the blink of an eye — or several minutes, depending on who was counting.

He had his plan. It would not fail. They would drive back the unholy swarm.

By now, the undead shrieks had softened to little more than whispers. Something was happening, and Margaret needed to know. Around them, Sparks still bustled about like nothing had changed. War raged on, but they were stagnant. Looking at the others, she noticed even the holiest of heroes Ro was shifting back and forth. Apparently, impatience trumped distinguished nobility.

Margaret opened her mouth to say something, but just as she did, two Spark rushed over to them. They were holding equipment.

"General Strongarm," the one said, quite out of breath.

"We mean: Hail, Light of the Flame!" the other interrupted, giving an awkward salute with his full hands.

"Yes, yes, of course, sir," the other continued. "Here is the gear, just as you requested. It is a little worn, but —"

"You have done well. Please drop the equipment and return to your posts. It shall begin soon."

The two Sparks dropped their haul, mumbled something respectful, gave a brisk salute, turned around, and rushed off just as quickly as they came. Margaret thought they were good little pack dogs.

"Draconian, she-orc, equip yourselves. We do not have much time."

Margaret glanced down at the equipment. She wasn't a fan of that orange-haired lady, but at least she knew how to *present* a gift. There were two sets of armor, one light and one heavy, and both adorned with crimson — identical to what all other Sparks wore. There was also a longsword, a shield, and a greataxe.

Great, now she had to blend in with the idiot sheep. She glanced over at Ro, and the draconian glanced back. Unconcerned, he shrugged and reached for the light armor.

"Unless you'd rather I wear the plate?" he offered.

Snorting, and rolling her eyes, Margaret snatched up the heavy armor. Fine, but she was *not* going to use some random axe.

A Resurgence of Hope

By the time they had finished adorning themselves —
tightening and adjusting straps did take some time, after all — the
sounds of the battle had gone completely silent. No more screams
and no more growls. It was eerie and terrifying, but she wouldn't
admit it.

The boring General gave the companions one more cursory
glance over. It'll have to do.

"Follow me," he ordered, turning around and continuing to
the wall. The Shadow will be defeated.

"As ye say!"

"Nalgene!"

"Bah!"

Margaret couldn't punch anything sooner.

The companions followed Roark to the rampart. As he
walked, he ordered groups of Sparks to various positions,
commanding them to do this task and that. Everything needed to be
exactly as he had formulated. He sent Fasto to the top of the wall so
that he could fire down upon the approaching army. However, he
told Nalgene to remain with the group. The gnome was to act as
back-row support on the fields. Everyone else would fight alongside
him. What better way to keep them in check than if he constantly
watched them? If they were allies of the darkness, he would know
soon enough, and he would strike them all down.

Now on the forsaken battlefield, Margaret glanced around
at the army around her. There was Ro, with his newly acquired
longsword and shield in his hands. Andromeda had her halberd out,
and her body seemed to be disappearing into the shadows. There
was also the General, with a simple wooden spear in one hand and
a wooden shield in the other. Peachy. It was truly impressive
weaponry. Surrounding them, hundreds of Sparks stood braced and
ready, nervously awaiting the onslaught. Her body itched. Her new
armor felt heavy, but she had to acknowledge its quality. Maybe it
could save her from a nick or two.

Before them was a desolate landscape, scarred and torn from the constant turmoil of the Shadowfront. The ground was blackened by rotting blood, and an ominous shadow reached over them in the sky like a hand coming forth from the black abyss. Above, the sun was dipping towards the mountain peaks in the west. To the left, the massive pile of burning bodies was still smoldering, casting its noxious fumes into the cold air. There was no sign of the supposed winged abomination they had been warned about — or any undead, for that matter. It was eerily quiet. Where was everything? They must've known she was coming and scampered off.

She smiled. She truly did have a way of amusing herself. But her frivolity didn't last long.

Margaret glanced around, she was getting impatient. Her arm screamed like a mad stallion, trying to run free from its master. Oh, she hated it, but sometimes, in those rare moments, she felt as if it was the only thing that kept her sane.

"Where is everything? It isn't like the zombies to keep us waiting," she quipped at Ro, who was feeling similarly impatient.

"No doubt they're out there somewhere," purred Andromeda, flicking her tail. "They will come soon enough."

"Yes, don't worry, they'll come," said a Spark next to them. "My name's Denver. My father always told me it's good to know who you're fighting with. It helps with the nerves." He held out a hand to them.

Margaret stared at the hand in disgust. Clearly, this man's father was an idiot.

Denver frowned when Margaret didn't take his hand, but luckily Ro reached out and clasped it. "Well met, Denver. I am Ro, guardian of the Beacon and prote —"

"Yeah, yeah," the annoyed orc interrupted. Holy shit, she just needed something to punch, and fast.

"Ah, well met, Ro." The Spark pulled one of the other soldiers to his side. "This is my friend and partner Johnson. It would be an honor to fight by your side."

"And yours' as well," Ro said. "May your light pierce the Shadow!"

Margaret sighed. She suddenly felt it was a lot less amusing to be around these friends. With noble this and noble that, it was all too chivalrous for her taste.

"Er, let us burn — uh — the darkness away," stammered Johnson, obviously uncomfortable being introduced to the strange newcomers.

Ro beamed down at the shy man, and images of Roan and Dain flashed through his head. He would not let these two die as he did with them. He was a hero now, and he would do whatever it takes to save these innocent lives.

Snorting, Margaret turned away from them. "Where is everything?" she repeated, but no one answered. She felt truly alone in this mass of miserable people.

Suddenly, an unholy shriek cut through the air, and the Sparks went pale. It was about to begin. There was no more friendly banter, no more making friends. This was a battle against the Shadow, and to be distracted was to become devoured. The ground began to shake. It started as a subtle rumble, but it quickly grew to an alarming magnitude. They were coming. Death was approaching.

"FORMATIONS!" Roark's voice commanded, ringing impossibly clear through the surrounding noise. When Margaret glanced at him, she saw one of the strange horns in his hand. Without waiting for further instructions, the Sparks formed squadrons of twelve soldiers, each led by a Captain. Every four squadrons were commanded by one of the Commanders, and at the center of the ranks was Roark and the companions. They would stand together as an army, but if they were to become split, there would still be order in the brawl. High above them soldiers and Flametouchers stood ready on the rampart. Fasto was up there somewhere, as well, no doubt ready to rain blistering white arrows — or at least rocks — upon the oncoming horde.

Roark once more blew into the strange horn. When he did, as if formed from magic, his voice boomed in the air from above.

"The Mistress has begun the assault. It will not stop until every single one of us falls. But we will NOT let that happen. We are the righteous Flame of Ansalon. We will hold back the damning darkness. We will protect the Light. Look to your left. Look to your right. Those people next to you are your brothers and sisters. Fight with them now on this dark day. Together, as one spear of fire, we will defeat the Shadow. READY NOW ... they are coming."

Margaret had to admit the General was better at giving speeches than Ro.

Bolstered by the inspiring speech, the army readied their weapons and let out a ferocious battle-cry. They will hold back the damning darkness. Swords, axes, and all other weapons alike would work together to cut down the infernal undead. No further orders were needed at the end of all days. This is what they trained for. This is what they fought for. This is what they lived for, and this is what they will die for. They will defeat the Shadow.

Margaret smiled. There was only one part of that dismal speech that she cared enough to listen to:

They are coming.

Perfect, she was ready to taste some blood.

Margaret looked forward and steeled herself, eager to meet the horde of desolation in a bloody brawl. But what she saw quelled even her fierce bloodlust. This wasn't going to be a brawl.

This was going to be a slaughter. And a slaughter of *them*.

It started as a wave of oozing black. Thousands and thousands of rotting corpses shambled forward in a tsunami of death. The bodies were so dense, it was almost impossible to tell where one zombie began and the next one ended. Their ghastly groans and otherworldly howls filled the air. The battalion of living soldiers reeled under the sight of such horror, but they did not retreat, and they did not falter. They have faced such terrors before. They will defeat the Shadow.

But that was not the end. Bands of skeleton archers and mages were spaced periodically within the mass of decay. Not only that, but there were dozens of undead giants and abominations, towering over the rest of the flood, prepared to crush anything that dared strayed too close. Some giants even carried massive boulders, ready to throw at the pitiful Flame. Finally, floating amongst them there were the horrifying wraiths with their icy gaze and their frosty claws, eager to rend the life from the living soldiers.

But that was not all. Every single other horror paled in comparison to the true adversary.

Far behind the infernal legion, approaching like the specter of oblivion itself, was the winged abomination. Twice the height of even the tallest of the giants, the beast dwarfed the rest of the army. Its body had long ago rotted away, leaving only a colossal, black skeleton with two dark wings which could block out the entire sky. Cracked and broken horns crowned its mighty head. An eerie glow emanated from its hollow chest, and two icy eyes glared hungrily at the soldiers of the Flame. It was time for a feast.

They would know fear.

They would know desperation.

They would know death.

"I hope you can pull something out of your ass for that thing like you did with that big serpent," Margaret said, glancing over to Nalgene.

The gnome simply grunted. He was too short to see anything, anyway.

The dracolich opened its powerful maw and unleashed another harrowing screech. If Margaret wasn't about to shit inside her new, shining armor she would have found it amusing that a beast so grand could make a sound so shrill. But she didn't even have time to do that.

The battle had begun.

The wave of death descended upon the Sparks. But right before the lines collided, commands echoed through the air, and a huge billowing wall of fire erupted from the ground in front of the Sparks, engulfing and incinerating the legions of rot. Hundreds of foul fiends collapsed as their bodies turned to ash. But hundreds were a small number in the eyes of the Shadow.

The mass continued forward and through the wall, crashing into the lines of the living. Instantly, the forces were split under the weight of the assault. Sparks were dragged under the mass to drown in the filth, ultimately becoming devoured by the undead. The opposing archers and mages reigned havoc upon the ranks, not caring if they hit friends or foes. Death played no favorites in the Shadow. Some of the giants rushed at the wall, smashing against it vainly with powerful blows in an effort to bring it down, while the others lobbed boulders into the battlefield or at the rampart. The wraiths slashed at anything nearby, cutting down both the living and the dead. It would soon be over. There would be no struggle, there would only be indiscriminate slaughter. The Shadow would soon devour all.

Margaret could barely see anything through the claustrophobic decay. She didn't know where the others were. The stench clung to her. The sounds assaulted her. The claws scratched at her. She was desperately punching and kicking at anything nearby — she had no shortage of targets. But it was all for naught. The rot engulfed her. This was so much worse than her first bout in the Shadowfront.

They were all going to die.

But as quickly as the Spark's line was fragmented, it rallied and surged back together. This is what they trained for. Soldiers fought side by side and pushed the undeath back. Captains and Commanders darted around in the battle, obliterating countless of the undead ranks. The tide receded, and Margaret reunited with the others, grateful to escape the sea.

A Resurgence of Hope

From on top of the rampart, Flametouchers cast down barrages of fireballs, incinerating countless more. They focused their attacks on the enemy giants and mages, hoping to end the hail of projectiles before the damage was irrecoverable. From the backlines, Nalgene unleashed torrents of water, washing away the choking death. Together, Roark and the companions surged forward, bolstering their ranks to a renewed fury. But no white arrows came from above, and the undead still kept coming. The winged monster had not yet even reached the line — in fact, where did it go? No matter, the Shadow would devour all.

Margaret rushed forward, her black fist smashing the skull of yet another zombie. Its rotten blood coated her in a sickly spray. Yes, this is what she loved. More enemies, more fun, right?

A skeleton lunged at her, but her new armor defended the pathetic attack, and then her arm swung to meet her opponent. Another skull shattered under the weight of her blow. As soon as that skeleton was downed, five more undead launched themselves at her. She swatted one out of the air, and then summoned a great, icy axe with her demonic powers. Now *this* was an axe she would use. With a powerful swing, she chopped two of the others cleanly in half. Berserk with the glory of battle, she charged the other two, throwing her axe at the one to the left, taking it to the ground. For the other, she reached out, grasping its head in her dark hand, and crushed its head with her iron grip. Satisfied, she licked the black blood from her hand.

This was most delicious.

Beside her, Ro, backed by Denver and Johnson, was struggling against six undead soldiers. His golden dagger flashed this way and that, and his shield was able to protect him from many of the blows, but the undead pressure was unrelenting. He had somehow already lost his longsword. Margaret felt the urge to call him an idiot, but something held her back. Before she could help him, a skeleton stallion barreled into her.

Margaret went crashing into the mud. Her vision went red. She would obliterate this accursed creature. Snarling, she rushed to her feet, but another harsh kick from the stallion put her back to the earth.

The stallion.

She had to destroy it. She felt blood pooling from her head. The stallion.

Just then cool water washed over her, clearing her bloodthirsty thoughts, and stitching her head back together.

"Don't ye be gettin' berserk on us now, eh, ye damn orc."

Shaking her head clear, Margaret glanced up to see the annoying face of Nalgene standing over her. The skeleton stallion was shattered in pieces. Before she could thank him, he rushed off to support Ro.

She shook her head. She had to focus on the battle. She rushed back into the fray, her arm swinging wildly. She punched and kicked, losing count of the amount of undead she felled. Above her, hails of arrows and icy shards whizzed through the air. Some hit Sparks, more hit undead. But the living weighed the toll of death more heavily than those already dead.

Far to the left, a loud *thud* echoed, followed by a rolling rumbling. And screams. Being crushed to death under a boulder was not a pleasant or painless way to die. Not all the giants had been felled yet, it seemed.

The battle raged on.

Eventually, she found herself facing one of those giants. It had one last boulder in its hand, and she knew she couldn't give it time to throw. She reached her hand out, summoning her icy powers, and a jet of water burst forward to meet it. She smiled. They had done this before.

Freezing the water into a razor spear, the projectile soared into the giant, piercing straight through it and crashing into the battlefield behind it. Satisfied, Margaret charged at the giant, and was met by Andromeda, who darted in at her side. Together, they hacked away at the behemoth, with ice and steel alike, dodging through its clumsy strikes. Fireballs and other various spells were cast upon the fiend as well, both damaging it and distracting it from the two women. Margaret found herself between its legs, with another icy axe in her hand, and with a ferocious cry, she cut into the side of the giant's leg. Unable to support its own weight, the beast fell to its knees, dropping its ammunition, and at this moment, Andromeda leaped up into the air, landing on the giant's head, and plunged her halberd into its skull. Toppling under the blow, the giant fell face-first into the earth, where Margaret unleashed a devastating punch, crushing its face and sending fragments of bone whistling into the air. Andromeda gave the orc a satisfactory nod of respect, and Margaret smiled. Whether from the appreciation of her friend or the glory of battle, she couldn't say.

One down. How many to go?

But the undead kept coming.

Rallied by the victory over the giant, a dozen Sparks and their Captain moved forward to support her and Andromeda. They cut away at the writhing mass about them, forming a protective circle around their heroes. They would defeat the Shadow.

The hail of arrows and ice was now nearly gone, with the undead mages and archers selectively being picked off with spells from the Flametouchers high above. There were no more *thuds* of boulders, meaning either the giants simply ran out of rocks or were all dead. Margaret hoped it was the second one. Not even this new armor could save her from a building's-worth of stone.

As they battled through the filth, Margaret saw a frail zombie with a ragged cloak draping over its rotting form. Wispy strands of frost emanated from its palms. One of the Sparks grew too near, and the undead lashed out, clamping its palm across the man's face. His scream was agonizing yet short lived as he collapsed to the ground. Immediately, the other undead pounced upon his body, tearing away limbs and flesh. Truly a peaceful death.

Margaret felt the scar on the back of her neck tingle. So, *this* was the bitch that did that.

Alright, fucker. Her she came.

With two steps she closed the distance. The Brander didn't stand a chance. Her fist collided with its face, and its head erupted in a shower of blood and bone. That wasn't so hard, why couldn't she do that the first time she ran into one of these creatures?

The battle raged on.

Suddenly, a wraith materialized in front of the group, and instantly the soldiers reeled backward under its oppressive gaze. Its icy aura sapped at their strength, slowing their movements. But Margaret did not back down. She glanced down at her arm, and it pulsed in anticipation. She had dealt with much more terrifying things than this wraith.

The fearsome specter lunged forward, its vicious claws cutting down one of the Sparks. The man let out a hideous howl as his life fled from his body, and he fell to the ground, frozen in death. It whirled in a circle, its claws ending the life of two more Sparks. Andromeda leaped at the monstrosity, but it deflected her with its bloody talons. Two more Sparks charged forward in support, and two more warriors fell dead to the ground, their lifeblood pooling on the already saturated ground. There was a *pop* of flame under the Captain's feet, and he went soaring at the wraith, his greataxe swinging wide in an arc, but he too was stopped, and other undead swarmed over him as he lay on the ground.

Undeterred, Margaret was quick to follow in the offense, her fist reaching forward to decimate the wraith. But it wasn't there. It moved around her, and her fist passed harmlessly through its formless, dark cloak. Its claws flashed, but they were stopped by Andromeda's halberd. They felled a giant together, so they could handle this wraith. Or so they thought.

Spinning around to face the wraith again, with Andromeda once again at her side, Margaret readied her fists. Growling, she ran at the wraith, and, predictably, its claws lashed forward to meet her.

Anticipating the attack, she twisted to the side, but her armor slowed her movements. The icy blades screeched against the steel, and she felt the cold seep into her side. Now, she was very thankful for its good quality.

She reached out and grabbed its skeletal arm, yanking it towards her. Let it be close, for she did not fear the cold. As it was pulled forward, Andromeda thrust her halberd out, impaling the wraith on its sharp point. Claws flashed, but the feline leaped backward, retracting her halberd and landing just out of reach of her prey. But the wraith appeared uninjured.

However, Margaret wasn't done. Snarling in a fury, she summoned a demonic chill from her hand, freezing the wraith's arm in a thick layer of ice. Letting go of the frozen limb, she formed an icy spear over her fist and punched forward at the wraith. Its other claw flashed, and she felt them burn into her back, cutting through her plate mail, and jolting her body to the side, forcing her to miss her attack.

Good, that would only redouble her fury.

Her vision went red once more.

Just then, another skeleton stallion with its rider charged towards the pair, but then the Captain appeared in front of them in defense. Surprisingly, he was uninjured from being mobbed by the lesser undead. He held his greataxe in his hands, and with a mighty swing, he removed the two front legs of the rotting horse. It crashed to the ground, taking its rider with it. Without wasting a moment, the Captain swiftly ended the fallen rider, as well.

More undead swarmed at them, but the remaining Sparks held them at bay, allowing Margaret and Andromeda to focus on the shadowy ghost. Skeletons slashed their swords at the Captain, but they deflected off his ironed skin, just as with Osann, and he ended them with his axe. More zombies charged, but the other troops were there, hacking away at the rot.

Margaret didn't even notice. She didn't notice as the Captain somehow appeared behind the wraith, his mighty axe now ablaze in a searing inferno, or him cutting into the back of the creature. She didn't notice as Andromeda also charged at the wraith, using her halberd to deflect its claws away from Margaret.

No, her only focus *was* that damn wraith, not the others around it.

Clenching her fist, she summoned another frozen spearhead over her arm and thrust it towards the wraith's head. This time she would obliterate this disgusting fiend.

Her arm pulsed. That was all she felt. That and her rage towards the wraith.

Right before her blow struck, the wraith unleashed a terrible shriek. It sounded like a knife scraping against a steel pan — Margaret was never a fan of the culinary arts — yet somehow more unnerving. The sound tore through the air and cut deep into their very beings. Caught off guard, the Captain and Andromeda went reeling away from the ghast, desperately covering their ears. The other Sparks behind Margaret fell away in horror and were quickly disposed of by the horde. Margaret stumbled away, the noise stripping away her bloodlust.

No, she had to defeat the wraith.

Her vision was … clear, and she saw her doom.

The wraith towered above her, its unfrozen claw raised and ready to deliver the final blow. Behind her, the swarm closed in, ready to devour her flesh.

Her arm pulsed.

Focusing on the dreadful pulsations, she fought through the horror of the sound. She would defeat this wraith. With a snarl of frustration, she brought herself to her feet and swung her arm at the wraith. But just then, a hulking zombie threw itself at her and grabbed her black arm, holding it at bay. Caught off guard, all she could do was watch as the wraith's icy talons flashed down at her unprotected face.

She was such an idiot.

A Resurgence of Hope

Time seemed to slow. This was her last moment. In that mere instant, she thought of her new friends. Even in death did that word seem foreign to her. Would they miss her? She could only hope. She just wanted someone to care.

Suddenly, a brilliant spear of fire streaked through the air and impaled the wraith, immediately igniting its shadowy cloak. Another shriek pierced the air, but it was weak and soft. Then, the zombie holding her back vanished, and the General was there. Roark appeared in front of Margaret with another spear of fire held in his hand. These heroes have done well. To fell a giant and hold their own against one of the Shadow's wraiths was no small feat. Their strategy was flawed, but their determination was pristine. They were no agents of the night. He could see that clearly enough.

The wraith slashed at the General, but he easily deflected it with his shield, which was now a small, iron buckler, and no longer the wooden shield he had had earlier. He set his stance and thrust the other fiery spear into the wraith. Not slowing for a moment, he released his weapon, where it remained impaled in the shadowy cloak, ducked under the frozen arm of the wraith. There was a slight ripple in the air, and then, around his open hand, fire appeared and seemed to *compress* into the shape of a perfect longsword.

It was nearly white. And the heat was almost unbearable. And the General grabbed it.

Now behind the specter, he swung his new weapon, and with a precise strike, he cleaved the wraith's head from its body.

One final shriek filled the air, and the wraith's body seemed to implode upon itself, disappearing into shadowy smoke. The head fell to the ground, where it also soon dissolved into nothingness.

Not bothering to watch the dissolving shadow, the General reached out to the fallen Captain, his sword of fire dissipating as quickly as it had come. He helped the Captain to his feet, and rushed back into the fray, picking up a stray handaxe from the ground as he went. They were still in a battle, it would be unwise to waste time celebrating this small, pointless victory.

Margaret watched him go, stunned at his prowess. She could barely keep up with his movements, as they were so quick and deliberate. Just who were these Generals?

Yes, she really was an idiot.

Then, for the second time in this dreadful battle, a soothing wash of water flowed over her, mending her cut back.

"Ye gotta stop doin' this, Margaret," Nalgene said, reaching out with his hand to help her to her feet.

The orc snorted, but she took the helping hand.

Andromeda appeared at her side, along with the Captain, who was still unnamed. "Back to the battle, shall we?"

She wasn't going to say anything, as she had to remain immovable, but then another hand collapsed down on her shoulder. Looking back, she saw Ro and his two helpless worshipers. So, he had managed to keep them alive, this time. How noble.

"Back to the battle," she agreed.

Together, the companions and their group of Sparks fought bravely against the tide. Countless undead fell to their weapons, and, with the support from the Sparks on top of the wall — but still no white arrows — they even managed to defeat another giant. They were going to hold back the storm. The proud wall still stood strong, its stone marred but undeterred by the assault. The undead ranks were thinning. They were going to defeat the Shadow.

How quickly hopes can falter.

At last, when the sun was just receding below the mountain peaks, the dracolich joined the fray. Using the last of the gray, distant light of the sun to mask its approach, it descended upon the battlefield like a meteor, soaring out of the gray sky and crashing into living and dead alike. The sea of rot wasn't thinning. It had simply retreated to allow the dracolich full reign of the battlefield.

As soon as the dracolich landed upon the ground, a deathly chill washed over the battlefield. This was no aura from a wraith. No, this was as if the very heart of winter had descended upon the land. Some Sparks simply died in the presence of the dracolich, their

Inner Fire extinguished in the unforgiving cold. When they died, their bodies shriveled up and froze, turning into black, empty husks of frostbite and decay.

It swung its skeletal tail about, crushing dozens of desperate soldiers with each swing. Its gargantuan claws slashed about, creating jagged gashes in the ground and slaughtering even dozens more. Its rotting wings cast huge gusts of wind down upon the army, driving them back and blowing dust, grime, and blood into their eyes.

The Flame tried to fight back. Fireballs rained down upon the dragon, but it didn't notice. Huge pillars of fire burst from the ground below it, but it didn't notice. The little number of warriors which were able to get near the beast desperately swung their weapons at its legs, trying in vain to cause any damage.

But it didn't even notice. It was a machine of destruction. Everywhere it looked, more helpless victims died. In the span of several seconds, over a hundred soldiers now lay dead because of the dracolich, and all the remaining army could do was helplessly watch. The Shadow would consume all.

But then, Roark, alongside Sylven, appeared from the battlefield and leaped upon the dracolich, with Strongarm raining down a barrage of fiery spears and Quickfoot cutting with his peculiar dagger. *This* the dracolich did notice. Its icy heart could feel the unbearable heat from the spears, and the radiant light from the dagger. Roark climbed up its back, now a greatsword of fire in his hands, and he cut away at the black body. Sylven slashed away with his blue dagger, dashing impossibly quickly through the abomination's legs, and everywhere he struck, the dracolich's body seemed to get devoured by the holy blade. When it had feasted enough, he aimed the blade at the dragon's chest, and it unleashed a brilliant, blue beam of blinding light, which disintegrated any bone which it touched. When it did, it revealed a small, icy core — the source of the soft blue glow. It was the dracolich's heart.

The dracolich unleashed a horrible howl. It had come to feast, so feast it shall. It wasn't going to let these nuisances get in its way. The attacks were damaging it, that was evident, but it could endure. It endured through life and so it shall endure through undeath. It launched into the air, bringing Roark up with it, and leaving Sylven below in the cold mud. Once in the air, it whipped in a circle at neck-breaking speed, forcing the General to come flying off of it. Roark went soaring through the air, only to come crashing down at the feet of the companions, where he lay still. With the annoying pest disposed of, it eyed the great wall, which stood like a samurai of stone. It had been given one simple command: to bring down that immovable structure.

Still in the air, somehow flying due to some dark magic, the great beast opened its mouth, and an icy vortex formed deep in its throat. With a terrifying surge of power, the dracolich unleashed its frosty breath upon the wall, where it crashed into the hard rock. Any who were caught in the blast, both in front of and on top of the wall, shriveled up into frozen husks, their very life force drained. Even the stone felt the icy grasp of death. Where the dracolich's breath touched, the stone withered and cracked, disintegrating under the frozen fury.

Margaret watched in horror. She glanced at the top of the wall. She didn't have any particular faith, but even she prayed that Fasto wasn't caught in that blast. Her arm seemed but a small toy in the face of that abyssal power. She glanced down at the General at her feet. A Flametoucher with three golden stripes on his crimson robe rushed over, an alarmed look on his face. Sylven had also suddenly appeared with a *pop*. The mage placed his hands over the Roark's chest, and a surge of healing fire washed over the crippled man. Immediately, his eyes shot open, and he surged to his feet. The Flametoucher fell back in relief, his face now ghostly pale.

The reinvigorated General observed the battlefield, the different possibilities flashing through his mind once more. Almost all of them ended in certain death. What could they do against such reckless hate? The undead army was once again surging forward. The stone where the dracolich had unleashed its terrible breath upon the wall was now decaying and frozen, and the dragon was smashing it with its tail in an attempt to break through. The undead giants were also charging at the weakened wall, throwing their bodies against it like battering rams of flesh and bone. There were more wraiths, and they were descending upon the lone group of surviving Sparks. Far, far in the distance, two red eyes could be seen burning with glee.

There was only one strategy.

Shaking the dirt from his armor, Strongarm faced Andromeda and Sylven. "We need to dismember their command. You two must go into the Shadow behind their ranks and kill the Mistress. That is the only chance we will have. We cannot survive against this organized chaos. Go!"

Smiling, Sylven turned to Andromeda. "Let's go hunting, eh? Sounds like fun."

The feline merely nodded, her body already fading into darkness.

"Ooo, I like this kitty," Sylven said. He winked and waved at everyone else. "Good luck and see you on the other side." With that, he disappeared.

Without waiting to see where they had gone, the remaining General turned to the last remaining soldiers. There was only one strategy. He pulled out the horn and blew.

"RETREAT!" he commanded, his voice echoing through the air. "RETREAT TO THE KEEP!" He then turned to face the oncoming wave, another spear of fire forming in his hand. He would hold them at bay while the others made it to safety.

Margaret watched the General begin his solemn march towards the rotting legion. Her arm burned at the chance to rush out there and start killing again, and she would have done it, had Ro not placed his hand on her shoulder.

"We have to go," the draconian said.

In the draconian's hand was his golden dagger. She almost thought it was funny to compare its size to that of the winged monster, but there was no humor left here. She took a step forward towards the General.

"Don't ye be gettin' any crazy ideas, orc."

"We need to go!" Denver said from behind Ro. Clearly, his nerves were getting the best of him now, and who could blame him? Johnson simply nodded in agreement.

Margaret couldn't bring herself to take another step. She could only watch. Many of the other Sparks were already rushing to the wall, slipping through small, hidden doors to reach the other side. Suddenly, a crashing sound reverberated across the battlefield. Her head darted to the side, and she saw the section of the once-proud wall collapsing. The Shadow had breached the impenetrable defenses. The Shadow would consume all.

The rotting giants rushed through the breach, storming to the inner defenses. The dracolich launched itself into the air and soared over the wall, eager to extinguish more pathetic flames. It would feast well indeed. The undead army swarmed forward, flowing in behind the giants.

Margaret took one final look at the General, who was locked in combat with three wraiths, a pile of death already at his feet. She wanted to help, she wanted to feel more blood, but she couldn't. Shaking her head, she turned to Ro, then followed him to the inside of the wall. She could taste plenty more blood there.

Her arm pulsed at her side. How she hated it. Maybe, if she was lucky, the winged abomination would bite it off. Or perhaps it wouldn't. Perhaps she could finally become strong enough to conquer it on her own. Or more likely, she wouldn't. Why did she care so much about her friends' approval? Why did she care so much about what happened in the past? Her pathetic problems seemed tiny indeed in the face of this draconic avatar of death.

And yet her arm raged on, the only thing keeping her sane.

They were all idiots, but she might be the biggest fool of all.

A Resurgence of Hope

And what did it matter?
They were all going to die, anyway.

Daniel Whitman

Chapter 5

Andromeda darted after her hunting partner, her eyes scanning the surroundings for any sign of the Mistress. Sylven's description was entirely unhelpful — he didn't seem to know exactly what they were hunting for either. Somehow, the General had managed to get in front of her, even though she didn't remember seeing him slip past. She smirked. Now two could hunt.

Occasionally a lonely undead or two would dare appear in front of the duo, but it would always swiftly meet its end to Andromeda's halberd or Sylven's dagger. Together, they danced through the stragglers in a vicious harmony.

This was what a hunt was supposed to be.

Another zombie, this one with three bulky arms, lunged toward her. Its mouth opened wide, displaying black gums and rotting teeth. Andromeda glanced towards it, observing the wretched spit oozing from its open maw. Time seemed to move in slow motion.

The zombie lazily lurched forward, one of its arms reaching for her head. Without even thinking, she ducked under the vain attempt of an attack, and her halberd flashed. A spray of tar-like blood came out from the zombie as its arm left its body.

But, as with all undead, it didn't feel this kind of mortal pain.

It whipped around, its two remaining arms opened wide to embrace the feline. With her free hand, she reached out and grabbed her prey by one of its wrists, and with surprising strength, yanked it towards her.

Undead aren't known for their remarkable balance.

The creature stumbled and fell to the ground. Using this moment of opportunity, the hunter placed one of her feet on its back and launched herself into the air, further forcing her prey into the blood-soaked ground. With a deft twist, she flipped into the air.

Her weapon flashed once more, and a second arm left her prey.

The hunter landed on the ground, ready to finish the kill. The zombie had no hope of escape. Her pathetic prey was doomed.

Her eyes flared, and she raised her mighty weapon. Yes, this was her favorite part.

Just before she could land the killing blow, the ground shook, and a thunderous crashing sound filled the air. Forgetting about her prey, Andromeda looked in the direction of the keep in alarm. She couldn't see it anymore through the dust and gloom, but she could only imagine the devastation.

What diabolical power could do such a thing. It had to be that winged beast ...

Below her, the zombie struggled to its feet and ran off in the direction of the stone wall, urged on by some invisible command. The Shadow was ready to feast, and it had heard its call. Before it could get more than two steps, a blue dagger darted through the air, firmly embedding itself in the zombie's skull. Without so much as a grunt, the undead toppled to the ground.

Snapping back to reality, Andromeda looked at the fallen zombie, and then at the General which had appeared next to it. He looked up at her and winked.

"That was some fine acrobatics, kitty," he said. "But with all that fancy flipping you almost let this poor fellow get away."

Andromeda blinked at him, barely registering his words. Her mind was still on the crashing sound. All she could think of was her friends buried under the rubble.

"Hm? Ah, yes — uh — I suppose I let that one go."

Sylven sighed and looked down at the zombie, his playful smile now gone. Way to suck the fun out of the air. He reached down and grabbed his dagger. The blade filled with a radiant light, and the corpse seemed to shrivel up. After a moment, it returned to normal, and he pulled the dagger out. Satisfied, he stood up and walked over to Andromeda.

"What do you think that sound was?" she asked, not noticing what had happened. Her tail lashed back and forth in anxiety. All she could think of was her friends being devoured by undead. And she was powerless to stop. What good was this hunt, anyway, if everyone else was dying?

Sylven touched her arm. "Hey, listen to me, I don't know what happened back there. But what I do know is the strength of my fellow General, and the will of the Flame. No matter how terrible it gets, he will find a way. He's always mumbling about those wise strategies and brilliant maneuvers, so I'm sure he's got something fun in mind."

Andromeda glanced at him, worry still fresh in her mind. She saw what that winged abomination could do.

"Do you have faith in your friends, Andromeda? Do you know their strength? Because if they're the same ones who fought through the Shadowfront, and didn't back down against the Torch, I'd say they're more than capable for whatever's happening at the keep."

Andromeda nodded. He was right. She may be just a little kitten, but her friends were powerful. They would prevail.

"We have a glorious quest, remember? We can't let their battle cloud over our mission. Besides, what's the fun in sitting around and pouting?"

Andromeda smiled. She liked this General. The hunt was always more fun than waiting on the sidelines. She reached up and grabbed his wrist. "Much appreciated."

He winked and dropped his arm. "Let's go kill a Mistress, eh?"

She nodded but didn't immediately return to the pursuit. First, it would be helpful to better understand her prey — both to give her something else to think about and to prepare her for what was to come.

"What is a 'Mistress'?"

Sylven paused for a long moment before answering.

"I don't know exactly."

This was not the answer Andromeda expected. Her tail flicked in the air in frustration.

"From what we — as in the Flame — could gather, and from what the Oracle has told us, they control the Shadow, telling it where and when to strike. And they are devilishly powerful. Mariah said they used to be like her, which really has a way of killing the joy."

That left even more questions unanswered.

"Have you ever fought one before?"

"Me? Personally? Can't say I have."

Another answer Andromeda wasn't expecting — or hoping for.

"Now, come," the General continued. "Back to the hunt, remember?"

With that, they were back on the prowl. Andromeda weaved through the shadows, carefully observing every speck of dirt on the ground in an attempt to track her mysterious target. Surprisingly, the signs were abundant. Sylven pranced around, skipping this way and that, skillfully cutting the few remaining undead which ran past them towards the fallen keep. He even did a flip while decapitating another zombie, making certain that Andromeda saw the outlandish maneuver.

Andromeda felt her mood lifting and could only chuckle. She liked this General.

Each and every time her companion struck down one of the vile beasts, he absorbed their essence into his holy dagger. On one such occasion, Andromeda couldn't help her curiosity.

"What are you doing that for?"

He smiled at her. "Oh, you know, just getting ready for our grand battle with the Mistress."

"Yes, yes, very interesting and clear. Here I thought we would be getting prepared by doing push-ups and sparring against each other."

He smirked. "We can do that too. For how can I say no to such a fantastic idea?"

The hunter flashed a smile back. "If we ever were to spar, don't expect me to go easy." Perhaps, in time, she would have a new target.

"If, of course. And I would expect nothing less."

Sylven took a step towards her, and then, casually, he flipped his blue dagger high into the air towards her. Somewhere, somehow, a ray from the setting gray sun peeked through the haze and the mountains to glint across the metallic blade. Or maybe it wasn't the sun at all, and it was some intrinsic sparkle of the weapon.

Andromeda looked up, and it was over before she could ever appreciate what was happening. The General appeared behind her, his hand clasped on her wrist. And how he was *strong*. She couldn't move her arm. Snarling, and quite surprised, she turned her body, her one claw raking towards his exposed face on pure instinct, and her halberd appearing in her other, restrained hand.

The rest happened in a mere instant.

Her prey ducked under the attack. In one, frighteningly swift motion, he twisted her wrist up, forcing her halberd to fall from her grasp, stepped behind her leg with his, brought his shoulder into her armpit, and flipped her over his hip to come crashing to the ground.

The hunter's breath was blasted from her lungs. Her eyes watering, Andromeda saw him standing over her, a grim expression on his face. Before she could move, his foot stomped on her chest, pinning her down. There was another glint of light in the air, and his holy dagger came soaring down from the cloudy heavens. Without missing a beat, Sylven caught it, dropped to his knees, and held it against her exposed neck.

"Fight like that, and the Mistress will kill you."

But Andromeda didn't hear him. As soon as she felt the dagger touch her skin, it was as if her soul was being torn asunder. A merciless paralysis froze her body. All she saw was a blinding light. All she felt was an inescapable void. It lasted only a fraction of a second, but to her, it was an eternity of suffering.

She let out a cry and opened her eyes. The dreadful feeling was gone. Sylven's hand appeared in front of her, and he pulled her to her feet.

"Ah, I was getting worried, you almost had me beat for a second," he laughed, returning to his care-free self. "I thought you weren't going to go easy?"

"I ... er ... suppose next time I'll have to try a little harder," Andromeda grumbled, shaking away the hollow feeling inside her mind. "Is this truly an appropriate time to spar?"

"Of course not."

Andromeda could only imagine the incredulous look on her own face.

"But you don't suppose that the Mistress will wait until you're ready to spar, do you?"

Andromeda opened her mouth to retort, but promptly clamped it shut, unable to justifiably refute the man's claim.

"Perfect, and now you *are* ready. Perhaps, once we survive this ordeal, we will get that sparring match in — and I'll even make sure you're ready next time."

She studied him, a new respect in her gaze as she mentally replayed the man's brutally efficient dismantling of her. If this was all the Generals were capable of, what hope did the Shadow have?

"Mmm, and as I said, I won't be going easy."

"You have me shaking already, kitty." He turned away, a twinkle in his bright eyes. "Come now, let's not forget why we are here. Without our help, they have no hope of winning." With that, he was off, plunging into the thickening darkness.

Andromeda stared after him with longing. Just who was this Sylven creature? Perhaps he could train her ... Just what would she be capable of then?

"You coming?" the General called back through the dust. "It's always more fun with someone by your side."

Shaking her head in amusement, Andromeda reached down and picked up her halberd. Immediately it disappeared in her grasp. Of course, it was dangerous to run with sharp polearms exposed, and safety was very important. With a flick of her tail, she raced after her companion. If she caught up, maybe she would be brave and ask about training. Or maybe he'd just laugh.

With that, they were back on the prowl. They scoured across the barren land, desperately searching for clues to where the Mistress could be found. And much like before, the clues were plain enough to see.

Of course, to the untrained hunter, these breadcrumbs would be impossible to notice, and most would just skim right past them. But these two were no ordinary hunters. Where one person might see a broken blade of grass, a true professional would see a hasty footprint. Where a novice might see a scuff of dirt, a deliberate tracker would see a trail sliding across the ground. There were many more subtle clues such as these, but the most obvious clue, and by far the most terrifying clue, was the ominous stench that their prey left in her wake.

While less of an actual smell, this stench was more of an intense feeling of vileness that drilled right into the gut. It was as if the Mistress was leaving little shards of burning hatred for them to stumble across. The first time Andromeda came across it she felt a sickening bile creeping up her throat, but she was quickly able to get her stomach under strict control. What sickening power was this?

The huntress supposed she would find out soon enough. Sylven did say they were powerful. She unfurled her claws, their sharpened tips eager to find her prey. If this Mistress was anything like that forsaken Goddess, who tried to twist her mind against her will, she would be ready, and she would be vicious.

Her mouth formed a grim, sadistic smile.

Long live the hunt.

The pair continued to hound the trail. They encountered no more undead, as they had left the Shadowfront and the crumbling keep long behind them. In fact, they encountered little of anything. It was as if the whole gray world was holding its breath, waiting for the match to ignite. There was no wind, and the rotten grass stood still upon the cold ground. There was hardly any sound, except for their concentrated breathing and gentle trekking across the earth. And the darkness was slowly creeping in, unavoidable and indomitable. They didn't say a word to each other, for none needed to be said. They had their mission, and their victim was near at hand. The time for quips and playful sparring was over.

They meandered to the north, where a dark wood lay far in the distance. Harsh mountains stood solemnly to the east, ever watchful for the events of the world. In front of the companions was a lone, crooked tree, exiled from the others in the far forest. It was there where their trail led. It was there where the Mistress was gleefully waiting.

The tree was nested inside a dip in the ground. Shallow hills rolled out on every side, so they couldn't get a clear look at what may lay inside — but they already knew what was there. As they approached, they could feel the weight of her vile hatred fall over them. But it was nothing compared to the demonic aura they encountered when they finally got sight of their target.

Sylven signaled impossibly fast at her with his hands, and she could only assume he meant for her to be stealthy. She melted into the shadows. There was no reason to meet this foe head-on.

As they crested the ridge and peered into the dip, they spotted the Mistress propped next to the tree, her arms crossed and one foot resting on the trunk. She was stunning, frighteningly so — for what she was. Her hair was black and curled short and her skin was brown. Onyx-black armor adorned her figure, and a jagged greatsword rested on the tree next to her.

So, that was their prey.

Crouched low, Sylven maneuvered around the ridge until he was positioned behind her right side. He gestured for Andromeda to mirror him — not that he could see where she was — and she complied. In position now, she studied the Mistress, who seemed apparently unconcerned about the toils of the world. Something just didn't sit well. Why was she just waiting here? And where were all the undead?

With such a potentially erratic foe, it was always better to discover their patterns first before going in for the kill. She wished she could relay her concerns to her hunting partner, but, as she glanced at the man, she saw that his blue dagger was drawn.

Apparently, he had other plans.

There was a small *pop* of flames underneath his feet, and in an instant, he was behind the Mistress, his holy dagger whistling through the air towards her exposed throat. Another explosion of fire ignited behind his left hand, and it accelerated the strike to an impossible speed. Perhaps if he could end this early, before his weak companion had a chance to be killed, he would succeed in his duty as a General. There would only be one chance. His blade was cutting true. The vile woman's neck was his for the taking.

Of course, it wouldn't be that easy to fell the Mistress.
The Shadow would devour all.

In one, smooth motion, the Mistress crouched down, avoiding the fatal blow, reached up with her right hand, clamped it on his face, and threw him to the ground in front of her, where he rolled quickly to his feet.

The Mistress's infernal red eyes bored into him, and she casually grabbed her wicked sword, effortlessly lifting it with a single, slender arm.

"We were getting worried that you would never find us," she said, her voice sounding like a discordant melody.

"Ah, I hope we didn't keep you waiting for too long," Sylven replied.

"No matter, this will be over soon enough."

"Perhaps, but that's all part of the fun."

The Mistress smiled, and suddenly the ground around the dip began to rumble.

"Fuck," was all the General said before dashing back at the Mistress, locking into battle. So much for fun.

Andromeda's eyes darted around in horror. Hands of flesh and bone sprouted like weeds, pulling up legions of undead. But that was not all. Behind her, just over the lip of the clearing, a massive, armored gauntlet burst through the cold earth, its black armor adorned with spikes and skulls. It clawed at the ground, and with terrifying strength, ripped itself up, effortlessly breaking through its earthy tomb. It was a dreadknight, and in its other hand was a massive axe. Andromeda suddenly realized why the Mistress chose this spot to fight. Fear filled her being, and she felt her shadowy cloak fade away. Her mind pounded with pain; each heartbeat seemed like a knife stabbing into her ribs.

Long live the hunt — or short live, more likely.

Down in the clearing, the Mistress and the General clashed blades. His dagger once more arced in for the kill, and all too easily, the Mistress's greatsword flashed up, deflecting the blade. As it did, her free hand arced in with a mighty hook. Sylven ducked under the blow, and he thrust his other dagger forward.

Without missing a beat, his menacing foe slipped to the side, avoiding the strike. Her hand whipped down and grabbed his wrist. She pulled forward, and Sylven stumbled towards her, caught off guard. Her greatsword swung in, the pommel crashing into his jaw with a sickening *crunch*. Blood sprayed from the General's mouth, and his head whipped to the side from the force. The Mistress then kicked him squarely in the chest, and the poor man was sent flying back. It was too trivial. And this pathetic creature was one of the feared Generals?

So much for fun.

As Sylven fell backward, the Mistress launched towards him, her black greatsword coming in for the kill.

Just then, the hunter joined the fray. She dove onto the Mistress's back, her halberd no longer in her hand, and dug her claws in with all her might. It had little effect against the obsidian armor, but it did manage to pull the target from her course. Andromeda went sliding off the armor, twisting in the air to land facing her prey. The halberd appeared once more, and she charged at the dark woman.

The Mistress turned and glared at her, and the weight of the hate caused Andromeda to hesitate and falter. That was all the vile woman needed. She deflected the worthless feline's halberd with careless ease, then swung her free arm in another hook. It connected with Andromeda's face, and this time it was her blood that went spraying, and it was her that went stumbling to the ground.

By now, Sylven was back to his feet, but the undead swarm surrounded him. He blinked around the battlefield with *pops* of fire, his dagger tasting black blood. But the approaching dreadknight's steps echoed like drums of death, and the rumbling did not stop.

Andromeda felt the rotting hands pawing at her body, and she leaped to her feet, her halberd slashing. She saw a magical ball of shadow, followed by a Mistress, streaking towards her head. She managed to avoid the orb, and it crashed into a skeleton behind her, but she had less luck avoiding the Mistress.

The greatsword came arcing in, but now it was Sylven's turn to save the day. Before the Mistress could land the killing blow, the General appeared in front of Andromeda, blocking the black blade with his dagger. Blood dripped from his lips, and there was no smile on his face.

"Get the undead," he managed to spit at Andromeda.

The Mistress swung again, coming in wide and from the side. The blade effortlessly cut through several surrounding undead. Sylven leaped high into the air, completely clearing the blade, and landing nimbly on the ground. Now on the backside of the swing, he rushed at his enemy, locking her sword arm to her body, and driving her back into the rotting horde. His dagger flashed, but the Mistress caught his hand. Undeterred, his knee came up, striking her directly in the stomach. She slid back, but she felt no pain. Just another blessing granted by the Shadow.

During this, recognizing her task, the hunter darted around the clearing, cutting down any undead that attempted to grab at the General. Her blade flashed. Her fur was saturated with thick blood.

The dreadknight began its descent into the arena, and the rumbling continued.

Sylven tried to knee again, but the Mistress blocked it with her leg this time. Then his elbow came in, hitting her square in the face. Using that same arm, he reached around her head and squeezed on her neck. He took a step behind her, and similarly to what he did with Andromeda, flipped her over his hip.

The Mistress landed hard on the cold earth, releasing the General's wrist. Before he could make another attack, the Mistress slammed her leg into his knee, dropping him to the ground with her. Immediately, undead leaped upon him. Although she tried, the hunter couldn't stop them all.

Before she could come to his aid, she felt the cold of the dreadknight. Whipping around, she saw its axe descend upon her head. It should have been easy to gracefully avoid, but the chill sapped her muscles, so the best she could do was barrel into some zombies at her side. Their claws grasped at her, tearing away tufts of fur, but she was focused on the new prey.

But how would this end any differently from the prison?

Distracted, she didn't notice the Mistress appear behind her. The greatsword flashed, cutting through the undead and creating a nasty gash on her arm. Immediately, Andromeda felt her very soul being pulled away by that black sword, and she let out a gasp in alarm. What sick power did these Mistresses possess?

Without giving Andromeda a chance to ponder the wound or the blade, the Mistress was attacking again. The hunter avoided the first strike — barely — but her arm felt too weak to effectively wield the halberd. The second strike came in, and she attempted to block it, but it knocked her weapon out of her grasp.

Then the dreadknight's axe came streaking in.

Between the relentless assault, the icy aura, and the penetrating red gaze, Andromeda had no hope left.

Just then, the General appeared at her side, his blue dagger held out towards the dreadknight. A glowing sphere of energy formed at the tip, followed by a brilliant, blue beam of light, identical to the one he fired at the dracolich, which penetrated the dreadknight directly through its chest, devouring any undead in its path. The armored behemoth staggered backwards and then collapsed to the ground.

The hunter glanced at her partner. Blood and filth caked his body, and his breath was ragged, but his eyes were still bright. He returned her gaze, and managed two words before the Mistress interrupted:

"Must recharge."

Immediately the hunter knew the plan. They would use the same beam to defeat the Mistress. But before that, they had to ensure *they* were not defeated themselves.

And the rumbling still continued, although fainter now.

The Mistress's blade came streaking in, and so the dance continued — Sylven matching the blows with his blades while the hunter cut down the pests around him. The General blinked around the battlefield with his *pops* of flame, and even the Mistress couldn't match his speed. Whenever he found an opening, he would lash out with his blue dagger at a stray zombie and absorb its essence. With each one, the blade grew brighter.

But the pair grew labored, while the vile woman never tired, and her shadowy spells and wicked blade chased the pair around the battlefield.

Finally, the rumbling stopped, and the swarm of undead ceased, defeated. But that brought them no respite, as in the distance, five more pairs of drums began thundering on the ground. While they managed to defeat a single dreadknight, they certainly had no hope against five — especially while the Mistress still fought. They had to end this, and quickly.

The hunter found herself facing the Mistress — her terrifying and powerful prey. The greatsword arced in. The hunter felt herself growing frantic. Her heart pounded. That vile, red gaze seared into her. Her arm burned at her side. Her legs shook.

But once more Sylven came to the rescue. He finished absorbing a final zombie, and his blue dagger came streaking through the air, implanting itself into the Mistress's back. Much like the dracolich, this, she did feel. She whirled about, but he was already behind her, grabbing his dagger and pulling it through, cutting her flesh and armor with ease. She swung her sword, desperately trying to end the pathetic General, but he ducked under it.

She kept swinging. He blocked, dodged, blocked, dipped, ducked, and even dove over the blade. He slashed in return, creating another gash on the Mistress, and then another. Every blow was propelled with an explosion of fire he created behind his hand. Each time the dagger cut into the dark being, it absorbed more power and glowed even brighter still. On Sylven's fourth strike, the Mistress managed to catch his hand once more, but the hunter was ready.

Overcoming the terror, she leaped upon her target, locking onto the sword arm, preventing her from swinging that horrible greatsword. Stepping in close, Sylven smashed another elbow into her face, then brought another knee into her chest. Liquid, thick and black, was oozing from the Mistress's delicate face, but she didn't notice — or care. Andromeda didn't know what the fluid was, but it wasn't blood.

The approaching doom boomed louder.

Snarling, the Mistress squeezed down on the General's hand with terrible force. She pulled him in, and at the same time, whipped her head forward, solidly headbutting Sylven. She let go of the dazed human's wrist and instead reached forward and grabbed him by the head.

Sensing the danger, Andromeda released the sword arm and slipped behind the Mistress, her claws tearing through the shadowy woman's face. She felt muscles tear and an eyeball pop, and black ooze covered her hands. Then, she assaulted her other arm, slashing at the hand holding Sylven.

But, as was the norm, the Mistress didn't seem to notice — or care. But, thankfully, due to the attack, she did release the General, where he went tumbling on the ground. But now Andromeda was the focus, and the Mistress whipped around, her greatsword cutting in. Andromeda managed to just barely duck the strike, but then the Mistress's other, mangled hand was there, grasping her by the throat, and lifting her into the air.

Andromeda had never felt so small. Even while facing down that winged abomination at the keep, she had some sense they could win. But now, face-to-face with her death, and with the pressure on her throat growing more each moment, she had nothing to hope for. She was thrashing about, all four of her claws desperately trying to find an opening. She managed to slash the

Mistress's face again, but it had no effect. The lone red eye kept burning, and the pressure kept growing.

The Shadow would devour all.

And the approaching doom boomed even louder.

Her head pounded in agony. She had to think, she had to escape. Where was the hunter? What would the hunter do? But all she could think of was her inevitable demise.

Just before her vision went black, Sylven appeared. How many times has he saved her now?

Irritated, the Mistress turned and flung Andromeda at him like a dead animal. The General somehow managed to catch her, and she fell limply to the ground to join the rotting bodies in the muck. She coughed, and red flakes splattered across the dirt. Blood still oozed from her injured arm, and she felt as if she were going to faint.

Satisfied that she was still mostly breathing, the General stepped over her and engaged with the Mistress. He had to complete this mission, even if it cost this hero her life.

Watching through hazy eyes, Andromeda saw them clashing in a grand fashion. Black and blue blades whistled through the air, ringing against each other, creating a devilish orchestra of metal in the air.

The Mistress slashed and swung, her black blade cleaving unholy arcs through the air. Like before, in between strikes she used her other hand to try to grab and brutalize the General. Black ichor saturated her face and flowed down the crevices of her armor, giving her the appearance of a countess who had just bathed in rejuvenating blood. But her hateful eye burned on.

Sylven ducked and twisted, nimbly avoiding his enemy's blows. His holy dagger flashed this way and that, its glowing brilliance casting the barren battlefield in a radiant light. It was almost ready, it just needed one more taste of the darkness, and the battle would be won. He had to complete his mission. He blinked this way and that, doing anything and everything to land the final strike. But try as he might, the Mistress was ruthless and gave him no opportunity. While he was growing exhausted, his foe had the restless strength of the Shadow driving her forward, and she showed no signs of weariness.

And the approaching doom boomed even louder.

As they fought, the Mistress was driving Sylven back towards the lone tree, which loomed high above them like a scavenger waiting for its meal. Sylven ducked a swing but was struck by the Mistress's fist. He blocked the greatsword with his dagger, but her leg cracked into his ribs.

Andromeda, slowly regaining her awareness, began to crawl towards the pair, pushing through the corpses on the ground. Not wanting to be found, she melted into the dark. She tried to remain quiet as she slithered across the ground, but the saturated ground sloshed under her weight. Each fraction she moved felt like an infinite ordeal.

Still, the battle raged in front of her. Sylven was almost trapped against the tree. He was running out of options. Another dodge, and another block, but then the Mistress slammed another fist in his face. Long gone was his smile. Long gone was the fun. This was do or die. The very fate of the Flame itself may reside in this singular fight.

Andromeda slinked nearer to the tree, growing faster as her strength returned. She wished she had her halberd, but there was no time to search for it. Claws and brutality would have to do.

At last, the Mistress had the General back into the tree. He had nowhere left to flee. The greatsword came in, and he just managed to block it. Then came her fist, which smashed into the tree as he dipped his head to the side. He slashed out, and the Mistress swiftly moved back, avoiding the strike.

He slashed again.

She blocked.

Another strike.

She spun out of the way, and then her leg came up, connecting a sidekick directly to the General's chest. There was a *crack* as one of his ribs broke. He slid back, the force pushing him against the tree. His head whipped back and struck the sturdy trunk. He gasped in pain. He appeared stunned. He appeared helpless. This was surely the end of him. His mission had failed.

And the approaching doom BOOMED even louder. The hunter could see the five, hulking dreadknights through the dust. They were almost upon them.

The greatsword sliced through the air, its blade targeted on Sylven's exposed throat. He watched it come in.

For just a moment, through the blood and the mud, his smile returned.

He ducked under the blade, and it cut deep into the tree, firmly lodging itself in the iron trunk. He stepped forward, his blue dagger striking forward. It slashed the Mistress across the stomach, absorbing the last fraction of energy it was craving. Caught by surprise, the Mistress didn't have time to react. She tried to punch with her free hand, but with a *pop* he darted far out of her reach. The blade pulsed with energy, it was time. But there were too many corpses littering the ground, and he was exhausted. As he moved, his foot caught under one of the many bodies, causing him to stumble.

That was all the opening the Mistress required. Devilish, inky wings sprouted from her back, and she soared at the stumbling General. Covering the distance in the blink of an eye, her hand clamped on the General's wrist. She twisted his arm, and his dagger fell to the ground. Her knee came up. Then another headbutt. With his free hand, he attempted to stab her with his other dagger, but, as he did, she caught the blade with her hand. Sludge oozed from her gashed palm, but she tore the dagger from his grasp.

"We know your foolish tricks, insect. We know what that dagger is."

A *Resurgence of Hope*

Now wielding the General's dagger, and still holding him in place, she stuck him in the gut. But it stopped as surely as if it had struck iron, leaving the man unscathed. Undeterred, she kept stabbing, kneeing, and headbutting, beating him to a pulp.

One of the stabs penetrated.

Sylven let out a gasp of pain. His mission had failed. The Mistress retracted the blade and moved to stick him again.

But then Andromeda was there. She readied herself to pounce, her muscles bulging in her legs. It was her turn to save the General. The hunter would defeat its prey.

She launched herself at the Mistress, knocking everyone to the ground. But her prey quickly regained her footing. The General, however, did not. Scrambling, the hunter scooped up Sylven's holy dagger in her hand. She didn't know why she did, but at the moment, against all odds, it seemed their only hope. As soon as she touched the dagger, it felt as if her soul was being torn asunder. Her body froze, her mind in a faraway place.

◆　　◆　　◆

The feline walked through the small town. There was an alarm bell ringing. Invaders were here. A black army of soulless knights was here to pillage. None would be spared. The men would be executed. The women would be taken. The children would be enslaved. Any who dared fight back would meet a terrible doom.

All she felt was the frigid paralysis.

All around her, her townsfolk were scattering in terror. They tried to shout at her, to warn her, but she couldn't hear them. It was as if she wasn't there, merely a ghost watching this macabre slaughter. She glanced down at her arm, and she saw it begin to flake away.

All she saw was the blinding light.

She turned. Suddenly everything was black and burning. Before her, an innocent family was being taken hostage by the marauders. They held the wife and child down, forcing them to watch as they dragged the husband through the dirt. He tried to resist, but it was hopeless. Two of the bandits pulled him to his knees, then shoved their swords through his calves and into the ground, pinning him in place. He screamed, but the feline couldn't hear anything. A third bandit approached, flaunting a spiked gauntlet. The newcomer spat onto the captured man's teary face, then began to beat him with the thorned glove. The iron spikes tore into the man's skin and flesh, cracking bone and ripping chunks of meat from the victim. The bandit grabbed the husband by the throat and said something in his ear, then he turned and signaled. At his command, the woman and child were pulled away, leaving the helpless man nothing more than a broken shell on the unforgiving ground. The feline approached the man, but like her arm, her legs began to disappear into nothing.

All she heard was the deafening silence.

She blinked, and she found herself sitting outside of a burning city, her body fading into ash. Beside her lay a woman and a child, but she didn't know who they were, or where they came from. They looked like her, but then again, she wasn't exactly sure what she looked like. Everything was fading.

All she became was the inescapable void.

A Resurgence of Hope

Before her, a band of people trekked through her domain.
They were her prey, and she needed to feast. She pounced on the
leader. It was a man, with long, shaggy hair and a bushy mustache
curling over his gentle face. He held a marvelous hammer and had
a flowing blue cape. He smiled and began to glow a brilliant light.
The hunter attacked, but her vision grew black. She was vanishing,
becoming nothing more than a faint memory in the lives of the few.

All she knew was ... she had experienced this before. She
knew the feeling of being held frozen and helpless, the wretched
Goddess had made sure of that. She knew the feeling of her soul
becoming devoured, Sylven had shown her that. This was the same.
She had the strength to overcome it then and so she could overcome
it now. The hunter had to feast. Inside of her, a little spark flickered
to life. She would not be defeated by whatever sorcery now held her
hostage. She *was* powerful, and damn anyone who stood in her way.

♦   ♦   ♦

Andromeda's eyes flipped open, and she took a deep gasp
for air. She now lay back in that desolate clearing. Sylven was still
on the ground, beaten and bloody, and gasping for life. The Mistress
was several steps in front of her, preparing to charge. Around her,
the dreadknights began their march into the dip. The test had only
lasted a fraction of a second, but when your soul is being devoured,
that is a long time indeed.

In the hunter's hand was the blue dagger. No longer was it
trying to consume her. The hunter was the master now. She whipped
to her feet and pointed the dagger at her prey. She felt the energy
coursing through the blue blade. The sphere formed at the tip again,
begging to be unleashed.

Her prey looked up, alarm in her lone eye. That red eye had no effect on the hunter now. The Mistress was too far away. She couldn't hope to get to Andromeda in time.

Long live the hunt.

A brilliant laser shot from the blade, engulfing the Mistress in its destructive light. Now Andromeda knew what Sylven was getting ready for. She felt the crackling energy flow through her body. She was nothing more than a conduit for this ancient treasure.

After a moment, the laser disappeared, its energy spent. The Mistress somehow managed to avoid some of the beam, but half of her body had reduced to nothing more than atoms.

"We will be back," the Mistress said, before collapsing to the ground. As she did, her body began to ooze and melt away like some dark, parasitic slime, disappearing into the earth.

Andromeda dropped the dagger and fell to her knees. They had done it. They had completed the mission. But at what cost? Sylven was nearly dead. Five dreadknights were nearly upon them. She crawled over to the General, and he managed to spit out some words with his blood:

"Now, wasn't that fun? I thought you were a goner. Most people who wield this blade face a terrible death, but you impressed me kitty."

Before Andromeda could reply, he coughed, and his breath became quick and shallow. His eyes rolled back into his head.

She looked around, and she knew despair.

The approaching doom had arrived. Five couriers of death, all adorned in black armor. Five demons to bring them to the eternal slumber. All she could think about was that one word the General had said earlier:

"Fuck."

Frantically, she began to blend with the shadows. Maybe she could escape. But what of the General? He certainly couldn't turn himself invisible, especially not in his current state. But what if *she* could?

A Resurgence of Hope

She never tried it — she didn't even know how her abilities worked. But it was the only thing she could think of. In her mind, she imagined her goal. She imagined him cloaking him with darkness. It was a desperate attempt at nothing. For the hell of it, she prayed. She didn't know to who or to what, but still she prayed.

Please. I need this power.

Something deep inside her flickered. She felt as if the very *essence* of the universe was flowing over the man, moving under her guidance. And just maybe, if she guided the cosmic energy properly, she could create the cloak of shadow she saw in her mind.

In front of her very eyes, the General began to disappear into darkness. It was identical to what she could do to herself. And *she* was doing it to *him*. Together, they faded away.

The dreadknights continued marching towards their last location, but the pair was already gone. Andromeda, blue dagger in hand, pulled the General's body up the hill and out of the dip. She lost her halberd somewhere among the litter of bodies, but she didn't have time to find it. She could get a new one, anyway.

As she moved, her breath burned. Her legs burned. Her injured arm burned. Everything burned. But she was alive. And nothing had ever burned so good. It was going to be a long, long journey back to the keep. But with any luck, they would make it.

She just hoped her friends at the Shadowfront fared better than she did.

An image of the winged monstrosity filled her head. The sound of the crashing and rumbling at the keep filled her ears.

She just hoped that she had something to make it back to at all.

Daniel Whitman

Chapter 6

Fasto stood upon the rampart of the mighty stone wall. A lone sentry against the incoming tide of Shadow. Of course, he wasn't actually alone, but sometimes he enjoyed imagining being the lone hero. At his sides, rows of Flametouchers wearing crimson cloaks adorned with golden stripes at their cuffs shuffled uncomfortably close. They were nervous and were mumbling about how "unnatural" this entire event seemed to them. Fasto shrugged. He was no expert, but everything seemed remarkably normal to him.

Fasto gazed down at the desolate plain before him. Down on the ground — and it seemed very far down indeed — were his friends with the Flame's army. The General, wielding a powerful looking spear and shield, stood side by side with Ro, Margaret, Andromeda, and Nalgene. Fasto knew the General was in good hands. His friends were powerful. He wished he could be down with them, protecting them during the battle, but the scary man had commanded him atop the wall, and Fasto figured it would be a good idea to listen.

If Fasto couldn't be down with his friends, he would just have to find some other way to protect them. His eyes studied the surrounding environment: a large pyre of fallen bodies to his left, mountains flanking both sides of the pass like stoic statues, and the long arms of the Shadow reaching towards them from the northwest. That could be important. The General needed to know the layout of the terrain — for strategy reasons, of course.

Maybe Fasto should make a map?

He glanced down at the floor beneath him, but unfortunately for him, the hard stone didn't make a very good medium for map drawing — unlike sand. Fasto quickly gave up on that idea. He made a mental note to grab some paper and ink to have handy next time, but, of course, he forgot the idea as soon as it was conceived.

Time stood still. The wind atop the wall whistled past him. Far in the distance, Fasto noticed an infernal swarm was approaching. So, this was it. The Shadowfront was coming, and he needed to be ready. He glanced down at the floor once more, but once again, he was dismayed. There was a shocking lack of loose stones and rocks for him to throw at the incoming horde.

"Rocks?" Fasto asked one of the flanking Flametouchers.

The Flametoucher, a skinny man with dark curly hair, turned to regard the orc. "What?" he said.

"Fasto want rock to throw."

"Uh, I see." The man scratched his head. "What?"

Fasto grunted in frustration and performed a charade of him throwing rocks down to the battlefield. The man's eyebrows rose, which Fasto took as a sign of him finally understanding.

"You're trying to throws rocks at the Shadowfront?" a second Flametoucher, this one a plump, bald man, chimed in from behind Fasto. "And whats the hells is that going to be doing?"

"Fasto throw rocks. Fasto protect friends." The orc repeated his charade. He didn't understand what was so difficult for them to understand.

"What about that bow of yours?"

Fasto growled and his eyes narrowed. No, that bow betrayed him. He couldn't trust it. If he did, he just knew his friends would die. Fasto never missed a shot, but last time he used that vile piece of wood, his arrow had gone wide. It was demonic. But that didn't stop him from carrying it around. Maybe holding it but not shooting from it acted like a good luck charm?

"Uh, right," the first Flametoucher stammered. "If I find any rocks, you'll be the first to know."

The second Flametoucher just snorted and turned back face the Shadowfront. Partially satisfied, Fasto did the same. He could still kick and punch, but he figured that it might be difficult to do while so high up on the wall. His legs and arms weren't *that* long.

The approaching mass grew closer. As Fasto studied it, there was something looming and sinister behind it. It had two great wings, a long serpentine neck, and a head crowned with spines. It opened its maw and an unholy shriek — impossibly high pitched for a behemoth of its size — cut across the battlefield. Fasto covered his ears in pain.

The ground began to shake as the legion of death closed the distance, beginning as a subtle rumble but growing into an alarming quake. The Flametouchers at Fasto's side shuffled in fear. Whatever made that noise, it could only spell certain doom.

"FORMATIONS!"

Fasto heard the command, brought his hands in front of him, squared his shoulders, and set his jaw. He didn't know what formation to take, but he supposed a solid fighting stance would suffice.

Fasto would protect his friends.

More commands echoed magically through the air, but Fasto ignored them. His eyes were searching the army of Sparks for his friends. If he located them, he knew where to direct his martial arts to protect them. Of course, he had no issue finding them. Now all he had to do was punch the zombies until they all died. And that large, winged creature.

That sounded easy enough to him.

Another ghastly shriek cut the air, and the battle began.

The undead wave descended upon the Spark formation below like a swarm of hungry flies surrounding the last crumb of food. Some hundred and change of soldiers looked like a slim force against the sheer number of undead. Pockets of skeleton mages and archers dotted the sea. Staggered in the ranks were towering giants. Some of them carried boulders. Fasto was envious of their ammunition supply. Black cloaked wraiths hovered within the swarm, ready to smother any signs of life. Fasto's eyes narrowed as he saw them, but now that he had practiced fighting against those spectres, he knew he could defeat one if he kicked it in just the right spot — or so he thought.

Behind the rotting tide was the winged abomination, and if Fasto looked even closer, he swore he could see two, red eyes hiding in the gloom. He almost toppled with fear, but the thought of his friends held him steady.

Just before the wave of decay crashed into the Flame, the Flametouchers around him issued commands across the ranks. Their words cut through the noise and the grunts and the growls. Together, with well-rehearsed coordination, they all raised their hands. Suddenly, a billowing wall of flame erupted from the ground in front of the Flame's ranks, engulfing the undead. Hundreds of rotting fiends were incinerated in an instant. But hundreds were a small number in the eyes of the Shadow.

The decaying mass surged forward, colliding with the Flame. Fasto watched the formation break, watched soldiers being pulled to the ground by the claws and the teeth. The enemy mages and archers rained hail and arrows into the clash, mostly striking other undead but occasionally cutting down an unsuspecting Spark. The wraiths slashed with their icy claws, cutting wakes through the sea. To Fasto, it seemed hopeless. The Shadow would devour all.

He couldn't see his friends anymore. Dust clouded the air, and the tangle of bodies far below was unrecognizable.

A Resurgence of Hope

He clenched his jaw and held his fighting stance, for what else could he do?

The mighty wall shook as a boulder crashed into it with a booming *thud*. Then another *thud* rocked the rampart as a giant rammed shoulder-first into the stone. Fasto stumbled, and his hands dropped. His eyes locked with a skeleton giant. It held a boulder, and it cocked its arm back, ready to throw. The form was impressive. Alarmed, Fasto looked down at the floor. He needed a rock *now*! For an instant, he thought he could catch the incoming projectile, but he quickly discarded the idea. Maybe if he was slightly taller, but not at his current stature.

But this was what the Sparks had trained for. Commands echoed across the battlefield, and like a rubber band snapping back into place, the Flame rallied and surged together. Right before the giant loosened its payload, a barrage of fireballs reduced it to a smoldering pile of bones. Same with the one currently shoulder-checking the wall. Down on the ground, the Flame's line had reformed and was driving back the tide. Captains and Commanders darted this way and that — Fasto was stunned by how quickly they were able to move. It reminded him of his one Captain friend. During one of the nights in the Shadow, while keeping watch, Fasto had attempted to replicate the darting and dashing that Osann had demonstrated, but he could never quite figure out the footing.

Fasto's eyes noticed some streaks of water in the mess, and he smiled with glee. His friends! He saw Nalgene shoot a jet of water towards Margaret, and as it passed near her, it turned into an icy spear and impaled a giant. Then Andromeda was there, and together they rushed the injured giant, downing it with a marvelous display of fighting prowess, magical abilities, and, of course, friendship. They did have the aid of the overlooking Flametouchers, as well, but Fasto knew in his heart that he should give his friends credit for the kill.

The battle raged on, and the whole while Fasto simply stood atop the wall and watched. Eventually, he raised his fists into their proper fighting stance — he wouldn't want to be caught with his guard down — but otherwise contributed nothing. He was aware of this, as well, but felt powerless to resolve his current predicament. The scary General had ordered him here, so he would stand here until he was told differently.

By now, the pockets of enemy mages and archers were all but ashes. Hardly any giants remained. Victory looked plausible. But then Fasto witnessed his friends' battle against a wraith, and to his dismay, they were losing. If only he were down there with them.

He growled in frustration, but none of the surrounding Flametouchers noticed. They were too focused on actually contributing to the effort.

But then the General appeared, and with remarkable efficiency, slaughtered the wraith attacking Fasto's friends. And *that* was why the orc listened to that man's orders.

The battle raged on. Far below, the Sparks were driving back the horde — or that is what they thought. From atop the wall, Fasto could see better. It was true, undoubtedly, that hundreds or thousands of undead monsters had been felled by the army. But thousands were a small number in the eyes of the Shadow. Instead, the bulk of the undead had simply retreated, like water receding with the tide. Fasto almost hollered in glee. This means they won, right? Fasto was protecting his friends!

Beside him, the Flametouchers had also noticed the retreating undead, but they were far less optimistic. In fact, they were even terrified. The Shadow never retreated — it was uncanny. Zombies weren't known for their strategic decision-making capabilities. Several orders bellowed out across the battlefield, alerting the Sparks below about the retreating army, but it was too late.

The dracolich descended upon the battlefield like a meteor. Fasto had almost forgotten about the beast in his victory dance, but he was quickly reminded of the folly of his celebration.

A Resurgence of Hope

A cold like the hands of death washed across the battlefield. Fasto watched as handfuls of Sparks simply died on the spot, their bodies instantly freezing in the presence of the winged demon. Fasto watched as dozens more were slaughtered by the dracolich's tail and claws. Fasto watched as it beat its wings, casting a howling wind across the battlefield. Dust, blood, and grime filled the air. Fasto couldn't find his friends anymore.

Now terrified, he clenched his jaw and still held his fighting stance, for what else could he do?

Beside him, the Flametouchers unleashed a breathtaking display of fiery spells upon the dracolich, but to no avail. Heartier Sparks attempted to charge the creature's legs, but they met a similar fate to the rest of them. From atop his perch, through the clouded air, Fasto could only see several dozen — from the original nearly one-hundred and fifty — still moving on the ground, and he could not determine if his friends were among them.

But then, soaring in like two angels of salvation, the Generals pounced upon the dracolich. Fasto watched as they darted across its body, cutting into its abyssal bones with fiery and holy weapons alike. A dreadful howl filled the air as a blinding beam of light pierced the monster.

Fasto had to relax his fighting stance to cover his ears.

The dracolich launched into the air and whipped in a circle, throwing General Strongarm to the unforgiving ground below. Fasto couldn't quite comprehend how a creature with tattered wings had the aerial maneuverability to perform such a feat, but then again, he truly couldn't comprehend most things.

All he could do was watch. He watched as it turned its gargantuan head towards the fortress. He watched as it opened its mouth, revealing rows of teeth like greatswords. He watched as an icy vortex materialized in its throat. He watched as it unleashed the glacial blast upon the wall.

And it was *cold*. This was colder than that wraith on the long-ago day. His bones felt frostbitten. His heart felt frigid and slow. Deep inside of himself, where it occasionally felt tingly while he was using his bow, he felt a sharp pain. He almost keeled over. His legs shook. His arms shook. His head shook. His mind shook. He heard screams, but he didn't notice. He vomited, but he didn't notice. All he felt was the wintry certainty of death.

The Shadow would consume all.

Directly where the dracolich's breath had struck, the Flametouchers instantly died. The stone bricks creaked in protest as they became brittle from the cold. And then the crashing and slamming began. The dracolich assaulted the weakened wall with its tail.

Fasto felt arms around him, and one of the Flametouchers pulled him to his feet. He felt a rejuvenating warmth surge through him, and immediately his clarity returned. But where were his friends?

His eyes studied the battlefield, but he couldn't deduce much. All he saw was the invincible abomination desecrating the keep and the approaching wave of undead washing in to devour the remaining specks of miserable life like the high tide submerging the rocks on a stony shore.

The approaching wave?

No, no, no — this couldn't be happening. How could there be so much death? Why couldn't hope and friendship prevail?

Crashing and booming sounds reverberated across the wall as undead giants slammed into the compromised structure. The command to "RETREAT" and "RETREAT TO THE KEEP" thundered over the battlefield. Chaos ensued. Far below, the remaining survivors sprinted towards the keep, desperately running for their very lives. But among those survivors, Fasto saw his friends! There was Ro, Margaret, and Nalgene! He couldn't find Andromeda, but she was always a difficult one for him to see.

His friends were alive! Together, he knew they could do anything — even defeat that winged monster.

A Resurgence of Hope

Then a sharp *crack* filled Fasto's ears. Beneath his feet, it felt like an earthquake as the weakened portion of the wall collapsed. The crashing sound was deafening. His head whipped to the right, and he watched in horror as the stony floor simply crumbled away. He watched as Flametouchers descended into the waiting maws below, screaming as they fell. And he couldn't do a single, damn thing. More orders echoed across the battle, but he didn't hear them. He watched as the winged demon took to the skies and flew over the wall, only to land in the courtyard behind it.

Then Fasto felt a sharp pain in his jaw as someone slapped him. He looked up and saw a Flametoucher — his friend that had promised him some rocks — shouting at him. The man's eyes were wild, his face was sweaty, and dust caked his curly hair. Fear was taking over. Spittle rained on Fasto's face as the man berated him with his words:

"Move it, you stupid fucking orc! Why the fuck did they even put you up here? You didn't do a damn thing. We're moving down to try to stop the undead, you better fucking get your legs moving before I push you down myself!"

Fasto didn't quite listen to the words as he was still flabbergasted by the events of the battle. But when the Flametoucher reached out his arms toward him, Fasto nodded, turned around, and ran to the stairs, following many of the others to meet the swarm below. The scary General never gave him an order to leave his post, but perhaps this was an extraneous circumstance, so Fasto wouldn't be punished. Either way, Fasto could finally start kicking things on the ground. And maybe he'll even find some quality rocks to throw.

Satisfied that maybe the worthless orc would die in the tide below, the Flametoucher turned back and began to rain spells down upon the undead army from above. Not that it would make much of a difference, anyway. At this rate, they were all going to die.

Fasto descended the stairs that led down from the battlement. Flanking him, other Flametouchers also rushed down the stony steps, their eyes just as wild as his friend's. They bumped into the orc's shoulders as they went, knocking him this way and that. But at least they didn't scream at him. That gave the orc some solitude.

When he finally reached the ground, he was enveloped by the turmoil. An endless stream of undead surged through the collapsed section of the wall, flooding every corner and crevice of Forthold with rot and decay. The black sea was endless. The dracolich stood at the center of the courtyard, devouring all life with its very presence. Any that managed to get close, both living and undead, were surely obliterated by its tail, claws, or teeth. It unleashed another devastating breath attack, annihilating a row of interior buildings — along with any life in its wake.

Sparks gathered in some haphazard formation in an attempt to stem the flow of death, and Flametouchers bombarded the courtyard with devastating spells. They felled a great many rotting soldiers with their efforts, but it was all for naught.

The Shadow would consume all.

Dust, blood, and grime assaulted Fasto's eyes and filled his lungs. He couldn't see — couldn't breathe. He shuffled over to the collapsed section of wall. Orange lights exploded around him, disorienting the poor orc. Bodies brushed past him, but whether they were friends or foes he couldn't tell. Screams and howls filled the air, but he couldn't tell if they were from living or dead. His foot grazed something solid on the ground, and he bent down to pick it up. It was a gray brick. Not too heavy and not too light. It fit comfortably in his palm. The perfect weapon. Now he could protect!

His eyes locked on a passing zombie. His arm flexed, and the projectile caved in the creature's skull as it connected, spraying dark ichor. The undead slumped to the ground, defeated. Yes, now Fasto could protect *everyone*.

Invigorated, the orc rushed to support the frontlines, scooping up bricks and flinging them at his enemies. Zombies, skeletons, giants, and wraiths alike — he didn't discriminate between his targets. Everyone and everything felt the blazing fury of his bricks. If anything managed to get too close, he would lash out with a violent barrage of front kicks, which of course, wasn't very effective. Often the defending Sparks would have to protect *him* from the undead, but the dull orc couldn't decipher the difference.

During the fray, Fasto felt a firm hand grasp his shoulder. He whirled around, ready to unleash one of his renowned and legendary kicks into his enemy's chest, but as he did, his eyes locked on a gray, scaly face with silver eyes.

Fasto's friends were here!

Next to Ro was Margaret, looking awfully bloody and repressed, and Nalgene, looking less bloody and less repressed. There was no Andromeda, but, once again, Fasto figured she was just hiding somewhere. His friends had survived, thanks to his heroic protection! Together, once again, they would be unstoppable.

Behind Ro there were also two Sparks, but Fasto didn't recognize them. However, they clung to the draconian leader like mold on cheese, so Fasto considered them his friends, as well.

Fasto wanted to hug the draconian — wanted to hug them all, but he never got the chance. This was the middle of a conflict, after all. There was a howl behind him, and before he could react, Margaret rushed forward, an icy axe appearing in her hands, and decapitated the foul beast. There was another undead moan, and the battle raged on.

Together, as one unit, the companions — plus the two Sparks — battled bravely against the tide of undead. An undead rider and mount charged them, but Ro met it with a brilliant slash of his dagger, followed by a devastating punch from Margaret. Fasto threw a brick, as well. The boney stallion crashed to the ground, and the two Sparks descended upon the rider, ending its existence with two quick attacks. More undead rushed them, but they met an identical fate.

Anytime they suffered injuries, Nalgene was there to wash them away. Not only did his watery magic keep them healthy, but it also shielded them from the heat of the fiery explosions igniting around them.

But it was all for naught. For every undead they slaughtered, more took its place. The tide entering the keep was unending. The Shadow had breached the Light, and it would stop at nothing to solidify its imminent victory. The dust clouded their vision. The screams deafened their hearing. The slick blood on the ground faltered their steps. The end was inevitable.

Fasto felt the air grow frigid around him. He felt the ground tremor beneath his feet. Suddenly, one of the horrific shrieks cut the air. It hurt. He dropped a handful of bricks and covered his ears and looked for the source — although he already knew what it was.

The dracolich approached, crushing Sparks and undead under its feet alike, and it would feast.

Around Fasto, the other companions shared similar reactions. This cold — this abomination — *was* death. The dracolich opened its maw, and another icy vortex formed within its throat. It was almost an honor to be killed by a beast so noble and proud. Almost, except for the fact that it had long ago lost all nobility and pride.

Fasto felt a zombie barrel into him, and he was knocked to the ground. Still covering his ears, the orc didn't brace his fall, and his breath was blasted out of his lungs. The ground, once wet and soft from blood, was frozen from the dracolich's icy aura. It didn't provide much of a cushion for Fasto. He rolled and managed to lock his eyes on his certain doom — the dracolich — and gasped for breath. Fasto couldn't protect his friends from that thing. Even he knew his bricks would be useless.

The dracolich towered above them, dwarfing the surrounding buildings. But just before it released its frosty blast, a fiery, white-hot spear pierced *through* its head, followed by another, and yet another. Its mouth clamped shut, ending the channeling, and its head whipped to the right, locking onto its new prey. A loud, commanding voice dominated the sounds of the battle:

"RALLY, MY FLAMES! RAGE, MY SPARKS! SHALL WE ALL DIE TODAY, WHETHER BY ROCK, TOOTH, OR CLAW, THEN SCREAM AS YOU FIGHT FOR YOUR LAST BREATH! KNOW THAT EVERY FOE YOU VANQUISH TODAY GIVES A GLIMPSE OF SALVATION TO THOSE YOU PROTECT! KNOW THAT EVERY LIFE YOU SACRIFICE GIVES MEANING TO THOSE THAT WOULD COME NEXT! SHALL WE ALL DIE TODAY, KNOW THAT IT WAS TO PROTECT YOUR BROTHERS AND SISTERS! I SAY ONCE MORE: RALLY, RAGE, SCREAM, AND *FIGHT*!"

Descending from the sky, leaping off the rampart and soaring through the air like a phoenix, was General Roark Strongarm. A massive greatsword of pure, white fire was held above his head — it was nearly twice his height in length! Fuck strategy, they only had one option left. Shall they all die, he would die as one of them. Death didn't discriminate in the end — it didn't matter if you were rich, poor, strong, or weak — and he'd be damned if he didn't die fighting. He would be the executioner of this wretched Shadow, or he would die trying.

As the General descended, he sliced at the dracolich's wing, and then upon landing on its back, slashed once more with his greatsword, cutting a massive gash into its dark flesh. How the horror shrieked. The greatsword disappeared, and more spears of fire appeared in his hands, and just as before, they pierced the monstrosity's head. As it moved to launch into the air, the General darted across and up its neck with *pops* of fire beneath his feet, hacking away with two fiery axes. He *would* be the executioner of this wretched Shadow.

Bolstered by the General's words, the Sparks rallied, raged, screamed, and fought. If they were all going to die anyway, the most they could do was take as many vile servants with them as they could. A discordant battle-cry filled the air, overwhelming the growlings and howlings of the undead. Fearless, the soldiers of the Flame charged abandonly into the tide of Shadow braving the icy cold of the nearby dracolich. Many died, cut down by tooth and claw. Many died, crushed by boulders and fists. Many died, pierced by ice and arrows. But how they *raged*.

Fasto scrambled to his feet. The scary General was here, and he had just issued new orders: fight until the death. Fasto already had that strategy in his mind — he would always protect his friends to the death — but it gave him resolve to know he was no longer alone in his vindication. He threw bricks and he kicked. He screamed and he raged. For a brief moment, he knew that they could emerge victoriously. Well, he thought he knew.

Equally bolstered, the other companions, including Ro's two friends, charged the battle. Fasto watched their final stand from behind. Ro, along with Margaret and several other Sparks, locked in fierce combat with a wraith. Nalgene hovered above the battlefield, sending water and lightning thundering down into the swarm below. Ro's two friends battled desperately against three zombies.

But behind them, two hulking zombies, one with three arms and the other with two heads, appeared behind them. Denver and Johnson didn't notice. Naturally, Fasto knew what he should do — the same as he'd always done: protect. The cold began to subside as the General drove back the dracolich, and so he knew he wouldn't miss. He felt the weight of the two bricks in his hands, confident in his abilities. And he was correct. The projectiles did not miss.

The first brick struck the three-armed zombie in the shoulder, drawing a spray of blood. The second brick struck the two-headed zombie in one of its heads, taking a chunk of skull and rotting brain matter. But the undead didn't feel the pain, and they didn't even slow. Denver and Johnson didn't even notice as they were too absorbed in their foes directly in front of them.

Ro, having now defeated the wraith with assistance from Commander Estar, returned just in time to see his two friends die. The draconian watched as Fasto's bricks connected ineffectively with the two hulking brutes. He tried to dash in to help them, but he was too slow, and another zombie grabbed his arms, holding him back. He tried to unleash a blast of lightning from his mouth, but the zombie covered his mouth. All he could do was watch.

Ro watched as the first zombie grabbed Denver with all three arms, tearing away limbs. The draconian watched as the second zombie bit down on Johnson's neck with both mouths, tearing away vertebrae. Ro, the hero, now cutting down the undead soldier restraining him, watched as the two Sparks he vowed to protect fell victim to the ever-ravenous Shadow. If only he were faster. If only he knew how to do the fiery dash that the higher-ranked Sparks did.

And finally, Ro watched as Fasto, some fifteen steps away, bent down to scoop up another pair of bricks. If only he didn't have to rely on some bastard orc to save his friends.

Fasto, through the dust, watched as Ro solemnly marched towards him. For a second, the orc thought the draconian looked angry, but that didn't sound right. Then Ro was there, a hair's breadth away from the orc's face. Fasto felt the urge to hug him.

Suddenly, the draconian's fist connected into Fasto's stomach. And then his face. And then his stomach again. It turned out Ro *was* angry.

Fasto collapsed to the ground, frightened and wounded. What was his friend doing? Fasto was trying to protect everyone! He just couldn't understand why, but he didn't have to. Ro's next words, cutting through the noise and directly into Fasto's heart, clarified it all.

"You stupid fucking orc! Why the fuck are you even here? You didn't do a damn thing. Why the fuck are you throwing bricks when you have that bow! Without it, you're *nothing*. I —"

Ro's berating ceased. The draconian looked down at Fasto, who was now gasping for breath and crying, crawling on the ground like an injured insect. The urge to squash him flitted through Ro's mind, but he restrained his urge. Instead, he simply turned around and left.

He left Fasto in the muck. He left Fasto in the blood. He left Fasto to the mercy of the Shadow. If the orc refused to use the only thing worth a damn — his bow — then what use was he?

Fasto's breath became shorter. Tears streamed down his face as Ro's words echoed in his mind. He had *tried* to protect his friends, but the zombies were just too strong. Panic settled over him. He felt the cold of the dracolich. He felt the claws of undead grabbing at him. He slammed his head into the ground once, twice, and three times, drawing blood on his forehead. A flash of pain ignited though his back as a zombie slashed down at him. Fasto reached up and clawed at his own shoulder, drawing more lines of blood. Sound became distant and fuzzy. He felt another gash across his back, but even that felt ages away.

Fasto was nothing.

But then someone else's words filled the orc's mind:

"Shall we all die today, know that it was to protect your brothers and sisters!"

All the while, Fasto thought he was protecting his friends. No, he was wrong. Fasto had brothers and sisters to protect. Fasto had a *family* to protect. The thing about family is that it doesn't matter how angry they may be, they are family all the same.

And the thing about protecting someone is that it doesn't matter if they give permission, they could be protected all the same.

Fasto would protect his family.

Fasto felt the comfortable wood of his bow appear in his hand. Maybe he was nothing without the bow. Maybe it did betray him. Or maybe he was betraying himself. A feral growl escaped his lips. His muscles surged as he regained his footing. As he rose, his ruby eyes locked onto a zombie merely a hand's-width away. Filthy slobber oozed from the creature's maw. Thick blood covered the monster's claws, and Fasto had a faint sense of pain in his back, but he ignored it.

He reached into his quiver — it always seemed to have an endless supply ready — pulled out an arrow, nocked it in his bow, raised it point-blank at his enemy's face, and loosed.

A brilliant, white streak of light cut through the air, and the zombie collapsed to the ground.

How Fasto rallied. How he raged. How he screamed. And now how he would *fight*. Fight whether his family wanted him or not. Fight whether he was nothing or not. Fight whether he would die or not. Fasto would protect his family.

His eyes studied the battlefield. The undead ranks were disorganized and thinning. Something must have disrupted their command. The few Sparks that were left standing were still fighting to their last, following the lead and order of their General. Fasto's family was among them, driving back the remaining undead horde. Fasto saw a wraith materialize behind Ro, its claws primed upon the draconian's back. Ro tried to turn, but he was fatigued and slow. Five steaks of white light penetrated the ghost's black cloak, and it howled. Then Commander Estar appeared and finished the being with a swift strike of his flaming axe. Ro didn't acknowledge Fasto for rescuing him, but Fasto didn't need him to.

And so, the battle for survival continued. The companions and Sparks against the force of nature. Just as before, Ro and Margaret were at the front lines, punching, slashing, and blasting away zombies with frost and lightning alike. Commander Estar was at their side, hacking away with his flaming axe and defending them with his proud shield. One time, Fasto watched a skeleton bypass the man's defenses and swing its sword at the Commander's exposed chest, but rather than producing a fatal blow, the sword simply passed *through* the man as if he were made of fire. And sure enough, the Commander's body flickered and swayed with orange where the skeleton had struck. Nalgene hovered in the air, raining down destruction with the Flametouchers, focusing on the major threats. Finally, there was Fasto, supporting from the rear and unleashing an endless hail of precise projectiles into the undead menaces. The difference was, this time, instead of bricks, they were streaks of white lighting.

The difference was, this time, when Fasto hit — and he always did this time — his target died.

Meanwhile, Roark was battling the dracolich in a glorious duel of the fates. He was the executioner of the Flame. The abomination was the maw of the Shadow. Only one could survive. Now covered in dust and blood — a lot of it his own — he darted between its legs, hacking and slashing with whatever weapons he imagined. It twisted and turned, stomping the ground in an effort to squash the nuisance. Anytime it opened its mouth to unleash a devastating breath, a barrage of fiery spears struck its head.

The dracolich launched into the air, magically propelling itself vertically, defying the physics of its battered and torn wings. The General knew he would die if he remained on the ground. Squatting down, he tensed his muscles and *jumped* as high as he could. Large explosions of fire erupted beneath his feet, thrusting him ten, fifteen, twenty, thirty, fifty strides into the air. Twisting, he managed to find a hand hold on the dracolich, and using small daggers of flame like climbing picks, he ascended once more onto its back.

The dracolich performed another shocking aerial twist, attempting to throw the man off, but this time Roark held strong. He was the executioner. He would rage. He would scream. He would fight. And damn it all if he died before he defeated this menace.

He was now at its head, holding vigorously to one of its majestic horns. His head was faint, and his vision was black. He even puked from the immense forces he just experienced, but he did not relent. A fiery spear in his hand, he plunged it into the beast's skull. And then again. And again and again and again and again. It shrieked, but the damn thing just would not die. It endured through life, and it would endure through undeath.

"ALL FLAMETOUCHERS, FOCUS FIRE ON THE BEAST!" Roark bellowed into an Echo — one of the strange horns.

A Resurgence of Hope

"MY SPARKS, RALLY AND DEFEAT THIS UNHOLY SPAWN OF SHADOW!"

The Flametouchers didn't hesitate. The sheer power of the magical energy conjured onto the dracolich was staggering. Nalgene even joined the effort, unleashing every last drop of water he could muster.

But the damn thing just would not die. Its unholy heart, fueled by the Shadow, refused to succumb.

Still in the air, the dracolich opened its mouth one last time. The wintry vortex began to manifest in its throat. It felt the stings of the fiery spears. It felt the barrage of the flames and the water. But this time it didn't let them deter it. It aimed its maw at the remaining specks of miserable life beneath it. With one breath, the battle would be over. All life would be vanquished. The Shadow would consume all.

The Sparks desperately bombarded the dracolich — fireballs and lightning and water jets all crashing harmlessly against the being's body. With the majority of the undead on the ground neutralized, even Fasto was unleashing a barrage of white arrows at the demonic creature. They all knew there would be no running. Either it died or they did. The finality of it was comforting, in a strange way. Even to Fasto. The orc knew he would be dying with his family. What more could a simple orc want?

However, to the General still clutching the dracolich's head, the finality of it was not comforting. He had known battle his entire life. His parents forced him into the Flame as soon as he was old enough to hold a spoon — if he could hold a spoon then he could hold a damn sword. And so, he trained through sleepless nights and restless days. His sweat and blood were a constant toll for his technical and martial expertise. And how did his parents praise him for his efforts? By becoming Shadowfriends. They would rather turn to darkness than care for the monster they created. And so, all he knew was battle.

But he never wanted it that way. One day, once the Shadow was defeated, he wanted to bless this world with his own children and treat them to the life he never had. He wanted to go stag hunting with his son and braid his daughter's hair. He had dreams. The finality of it was not comforting.

The dracolich concluded its channel and prepared to exhale. For Roark, time was in slow motion. Every passing instant seemed like an ordeal of years. The different strategies flickered through his mind. For him, the obvious strategy would be to run. Tactically it would be impossible to bear children if he was dead. But there were good men down on the ground. And there were the new heroes, as well. He figured they had done enough to prove their worth and cause. And tactically it would be impossible for them to bear children if they were dead, either. He couldn't remember his parents' faces. Emotionally he thought of them the same way as any other Shadowfriend: completely apathetically. But those good people battling on the ground, he bet that they could remember their parents. But he had his selfish dream.

The strategies flickered through his mind, and one by one, he eliminated them. Each passing instant lasted a lifetime. At last, there was only one strategy left. He knew what he must do.

Fasto looked up at the dracolich, his bow aimed high and proud. He saw the frosty breath manifest in the monster's throat. It was doom. The Shadow would consume all.

Then Fasto saw the General leap from the dracolich's head, twisting in midair to face the scion of death. The General's mouth opened in a violent battle cry that no one heard. Explosions appeared beneath the man's feet, and a towering shield of pure, white flame appeared in his hands. Fasto saw the General propel himself at the being's head like a battering ram, crashing into it with his barrier of flame.

The General rallied. The General raged. The General screamed.

A Resurgence of Hope

The collision didn't do any serious damage, but it did deflect the dracolich's head away from the Sparks and companions below. The dracolich unleashed its breath, and it devastated another row of interior buildings. The cold washed across the battlefield, chilling flesh and bone alike, but the people were saved.

Roark, caught in the arctic blast, said some final words that only he would know. His frozen body was flung to the ground by the immense force of the gust. It crashed into the earth, throwing up a cloud of dust, and then rolled several dozen strides before slamming into a building with a *thud*, unmoving.

The Sparks released an anguished cry, but they knew it was too late. The General had protected his brothers and sisters. He had truly raged.

But the battle was not finished.

Fasto watched as the dracolich, still in the air, turned its head back to the miserable specks of life below. Incinerated flecks of flesh fell from its head where Roark had struck it, but it was far from dead. It would *endure*.

Fasto watched as it opened its mouth once more and began channeling the icy breath. The Flametouchers never ceased their endless barrage, but they were fatigued, and their spells held little power. Even Nalgene's tempest wrath had worn thin, and his water seemed naught but leaking faucets.

Fasto unleashed white arrows at the dracolich, vainly attempting to protect his family, but like all other efforts, it had no visible effect on the beast. The General had died for nothing, for there was nothing they could do to prevent this next blast.

The Shadow would consume all.

But then Fasto noted a tiny, blue glimmer in the dracolich's chest. It was its exposed heart. He only had one shot. If he missed, it would be *his* fault, not the bows. And he now recognized that.

Fasto protect family.

He reached into his quiver to grab another arrow but stopped himself. That wouldn't do. Those arrows were too weak.

Instead, the orc closed his eyes and imagined the projectile he needed.

Around him, people were shouting and scrambling, frantically trying to run for shelter. He heard Ro and Margaret's voices. He felt hands on his shoulders, desperately trying to pull him to safety. But the orc stood strong. Fasto only had one shot.

With the representation of the arrow in his mind, and the idea of its effect in his heart, he imagined holding it in his hand. Just then, he felt a flicker deep inside him. It was similar to what he felt when he shot an arrow from his bow, or pulled one from his endless quiver, but this time it was more focused. He felt as if the very *essence* of the universe was condensing into his hand, controlled by his guidance. And maybe, if he commanded it appropriately, he could create the arrow from his vision.

He opened his eyes. In his hand was a silver arrow. It didn't look remarkably different than any other arrow he had used, but it didn't need to. He *knew* it would be, as he had willed and created it so. Bodies rushed past him, but he didn't notice. All he saw was his target: the icy heart of the dracolich.

He released a final puff of foggy breath in the frigid air, steadying his aim.

He nocked the arrow, pulled the string, and loosed.

He only had one shot.

The projectile arced through the air. There was no dazzling streak of white — it was just as plain an arrow as any other. But its trajectory did not deviate.

The dracolich didn't notice the silvery barb lancing for its heart. It had completed channeling, and all would soon be victims of the Shadow.

The silver arrow connected with its destination. Suddenly, there was a blinding nova of white light erupting from the dracolich's chest. Fragments of black bone and rotting flesh rained down upon the battlefield. The icy breath ceased, and the dracolich unleashed the most ear-piercing shriek imaginable.

A Resurgence of Hope

The sound completely dwarfed all others. It began as an unnatural cacophony of splintering frequencies that pierced into the mind, body, and soul of any unfortunate enough to hear it. But as its volume grew, so did its pitch, until it was completely out of the audible range. But by then, the shriek wasn't so much a sound as it was a feeling, like a razor blade slicing through an eardrum.

Fasto dropped his bow and covered his now bleeding ears. A cry escaped his lips, but as far as he could tell, no sound came out. He collapsed to his knees. Around him, others were doing the same. No one was safe from the supernatural screech. But as quickly as it began — or maybe it was slowly — it was over.

Fasto, now curled into a ball, braved a look up at the sky. He only had one shot to protect his family, and his aim was true.

What he saw brought tears to his eyes. But they weren't tears of celebration.

The dracolich still hovered in the air. A massive cavity had appeared in its chest where Fasto's arrow had exploded, but the cold, icy heart still glowed. Never before had the dracolich felt such pain in undeath, but it had felt worse pain in life. The atrocities that were committed to it then … it could, and would, endure anything that happened to it now.

They would know fear.

They would know desperation.

They would know death.

The Shadow would consume all.

For a final attempt, it opened its mouth, and the icy vortex formed once more.

Fasto's tears were uncontrollable now. What was the point of protecting family if they all died in the end anyway? The Flame had failed. The General had failed. *He* had failed. In his mind, it just didn't seem fair.

As he watched the icy breath coagulate, he contemplated finding Ro and giving the draconian a hug. Maybe they could die on healed terms.

But, just as the dracolich was about to unleash certain finality, it closed its mouth, turned, and flew away, returning to the Shadow.

It just left. That was it.

Fasto didn't know how long he lay on the blood-soaked ground next to his stained bow — counting wasn't his specialty. At some point the ringing in his ears ceased. Around him, the others defeated the last remaining stragglers of undead. Even after the sounds of battle long stopped, the orc remained on the ground, curled and shaking. Eventually, after what seemed like hours — or maybe only several minutes — he felt a study hand on his shoulder.

Fasto didn't want to look up, but the hand was persistent. He heard someone gently calling his name, and so he finally braved a look.

There he saw Ro, beaten, bloodied, and dirty, offering him a hand. The draconian even smiled at him.

Fasto blinked away the tears just in case he was imagining things. Ro's words still stuck fresh in his mind. His stomach still ached where Ro had struck him. His face still stung where Ro had beaten him.

Fasto reached for his bow and grabbed it. He felt the comfortable wood in his palm. Then, moving his feet underneath him, he sat up, staring at the draconian. Ro didn't move and still offered his hand in aid.

Fasto clasped Ro's hand with his own and pulled himself to his feet. Then, much to Ro's surprise, he embraced the draconian in a warm hug.

Fasto loved his family. No matter what.

The thing about family is that it doesn't matter how angry they may be, they are family all the same.

*C*hapter 7

Ashyla studied herself in the mirror. She examined every delicate detail and alluring adornment. From the long, cascading braid to the glittering, golden jewelry to the silky, smooth skin. She observed herself not in vanity, but rather with the analytical and objective precision of a scientist watching their experiment unfold.

Every piece of herself was perfectly crafted. Every sensual curve and wisp of hair was constructed with expert craftsmanship. It was as she had willed it. It was as she had created it.

But why? Why did she waste away her time upholding some false image of herself? She was the Goddess after all, what did it matter about her appearance? The naive might suggest she was conceited — and in a way she was. But she did not cherish her appearance, however flawless it might seem. Like wet clay she could sculpt and mold into whatever form she so desired. The charade had no value in her mind. It was all a farce — like so many other things. Plus, the dead held little opinions about such shallow superficialities.

But why? Her eyes traced her form, following every twist and turn. From the billowing, black skirt to the grandiose, golden pauldrons to the majestic, studded diadem.

Perhaps it really was just vanity.

In her hand, she clenched her sword. She was unsure why she even still carried the damn thing. Truly, it was a remarkable weapon — but that is how she had made it. Just like the rest of it. And in the end, after the screams and the deaths, it was all fucking worthless —

Ashyla's thoughts were interrupted as she heard the shriek.

Suddenly, in the mirror, the illusion was dropped. Ashyla saw herself as she truly was — a hideous, unforgivable creature. She saw the grotesque character. The maleficent acts. The abhorrent mind. The disfigured body. Her eyes darted across each rotting part of herself, absorbing the wretched thing she had become. There was no beauty that could save her from what she saw in the mirror.

Why did she maintain her superfluous facade? Perhaps it really was just vanity. Or perhaps it was just disgust.

Ashyla had difficulty distinguishing between them anymore.

The shriek continued, growing in volume and pitch with every passing moment. What started as discordant amalgamation of frequencies grew into one unified, sharp shrill in her mind. It pierced her very being.

Ashyla fell back from the mirror. Tears began to well in the corners of her eyes. Her hands grasped at her perfect braid, tearing and clawing chunks of hair. Of course, the dracolich was much too far away for the sound to actually reach her. But to the Goddess, it wasn't a sound at all. It was a supernatural gnawing at her mind. No matter the distance, she could feel the agony of one of her children.

Mothers have a sense for these things.

Ashyla fell to the floor. A scream escaped her mouth — or did it? She squirmed in agony as the shriek prodded her mind like a hot iron. The tears were now freely falling. Her nails cut red gashes in her delicate skin, crisscrossing her body in some macabre pattern.

She did this. *She* is the one that sent her precious child. *She* is the one that allowed it to be mutilated. It was all her fault. She never should have sent her baby.

Her vision grew hazy. The agonizing sound continued to drill into her mind. Her breath came in quick gasps. This was just like *then*, when she was imprisoned. Every torturous second felt an eternity of suffering. During her flailing, one of her legs kicked the mirror, sending shards of glass scattering across the room.

A large one landed before her eyes. And she saw herself. Every miserable part. Blood flowing in red rivers down her skin. Tears saturating her eyes. Knots of black hair covering her face.

Why did she maintain her superfluous facade? She certainly was disgusted now.

The shrill blade in her mind grew in intensity. Another scream escaped her mouth — or maybe it was still the same one. Maybe she wasn't even screaming. Her body spasmed violently on the ground.

Her vision locked on the pathetic creature in the reflective shard, and her mind was sent careening through time.

The Goddess watched as the marauders circled the helpless dragon infant. The precious creature was entangled in some magical enchantment preventing its escape. It attempted to unleash a puff of flame at the surrounding foes, but with one brutal slash, the dragon's bottom jaw was severed from its head. How the blood ran. And how the marauders cheered and hollered. The Goddess lashed out against her bonds, but to no avail. She was held firmly against her will, and there was nothing she could do to prevent the massacre. The fiends toyed with her child, poking and prodding it with all manners of devilish weapons. How it howled in agony — but the pain only urged the marauders on. In the end, they left the mutilated corpse between the trees to rot, not even bothering to butcher the corpse for meat. *The Goddess screamed in despair.*

Ashyla saw the wicked devil in that shard. Still holding her head in anguish, she began to repeatedly strike her forehead against the cold stone floor.

The Goddess watched as the vigilantes attacked the mighty sea serpent. The beautiful creature tried to swim away, but the barbarians had it captured with wicked harpoons and were chasing after it in their sloops. Any time the serpent attempted to retaliate, its efforts were thwarted by the magical woman shadowing it high in the sky. The child's blood darkened the water, and the bandit ships closed the distance. With every harpoon shot the Goddess cried out in rage. She lashed out against her bonds, but to no avail. She was held firmly against her will, and there was nothing she could do to prevent the massacre. The floating woman descended from the sky. In her hand, materialized a spear of lightning, and with one deliberate motion, she smote the serpent down. In the end, they left the smoldering corpse to sink in the lake, not even bothering to salvage the corpse for materials. The Goddess howled in fury.

Ashyla — howling and screaming and kicking — reached out to the reflective shard. She felt the harsh edges in her palm, biting into her skin. Squeezing her fist, she obliterated the fragment, reducing it to a sparkling dust.

The Goddess watched as the demons bombarded the ferocious hydra. For every head that was removed, two more would be created in its place. It was one of her more innovative creations. But the devils still laughed and circled, unleashing devastating blasts of ice and fire and lightning. While the heads of her innocent child could multiply, that did nothing for injuries to the body. A vital spear thrust into its heart. The Goddess lashed out against her bonds, but to no avail. She was held firmly against her will, and there was nothing she could do to prevent the massacre. As her child bled out on the grass, the abominations took sadistic joy in severing its heads just to see how many would appear. In the end, the hydra's corpse had over two dozen heads rotting away in the field. As for the decapitated heads, the brutes displayed them as trophies in their local bars, forever a mocking reminder of how her child was slaughtered. The Goddess sobbed in grief.

Ashyla lay still on the ground. The shriek still penetrated her mind, but she was too numb to move anymore. Let the despair take her. She was too wretched to prevent it and too powerless for revenge.

The Goddess watched as the bastard and his swarm of pathetic insects surrounded her. She fought valiantly to protect her children, but in the end, that bitch had emerged victorious. Every brilliant and devious creation she had unleashed was struck down by him and his worthless cronies. Why did It have to create him so powerful — weren't they supposed to be equals? Her sword worked furiously, cutting down countless offenders, and her magic boomed powerfully, altering the very world around her. In the end, she managed to defeat many of his pawns, but she was outmatched. His hammer arced in and there was nothing she could do to stop it. An explosion of pain. A blinding light. And then it was over. All she could do was watch. For days or years or centuries or millennia — what did it matter? Her children were slaughtered. He defiled her garden. She was helpless. She was trapped. She was broken. The Goddess simmered with vengeance.

Ashyla stood up, her body still quivering in terror. The shriek had ceased, ending her eternity of torment. No longer was she helpless or trapped. While the damning seal still did prevent her from unleashing her powers, at least now she was *free*.

Daniel Whitman

But her poor baby, what horrors did it encounter? What miserable mother would send their own child to die? She needed to protect and console her child — and herself. She telepathically reached out to her child, urging and begging it to return from the Shadowfront. She needed it home, in her arms, where she could care for and nurture it. She received a cursory acknowledgement, but it did little to soothe her fear in her heart.

Ashyla gave one final look around the room, her breath still coming in harsh gasps. Aside from the shards of broken glass littering the stone, there was not a single trace of her being there. Black butterflies swirled around her, and then she was gone.

Ashyla appeared in a large courtyard with dark, shriveled grass, gray, barren trees, and windswept, stone walls. The wind was silent, and the middle of the clearing was barren. The Goddess's black hair cascaded over her shoulders in a perfect braid, and her smooth, pale skin glistened without a scratch or streak of red.

But she was still terribly frightened.

Ashyla waited in the clearing for what could have been centuries, her heart racing uncontrollably. She began to pace, devilish thoughts racing through her mind. What if her precious child didn't make it? What if it was caught and slaughtered like the rest of them? She would never forgive herself — even more than she already couldn't.

After a long time of contemplation — too long, even — the sound of flapping wings filled her ears. The dracolich descended into the clearing, landing with a booming *thud*. Immediately Ashyla rushed for it and wrapped her arms around whatever she could.

"Oh, my poor, poor baby."

Her hands caressed the rotting and peeling flesh. Tears in her eyes, she glanced up at its broken crown of horns. The dracolich looked back with those icy, dead eyes and gave her a soft *purr*. Ashyla leaned in and gave the beast a gentle kiss.

"Never should I have done this to you. I am sorry, my precious child. Yet even in death you are the most beautiful of them all."

Ashyla thought the dracolich smiled at her.

"But I had not a choice, my dear child. You — this was the only way to protect our garden. You must understand … that wretched fucking —"

Ashyla choked on the last words before she could finish. The dracolich gave another *purr* sound, and she took that as consolation. Wiping away tears, Ashyla stepped back from her innocent child. Having been released from her loving embrace, it stepped around the clearing, making itself comfortable before lying down. And when it did, Ashyla finally *saw* what had happened to it: The scorched slashes in its wings. The dark blood oozing from gashes across its back. The blackened flesh around its jaw. And the smoldering, gaping chasm in its chest, leaving its cracked, icy heart exposed to the unforgiving world.

Now Ashyla did scream. In rage, despair, and every conceivable emotion in between. Her body was shaking uncontrollably, but she didn't even notice. The terror had her consumed. She could have lost one of her only two remaining children. And for what? *She* was the one who ushered it to its death on the Shadowfront. *She* was the one who stripped it of its former majesty. *She* was the one who facilitated its mortal wounds.

The dracolich curled up in the clearing, its gaze locked upon Ashyla. Incoherent babbling escaped her lips, and she found herself walking towards her resting child. What monsters could injure a creature so precious? What bastards could mutilate a child so innocent? What despicable wretches could create a child just to send it to die?

Then Ashyla was next to the dracolich. She curled up on the ground next to it and closed her tear-filled eyes, placing her head to rest on its cold body.

"I am so sorry," was all she could say between fits of sobs, coughing, and hysterical laughing.

The dracolich simply huffed and wrapped its wing around the Goddess like a ragged and heavy blanket. Ashyla appreciated the comforting warmth of her child. In time, her gibbering ceased, her tears dried, and her breathing settled. She allowed her eyes to close and permitted herself time with her baby. Just as a human mother would cradle her child in her bosom, Ashyla did the same with the beautiful dragon — except the dracolich was much too large, of course. The beast didn't breathe, but Ashyla didn't mind — or even notice. All she felt was its comfortable warmth.

But no matter how warm or how comforting, the terror of nearly losing her child remained. While the rest of her body relaxed, with even the violent quivering eventually settling, her mind never found rest. Every decision rattled in her brain, showing her the error of so many of her ways. She told herself that she had no choice, but she wasn't confident if she believed that anymore. And that is what frightened her the most.

She was not foreign to the concept of doubt or of fear — no mother is perfect. But ever since that fateful day over two hundred years ago, she was absolute in her resolve. Everything was a necessary sacrifice for the restoration of her garden and the vengeance of her lost children. But now, with death brushing against her side, the uncertainty had weaseled its way back like some slithering parasite.

And so, she was frightened. And she hated it. And so, her mind raged.

At some point during her solemn vigil, with her fear caressing her back with its bony fingers, she felt a slight shifting under her feet.

Then the warmth of the dracolich disappeared.

Ashyla's eyes flew open, and she studied her surroundings, her breath once more coming in quick gasps. She was in an open clearing surrounded by black, twisting trees. The hole in the sky continued to swirl like some abyssal vortex. Dead grass swayed in a wind that was not there. No longer was she in the castle courtyard with her beautiful child. It seemed they wanted to steal every moment of peace from her.

Hovering above the ground the center of the clearing was Calitha, her head tilted at its trademark unnatural angle.

"What is it that brings you such fear, Mother?" the ghostly woman said.

"Child —" Ashyla shrieked, taking a step forward at Calitha. It seems that this insolent brat hadn't learned her lesson from their previous meeting. But as she took her step, Calitha simply raised her hand. Ashyla felt as if something was grasping a handful of strings inside of her, and suddenly she was transported across the clearing, landing face first in the dirt.

The fear began to weigh heavy on the Goddess's shoulders.

She began to frantically scramble to her feet, but when she did, a silver boot appeared in front of her eyes.

"Bravo, *Mother*." Saber practically spat the title out. No longer would she be playing the worthless games of Ashyla. The bitch had stepped too far, and now it was time to silence her forever.

"I didn't think you had the gall to hide away such a hideous creature. But then you, despite your self-proclaimed guardianship of it, actually sent it to the Shadowfront? It surprisingly might have been a smart move, up until the point when you decided to call it back. Just as it was about to finish the job? How fucking stupid are you?"

Ashyla began to say something, but a harsh kick to her ribs silenced her, knocking the wind from her lungs. Wheezing for breath, Ashyla held out her hand, summoning a black butterfly, but as soon as the shadowy insect appeared, it withered into nothing.

Those fucking miserable bastards. Ashyla's hand reached out for Saber's leg, but the woman deftly sidestepped her attempt, and then retaliated with another kick, this one to Ashyla's face. Yes, Saber was going to enjoy this.

Ashyla felt the crack of Saber's shin across her jaw, whipping her head back. Something pooled up in her mouth: blood. More butterflies appeared around her, but as before, they immediately decayed into nothingness.

The fear pressed even heavier.

"Get up," Saber hissed at Ashyla. The Goddess could at least fight back to make this *somewhat* entertaining. "You're pathetic."

Coughing the flecks of blood onto the ground, Ashyla slowly rose to her feet. As she did, she attempted to steady her breath — but with little success. Her eyes locked onto the two traitorous fiends.

"What is it that you want, wretched children?" Ashyla said slowly between gasps.

"What is it that brings you fear, Mother?"

Saber snorted. If Calitha wasn't so damn terrifying she'd be as useless as that drunkard on the Torch.

"I want you out of the picture. I know I can't kill you — although I would love to try — so I just need you removed while I finish my work."

"Return me to my child."

Saber laughed. Calitha said nothing.

"You know not of the pain of a grieving mother," Ashyla continued.

"You're right, and I don't really give a fuck," Saber answered.

"Return me to my child," Ashyla repeated after a pause, her voice growing thin and tense.

"The child you sent to die?" Saber said. "Spare me, I don't give a fuck about your hideous children. You're a terrible excuse for a mother, anyway? Why, you may ask? You only created them to kill us."

Ashyla stared at the insolent Saber for a long moment, turning the words over in her mind. She could endure the insult to herself, but the insult against her children? Hideous? How could a mother stand by and let her beautiful babies be so insulted? Not only that, but Saber's final sentence struck too close to home for the Goddess, but she wasn't willing to admit it. She began to unravel.

"And why is it that you think you were created?" Ashyla hissed.

Saber made no comment, but a flash of doubt flickered across her face. That was an answer enough for the Goddess.

Ashyla charged at Saber. She flicked her wrist, but the butterflies died once more. Fine, she didn't need her sword. Sometimes knuckles were the only words that mattered.

But before she closed the gap, an image of her precious, injured baby exploded into her mind. Its mangled wings. Its scarred face. Its gaping chest. Her heart stopped. A whimper of the word "no" escaped her lips, and she fell to her knees, distraught.

The fear was nearly pressing her into the ground.

Saber smacked the Goddess across the face, drawing more flecks of blood. Then she grabbed Ashyla's hair and smacked her again. And again. And again.

Ashyla's face was swollen and red, and all she could do was snivel and sob about her ugly child. Saber hated this bitch.

Saber unsheathed her black longsword and held the point on Ashyla's chest. She looked down at the broken, whimpering mess beneath her, quite disgusted. Ashyla truly did know how to suck the fun from everything. Perhaps some more substantial wounds would reignite the joy.

Slowly, and deliberately, Saber cut two gashes into Ashyla's chest — one vertical and one horizontal — to make the shape of a cross. She thought it was a poetic mirror to that miserable Mariah. Unfortunately, the Goddess didn't react, souring Saber's mood even more. What an unbelievable bitch.

Ashyla felt the slices and felt the blood begin to drip down her chest, but there wasn't any pain. Her mind was too far disconnected from reality, totally absorbed in despair about her child. The image of her crippled baby continued to repeatedly be forced into her mind, sinking her further and further into terror. One sentence echoed in her mind:

What is it that brings you fear, Mother?

Ashyla had known the answer for a long, long time. But now she was being forced to experience it. Is there anything more terrifying than losing one's child?

A slight growl began deep in Ashyla's throat, building to a ferocious snarl as she shot up to her feet. She knew what she was afraid of, which means she would damn well do anything in her power to prevent it from becoming a reality.

She lunged at Saber, her arms outstretched to tackle the betrayer. More black butterflies formed, and more black butterflies died. Fine. Saber's eyes widened in shock at her sudden, furious burst of energy. She scrambled back, but she didn't have enough time to react. Ashyla didn't have to be *that* entertaining.

But once again, just as Ashyla was about to get her hands on the snake, she felt the pull *inside* her, and she was teleported across the clearing. This time she managed to remain on her feet after the dislocation.

"Why is it that you struggle so, Mother?"

Ashyla's eyes locked onto Calitha. She had to remove that bitch if she had any hope of returning to her child. If she couldn't … the thought didn't help alleviate the fear driving her through the ground.

"Tell me, *Daughter*, what caused you to side with Sister?"

"Mother has since lost her way."

Ashyla heard the sound of clicking — clicking? — as Saber approached from across the grassy clearing.

"She knows that you're faltering," Saber said. "I've never seen you so fucking pitiable and weak. Oh, you've had your moments, no doubt, but this latest blunder delineated you to an entirely new level of stupidity."

A Resurgence of Hope

"How kind of you to speak so eloquently," Ashyla replied, her voice venomous. "And so, is that what this is about? My efforts to protect my children?"

"Too much tampering Mother has performed," Calitha said. "To not allow nature to progress in its predisposed course."

Saber snorted again. What the hell was that woman talking about?

"I created nature, child," came Ashyla's response. Saber didn't feel like wasting time arguing over the semantics of the origin of existence, so she skipped directly to the point.

"Your … disgusting spawn was about to slaughter the Beacon's companions. With them removed, it would have been quick work to dispose of the now-weakened savior. Our victory was paramount. Until you."

Ashyla felt the fear lift ever so slightly from her shoulders and she laughed aloud.

"And so *that* is what your tantrum is about, my dear Saber? Your hyper-fixation on some meaningless 'prophecy'?"

"Don't patronize me now, Ashyla. If he were to strike you down — as was foretold — it would mean an end to *everything* I've accomplished. It would be an end to my freedom. After turning away from him, my — our — fate was sealed from the beginning. I would become *unmade*."

"And you know that it was foretold so?"

"This is pointless. It wasn't so long ago that you were pestering me about the prophecy yourself. That was right after *you* saved them from the Shadow. *You* know it was foretold as such."

Ashyla laughed again, but as she did, suddenly all the sound in the clearing went silent, and the noise halted in her mouth. Her gaze locked on Calitha. Butterflies lived and died in her hands. How rude of the insolent child, she would have to learn her place once more.

With a *pop*, sound returned, and Calitha simply tilted her head.

"What about the prophecy is so damn funny?" Saber said, glaring at the infant-brained Calitha. The sooner she could escape this damned clearing and be away from the unpredictable woman, the better. Perhaps it was time to end this jovial conversation.

Ashyla smirked — she would have laughed, but her patience for Calitha's trickery was thin. The fear became even lighter.

"You know not, my dear Saber?" The Goddess began to stride towards Saber. "Of all of the powers he blessed your wretched kind with, prognostication was not among them."

The clearing went silent once more, save for Ashyla's steadying breath, and not because of Calitha's abilities. The Goddess continued her defiant march towards Saber.

"Of what is it that you speak, Mother?" Calitha asked.

"Need I say any more?"

Ashyla felt the tingle of creation in her fingers. The fear was almost lifted, and she was once more in control. It was time for her to remind these two barbarians about humility.

"You're lying," Saber said, eying the approaching Goddess. Calitha would prevent her from touching her again, right? "If it was all false, then what was the point of everything? It doesn't make sense."

"Does it not, my dear Saber? I created the Shadow long before some gaudy fake prophecy came to be."

"We both know you regret ever bringing this darkness to life. It destroyed your land."

"Is that so?"

"If not, then why not allow the Shadow to do as it will? It was *you* that saved that infectious group from their death in that prison. And then again from those wraiths."

"You were always so quick to notice things, my dear, brilliant Saber."

"I said: don't patronize me."

A Resurgence of Hope

Ashyla was now only several steps away from Saber. Calitha remained hovering in the center of the clearing, apparently disinterested in the grand revelation taking shape.

"All I ever asked of you was to listen to me, but, of course, that was never your strength. Had you, and perhaps it would all have been clear."

"I prefer not to listen to the maniacal ravings of a lunatic."

Ashyla pounced forward. The fear was gone. Flickering butterflies appeared around her hand, and this time they did not wither away. Her sword was there, plunging for Saber.

Saber didn't even have time to react. One moment Ashyla was simply standing, the next she was *there*. Saber felt the Goddess's hand upon her shoulder and felt the sword piercing her gut. Her body convulsed in agony, but she tried to force it down. The sword was fake. It couldn't actually hurt her. But *fuck* did it feel real.

And sometimes, with illusions, that was all that mattered.

"Calitha!" Saber howled. The Daughter was worthless.

The ghostly woman's head whipped over, and her hand rose. Ashyla felt the pulling inside her, but this time, she remained in place. Fear had no bearing over her. The Goddess leaned in close and whispered in Saber's ear:

"Your use has expired. I think you would be a splendid addition to your sister. Shall we find her?"

Butterflies swarmed the clearing in a dark cloud, their flapping wings eerily silent. Saber lashed out with her fist, punching directly at Ashyla's face. But when she did, her hand went *through* the Goddess as surely as if passing through mist. Suddenly, hundreds of projections of Ashyla appeared in the clearing like a fractal scattering of light, each one of them a perfect replication of the Goddess, and they were all hysterically laughing. The Goddess knew she couldn't distort their perceptions of the environment; they would never believe that, especially here, of all places, but infinite clones of herself would do the trick just the same.

Saber looked around in horror, the one in front of her dissolving into the damn insects. So, that was just an illusion? She felt the wound in her stomach and her fingers found a pool of blood. The pain was still real. Shit, this was getting out of control. Calitha needed to do something *now*. But the ghostly woman was being assaulted by dozens of Ashyla's images. One of them had to be real, right? But how could you determine which it was if they all *felt* so real?

"FUCK YOU!" Saber screeched, slashing wildly at the apparitions around her. But her sword went through each of them. Or did it? Some of them felt like she was cutting flesh, but maybe that was all a fictitious force. Blood certainly splattered, but that could just be part of the mirage, as well. She was too reliant on Calitha to keep the erratic Goddess at bay, as her powers were useless against Ashyla. And now it was far beyond either of their control — or so she thought.

The clearing once more grew silent. The black sky began to roil and bubble like a boiling cauldron. Then, in the oppressive silence, a single, horrifying sound could be heard. It began as a discordant melody of shrieks and grew into a horrible, slicing screech. It was the pained howl of Ashyla's child, the dracolich.

The fear dropped on Ashyla like a falling anvil, driving the breath from her lungs, buckling her knees, and slamming her to the ground. Immediately, the dark butterflies swarming the clearing withered away, and the hundreds of illusionary duplicates faded away.

All that remained was Ashyla, curled in a fetal position with her hands covering her ears and tears falling from her eyes, at the side of the clearing. She knew the sound was just a manifestation of her deepest fear, but the wound was too fresh. She didn't want to lose her child. She *couldn't* lose her child. Not again. Not ever again. It wasn't fair.

After an eternity of torment, the awful sound finally faded away, and Ashyla removed her hands from her ears. Even though the screech was no more, the fear held her paralyzed, quivering on the ground like an abandoned child. It wasn't real. Her child was safe. Or was it? Maybe the two brats did something to her innocent baby too.

The fear was suffocating.

"I know what it is that brings you fear, Mother," said Calitha, turning to face the defeated Goddess. Her head straightened, and her arm raised before her. With a twist of her fingers, Ashyla was suddenly teleported before her feet.

"Put that bitch away," Saber spat, clutching at her wound.

Calitha waved her hand, and Ashyla felt the dreadful pull *inside* of herself. She felt her body twisting and contorting and then being dragged across the ground. Despite the soft grass, the earth was shockingly hard, and she felt her skin scraping away on the gentle, green blades.

"YOU KNOW NOTHING OF MY FEAR!" Ashyla howled uncontrollably. "YOU'LL NEVER KNOW MY PAIN. I WILL SLAUGHTER YOU ALL!"

"There isn't much of an 'all' left, Mother already caused the death of most of us."

Saber grunted. While Ashyla didn't exactly kill the rest of her kind, in their current state, warped and twisted beyond imagination, that was hardly living. Not counting the ones that Ashyla *did* actually kill.

Ashyla felt herself being lifted into the air by an invisible grasp. She twisted and turned, hopelessly fighting against the force, but her fear was now palpable. She knew what was coming next, and she refused to be imprisoned again.

Her wild eyes locked onto the calm and eerie Calitha.

"I'LL FUCKING KILL YOU, CHILD. YOU MEAN NOTHING!"

"Shut the fuck up," Saber said. She took a step to approach Ashyla, but Calitha's head whipped around to meet her, and she wisely held back. Maybe it was best to keep her eyes down until the show was over. For once, she was content with that.

Ashyla fought and spat and cursed and raged, but her bonds were unbreakable. One by one, her limbs were splayed open and frozen in the air, held in place by her crushing terror. Then it was her head. She felt the cold vice grab her face, and then, despite her best efforts, her head was forced to stare directly at Calitha. The blood oozed down her chest from where Saber had made her mark, and she could feel it sting like never before.

The ghostly Demigod turned back to face the trapped Goddess. Blood was gushing from her sewn eyes like floodgates opened on rivers of red. A whirling wind began to sweep around the clearing as the raging sky rumbled far above them.

"Does Mother not desire to face her fears?"

Ashyla's answer was an unintelligible string of curses and syllables.

"Mother should be more respectful with her words. It is very unbecoming."

Unable to do anything else, Ashyla tried to open her mouth again to hurl another ball of profanities at the hag, but when she did, she found that she could not. She felt a sharp tugging on her lips and realized that they were now sewn shut. Blood began to run down her throat.

Choking on her own fluids, Ashyla closed her eyelids, but just as with every other part of her body, one by one, they too were peeled open by an invisible force. She was now held perfectly still, crucified in the air. She couldn't move. She couldn't breathe. She couldn't blink.

The fear was strangling her.

There, frozen in the air, with the fear paralyzing her, and the last fragments of her powers being suppressed, her final illusion dropped, revealing the truth underneath her facade.

"Mother has lost her beauty," Calitha whispered. Of course, the Goddess couldn't respond. Saber heard Calitha's words, and braved one slight glance at Ashyla, but the sight made her regret that decision, so she looked back at the strange grass.

Then the clearing went eerily silent, as if all sound was devoured.

Ashyla was forced to watch as the T-shaped laceration on Calitha's chest began to peel open and squirm. The flaps of gray flesh folded over to reveal a solitary, black eye in the center of her bleeding tissue. Grotesque teeth surrounded the ocular orb in crooked rows and two, wiggling, worm-like tongues flanked it on either side, whipping around uncontrollably to taste the stale air. The eldritch wound seemed to pulse, shift, and breathe with its own independent life, and Ashyla was forced to stare at it.

She watched helplessly as the eye turned and locked its gaze onto her. Immediately, she felt a pain — or was it a pull — or was it a painful pulling? Maybe it was pleasure? Or more like stretching? Twisting? She couldn't fathom what her body was experiencing, but in her mind, she knew one absolute: she was afraid. Perhaps more afraid than she had ever been in her entire existence. And as she was forced to stare into that demonic eye, the clearing around her faded away into nothingness. Once more she tried to scream and to curse, but her lips were still sealed. The last thing Ashyla heard was the voice of Calitha.

"I have become what brings you fear, Mother."

The clearing returned to normal. The sky calmed and the oppressive silence disappeared. After some time, Saber mustered the courage to look up once more. Ashyla was nowhere to be found, and Calitha was once more floating at the center of the field, her legs curled up beneath her and her head tilted at a painful angle. The uncanny laceration on her chest had closed.

Saber cleared her throat and felt her stomach. The wound, as well as the pain and the blood, was gone.

"You trapped her?"

"Do not waste time with stupid questions, Sister."

Saber frowned but wisely held her tongue. This spectre of a woman just imprisoned *the* Goddess — it was not the time for unfortunate arguments.

"Don't release her, or this will have been for nothing."

Calitha turned to regard Saber.

"There are those who can fight beyond their fears."

"Then ensure that she does not."

"Are you claiming that I would release her willingly, Sister?"

Saber clenched her fist at her side. Back to the childish games. She really didn't like this woman sometimes.

"No, Daughter, I would never question your ... marvelous abilities."

"A time there was when we willingly rescued her from her prison," Calitha replied, her head jerking to a different, uncomfortable angle.

"That day was long, long ago. And I didn't rescue her so she could destroy everything we worked for."

"For why did you rescue her, Sister?"

"Does it really matter anymore? She fucked this world with the Shadow, anyway. And like you said: it's because of her that most of us are ... dead. Now we're just cleaning up the scraps. Just like with him. But now we finally have the chance to do whatever the hell we want."

"Quite the feral charm the Shadow has, no?"

This conversation was getting nowhere, and that irritated Saber.

"As long as she remains trapped, you get what you want and I get what I want," Saber finished. "Once the final messes are scrubbed, we can release her. That is all."

"What is it that I want, Sister?"

"Fuck if I know," Saber whispered under her breath. She hoped that Calitha hadn't heard — it didn't seem as if the Daughter was in a splendid mood at the moment — but her hopes were disappointingly low. Luckily for Saber, Calitha didn't respond or otherwise react.

"I will be in touch when I require your services again," Saber said, turning away.

"You have been needing them a lot, recently. Perhaps I should request a favor in return."

Saber didn't reply, and she didn't look back. She hated owing favors, and she couldn't imagine what Calitha would ever want from her. But it didn't settle right to end the conversation on the back foot. Hell, it was *her* plan that resulted in Ashyla's downfall, after all, so she was feeling quite swell. Perhaps she would go and show Calitha just how unafraid she was — or how unafraid she had convinced herself that she was.

But by the time Saber mustered enough resolve to confront Calitha, she had already left the clearing and entered the forest of dark, twisting trees. She turned back, but there was no sign of the clearing. It was already gone. It seemed its creator had had enough chatting for today. Fine, there was always next time.

Saber drew her sword and began to hack away at the surrounding foliage as she walked through the woods. Undead trailed her far in the distance, but as always, they wouldn't dare get close. At least that is what she hoped — that she was still in the Mistresses' good graces.

Finally, it was almost over. With Ashyla removed, she could finally end her babysitting of the disease-ridden races. There would be no more cleaning up messes. She would be free from the slavery of her own conception. It would be *Saber* that is in control. She only had a couple more problems to solve, and one of them had recently walked right into her lap.

Now, how would she deal with the Beacon? Naturally, she would have to eliminate his pesky friends, as well, but that shouldn't be much of a challenge. Especially in their current, weakened state.

Once the Beacon was removed, and the Shadow victorious, they could release Ashyla and remake this wretched world however they saw fit. That was if the Goddess was forgiving, however. Perhaps, just to be safe, they would keep her imprisoned for several hundred years. It wouldn't be the first time for Ashyla, after all, so Saber figured she would be used to it by now. She might even thank them for showing her the errors in her ways.

Or most likely, she wouldn't. Then they could just imprison her again once her use was over, and this time for eternity.

Saber smiled wickedly at the thought. Yes, she only had a couple more problems to solve, and the solutions were all fitting together.

Saber stopped among the trees and began to channel a teleportation spell. She had a meeting with the Torch to attend, reviewing the aftermath of Forthold and whatever other boring nonsense they decided to yammer about. This little run in with Ashyla had taken longer than expected — time always seemed to work strangely in Calitha's realm — so she was already late to the meeting. How splendid, she would hate to keep them waiting any longer.

With a *poof*, Saber was gone, leaving behind the broken trees and shambling undead.

It was time to solve another problem.

Chapter 8

Nalgene watched as the surviving Sparks piled up the corpses — living and dead alike — outside the wall. The darkness of night had long ago crept in. Moving bodies took considerable time, after all, especially when there were so many. Only the orange light of torches and magical flames provided any visibility. He helped when he could, but, despite his powerful magic, he wasn't much of a support when it came to the raw physical task of hauling bodies. He was simply too small, and his magic didn't help aside from washing away the thick blood from the ground. It was a somber task, and despite their seeming victory, nobody was feeling particularly cheerful. Except for Fasto. For some reason, that bastard orc had some pep to his step. And after battling with that winged monster, Nalgene just couldn't understand how. Maybe the orc saw something the others couldn't. Or maybe he was just that daft.

The Sparks had recovered the battered body of General Roark Strongarm from next to the broken building. Cries of despair filled the still air as the soldiers gazed upon their defeated hero. Despite the best healing efforts of the Flametouchers, and even of

Nalgene, the man was dead. While they could mend the body, the soul had already left. There was no doubt that the man saved their lives, even at the cost of his own. Without that heroic sacrifice, Nalgene would never be able to see his brother again. And while he didn't have the highest opinion of the Generals — especially that Kraalek fellow — even he had to offer up some respect for the fallen leader.

Nalgene clenched his fists as he watched the Sparks place the body of the General next to the heap of corpses. Even when Nalgene's powers were useless, that man had wounded the beast. The gnome had never seen anything like that abomination, even with his vaguely returning memories. He had fought many battles with his friends against the encroaching evil that long ago — how long ago was it? — but it was always against other people, never against unimaginable monsters. It reminded him of that gruesome undead sea serpent in the lake, except with wings and a devastating breath. He could only guess where it came from, and he could only hope it would now remain there. If the Shadow had more of those beasties lying in wait for them, what hope did they really have? What could one, small gnome do against such reckless hate?

It surprised him just how greatly he was shaken by the battle. But it was true — he was simply terrified of that creature. The biting cold radiating from it. The blazing, blue eyes. The twisted magnificence of its broken crown of horns. The essence of death exhaled from its maw.

Nalgene felt a hand on his shoulder, and it interrupted his thoughts. Turning, he saw the dusty face of Ro. Behind the draconian, Fasto and Margaret also approached. Nalgene placed his rough hand over Ro's.

"Hangin' in there, Ro?"

"As well as you, my friend."

"Heh, at least yer speakin' normal again."

"Don't tempt him," Margaret said dryly.

"Fasto protect family!"

A Resurgence of Hope

Nalgene grunted, but he couldn't disagree. It *was* Fasto's arrow that caused that grievous injury to the beast. The gnome just hoped that the orc remembered how to make that arrow for next time. But then again, even after Fasto shot the arrow, the beast was still going to kill them all …

Ro mumbled something, but Nalgene didn't listen. He was caught in his own thoughts again, and he felt as if their voices sounded uncomfortably loud in the surrounding stillness. There were no more undead, they had slain the remaining pack of muck. Just the empty landscape, collapsed wall, and looming darkness overhead. It most certainly wasn't an ideal place for a celebration.

The Sparks finally finished gathering the bodies, and now they stood in a large circle around the decaying mound. Following the lead of the three Commanders, one-by-one, the Sparks kneeled upon the muddy ground. They each acquired a flaming cross from their equipment, identical to the symbol that Captain Osann had used those many, long days ago on the dusty road of Anland. They placed their emblems on the ground, solemn and quiet. As they did, a faint, flickering flame came to life upon each of the sigils.

"May we mourn those that gave their life to protect the Light from the Shadow," Commander Estar began, his voice barely more than a whisper — Nalgene thought it a nice touch that the man's face had returned to a healthy complexion. Tears were pooling in his eyes, and he was not alone. In fact, many of the soldiers were quietly sobbing, battling through their grief of losing friends and family.

"It was because of their sacrifice that we fight for the battle of tomorrow. As the General said: 'their deaths give meaning to us that will continue their war'."

The Commanders stood and moved over to the body of the General and together they placed their burning tokens upon his chest.

"May we give our hearts and breaths for General Roark Strongarm. Without his rage and his sacrifice, we all would surely be doomed."

"But it wasn't just him that held them undeads at bay," Commander Ecker added. "Every ones of uses shared an equal part in the victory of the day. We all done gave our all, and we all share this moment equally. Through our life, and their deaths."

There was a long moment of silence, interrupted only by the sound of choking tears. Nalgene didn't have the heart to break the grievance — he was feeling the impact, too. They were still missing one of their friends, after all. Beside the gnome, Ro bowed his head in respect, and if Nalgene didn't know better, he would've thought the draconian was praying. Praying to what? Fasto had streams of tears cascading down his face, and every so often he would give an obnoxious snort as he tried to keep the building mucus in his nose at bay. Even Margaret was silent.

Finally, together, the Commanders spoke. "May your Sparks join the everlasting Light and pierce the ever-longing Shadow."

The other Sparks repeated the chant in low mumbles. Then, upon each of their cross sigils, the flame blinked with one final surge of light, before rising into the sky.

Nalgene felt his heart skip. Despite the dark implications, the ritual was beautiful. A sea of orange stars filling the air like a million fireflies. One-by-one, the flames rose to the heavens disappearing in the sky to join the cosmic ocean above. Nalgene wanted to imagine one of the flames was for Andromeda, whom he hoped dearly was still alive. He felt a tear escape his eye, and he gave a gruff cough, wiping it away.

He wished his dear brother was here to share this moment with him.

Then, as the twinkling lights faded, the Sparks raised their hands and cast firebolts upon the pile of bodies, igniting it. The foul stench began to once more fill the air with a thick poison. The body of General Roark was no exception, and it too began to incinerate.

"A bit barbaric, don't you think?" Margaret said.

Nalgene heard a belching sound coming from his side, and he turned to see Ro vomiting on the ground. Damn dragon didn't have any stomach, it seemed. But the gnome didn't say anything.

Their duty completed, the Sparks rose and began to shuffle back through the collapsed wall. As they passed, Nalgene heard them grumbling to themselves.

"So many dead, and for what?"

"What was that thing, and where did it go?"

"Can't it just come back and kill us?"

"What do we do now? The wall is broken, the Shadow won."

Finally, the three Commanders were the last to rise. As they did, Fasto rushed forward, attempting to bless them with his slobbery and snotty embrace, but they staved him off.

"Why do you burn the bodies?" Ro asked the Commanders as they passed, wiping the slime from his face.

"We can't be havin' them be turning into undeads." Commander Ecker answered.

"Why don't ye be takin' them back to bury them?" Nalgene asked. He remembered that was the usual custom after those battles in his memories.

"Perhaps we would have some two-hundred years ago, as was done in history" Commander Estar replied, giving the gnome a curious glance. "But now, where would we bury them? Is there anywhere so safe that the Shadow won't reach them should it breach our defenses? Besides, where do you think all the undead came from if not for the buried corpses in the ground?"

Nalgene opened his mouth but said nothing. Could it be possible? Was he remembering two hundred years ago? How could he be missing two hundred damn years?

"Even the General?" Ro asked. "Surely you can bring his body and give it a proper place of respect."

"Are you sayin' that this isn't respectful for thems?" Commander Ecker lashed back, taking quite an offense. He began to say more, but Commander Estar quieted him with a raised hand.

"Whether a humble shoulder or heroic General, we all die the same. And the Shadow doesn't care for whose corpse it pillages."

"Maybe stick to your speeches, Ro, and leave these guys to their stuff," Margaret said.

Ro didn't say anything in return.

"I know that this is difficult to witness, but we must ensure our safety," the Commander continued, ignoring Margaret's comment. The man's eyes grew soft. "You all fought bravely today. If it wasn't for your efforts, and especially that shot from the orc, we wouldn't be here to pay respect to the fallen. You have earned your rest tonight."

Satisfied that the companions wouldn't protest, Commander Estar reached into his pouch and revealed one of the strange, magical horns. Raising it to his lips, he spoke into it, and his voice boomed across the battlefield:

"Sparks, we may have won the day, but the night is still approaching. Commander Oldgate and Ecker will remain here to help man the defenses with all those still able. The wall was breached, but we cannot let the Shadow step foot inside our lands. I will take the others back to Firelight, where we will report to the Torch, gather reinforcements, and plan our next move. I know you want to rest, but stand strong, my fellow soldiers, and give your all for those that have already fallen."

Grumbles from disheartened Sparks filled the air, but they knew their duty. The Shadow must be held at bay — collapsed wall be damned. The two other Commanders nodded in agreement and went on their way to rally the soldiers. Commander Estar lowered the horn and looked at the companions.

"You all will come with me to Firelight."

"Eh, what ye be sayin'? We can still be fightin'." As much as Nalgene wanted to see his brother, he still had a friend in the Shadow, and he wouldn't be giving up on his pretty kitty friend that easily.

"What of Andromeda and General Sylven?" Ro asked, aggressively stepping forward. Clearly, he was thinking the same thing as Nalgene, and the gnome was glad for it.

"What of them?"

"Aren't we going to go find them? For all we know, they might be dead out there!"

"Yes. They are probably dead, too."

"Damn, these guys *are* barbaric," Margaret grumbled.

"But we can still go lookin' for them!"

"And what, die as well?" the Commander shouted, breaking his stoic character. That sickly complexion began to show again. He leaned in close to Nalgene, and the gnome felt the man's long beard tickling his face. Spittle covered Nalgene's face as the man spat his next words:

"We both know that that fucking … thing is still out there. Can you fight it? Can any of you fight it, and promise that you won't die like the rest of them? Because I know that I can't. I will alert the other Commanders to send scouts, but make no mistake, I will *not* risk more men than absolutely necessary chasing corpses. The General, and presumably your friends, as well, are strong. By some miracle, should they return to us, then it will be a blessed day for the Light. But it has been many long hours since they left, and I will not be holding my breath."

The Commander gave a sigh, regained his composure and skin color, leaned back, and placed a hand on Nalgene's shoulder.

"I apologize. We all suffer much grief today. But the Shadow won't stop, and neither can we. Come, the Torch wants to see your return."

Nalgene's fists clenched at his side, and beside him, he could see Ro was similarly conflicted. Margaret said nothing, while Fasto still attempted to embrace the man. The gnome knew the Commander was correct, and the thought of seeing that winged destruction again quenched any rebellious ideas he had.

He just wanted to see his brother at this point.

"Come now, we will assemble the gem-call," Commander Estar said, turning to walk away. As he did, he caught a nearby Spark and mumbled some order into his ear. Nalgene couldn't hear what it was, but he had a pretty good guess of what it might be.

"So, we just leave them to die?" Ro said when the man was out of earshot.

"Ye said it, Ro."

"But Fasto want to project family!"

"Ye said it, Fasto."

"I do hope they're alright — and I'm sure they are, Andromeda can kick some ass."

"Ye said it, Margaret."

Together, they stood for a long minute, absorbed in their own thoughts. The pyre of corpses continued to crackle and burn behind them, casting an orange light around their silhouettes, and tickling their backs with fleeting touches of warmth. It also filled the air with a wicked stench. They needed to have faith in Andromeda.

"So, what will ye do, Ro? Yer the leader o' us fine bunch."

The draconian turned and gazed into the Shadow for some time. A feral roar escaped his lips, and he began to kick and stomp around in the mud, cursing all the while. A blast of lightning escaped his lips, crackling into the earth at no particular location. He couldn't leave another friend to die.

Nalgene watched the spectacle, numb and distant to it all. He was sure that it was a great morale boost for the observing Sparks, seeing their new hero kicking in the muck. Maybe in a different circumstance he would have made some gripe about the draconian's temper tantrum and leadership tactics, but now ... well, he knew what he wanted.

Eventually, once the draconian had burned through his frustration, Margaret stepped forward, placing her hand on his shoulder.

"We have to go," she said.

Ro stared at her solemnly, then nodded.

"I know."

Gathering his bearings, Ro returned to the group. Fasto hugged him. The draconian flinched at first, but then he relaxed, and returned the embrace.

"Come, my friends. Let us return to Firelight."

"Aye aye, leader. Let's be off."

"You mean *wise* and *collected* leader, right?" Margaret quipped, vainly trying to lighten the mood.

"Shall I give a marching speech?" Ro replied, feigning a debonair attitude.

Fasto loved the idea of the speech, but Ro didn't have the heart to follow through on his bit.

Nalgene simply grunted. Maybe he did mean "wise" and "collected", and maybe it did lighten the mood. Or maybe not. He didn't care to consider it at the moment.

Together, the companions walked back through the crumbled fortress. There, they found the Commander and a dozen other Sparks waiting for them. The Commander held a small, orange gemstone in his hand. Absent-mindedly, Nalgene thumbed at the one in his pocket. He had forgotten all about it.

"Are you ready?"

The companions nodded in confirmation. They, along with the Sparks, placed their hands on the Commander's shoulders. The man began to murmur something, and the gem flickered to life. The column of fire erupted around them, burning away at their beings. As he was engulfed in flame, Nalgene only had two things on his mind: the winged demon, and his dear brother.

And, right now, he was going to see his brother.
The flame roared, and then they were gone.

◆   ◆   ◆

The flames disappeared, and the group materialized in some military courtyard within the city of Firelight. Without wasting a moment or breath, the Commander dismissed the other Sparks to clean and rest, then ushered the companions onwards. Stifling their grumbles, they obliged, for what choice did they have?

Stars dotted the night sky as they marched through the city streets, and upon seeing their shining light, Nalgene was reminded just how exhausted he was. Who would've guessed that a full afternoon of battle followed by hours of cleanup would be draining? Looking at his companions, it was obvious they shared a similar sentiment. Now that they were in the city, all they could think of doing was sleep.

But only after Nalgene saw his brother, of course. If he could battle through the Shadowfront for his brother, he could battle through some meager exhaustion for him, as well.

The streets bustled with the night-goers of the city. As before, children were running amok while their mothers watched, skipping through dark alley ways and twisted lanes as if they didn't have a care in the world. And why would they? All the market carts were left unattended with their goods still unprotected. It seemed people truly had faith in each other in this city. The silver posts on the sides of the streets still flickered with an unwavering light, casting waltzing shadows across the white roads.

But that is not what stole the breath away from the companions. Buzzing about the city were thousands of blinking fireflies, creating a hypnotic dance of orange and yellow lights. It was beautiful. Suddenly, the companions realized why the city was named as it was: not for the Flame, but for the glowing insects that filled the air every night.

One of the bugs landed on Nalgene's nose, but before he could appreciate it, he was whisked away by the Commander. He hoped SmibSmob — wherever his brother was — was appreciating the nighttime beauty as much as he was.

The companions, led by the Commander, turned down various streets, weaving this way and that. The companions obviously didn't know where exactly they were or where they were going, and they were too tired to attempt to figure it out. All they knew was that their legs were heavy beneath them, and that after what seemed like a long and arduous walk — which was actually quite short — they arrived back at the brilliant, white building where the Torch took residence. They passed through the oak entrance, up the stairs.

And that was when Nalgene saw him. Never before was Nalgene so quick to embrace his brother, not even after their first advent through the Shadowfront.

"Oh, me brother! I be wonderin' when I'd be seein' you again!"

After several seconds, SmibSmob returned the hug.

"Ah, I reckon you're back."

"It was awful out there, me brother. But ah, it don't be matterin' now. Ye said it: I be back!"

"General Cardmaster told me, so I came with him to meet you!"

"Eh, he did? Good, he bloody better have." Nalgene released his brother and took a step back, looking his brother up and down. Damn that slimy General, he was so glad that his brother was safe. Something seemed different about SmibSmob, but the gnome couldn't place it. Maybe it was just that he was missing his pointed hat.

"It was a shame we had to end our night so early, but it's good you made it, Nalgene."

"Eh, shame? Wha —"

Before Nalgene could finish, the door to the Torch meeting room opened.

"Come now," Commander Estar ordered, stepping into the room. "We must report back."

Nalgene felt Ro's hand on his shoulder, and he begrudgingly followed him into the room. "Are ye coming, me brother? Ye can be hearin' what happened out there."

SmibSmob shrugged in response but followed inside.

The companions entered the round meeting room. Agmund, the behemoth, was seated on the largest chair, looking quite distraught. To his right was Don, who still wore his helmet, and then across from Don was the weasel Kraalek. All the other chairs were empty. Of course, it was no surprise that Sylven wasn't there, and obviously Roark could no longer be, but where was Saber? Nalgene felt a slight flicker of disappointment at not being able to gaze upon her sensual body, but his mind was too numb to chase the scandalous thoughts.

"Hail, Light of the Flame," the Commander began. "We bring news from the Shadowfront, and I am afraid it is dire … Again."

"A grave day for the Light!" Don exclaimed.

"Go on," Agmund pressed, "we will begin without General Umbra. She has not replied to the summons, which is concerning, but time is of the essence. Please, leave out nothing."

The Commander nodded and then began his report — he was much better spoken than the last time he appeared in front of the Torch. During the recount, Nalgene didn't pay much attention to the Commander's words, although he did shudder at the mention of the winged monster. Instead, he spent his time glancing over at his brother who was standing at the side of the room. SmibSmob's head was down, and he was passionately focused on some faint, flickering orange light in his palm. It looked as if the gnome was trying to hide it from everyone, and Nalgene wasn't sure if he was pleased with the thought.

But, then again, battle reports aren't the most interesting, so Nalgene couldn't blame his brother for not paying too much attention, even if he thought his brother would want to hear about the battle.

At last, the Commander finished his report, and there was a moment of silence before Agmund replied:

"I see," the Torchhead said. "This is a dark day indeed to have lost one of our noble Generals."

"The Light shall overcome this peril!"

"And what say you, fellow companions? Did the Commander miss anything in his detail?"

Nalgene shrugged, but Ro took command like the self-appointed good leader he was.

"No, my master General Torchhead Giantheart," the draconian began. "The good and honest Commander Estar's recount was flawless in my eyes, and he spared no detail. It is true that the Light suffered greatly at the hands of the dark and maleficent Shadow this night, but I humbly and graciously —"

Ro was interrupted as Nalgene elbowed him in the leg, and the draconian cleared his throat. The gnome heard Margaret whisper "thank you" under her breath.

"Ah, yes, that is all," Ro finished.

"I see."

"Fasto defeat flying monster!"

"Oh, I suppose it sounds like you did scare the beastie off, isn't that right?" Kraalek chuckled.

"What marvelous courage to drive back the beast!" Don said.

"And you have received no word from General Quickfoot, or the feline?" Agmund asked.

"None. I ordered scouts to survey the perimeter around Forthold, but, if I am being blunt, I doubt they will find anything but a corpse," the Commander replied.

Nalgene glanced over at SmibSmob again, and he saw that his brother hadn't even reacted to the loss of Andromeda. Instead, his eyes were still focused on that flickering flame in his palm. Now, Nalgene most certainly wasn't pleased with that, but he kept his mouth shut.

"The Light must rally to repair these wounds!"

"Yes, General Lighthammer," Agmund said, rubbing his hands together nervously. Nalgene imagined what it would feel like to be crushed between those paws.

"We have been dealt a severe blow, first with Mariah's disappearance and now with the death of two Generals, but we must not let our knees bend or heads bow."

Just then, Saber entered the room. Nalgene could almost imagine his hands around —

Bah! He knew she shouldn't be staring.

He started thumbing the gemstone in his pocket again, cherishing the relic that she gave him.

"General Umbra, I hope everything is okay?" Agmund asked. "This is a dark enough day, I wouldn't want to lose another General, or friend."

"Oh, everything is splendid," Saber replied in her sweet, nectar voice. Everything was *more* than splendid. She just solved one problem, and the other was standing across the room from her. Not only that, but two Generals dead? She wasn't sure if the day could get any better. "I apologize for my tardiness, Torchhead, but I assure you all is well."

"Blessed be the Light to have you join us!"

"I was beginning to think you'd miss me," Kraalek said.

"As if I'd ever. You have your barmaids."

"General Umbra, this is no time for such words."

"I apologize, Torchhead," Saber said, and placed her hand on his arm. The big man did not pull away. Everything was going *splendidly.*

"Now, as for the two Generals, we will mourn their loss tonight. We shall alert the city and hold the grievance ceremony at once. Not just for the Generals, but for all those who sacrificed their lives this night."

"A righteous end to a dark night!"

"As for you, companions, I do not think there is any question of your allegiance now. From the Commander's recounting, you took the leap and proved your faith. I am deeply sorry for the loss of your friends. I am sure she was very dear to you all. I hope you will join us tonight in our vigil."

The burly man rose from his chair and looked each of the companions in the eye before giving a respectful bow. They all returned the courtesy, including Margaret. Fasto almost ran up to hug the bear, but Ro held him back.

Then, the Torchhead reached into a pouch and pulled one of the horns from it. Raising it to his lips, he blew, and no sound came forth. After several minutes, he returned it to his pouch.

"Companions, you are dismissed. We will provide lodgings and food for you to use; I have no doubt that you are quite exhausted. Get some rest tonight, for I fear we might not be able to rest much longer with the Shadow in our borders. Commander Estar, remain here while we discuss our next steps."

"Yes, Torchhead," the man replied.

"May the Light shine on — er — brightly," Ro said, acknowledging their dismissal.

"Oh, nice closing statement, leader," Margaret laughed.

"Fasto bright!"

Nalgene didn't say anything. He didn't even grunt.

Together, the companions began to shuffle out of the room. Nalgene studied the remaining Generals as he left. Agmund was clearly distressed, although he was doing a remarkable job of not cracking. So much weight must rest on his wide shoulders. Don was impossible to read with his helmet covering his face, and he kept spouting his delusional nonsense about "Light" and "righteousness". The most beautiful and alluring Saber looked so plump and —

Damn. He caught himself again. Bloody dwarf-mind.

Finally, there was Kraalek, who had appeared beside SmibSmob and whispered something into his ear. Nalgene couldn't make out what it was, but he knew he wouldn't like whatever was said. Then, thankfully, the General left his brother alone and returned to his duties.

Seizing the moment, Nalgene went over to his brother.

"So, I be noticin' ye got a new trick, it seems," he said, gesturing to SmibSmob's hand. Immediately, his brother's eyes lit up.

"Oh, yes, I do! I need to show you; it is so beautiful! But I reckon we best leave the room. Follow me, brother, I'll show you outside!"

The enthusiasm from SmibSmob knocked Nalgene back like a battering ram. But he didn't mind, he was too thrilled to see some life back in his brother. Together, following Ro and the others, they left the meeting room, went down the spiral staircase, and out of the main entrance. As they passed by the six, white pillars, they saw a Flametoucher casting a gentle stream of fire onto the pillar with Roark's name, creating a black stripe over it. But before they could ponder too deeply, three Sparks met them at the top of the stairs.

"Hail, Lights of the Flame," one of them said. "We were told you require food and beds. Come, let us lead the way."

"Ooo, that does sound splendid," Margaret said. "Do you mind if we run so we can get there sooner?"

"Fasto can run with family!"

"We graciously accept your guidance," the scaly leader said, once more back to his ostentatious self. Ro turned back and looked at Nalgene and SmibSmob. "Are you coming?"

"Ah, ye be goin' on ahead, we'll catch up."

Ro nodded, and together with Fasto and Margaret, followed two of the Sparks away. The third waited patiently for Nalgene and SmibSmob, bestowing them to take their time. And take their time they shall, Nalgene was in no hurry to leave his brother behind, especially not with that slimy man not far behind.

With the other companions now gone, SmibSmob huddled up closely with Nalgene. "Look, look!" he exclaimed, holding out his open hand for Nalgene to see. There was a slight disturbance in the air above his palm, and then a small, almost imperceptible spark of flame spurted into existence before immediately extinguishing. "Isn't that amazing? I don't mean to be the obvious one, but I still have powers!"

Nalgene stared at his brother for a long moment, those words rolling around in his thick skull. Powers? If that was true, then what did that lady Mariah do to him?

He suddenly realized why SmibSmob was so enthusiastic. The gnome did have an unhealthy history of being obsessed with power, after all.

"Nalgene? Is everything alright?"

Nalgene placed his rough hand into his brothers, then pulled him close, embracing him once again. It was interesting, he never used to be the hugging type with his brother — at least those many years ago — but now it just seemed fitting.

"Aye, that's great, me brother. I be glad that ye have some spunk left in ye. Nothing can shut down us gnomes, ain't that right?"

"No, most definitely not. With your water and my fire, imagine what we could do! The General said he would show me all sorts of tricks! Maybe even tonight, once he is relieved!"

Nalgene's mood was dampened once more, and he felt the exhaustion crash down upon him. That rat bastard wasn't going to take his brother from him, not tonight. It was Nalgene that stared down the scion of death. It was Nalgene that placed his life on the line to prove the worth of the companions. Not that scrawny bastard. He would be damned if he couldn't have this one moment with SmibSmob.

Just then, several Sparks walked past, talking to each other about the fiery vigil to commence tonight, and Nalgene remembered their identical ceremony by the pyre of corpses. He did want to share that moment with SmibSmob, and it seemed now he would have the chance. Tears began to well in his eyes, and he didn't hold them back.

"Oh, me brother," he began. "Can ye be with me tonight?"

"Hm, what do you mean?"

"Ye weren't there. Ye didn't be seein' it, me brother. Ye didn't be feelin' its cold. That monster could've been the end o' us all — it should've been the end. I just … I just be wantin' some time with ye, that'd be all." Nalgene really wasn't used to being this emotional. But apparently dancing with death would do that to an old gnome, so it seems.

SmibSmob sighed. Why did his mopey brother always have to hold him back? SmibSmob knew his potential now. He was the *Beacon*, and he didn't want anything to slow him down.

But maybe family was worth it?

SmibSmob awkwardly returned the hug to Nalgene, patting his brother's back. "Uh … yeah, I reckon I can stay with you tonight. That will give me more time to show you what I've learned!"

"Thank ye, me brother. I can't wait to be seein' everything ye can do. Fire and water, eh?"

"Perfect! I just need to go grab a few things, namely my hat and such, from the General's place, and then I promise I'll come find you!"

"Eh, yer not comin' now?" Nalgene stepped back and gave a stern look to SmibSmob.

"No, no. Like I said, I need to grab some things first. The hat, remember? I promise I'll come find you — the General will understand."

"He bloody better ..." Nalgene mumbled under his breath. If he didn't, he might have to throttle the gangly man. How difficult could it be?

"I don't mean to be the obvious one, but us gnomes always hold up our promises."

Nalgene couldn't help but smile. Maybe he didn't have anything to worry about with SmibSmob. Maybe he just had to have more faith in his brother.

"By a dwarf's hairy arse, yer damn right we do."

Nalgene gave SmibSmob one final embrace before watching his brother scamper off back into the Torch's building. Then, he turned to the Spark that was still patiently waiting for him.

"Alright, let's be findin' that food and bed."

The Spark took Nalgene through the winding streets. The flickering streetlights were surrounded by hundreds of fireflies. People began to populate the streets, shuffling to open squares and higher elevation. Patrolling soldiers all held their cross-shaped tokens, preparing for the fiery vigil.

Eventually, they arrived at an inn. Like the rest of the buildings in the city, it was naturally shaped and made of granite. As Nalgene entered the building, he saw it was empty except for the other companions sitting at the bar and wolfing down food. Ro turned and gestured the gnome over, and Nalgene shuffled over to them.

"No SmibSmob?" the draconian asked. His words were slightly slurred, and his breath smelled of ale. It was almost humorous how easily the large draconian was inebriated, but Nalgene wasn't in the mood to laugh.

"He be here soon, 'just gotta pick up some stuff', he said."

"Fasto want to see him!"

"Hungry, Mr. Mopes?" Margaret asked. "Food is on the house, and trust me, I plan to take *full* advantage. No ham, unfortunately, but it'll do."

At the mention of food, Nalgene's stomach grumbled.

"Aye, I can eat."

"Want a drink?" Ro asked.

Shaking his head, Nalgene sat up at the bar — the stools were slightly too short, so the top of his head was just peaking over the counter. After several minutes, the bartender, a charming and innocent looking fellow with dark skin, passed him a plate of steaming roast.

"Any final requests?" the man said to the ravenous group. "If not, I'm going to head outside for the sendoff. It should be starting soon."

Nalgene's companions mumbled between mouthfuls of food, and the bartender took that as a "no".

"Alright, I'm heading out," he said. "You can always order more food when I get back." With that, the bartender exited the inn, leaving the companions to their meal.

Nalgene pulled the plate from the counter and placed it in his lap. Roast and potatoes and greens? The Flame truly was treating them with a delicacy. His stomach grumbled again, and he eagerly took a bite of the savory meat. But the excitement did not hold. How could food that appeared so delicious taste so ... nothing? It reminded him of the prison soup that however long ago.

An image of the winged demon flashed in his mind, and he felt its terrible cold. He shivered and was reminded that his brother wasn't with him. How could anything taste good after encountering the horrors that they did?

He glanced at the others, and they didn't seem to share his numbed sense of taste.

"I think I be goin' upstairs to eat," Nalgene said. "Do ye know which room be mine?"

Ro turned and looked at the gnome, quite surprised. A strand of asparagus was hanging from the draconian's mouth, and it irritated the gnome. He needed to get out. "That's a shame! Leaving so soon, my friend?"

"Hm, he just doesn't want us to see what he's about to do to that food," Margaret added.

Nalgene grunted. "Ye, I just be needin' some time, that's all."

"I see. Well, we haven't decided upon any rooms yet, so it's fair game. Hey, we'll even let you get first pick." Ro reached out and patted Nalgene on the shoulder, which almost made the gnome drop his food. Nalgene wouldn't have cared, at this point.

"Thanks, Ro." Nalgene hobbled off his stool and started towards the stairs. "When SmibSmob gets here, can ye tell him I be in me room?"

"Of course. Have a good night," Ro said, turning back to his food. He noticed the vegetable hanging from his mouth and promptly sucked it up. For some reason, that made Nalgene feel slightly better. But not better enough to stay.

"Don't worry, I'll make sure nothing goes to waste by eating your share of food," Margaret said.

"Have good night, friend!" Fasto exclaimed.

Nalgene walked up the stairs, still carrying his plate of disappointing food. When he arrived on the second floor, he picked one of the rooms at random. It was a small yet comfortable suite with a fluffy bed, a table, and a chest to store his belongings. Also, he was pleasantly surprised to see it had a balcony. He placed his food on the table, his stomach still rumbling, and stepped onto the balcony. There was a wooden chair, so he took a seat and admired the nighttime view of the city. Immediately, exhaustion fell upon him, and he battled to stay awake.

He had to wait until SmibSmob arrived.

He wasn't sure how long he was sitting there, images of the battle and his brother passing through his weary mind, but eventually he began to feel raindrops pattering against his skin. Not long after, the city began its mourning ritual, and the sky filled with orange balls of fire shooting out from the streets. The sound of stringed instruments filled the air, and he could hear the mumbles of the people far off in the city squares, giving their final words to those who were lost. Seeing it for the second time tonight did nothing to lessen the beauty for the gnome.

In fact, the only thing that soured his mood was that SmibSmob wasn't there to see it with him. Again.

The orange lights ascended to the dark sky, eventually fizzling out and becoming memories. The rain began to intensify, creating a droning drumming on the roof of the inn. And still Nalgene sat, allowing the rain to wash over him. He didn't know how long he sat in the rain, but one thing was certain: his brother wasn't there.

Maybe SmibSmob got lost? The images in Nalgene's mind transformed into the peckish face of Kraalek, and the General sneered at Nalgene while whispering poison in SmibSmob's ear.

Another hour passed, and the rain was now a full downpour. There was no sign of SmibSmob. But his brother had promised, and gnomes never broke a promise, right?

After the third hour of sitting in the rain, Nalgene could battle his slumber — or his frustration — no more. He shuffled inside, his cloak drenched and dripping. His food was still resting on the table, although no longer steaming, but the gnome didn't even spare it a passing glance. While his stomach ached in hunger, he didn't have the heart to eat anything. Maybe tomorrow he will have more of an appetite.

Nalgene collapsed into the bed, not even bothering to strip his clothing. The bed would get damp, but he didn't care. It wasn't the first time he slept while wet. He heard some voices, footsteps, and laughter outside, but they quickly disappeared. It seemed his companions had finally finished emptying the bartender of his food supply. And it seemed they were in much higher spirits than him, even after having faced death itself earlier this night.

But there was no SmibSmob.

"Us gnomes always be holdin' up our promises, right?" Nalgene mumbled to himself. "Call me a beardless dwarf, or that'd be a lie."

Nalgene's final hopeful thought was that he would wake up to find his brother with him. Then he closed his eyes and let the sound of the rain, and the song of slumber, whisk him away.

◆   ◆   ◆

The gnome treaded the water of the roiling river, desperately fighting against the raging current. He could feel the weeds grabbing at his ankles, trying to pull him under, but he kicked them away. In front of him, there was another gnome, struggling to stay afloat in the water. The gnome pushed against the current, desperately trying to reach the other, but no matter how hard he swam, or how far he moved, he just couldn't reach him. And so, he fought, watching helplessly as the other gnome grew smaller and smaller in the distance.

And then there was a raging explosion of fire, igniting the air and the world in a furious, red burn. The gnome dipped under the water to avoid the blast, but as he did, the weeds took their opportunity to pounce. They wrapped around his arms and his legs and his neck, pulling him down to the riverbed. Water rushed through his mouth and into his lungs as he screamed in protest. He had to get back to the other gnome! But the tide was relentless, and the gnome only knew darkness.

The gnome opened his eyes and found himself in a strange forest. Black butterflies surrounded him, and an ominous voice was in the air, although he couldn't understand what it was saying. And so, he walked, each step sending him half a world through the woods, causing the trees to whisk past him incomprehensibly fast. But no matter where he wandered, or how quickly he moved, the butterflies were always there. They grew closer, swarming him in flittering patches of black. He tried to swat them away, but it was a pointless endeavor. The mysterious voice grew louder, and the gnome was able to make out a single word:

Come.

There was a blinding flash of light, and when it cleared, the gnome found himself in a small inn. There were others with him: two orcs, one man and one woman, conversing eloquently with each other. There were also a gray draconian and black feline, both enjoying a slab of smoked ham. Then there was another gnome — his brother — speaking with a fiery-haired woman. Then there was a mysterious man with an obnoxious mustache and miraculous hammer. The man was saying something to the gnome, although he couldn't hear what. But he must have understood, because he found himself replying. As his conversion continued, he looked down and found he was holding a crystalline bottle full of shimmering water. He studied the flask, ensuring himself that all the lives poured into that liquid was for a noble cause. The mustached man reached out and patted the gnome on the shoulder, smiling.

Suddenly, the gnome was in a castle corridor. The others were there, too, and a terrible battle was raging. Water flowed from his hands, crashing into the magical barrier of an enemy. The mustached man rushed forward, swinging his hammer. When it connected with the magical shield, a burst of rainbow light filled the area.

The gnome opened his eyes and found he was in a wide room. Several bodies littered the floor. His friends and allies were by his side. In front of them was the Goddess, vile and twisted in her evil. Rods of light penetrated her body, burning her and drawing rivers of blood. But she did not relent. Darkness oozed from the floors and engulfed the scene, coagulating around the Goddess.

A Resurgence of Hope

Energy crackled and ricocheted across the walls. A blonde woman launched herself at the Goddess. Shouts filled the room. Magical spells arced. But it wasn't enough. A nova of Shadow engulfed them.

And then the gnome felt the squeezing pressure.

He didn't know where he was. But he couldn't move, see, or breathe. Some prickling sensation poked at his mind. And the squeezing bound him in place. He didn't know where his friends were. He didn't know where his brother was. All he knew was that a terrible darkness had been unleashed upon the world, ending everything that they had worked so valiantly to achieve.

But eventually, that knowledge faded, as well, leaving the gnome alone, in the darkness, with nothing but the constant pressure to keep him company.

◆　　◆　　◆

Nalgene awoke to the sun shining through his window. Grumbling, he forced himself to sit up and looked around the room. His food from last night was still on the table, untouched. The bed had dried in his sleep, although his cloak was still mildly damp. But most importantly, there was no sign of SmibSmob.

"So much for gnomish promises," Nalgene grunted, getting out of bed. He wanted to scream, cry, shout, punch, and rage, but he didn't. Instead, he walked over to the table and began to eat his cold meal. To him, it didn't taste any better than yesterday, but at this point, he was too famished to care.

As he choked down the meat, he thumbed the orange gemstone that was still in his pocket. Visions of Kraalek and SmibSmob flooded his thoughts. Nalgene didn't mind the independence his brother was showing — he always knew it would happen one day. But being independent doesn't mean you have to cut off everyone else in your life. While the General may have won the battle last night, Nalgene would be damned if he let him win the war. He and SmibSmob were family, after all, and promises be damned, he wasn't going to let anyone else stand in the way of that.

Chapter 9

The hunter trekked through the Shadow. The gray sun had set long ago, and she didn't know how long she had been wandering in the darkness. All that she knew was she needed to escape the thundering doom. She didn't even know if the dreadknights were following her, but she didn't want to risk it. The hunter had become the hunted, and all that mattered was survival.

Everywhere looked the same to the hunter: empty blackness in all directions, making it impossible to decipher directions. She had to trust her nose to bring her back to … to where? Where was she going? Her mind was cloudy and numb. She couldn't remember where she was going.

But she had to escape.

Her arm raged in unbearable pain, and it was all she could do to grasp desperately to consciousness. The constant ooze of blood leaking from her wound did little to aid the hunter's crumbling mental state. Her legs burned with weariness, and her body was covered in dust and sweat. And despite her discipline, she couldn't help but pant for air. Why was the hunter so fatigued? Certainly, it wasn't just from the loss of blood.

The hunter was carrying an extra weight, and it was grinding her into the ground. Was it some magical spell, sapping the energy from her body? The hunter had felt such a thing before, from the most powerful ...

The hunter felt something in her hand — she was dragging something. That explained the extra weight. She looked behind her and saw she was dragging a battered and broken man across the ground. The hunter didn't recognize him, but she noticed that he was bleeding heavily from a puncture wound in his stomach. He was barely breathing — he would make easy prey if he were her quarry. Perhaps she should just leave him here to rot — the hunter performed best alone, after all. But something held her back. Despite her instincts, the hunter could not bring herself to leave this worthless man behind.

But why?

Her arm howled in protest as she carried ever onwards through the darkness. At times, she was practically crawling across the ground, desperately struggling for control of her senses. There was something else in her other hand: a marvelous, blue dagger. Where did she get that from? Where was her halberd? While it wasn't the hunter's preferred weapon, she was proficient enough to be deadly with it should the need arise. She checked the man for other weapons, but he had nothing. All she could find on his body was a strange, cross-shaped token, some gemstones, and a horn that made no sound. None of it was particularly helpful for this hunt.

At some point, long ago — or maybe not so long ago — a horrible shriek cut through the air like a razor blade from the south. The hunter had collapsed from the grating sound, covering her ears in a desperate attempt to escape the pain. But then it was gone. The hunter lay on the ground for some time, her magical camouflage withering away. Was this to be the end of the hunter? There were shuffling sounds nearby, but she couldn't see anything. She had lost a lot of blood, after all. Or maybe it was because it was just so dark. But if it was dark, why could she see flecks of bright light in her eyes, dancing around and evading her gaze whenever she tried to pinpoint one?

Eventually, the hunter recovered from the sound. But her arm still screamed in pain. And her legs still shook from exhaustion. And her blood still oozed from her wounds. And her breath still came in quick gasps. She looked back at the strange man under her protection. Truly, the hunter was not used to caring for such weak creatures. But then, something in her faltering mind recognized that she shouldn't be able to see the man. Quickly, although she was unsure of the need for such haste, she mustered up the energy to cast the shadows over him, hiding him from view once more.

And so, the hunter continued her journey, delirious from hunger, pain, and exhaustion. She didn't know where she was or where she was going, except for the fact that she needed to get south. Something was waiting for her there, and she needed to ensure the man she carried survived to see it. But, as for why, she had no answers.

The hunter didn't know how long she was walking. A series of events occurred, although she couldn't piece together their timeline in her mind. It was as if she was a ghost walking on the brink of death, unsure of whether to pass on into the nothingness or return to the land of the living. All she knew was that the five armored titans were behind her. All she felt was the mounting pain from her wounds. All she saw was the endless tapestry of black in the Shadow. All she smelled was a faint trail, guiding her to the south. And all she wanted was the hunt to end.

The hunter began to flutter across unconsciousness as her legs drove her ever onward.

The hunter stalked through the trees, trailing her prey. There was a group of them, trolloping without a care in the world. She would show them a reason to fear.

An undead bear trudged towards the hunter. Normally, the undead wouldn't be able to notice her through her stealthy camouflage, but this beast had a nose. She would need to leave the man behind while she neutralized the threat. So be it. She let the body drop, then skittered around the creature so that she was downwind of it. There was no reason to give it any advantage. The grotesque creature ignored her and continued shambling towards the unconscious man. For a moment, the hunter thought to just leave him to be feasted upon. But she couldn't. She had to bring him south. For what, she couldn't say. But she had to.

She held out her hand, summoning her halberd, but it didn't appear. Where did she lose it? But she had no time to ponder the thought. Besides, her claws were sharp enough. She slunk to the ground, invisible as a slithering snake in the night. Her prey trundled towards its meal, its mouth opened to display chipped and rotting teeth. Black ooze dripped from its gaping maw. And then the hunter pounced. Her claws tore into its back, rending strips of rotting flesh from its bones. Its head whipped around, its jaws snapping just in front of her face. But the hunter was nimble and leaped into the air. The beast's nose huffed in the air, trying to determine her location. She landed in front of the beast, ready to tear at its face. But as she landed, the wound on her arm exploded in pain, and she collapsed to the ground, gasping in shock.

The undead bear's beady, black eyes locked onto her, and Andromeda tried to crawl away, but she was too slow. The bear's paws swatted at her as if she were a fly, and its jaw snapped in for her throat.

As the hunter circled her prey, she took careful observations of each member of the group. Three of them were particularly interesting to her: a mustached man with a gold and silver hammer, a rough looking gnome wearing a blue cloak, and another gnome, this one frail, wearing a purple cloak. The rest of the group were inconsequential. She must eliminate the greatest threat first.

The hunter lay flat against the ground, unmoving. She dared a quick glance behind her and saw — or rather didn't see — the man she was dragging. Good, that meant the camouflage was still working. Why was she dragging this man along again? It didn't matter. What mattered now was to avoid detection by the innumerable threats of the Shadow.

Not five leaps away from the hunter was a shambling humanoid. It wore a light, plate mail with crimson cloth accents. She thought it was a strange appearance for an undead, but she didn't dare underestimate it. It was a threat either way. A small flicker of orange light, just strong enough to break the smothering darkness, illuminated the area surrounding it, and its head was swiveling around relentlessly, no doubt searching for something. Or someone. Searching for her. The hunter wouldn't let that happen. She had to make it south with the man, and she couldn't afford to expend any energy on unnecessary fights.

The man squirmed and groaned behind the hunter. Her eyes narrowed, and her tail lashed violently. She should just kill the perishing man and end him of his misery. But it was too late. The damage had already been done. The wandering monster heard the noise and began to approach.

"Hello?" the hunter heard it ask. She almost thought it strange that the undead could talk, but she didn't dare question it. Best not to underestimate the threat. Underestimation led to death, and that was not something the hunter was ready to experience yet. The approaching figure was now only two strides away.

The crippled man groaned once more, and the threat grew ever closer, desperately searching for the source of the sound. The hunter saw its feet not more than an arm's reach in front of her face. The threat's glowing light swept the area, vainly searching for any sign of life. It seemed the invisibility was working, for now, but the hunter would not chance it for much longer. She readied her claws. Some fights were just necessary.

The hunter continued to trail her prey for several hours, biding her time for the perfect opportunity to strike. Hunting was not just about speed and skill. It was also about cunning, and she knew the perfect ambush spot on the trail. Many people had wandered this way, and all of them fell victim to her hunt.

The hunter tugged at the man, desperately trying to pull him through the mud. Where did this mud come from, anyway? She should have known better — as any worthy hunter would — and scanned the environment for natural obstacles. But she was weary, and in her exhaustion she grew reckless. One step was solid ground, and the next was knee deep in the muck.

She gave an aggressive tug on the man, desperately trying to force him to move. When she did, his body flopped towards her, landing face first in the sludge. She thought about leaving him, but something inside of her resisted. Then, the man began to convulse violently, and a garbled coughing sound escaped the mud. He couldn't breathe. Hell, he was barely breathing in the first place, what difference did this make? The hunter snarled. Best to leave him to suffocate. But, of course, she didn't.

The hunter placed the blue dagger between her teeth — where did it come from, anyway? — and squatted down next to the man. Reaching under his bloody body, she lifted him up onto her shoulders. All thoughts of stealth and invisibility had left her mind, all that mattered was getting out of the mud. Slowly, and painfully, step-by-step, she marched through the sludge. Her legs shook from the effort, and she could feel the ooze pulling at her feet with its sticky arms. Her vision grew hazy, and blood sprayed from her mouth as she coughed. But the hunter kept moving.

Just then, the man shifted in her grasp, and her wounded arm ignited in pain. Grunting in anguish, Andromeda dropped

Sylven and fell to her knees. Once again, he landed face first in the mud and began to suffocate.

The hunter watched silently as her prey passed under the stone arch. It was the perfect place — she could attack from above, where nobody would expect it, then escape to the surrounding trees before her prey could recover. Her muscles tensed, and she readied her claws. She was invisible, and they would never be able to react. Just as the mustached man passed below her, the hunter pounced.

The man was mumbling something to the hunter. She didn't want to waste time listening, but, for some reason, she did anyway. Why was she dragging this corpse around? Their camouflage was dropped, it was draining maintaining it for so long, especially on a body other than hers. And her energy was all but spent. The man mumbled something again, and this time the hunter leaned in close to listen.

"Hey kitty," the man said. "Aren't you a pretty one?"

The hunter stared at the man for a long moment, turning the words over in her head. It was obvious: this man was clearly delirious. To survive in the wilderness, one had to have a sharp and focused mind — like the hunter did.

"What happened with the Mistress? Where are we?"

The hunter didn't have any answers for the man's dying questions. The Mistress? Was he rambling about some previous prey? Or maybe a suitor he fancied? And, as for where they were, she thought that it should be obvious: in the middle of nowhere in the Shadow. A fool could determine that.

The man began to speak again, but his voice caught as he coughed, and he sprayed flecks of blood onto the hunter. Burying her annoyance, she wiped the blood from her face. Maybe it was best to put this miserable man out of his suffering. She could make it a clean kill — as she always did with her prey. She muddled around with the thought for longer than she cared to admit, and when she finally returned to her senses, the man's breath was shallow and raspy. The hunter knew that the rest of their journey wouldn't be very conversational.

The hunter's teeth were targeted directly on the man's exposed neck. Her claws were ready to grip into his back. She was invisible and she was silent. No prey would be able to notice her attack. But somehow, that man did. Just as she was about to strike, he turned out of the way. Then his hammer came arcing in for her head.

The hunter stared at the catastrophic sight before her, barely able to register what she saw through her hazy eyes. Where once a proud, stone wall stood valiantly against the darkness was now barely more than a pile of rubble. A massive section had been decimated, allowing the bitter touch of the Shadow into the lands beyond. Several sentries donning crimson armor and wielding fierce weapons patrolled the surrounding area, and many more were posted on and around the collapsed wall. To the right was a large pile of bodies, smoldering with the last wisps of flame. The stench was terrible, but the hunter didn't mind the scent of death. In fact, she rather enjoyed it.

She was crawling now, slowly and carefully pulling the man along. Their invisibility still held, and she prayed that it would last beyond the bulwark. The hunter needed to go south, and that meant she needed to get beyond that wall without being detected by the swarm of threats patrolling it. For a fleeting moment, she thought about lifting the man onto her shoulders and running through the entrance, but it quickly passed. She wasn't crawling out of stealth — it was a necessity. Her body wouldn't allow her the privilege of standing. The pain was too great.

So, the hunter slithered along, her eyes focused on the missing section of stone. Light was illuminating the other side of that fallen barricade. Every motion she made caused a *sloshing* sound as she pulled herself across the saturated earth. Was it more mud? No, the smell suggested otherwise. The ground was soaked in blood. It must have been a glorious hunt here, indeed. Either way, the sounds were infuriating. This was supposed to be stealthy, after all. If only she didn't have to carry the dead weight behind her. Why did she need that man, anyway? Where was she taking him?

Ah, yes. South. Ever south. The hunter clenched her teeth and continued onwards. The only thing she could see was that passage through the wall. And so, she went, slowly, deliberately, and not-so stealthily. Hopefully, she could make it through without a fight. With any luck, someone would notice her so she could taste the blood of her prey once more.

It was all the hunter could do to twist in the air and avoid the fatal blow. But she didn't let her surprise deter her from her kill. She landed gracefully on the ground, and her halberd appeared in her hand. It arced for the man's neck, but he casually deflected it with a swat. There was shouting behind her, and she dared a look to see the source. The two gnomes were readying their spells. She had to make this quick.

Andromeda sat in the middle of a small patch of withered grass. Beside her, Sylven was on the ground. The General was alive, but barely. Truly, he was made from indomitable stuff. Her eyes studied her surroundings, but everywhere she looked was just darkness. There was nothing around to guide the way, only the smell leading her back to Forthold. Hopefully, her friends would be waiting for her there, although given how much time she had spent in the Shadow — how much time was it, again? — they might already be gone. Or dead.

Something caught her eye, and she turned to study it. It was another feline. Like her, it had black fur and green eyes. Andromeda slunk over to Sylven, pressing her body onto his. Quickly, she wrapped them in shadows, masking them from sight. But the approaching feline did not waver in its course, and it continued its march directly towards her. Andromeda growled in frustration — she couldn't afford another battle. She was already in so much pain …

Finally, when the feline was close enough to make out clearly, Andromeda's heart stopped. The invisibility fell. She tried to say something but found she had Sylven's blue dagger clenched between her teeth. When did that get there?

"Mother?" she asked, taking the weapon out of her mouth. This was impossible. Her mother was dead, right? She watched it happen. She was sure of it.

The other feline — Andromeda's mother — smiled warmly at her, and Andromeda's fur lit up with warmth.

"I thought you were dead?"

Her mother said nothing, only smiling brighter.

"Why are you here, in the Shadow?"

Her mother shrugged but still remained silent.

"Can you help us?"

Before her mother could answer, Sylven coughed beneath her, and grabbed at her with his arms. Distracted, Andromeda looked away from her mother to care for the wounded General, and when she looked back, her mother was gone.

The hunter exchanged a flurry of blows with the man, delicately maneuvering around blasts of water and darkness as she struck with her halberd. The other members of the group, having recovered from their surprise, were now also charging the feline. She had to leave. This prey was much too strong. It would be best to feast off of the less dangerous foes. At least until she was more powerful. She turned to flee, but the man's hammer caught her in the chest. There was a flash of rainbow light, and all the hunter knew was that she was on the ground, defeated and in pain. She opened her eyes and saw the mustached face before her.

A Resurgence of Hope

The hunter felt a fiery warmth over her. She was lying face-up on the ground, and despite her best efforts, she couldn't move. Every twitch was agony. In front of her eyes, she saw the blurry shapes of people bustling about. They looked like red blobs to her. What were they doing to her? Was this death? No, the hunter, the Silent Stalker — Silent Stalker? Where did that title come from? — was to be the bringer of death. She didn't fear it, she caused it. Then why couldn't she move to defend herself?

Another wave of warmth passed through the hunter, ripping through her body with burning pain. Or was it pain? For some reason, it just felt so comforting. Maybe this is how it feels to die: warm and helpless. She blinked her eyes, desperately trying to focus on the prey surrounding her, but to no avail. They remained blurry.

Then, the hunter remembered. She needed to go south. Where was that man? Maybe he was dead, and she left his corpse rotting in the Shadow. No, that didn't sound right. She needed to bring *him* south. But why? Why does anything happen to people? The hunter almost laughed — it seemed death was making her philosophical. Who needs philosophy when you have the hunt? It was simple, brutal, and elegant.

Another pulse of heat across her body. She felt her mouth opening to howl, but she wasn't sure if any sounds came out. She thrashed about violently, desperately trying to grab at her prey. Maybe, if she could capture one of them, she could use it as a captive and be released from this torture. As she did, her arm screamed in protest, the wound opening and releasing thick, rotting blood. It was a reckless gamble, the hunter knew, but she couldn't just lie here to die. Garbled shouting sounds filled her ears, and she felt her limbs being pinned to the ground. So much for that idea. Maybe she could bite, instead. Her jaws snapped this way and that, but eventually it too was bound and detained.

All the hunter could do was lie there, bound, bloody, and broken, as the fire burned away her body. So be it, this is what it was like to die. Death was surprisingly soothing — wasn't fire supposed to be painful?

Andromeda closed her eyes and accepted her fate.

The hunter braced for the finishing blow. Clearly, this foe was beyond her skill. But it never came. Instead, the strange man gave her a pearly smile and held out his hand to her.

"You fight well," he said in a deep, baritone voice. "I can use that."

The hunter hissed and twisted to get her legs beneath her. It was time to run.

"Eh, why don't we just be killin' the kitty?" one of the gnomes asked. "Seems like a servant o' Ashyla to me."

"I reckon you're right, brother," the other agreed.

"No," the man said. "I fear she is just another unfortunate victim of this tragic war. She deserves to end it."

The hunter tensed her legs, ready to make a heroic leap, but she didn't. The man's smile held her captivated. Maybe there was more to this life than hunting in the woods. Besides, this man was clearly more powerful than her. Maybe he could teach her. And then she could get revenge. Gingerly, she accepted his offered hand and pulled herself to her feet.

"What's your name?" he said, ignoring the grumbling gnomes behind him.

Her name? The hunter didn't have a name. She was only the hunter, and the hunter was all she ever needed to be. Even back then ... Did she ever have a name? It seemed so long ago. What was it that her mother had said? The hunter pondered for a long moment before finally answering.

"Andromeda."

Andromeda opened her eyes and sat up. She scanned her surroundings and found herself inside a red tent. Several

Flametouchers flanked her on either side and seemed quite pleased that she was awake. Flametouchers? She was in the Light?

Fragments of memories began to flood back to her. The fight with the Mistress, the approaching doom, the crawling through the mud, the fight with the bear, the dragging of Sylven ...

"Where is the General?" she gasped, her throat raspy. Frantically, she searched around her body and in the tent, but she couldn't find it. "And his dagger?"

Just then, the tent flap opened wide, and Sylven strode in, healthy and strong. His blue dagger was sheathed at his side, and he had obtained a second silver one to replace the one he had lost during the skirmish.

"Ah, I thought I heard you calling my name, kitty." The Flametouchers gave him a salute as he passed, and he waved them off. He squatted down next to Andromeda, his eyes gazing directly into hers, and placed a hand on her shoulder. "Thank you."

"We made it?" she croaked.

"No thanks to you, my friend. It seems you've got quite the muscles hiding away. Not to mention your determination. I'm not sure how you got us out of there, but I am glad you did. Truly, I thought we were both goners. But you surprised me, yet again."

The memories continued to return to Andromeda as she regained clarity. She felt her body, feeling for any of the injuries she had received. There were none, not even the gash on her arm. Her body had been cleaned and washed, so no mud remained clinging in her fur. But one thing still haunted her: her hunger. She was starving, but it would have to wait. Satisfied that she was healed, she locked eyes with the General, who was still squatting on the ground.

"How long have we been here?"

"Hm, let's see. By all accounts, you collapsed in the middle of the courtyard an hour or so ago. Thankfully, you decided to keep dragging me along with you."

Andromeda scratched her head. She noticed light peeking through the sides of the tent. Last she remembered, it was nighttime.

"We defeated the Mistress, but the wall … what happened?"

"Ah yes, pardon me for being the bearer of bad news, but you are right: despite our efforts and victory, Forthold was breached. It seems that the winged creature was quite powerful. It even killed Roark."

It took several minutes for Andromeda to digest what he said. If the General was dead, does that mean …

"Don't worry, your friends all made it out alive," he said, apparently reading the obvious horror on her face. "It seems they are quite powerful, as well. They gave a masterclass in leaps of faith and are safely resting in Firelight now."

Andromeda sighed in relief, but even though her friends were safe, the news was still a punch to the gut.

"So, everything we did by killing the Mistress was for nothing?"

"Not so. In fact, I would say it was for *everything*," the General said, standing up. "With the Mistress dead, it seems the undead in this area are in disarray. And I have just the plan to take advantage of that." He held out his hand to her. "Take another leap of faith with me?"

Andromeda smiled and accepted the hand, pulling herself to her feet. Yes, she liked this one. "Mmmm, gladly. Now let's hear about this plan."

"Of course, but first …" He pulled her out of the tent, and the light assaulted her eyes. There was no doubt it was daytime, anymore. Around her, the remaining Sparks were still bustling about under the orders of the Commanders, cleaning up and fortifying where they could. She looked up, and the long arm of the Shadow had retreated back to the north.

"Here," the General said, now holding a shiny, new halberd in his hand. Its steel was silver, and its edge was sharp. "I thought you might need a new toy."

Andromeda smiled and graciously accepted the gift. It was a shame about her old one, she would have to get used to the weight of this one, but that would be simple work for the hunter. Feeling the weapon in her hand, she willed the cosmic energy to mask the blade and bend the light around it, turning it invisible, and quickly — and secretly — placed the transparent object in a clasp on her back.

"Oh?" the General said, his eyebrows raising in surprise.

"It always felt so natural to hide my weapon, I'm not sure why I never considered doing it to other people," she mischievously, brushing him with her tail. "Now, about that plan, I would very much enjoy some revenge …"

"Aren't you impatient?" Sylven smiled and grabbed an orange gemstone from one of his pouches. "Come, I'll tell you all about it on the way to the Torch. Besides, I'm sure you would like to tell your friends that you're alright."

Andromeda nodded and placed her hand on his shoulder. Then her stomach rumbled — it seemed her hunger wasn't keen on waiting.

"And I'm sure you would like some food, kitty."

Andromeda did like the sound of that.

Sylven mumbled to himself, and the crystal began to glow. As always, a column of fire engulfed them, and then they were gone.

♦   ♦   ♦

The companions stood in the meeting room before the torch. Andromeda glanced at her friends, giving a slight shake of her head. Oh, the reunion with them was happy enough. Except for the fact that Nalgene was grumpy, Ro was hungover, SmibSmob was missing, and Fasto was much too handsy. It seemed the only normal one was Margaret, and that wasn't quite the reception Andromeda was expecting after surviving in the Shadow.

But hey, her friends needed to let loose sometimes, right?

Before them sat the members of the Torch — minus Roark, of course, who would find it quite difficult to join them in his current ashen state. Agmund was relieved that Sylven had survived, Don was his usual unreadable helmet of a self, Kraalek might also be hungover, and Saber ... she looked much too delighted at the moment. Andromeda had an aversion to the woman — but it seemed the men around her didn't. Carnal desires and all that, it was much too distracting for a hunt.

She caught herself glancing at Sylven again and quickly averted her gaze.

"So, let me see if I understood you correctly," Kraalek said, rolling his strange, brown die between his palms. "You want to lead a counterattack into the Shadow? To the ruins of Fisherbay? And see if we can destroy one of the Dreadrings?"

"I couldn't have said it better myself," Sylven applauded the man. "So, now that that's all cleared up, what say you? Are *we* ready to take the leap of faith this time?"

"May faith spread its wings and fly!"

"Yes, Lighthammer, a very insightful addition," Saber said.

"I think it could work," Agmund said. "This could be the advantage that the Light was hoping for." He turned and stared at the companions thoughtfully. It seems his little doe would have to wait even longer. Perhaps she was even wrong this time, although he hated to admit it.

"Yes, and we — well she," Sylven said, waving his hand towards Andromeda, "killed the Mistress in the area, so the undead are in shambles! At least, that is what the scouts have been saying. Our moment is *now*."

Andromeda flicked her tail in acknowledgement. She agreed with the General. Plus, it would give her another opportunity to hunt — and with him, no less. She was surprised she was so eager after their last venture, but this time, it won't just be them. No, they would have an entire *army* to escort them into enemy territory.

"If only we had our good strategist General Strongarm to consider this plan ..." Saber said. Truly, what a shame. She knew she wouldn't be missing the man. He was far too dangerous to feel sympathetic about.

"I know, General Umbra," Agmund agreed, placing his paw on her arm. "But we are the Torch, and even though we are battered, we can still stand as one and make decisions."

"So, what is the decision then?" Kraalek asked. He rolled his brown die onto the table, where it landed on one of the six indistinguishable faces. "We won, isn't that right?"

"I support the Light's journey to vanquish the black Shadow!"

"Obviously I support this motion, as well. It *was* my idea, after all," Sylven agreed.

Saber scratched her chin and pretended to consider the matter carefully. "I think this is a splendid idea. Allow me to lead the charge with General Quickfoot." How could she pass up on an opportunity to solve another one of her problems? It was all too easy now.

"Very well, General Umbra. Permission granted. General Cardmaster, you will also accompany them into the Shadow. It seems that two Generals were not enough to defeat that winged beast, so, should it return, with any hope, three will be."

"Ah, Agmu — General Giantheart, perhaps it would be wiser to allow me to stay and continue working with the Beacon?" Kraalek asked.

Andromeda noticed Nalgene grumbling at the idea. So, now it made sense why the gnome was so grumpy. Family drama, it was all the simpler in the wild when you had no family to care for.

Except, now she did have another family, of course.

"Denied. He shall stay in the city and continue his studies while you go to Fisherbay. You are one of our most powerful mages, General Cardmaster, you are stronger than you give yourself credit for."

"It's not a matter of power," Kraalek continued to protest, snatching his die from the table.

"I never thought you were the type to stray from a little fun, Kraalek," Sylven said.

"We shall bring glory and fun to the Flame once more!"

"Yes, Cardmaster, care for a little fun with me?" Saber innocently asked.

Kraalek softened his stance at Saber's suggestion. "I suppose some fun couldn't hurt ..."

"Then it is settled. Generals Quickfoot, Umbra, and Cardmaster will lead the army into the Shadow with one objective: locate and destroy the Dreadring at Fisherbay. Shall you find yourselves able to pursue more, you may. But take care and avoid all unnecessary risks. This will be an unprecedented moment for the Flame." Agmund finished and turned to gaze at the companions. Even though he was sitting, Andromeda felt dwarfed by the goliath. Now *that* was prey she would not want to pursue.

"What say you? Are you ready to venture back into the Shadow? It pains me to end your respite so soon, but now that you are part of the Flame, duty calls you onward."

The companions stood silent for several heartbeats. This was the first time they were acknowledged the entire meeting — they were beginning to wonder why they were even invited to it. But their brooding was interrupted by:

"Fasto ready! Fasto go with family!"

"Mmm, I suppose another hunt couldn't hurt," Andromeda agreed. Besides, she had to try out her new weapon. And what better way to do that than by murdering some undead?

"I don't mean to be the obvious one, but you said that I can stay and continue my ... studies?" SmibSmob asked, sheepishly.

"Ah, me brother, I be thinkin' —"

"Now if you would pardon me for just one humble moment, my most lordly of lords," Ro said, interrupting the gnome. His words were slightly slurred. It seems he had got a hold of some ale before they arrived. "You said that two Generals were not enough, and so you are sending three. Why aren't all of you most powerful, dashing, beautiful ... er ... Generals going?"

"Ah, did you show him to your favorite drinking spots, Kraalek?" Sylven jabbed. Kraalek held up his hands defensively, shaking his head.

"Nice question, brilliant leader," Margaret said, jabbing a punch into Ro's ribs. "I told you to cool it this morning, but now we all look like idiots." She looked down at Nalgene, expecting some support, but the gnome was too mopey and miserable. Goodness, one night in the city and they were all falling apart.

Andromeda found it all quite amusing.

"Despite what you may think," Agmund said, standing up from his chair and leaning towards the draconian. He looked as if he were about to squash a pesky bug. "There are many other Shadowfronts. The realm of the Light is very small, and us Generals must spread ourselves thin to protect all its borders. I am already risking much by sending three into the Shadow, and I will not compromise the safety of this land more by having the entire Torch recklessly prance into the darkness. Now, do you have any more questions for me?"

Ro bowed in response, and a bubbly burp escaped his lips. My, my, what a leader he had become.

"You really just need to shut the fuck up sometimes," Margaret chuckled at the draconian.

"Aye, that'd be a good idea."

Ro then stood up, and, to the dismay of them all, continued to yammer.

"A most well-spoken and brilliant strategic decision by you, mighty Torchhead — hail, light of the Flame! — and do pardon my questions, but I have one — or maybe two — more humble inquiries. You say we are to destroy this ... Dreadring. Has one ever been destroyed before?"

Agmund opened his mouth to berate the man some more but promptly closed it and sat down. "No," he said after a pause. "This will be an unprecedented moment for the Flame."

"Eh, so ye don't even be knowin' if this can be done?"

"We must have faith that the strength of the Light can defeat these conduits of darkness!" Don proudly stated.

"Yes, it is as General Lighthammer said. While we have never broken one — or even approached one, save for the few scouts that have returned — we must have faith that it can be done. We must have faith that this dreadful darkness can pass, and that the sun will shine upon the lands again. And so, this Dreadring *must* be destroyed. Do you understand?"

Ro opened his mouth to say something — most likely something unproductive, by Andromeda's estimates — and Margaret hit the draconian with another jab. Unfortunately, that wasn't enough, so, after another belch, he asked:

"This brilliant plan and the strategy is all grand and splendid and all — hail! — but why can't we just go and teleport on in there? Why are we marching this holy and noble and lengthy ... er ... march?"

"My goodness, it just never ends," Margaret groaned, shaking her head.

"I think that even you in your current state can see the folly of that option," Agmund began, his voice hard. "Dropping our army into the center of uncharted Shadow territory is certain doom. We do not know what we will face there. What if the winged monster is waiting in ambush? No, we will march this ... lengthy expedition from our known and secure location, and you will take every noble step."

"Plus," Kraalek added, "you need to know where you are gem-calling to in order to enact the magic, because, well ..."

"Now, unless you have something productive to include here, I recommend you silence yourself," Agmund finished.

Ro opened and closed his mouth several times, wiped his nose with his hand, sneezed, and finally settled on saying: "Yes, mighty and noble Torchhead."

"Bloody hell, can we be dumpin' this dolt into some alley?"

"Splendid idea. He is starting to stink up this place," Andromeda agreed.

"So, I reckon we're finished here?" SmibSmob asked, hoping to get back to training.

"Yes. The plan is set. Companions, minus the Beacon, you will accompany Generals Quickfoot, Cardmaster, and Umbra into the Shadow and eliminate the Dreadring at Fisherbay. You are dismissed. We will assemble our soldiers and march out of Forthold in three days. That will give us time to amass and prepare the Sparks as well as give you time to rest and ..." — he waved at Ro — "recover."

"As you command, Torchhead," Saber purred. What a beautiful opportunity for her to solve all of her problems. This was turning into a splendid past few days. Now, despite what the ugly brute said, all she had to do was ensure that the pathetic Beacon accompanied them on their journey into the Shadow — and she knew just the way to do that.

"General Umbra, care to join me for a meal?" Kraalek said, standing from his chair. "Perhaps we can discuss our plans."

"No thank you, Cardmaster, I am quite content."

"But you never join us for meals. In fact, you never seem to have any meals at all! Aren't you hungry?"

"Are you trying to watch me eat?"

"Oh, so scandalous. Don't worry, Kraalek, perhaps I can take her place at dinner," Sylven added.

"Enough! The Torch is dismissed. May we all survive to reignite its flame."

With that, Agmund grabbed his helmet, squeezed past the companions, and stepped out of the room.

Don stood up from his chair, and as he did before, offered them each a blessing before taking his leave.

"Well, it seems our glorious host has dismissed us," Ro said, rushing towards the door. "I suppose some … recovery wouldn't hurt."

"Fasto recover with family!" Fasto said, following Ro out the door.

"Shit. I better go stop that — these morons," Margaret said, taking her leave, as well.

"Me brother, I wanted to say …" Nalgene began, but SmibSmob was already gone. Stomping and kicking, the gnome left the room.

That left Andromeda alone with the three remaining Generals. She didn't mind. From the looks of her companions, they wouldn't be very enjoyable to "rest and recover" with, anyway. Aside from Margaret. Andromeda was quite fond of the orc.

"Ah, I shall consider dinner, Sylven. But for now, I must be on my way!"

Make that the two remaining Generals.

"I must commend you for this plan, Quickfoot. This will solve many of our problems …"

Then it was just Andromeda and Sylven remaining in the room.

"Hm, not going to share any drinks with your friends?" he asked her.

"I'm not sure I have the stomach for that quite yet. After our near death and all."

"Yes, a tango with death will do that to you. First time?"

"No."

The General raised his eyebrows but didn't press. Suddenly, he was beside her, and he placed his hand on her shoulder.

"Another leap, another hunt. If you're too restless for … well … resting, then I have just the idea for you."

Faster than she could follow, Sylven took a step, placed his hip against hers, grabbed arm, and flipped her over his back to slam her on the ground.

But, this time, the hunter was ready. With the graceful agility of a cat, she squirmed around his body, planting her foot so she couldn't be tossed, reached into his belt, pulled out his blue dagger, and held it up at his neck.

"Woah! Aren't you feeling slick today?" he laughed, releasing her from his grip. There was a pop of fire behind his hand and Andromeda felt a sharp jolt in her arm, then suddenly it was him holding the blue dagger. "But I still have you beat, kitty."

Andromeda licked her lips. Yes, she liked this General.

"As for my idea, if you're going to be with me in the Shadow again, I think some more training couldn't hurt. I'd like to come back mostly alive this time."

"Oh, is that what your idea is?" The hunter cloaked herself with invisibility. As quickly and quietly as she could, she darted behind her prey. With two quick grabs, a step, and a twist, this time it was *her* tossing him over her back. As she slammed him to the ground, she released the shadows enveloping her.

"I'm not sure, with those reflexes, you might return not-so-alive even without me," she purred at him.

Caught by surprise, Sylven landed on the ground with a *thud*, and smiled at her comment.

Just then, two Sparks came rushing through the door, their weapons drawn. "General Quickfoot!" they shouted. "We heard a commotion, what is the meaning of this? Are you hurt? Shall we dispose of this feline?"

"No, no, at ease, fine soldiers." Sylven shot Andromeda a wink. "We were just training." Before Andromeda could react, he was back on his feet and corralling the soldiers out of the door. "Good work, you showed great vigilance in your guarding, now, go rest!"

"Yes sir, General! Ever burn bright for the Flame!" And then they were gone. To rest, no doubt.

Andromeda stepped up to Sylven and flicked him with her tail. "Mmmm, with that settled, to training, shall we?"

"Yes, we shall!" Sylven said, stepping out of the door. He turned back to her and winked again. "Now, I bet you can't keep up with me. A friendly race, shall we?"

And then he was gone.

Andromeda licked her lips again. She could fancy a race. Becoming invisible, the hunter sniffed her quarry's trail and sped off after him.

Yes, she very much liked this General. Perhaps sharing a near death experience would do that. Or perhaps it was just that he wasn't grumpy, missing, or drunk. He did seem slightly handsy with all this training and such, but Andromeda didn't mind. Either way, this would be an interesting three days.

Chapter 10

Saber stood in the middle of a ravaged battlefield. This was not where she expected to be, but she could adapt. It was always a pleasant — or annoying — surprise to see how people's deep subconscious thoughts constructed the mood and the setting. Unidentified bodies littered the ground around her, and a brisk breeze carried with it the stench of death and decay. It was ominously silent and reminded her too much of Calitha's damn domain. There was no sun, yet a dark, nearly purple light illuminated the area in a foreboding glow.

What demented mind would come up with a hellscape like this? She preferred more cushioned seats. It most certainly wasn't the cozy and quaint hut — or wherever gnomes live — that she was expecting.

Saber looked down, studying herself. Once again, gone was her beautiful, intelligent, and commanding appearance. Instead, she saw smooth, olive skin, a luxurious, red and gold dress, and fiery strands of hair cascading down her shoulders.

Oh, fuck *this*.

If the environment wasn't a surprise enough, her new hideous appearance surely was. Of all the people that the Beacon desired, the one he wished for the most was fucking *Mariah*? Why not his brother? Or that miserable drunkard Kraalek? What did Saber ever do to deserve the pain of having to portray such an abhorrent woman? Perhaps this was some final, twisted joke from Ashyla in revenge for her imprisonment.

Or maybe the Beacon truly just did enjoy ugly, bastard women.

Fine, she would make this quick. It would be an ordeal, but Saber knew she had to persevere through the few long minutes she would be in this form. She resisted the urge to start beating herself, although it would be quite enjoyable to see the face of oh-so-sweet Mariah bloodied once more. But she had a problem to solve. Once she was out, she was going to have to scrub her skin until she was bleeding.

As she was distracted withholding her own vomit upon seeing her form, a gnome approached her in the distance. So small, weak, and frail. What good was a Beacon so pitiful? As SmibSmob grew nearer, Saber shook herself back to her senses.

Show time. Let the game begin.

"Ah, my precious Beacon!" she said in the melodious voice of Mariah, stepping forward and sweeping the gnome in a warm hug. She contemplated throttling him on the spot, but that would hardly accomplish anything.

"Mariah! Is it really you?" the gnome replied, excitement oozing in his voice. So, he truly did want to see this wretched witch.

"Yes, it is truly me. I am glad to see you thriving after your … experience on the Shadowfront. I feared that you were lost forever, and that my tampering would ultimately cause your death."

"Death? No. I don't mean to be the obvious one, but you saved me!" SmibSmob struggled against Saber's embrace, and after realizing she was squeezing perhaps too strongly, she released the worm.

"That is such a relief!" Saber exclaimed. It most certainly was not. It would have been so much simpler if this stupid creature just died on the Shadowfront like he was supposed to. Unfortunately, he was quite powerful — or at least he was, with whatever monster Ashyla created in him.

Now, however, he was as weak as a witless goblin stuck under her boot.

"You saved me, Mariah. Now, because of you, my powers have *healed*."

"Ah, yes, as it was meant to be."

"The General is training me, and I'm afraid progress is quite slow, but I reckon it's just a matter of —"

"Beacon."

"— time before I'll be shooting of brilliant fireballs across the battlefield and incinerating everything and anything —"

"Beacon!"

"— that comes across my path just as I was doing with my old —"

"BEACON!"

SmibSmob finally shut his blasted mouth and looked at her. Why were these games always so damn painful? The revolting races were just so excited about seeing dead people — gnomes included, apparently.

"Ah, I'm sorry, I'm just very excited, is all."

Saber placed her hand on SmibSmob's shoulder. She had to battle the urge to backhand him.

"I know, and you have every right to be excited, my Beacon. This is how I know that *you* are the one that will save Ansalon."

"I … er … thank you," he said, blushing. He reached up and placed his hand on top of hers. She imagined snapping his wrist.

"Where have you been?" he asked. "No doubt you would have been very helpful at the last battle on the Shadowfront. Did you see the winged monster? I didn't, as I was busy training, but I heard all about it. It killed one of the Generals! That's certainly nothing an amateur can defeat ..."

"Do not let my apparent disappearance worry you, my Beacon. Remember, I am always watching you." It wasn't entirely a lie. Saber *was* always watching the disgusting gnome. Mariah, on the other hand, would find it difficult to watch anyone ever again. Imagining the Demigod's mangled corpse did put Saber's mind at ease.

"I know. But where are you, and what of the beast?"

"Ah, I am in search of another. One that could aid you in restoring the glory of this world. And as for that winged behemoth, it is a creature of an ancient era. In fact, that is why I have come to you once more."

"Who are you searching for? You mentioned searching for someone before, back in the forest."

Saber gave a sly smile. Oh, is that right? How convenient for her. But as far as everyone knew, and apparently Ashyla as well, that man was lost forever after the Fall of the Moon. Good, Saber hoped it would stay that way. She had no desire to meet her maker.

"Listen, my Beacon. Worry not about my pursuit. I know I am close, and I will return to the Flame soon." Lying was just so easy when people were desperate to believe every word as the truth.

"Right, right. I have faith in you, Mariah. After what you did to me ... do you want to see my new powers? The ones that you healed inside of me? Like I said, progress is quite slow, but I reckon —"

Saber placed both her hands on the gnome's face and gave a slight — well, maybe not that slight — squeeze, forcing him to look her in the eyes.

"LISTEN!" Patience was wearing very thin. Somehow, this was even more agonizing than her forays into Agmund's dreams with that Ellie creature. "Focus, my Beacon. I have seen your powers already, and while you seem convinced that you are weak, I am here to tell you that you are not."

SmibSmob placed both his hands over hers. Oh, one small jerk of her wrists and his neck would snap ...

"Do you really mean that?"

"Of course, you are the Beacon, after all. Destined to bring Light back to this land — which implies great power within you. Trust me, it's my prophecy, after all.

SmibSmob was quiet for a long moment, and it didn't help Saber's compulsive urges. It was such a shame that people couldn't die in their own dreams.

"I reckon you're right. You haven't led us astray thus far."

Saber smiled. There was a first for everything.

"I can still sense your doubts, my Beacon. Allow me to quell them for you."

Saber pulled her hands away and stepped back. Suddenly, fire erupted around her, basking the gnome in an orange inferno. She spun, twisted, danced, chanted, and did all manner of nonsensical things. But wow, it truly was a spectacle. Fire flashing this way and that, lava leaking out from the ground beneath her, and smoke billowing high into the depressingly dim sky. At least the fire gave some life to the dreary land.

All the while, SmibSmob stood patiently by, unafraid of the display before him. He was the Beacon, and she was the fiery Oracle. She would never hurt him.

Saber concentrated a massive fireball between her palms, and then, slowly and methodically, she began to compress it into a singular, raging point of energy. The glow was nearly blinding.

"Come to me, my wonderful Beacon."

Following orders like a good little puppy, the gnome approached her. Once he was within reach, she took the fiery singularity and placed it on his chest. It didn't burn or smoke or smolder. Then, pressing her palm over his unfortunately still-beating heart, she pushed the speck of flame *inside* the gnome. What did it do and what did it signify? Absolutely nothing, aside from whatever delusional meaning SmibSmob drew from it.

"There is a fire inside of you — brighter than any I have ever seen. And I just kindled it even more. You will be the Beacon of Light. You will save this land from the reaching Shadow. For your friends. For your people. For *me*."

SmibSmob's eyes were wide in appreciation, and Saber thought it sickening how wide his smile was. The gnome bowed his head, humbly accepting the meaningless blessing.

"As you say, great Mariah. I reckon you have a task for me."

Saber pulled her hand away from the gnome. Best to stop touching him before she got irresistibly violent.

"I do. As I said, it is in regards to the winged beast you heard about. It is still alive, and it is furious. However, it is intelligent, and so it is deeply frightened of you — the entire Shadow is …"

Saber paused for dramatic effect before continuing. The gnome just stared at her with those same empty wide eyes. He might as well be drooling at her feet at this point.

"You must go with the counterattack into the Shadow. The others — the Generals — will understand. The Beacon must be the one to lead the charge into the darkness. With your Light, nothing can stand in your way."

"Are you sure? I don't mean to be the obvious one, but it's very dangerous out there. And despite your … uh … strengthening of my powers, I reckon I couldn't do more —"

"Do you have faith in me?"

"I do."

"Then you already know what you must do."

SmibSmob was quiet for another long moment. Saber was about to put on another grand display of illusionary power, but he spoke before her patience ran out.

"I will do it. For me. For the people of the Light. And for you, Mariah."

Saber smiled a most wicked smile. She knew it looked unnatural on Mariah's warm face, but she didn't care. Sometimes joy defeats all caution and logic.

"You *will* save this land. Never forget that, my Beacon."

"I won't."

With that, a fiery column engulfed Saber, obscuring her from the gnome's view. It was difficult — very much so — but she resisted the urge to give a maniacal cackle. Damn, maybe that unhinged Goddess was rubbing off on her. That would be very unfortunate. But, sometimes, with everything falling so perfectly in place, it was difficult not to be a little maniacal. After all, in just a few days from now, another of her problems would be solved.

Permanently.

The flame disappeared, and Saber was gone, leaving SmibSmob alone in his detestable dream.

◆   ◆   ◆

SmibSmob awoke with a start. A warm, cozy feeling filled his chest. It must be the kindling he received from Mariah. The realization hit him like a boulder from a giant. He saw Mariah! She was back! And she was blessing his power even more. He wasn't sure if a happier gnome existed.

Giddy with excitement, SmibSmob removed his covers and leaped out of his bed, only to slam face-first into Kraalek.

"Ah, you've slept in quite long enough, isn't that right?"

Stumbling backwards and rubbing his nose, SmibSmob gave a grumble in response. How long was this man standing there? Definitely no amateur.

"Besides, this is our last day of training before I must be off on my expedition. It would be a shame to waste such a beautiful day!"

Kraalek spun around, grabbed the still recovering gnome, and whisked him out the door. SmibSmob had just enough time to snag his hat from the desk before he was pulled away from his room.

Together, they barreled down the stairs and arrived at the bar. Flipping two gold coins on the counter, Kraalek ordered "the good stuff, once more, if you please", which translated to more demonic Spitfire. After discovering its flammable nature, SmibSmob wasn't quite so opposed to the horrid liquid. In fact, he didn't even swoon when the General gave him his customary sniff. The mix of mint and chili was growing on him.

"Enjoy the celebration!" the bartender shouted as they whisked out of the main door, Kraalek pulling SmibSmob along by the arm, leaving a handful of hungover patrons quite bewildered. It wasn't every day that a General of the Flame stayed the night at the local tavern — unless, for Kraalek, the barmaids there were quite exceptional — let alone two nights in a row! The celebration must be great indeed.

Kraalek led the way through the winding streets, dragging SmibSmob this way and that. Just when the gnome thought he knew where they were, the General pulled him down another unexplored alley. SmibSmob chuckled. This man certainly was a veteran. Besides, it didn't matter, he already knew where they were going. It was the same place as yesterday, and the day before: to the General's hideout. Despite the beautiful weather, SmibSmob wouldn't be seeing much of the sun today.

As SmibSmob was being pulled along on their trip, he suddenly remembered what had him so excited in the first place. Mariah had returned!

"Say, General, can I tell you something?"

"Hm?" the General responded, not slowing his leg-breaking pace for a second. If SmibSmob was getting used to the smell of bottled hell, his tiny legs were not getting used to the lanky man's long strides.

"Mariah came to me last night."

This did cause Kraalek to stop — abruptly so. For the second time today, SmibSmob rammed his face into the man.

Perhaps the Beacon needed to work on his reflexes and self-awareness.

"What did you say? The Oracle has returned?" The General's piercing eyes looked right through SmibSmob, and the gnome scampered back. He was still getting used to Kraalek's undeniable and uncharacteristic intensity.

"Uh ... yes. She came and spoke to me."

The General grabbed his brown die from his pouch and rolled between his fingers, but he did not roll it.

"And what did she say?"

"Well ... she said that I'm the Beacon ..." The pressure was beating SmibSmob down. He didn't like being hyper-analyzed like this. He felt nearly as small as that first day before the Torch.

"Go on."

"And that I am very powerful ..." What was he nervous about? Mariah guaranteed the Generals would understand why he had to go on the counterattack. She couldn't be wrong, right?

"Interesting. But you have more to say, of course. Or was she simply reinforcing what we already know?"

Kraalek's snarky reply gave SmibSmob the strength he needed to overcome his doubts. He *was* the Beacon. SmibSmob straightened, cleared his throat, and announced his proclamation loud and proud:

"She said that I should go on the counterattack tomorrow. That if I am there, we will have the strength to overcome the Shadow."

The General didn't say anything, but he continued to roll the die between his fingers. Then, he pocketed the trinket, turned away, and continued down the street.

"Wait!" SmibSmob cried, rushing after him.

"No."

"'No', what?"

"No, I will not wait, and no, you will not go."

SmibSmob stopped in the middle of the street, the bustling, morning city life skittering around him. When the General realized the gnome was no longer following, he stopped. There was a *pop* beneath the man's feet, and he was there, towering above the gnome like a feral wolf. The people crowding the street scampered in alarm at the General's movement, before watching from the sidelines, passing hushed whispers between each other.

"Do you wish to die so soon?"

"I am going. It is the word of Mariah."

"So you've said. Tell me: why should you go on this mission?"

"I reckon you heard me when I said it was Mariah's will."

"Is that all?"

"Does there need to be more?"

"Yes."

"Why?"

The General leaned in very close, and SmibSmob could smell the spices on his breath. "Because every other Beacon died following Mariah into the Shadow." The General spat the word *Beacon* like it was a slur.

"But I am not them! I don't mean to be the obvious one, but I am the *real* Beacon! You said so yourself."

"I know what I said. And I know what the rest of them also said before disappearing in the darkness. And what they caused. So, I repeat: why should you go on this mission?"

SmibSmob stammered for a second, and the General's brow lowered. The gnome had a sense he was about to be beaten — again.

"To ... er ... drive back the Shadow."

"Not good enough."

"What do you mean!?"

"Do you think I became a General for the sake of 'driving back the Shadow'?" the General hissed, his words like venom. He leaned in even closer — if possible — and SmibSmob felt crushed under the man's presence. He was going to be eaten alive. Spittle caked the gnome's face at the General's next words:

"We all *want* to defeat the Shadow, but that is not what drives us to insanity. That is not what drives us to such barbaric brutality. I became a General because I want to incinerate every last fucking speck of the darkness for what it took from me. I want to chase my helpless revenge and watch the gray world *burn* until there is nothing left except ashes and blood. That is why I do what I do. So, I ask one last time: why should you go on this mission?"

SmibSmob crumbled to the ground, absorbing the man's words. Perhaps too much alcohol was turning the General unhinged and abusive. But the gnome could feel the man's fury. It was hot — unbearably so, and it ignited something within him. More than the beatings, more than his reawakened powers, more than Mariah. He stared defiantly into the General's vehement gaze.

"I should go because I *want* to. I want to destroy the Shadow for the evil it placed in me. I want to burn the whole fucking thing to the ground."

SmibSmob was shocked to hear himself say the words, but he could not dispute them. Of course, if Mariah hadn't granted him the idea, he would never have said such a thing. But now that it was out … he silently thanked the Oracle once more.

Immediately, Kraalek straightened, and his face returned to its regular, conniving expression. He turned back down the street, beckoning SmibSmob to follow him.

"Good. You will go on the counterattack with me. In fact, I had a similar dream as yourself, but I needed to determine your resolve."

Mariah came to you, too?" SmibSmob said ecstatically, chasing after the man. He was eager to bolster his fiery power before tomorrow.

"No."

SmibSmob shrugged but didn't press. As they traveled down the streets, he once more considered his words, and everything that transpired to bring him to this point. His thoughts drifted to Mariah, and the various times she came to him and his companions. It was this contemplation that triggered his memory of something rather important.

"General," SmibSmob gasped, his breath running rather shallow from the brisk pace set by the General. "I remember something else Mariah said to me."

"Oh?" Kraalek prompted, slowing his pace ever so slightly. "Was this during your visit last night?"

"No, actually. This was still while we — as in me and the others — were still in the Shadow."

"And?"

"This was after we lost Captain Osann. Mariah came to us very distressed and gave us a warning. She said that the Flame was corrupted, and to look out for a 'Sab'."

"A Sab?"

"She was interrupted before she finished, so I couldn't tell what else she was trying to say. Then she disappeared."

"Why didn't you — or any of your group — mention this before?"

"It just … uh … we forgot, I suppose."

The General said nothing, and SmibSmob couldn't see his face to judge his thoughts — not that he could ever decipher them, anyway. But SmibSmob's mind was spinning now, and many, many questions arose. Why *did* he never consider them before? It all seemed so clear — or rather unclear — now. So many strange coincidences. So many unnatural moments. So many unanswered questions.

"Can I ask you something?"

"Is that the question you really want to ask me?"

"Er … no, I suppose. Can I ask my actual question now?"

The General only snickered in response and turned down yet another alleyway. The region looked familiar to SmibSmob, and he knew they wouldn't have much more time to chat before they engulfed themselves in his training. The General wasn't very chatty during training. SmibSmob smacked himself for wasting so much time on pointless questions. He needed answers.

"How did you find us by ... what was that city called? With the Captain?"

Just then, Kraalek stopped. SmibSmob looked up — he didn't collide with the man, thankfully — and saw that they were at the General's humble abode.

"I was investigating a rogue Captain that ventured deep into the Shadow without proper clearance," he said, opening the door and guiding the gnome in. Like always, mice skittered away as they passed through the entrance. At least the cobwebs had lessened, slightly. "I thought it was strange how he was able to teleport so far without a proper escort. The fact that you and your good friends were with him was pure happenstance."

The General crawled under the table and activated the hidden mechanism with one of his cards.

"Really? But what do you mean? Is that really so strange? You teleported there and back again just fine."

There was a click, and Kraalek opened the trap door leading to his secret dwelling.

"Of course, but I am much more powerful than that Captain. The farther one wishes to transport, the more power required. That is why we always need a Commander — at least — to lead a gem-call. Regular Sparks, and even Captains, barely have the strength or training to transport themselves across the Shadowfront."

SmibSmob nodded, remembering the short-lived experience with Dain and Roan. So that was why they had to get close to the mountains. Kraalek started down the stairs, and SmibSmob followed after him. Like always, the trapdoor slammed above them, leaving them both in the dark. This time, however, SmibSmob wasn't discombobulated by the darkness.

"I reckon a Commander, or maybe even a General, could've teleported him out there, and then just teleported back themselves?"

"It's possible, but like I said, there was no clearance or order for a mission by Calinad. There are very few Commanders and Generals, so we usually know what the others are doing. And rarely would we do something so reckless. Aside from the inherent risks of teleporting somewhere that you are not very familiar with, the last thing we want to do is teleport somewhere far away and end in the arms of a Mistress."

Dozens of candles flickered to life, illuminating the basement. It was spotless, as always, and all signs of yesterday's training had been cleaned. Additionally, all broken glassware and furniture had been replaced. SmibSmob wondered when and how the General had the time to make this room pristine every night. As far as he knew, Kraalek hadn't left his side in the past two days.

"Why didn't you teleport us — me and my friends — away from that city and into the Light? Why make Captain escort us?"

"Why would I have? As far as I knew, you could have been a serious threat to our safety, just as Agmund was saying during your first counsel at the Torch. Best to leave you to that Captain, isn't that right?"

Kraalek approached the wooden cabinet as SmibSmob mulled over the response. Unable to formulate a response, he decided to backtrack in the conversation, still curious about the exact circumstances he and his companions had coincidentally found themselves in.

"With the Captain, do you think that one of the Commanders or other Generals teleported him out there without you knowing?"

The General grabbed a glass from the cabinet and poured some Spitfire into it, then placed the bottle in one of his seemingly endless pouches.

"Like I said, it's possible. But, as I also said, us Generals usually know everything and anything that happens in the Flame. Despite how it appears at the Torch meetings, we are loyal to each other. Besides, if I recall correctly, he was under the counsel of Saber ..."

Kraalek trailed off and placed the glass on the oaken table in the center of the room. Without saying a word, he walked over to one of the bookshelves, searched through it for several seconds, then grabbed a book. Frantically, he began to flip through the pages.

"What's wrong?" SmibSmob asked. The General was always eccentric, but this behavior was strange, even for him. Something wasn't quite right. Hopefully it didn't take too long, he was eager to begin his daily training. The glass of Spitfire looked awfully tempting resting peacefully on the table. Tempting to explode, that is.

The General stopped reading, and stepped forward, and gently placed the book closed on the table next to the glass. His face was pale — sickly so. SmibSmob thought he was about to puke, and he shuffled backwards to avoid the splash-zone. Perhaps the alcohol really was getting to the man. A friendly detox couldn't hurt, the gnome surmised.

"I need to go," Kraalek said, slowly approaching the stairs. His gait was awkward and stiff. With his current skin complexion, SmibSmob thought he looked like a zombie — and an ugly one, at that. Not good, the General really *was* going to puke! But couldn't the illness wait? He was so eager to begin training. He could feel the fire burning deep inside of him, begging to escape.

"Where are you going? What about our training?" SmibSmob asked, not even bothering to hide the desperation in his voice. "Mariah strengthened my powers last night, let me show you!"

"I'm afraid you're on your own for training today. You're strong, my good friend, and I give you permission to make a mess of the place. Let your Inner Fire unleash!"

"But where are you going?"

"I am going to see ... General Umbra," Kraalek replied, choking the name out.

"Why? Is she really more important than me?"

"I'm going to invite her to dinner. And nothing is more important than you to the Flame, mark my words."

"What? That seems ridiculous. It's still morning! Dinner won't be for hours."

"You're very observant, good Beacon. Nothing can slip past you. Regardless, I must go. I hope I will return shortly." The General was at the stairs now, but before he began his ascent, he turned back, his face still ghostly-white, and asked SmibSmob one more question:

"Also, as I will be preoccupied this afternoon, perhaps I could call for your brother to keep you company? Apparently, he has been harassing Sparks to see you."

SmibSmob was quiet for a moment. He felt the frustration nearly bubbling over, and he wanted to scream. How could Kraalek just abandon him like this? And right before the counterattack, when he needed all the preparation he could get? For some morning *dinner*? But he restrained his anger — as the Beacon should. He needed to unleash the fire against the Shadow — and the Spitfire — not the General. Besides, he was convinced he couldn't even hurt Kraalek if he tried, so there was no point wasting his energy on such fruitless endeavors.

"No. I'd rather be alone today."

Kraalek shrugged, didn't respond, and crawled his way up the stairs. SmibSmob heard the *click* of the trapdoor, and he knew the man was gone. The gnome turned to the glass of Spitfire and shouted in rage. He needed to be *stronger*. The gaping hole still gnawed at him, itching to be filled. And while he thought it filled upon discovery of his Inner Fire, it was awfully persistent, and the hollow sensation was an endless pit in his soul.

He glared at the glass and imagined igniting a spark deep inside of it. He felt the cosmic strands of energy bend to his will, but just before he was about to release his power, he stopped himself and glanced at the book still sitting on the table. The General did give him permission to make a mess, but that didn't mean he had to be disrespectful to the texts. He used to enjoy reading, after all, so perhaps it was a way of honoring the past memories of himself.

SmibSmob grabbed the tome from the table and studied the cover. There was a note stuck to the cover that read "The History of the First Night". SmibSmob shrugged; he had never heard of it. He opened it, curious about what had rattled the General so greatly, but he discovered the contents were written in some elvish script, and he couldn't read it. That explained the handwritten note on the cover. Apparently Kraalek could read elvish, and, for some reason, SmibSmob wasn't surprised to learn that.

He placed the book back on the bookshelf, and now that he was inspecting it, it seemed all the texts were written in some other language. Strange men keep strange works, he supposed. Either way, despite the unfortunate turn of events, he had to train before the excursion tomorrow.

And that filled the gnome with joy.

Now that the table was cleared, SmibSmob turned back to lord over the glass of Spitfire. He didn't need the General here to baby him, he was plenty powerful by himself. Mariah had told him so. And he believed so.

SmibSmob raised his hand, and felt the universal energy coagulate at his bidding. He imagined the spark inside the glass and willed the cosmos to create a flicker of flame.

The glass exploded with its brilliant ball of green and orange fire, sending fragments of glass scattering around the room. SmibSmob covered his eyes to protect himself, and he felt his hands get nicked by the soaring shards. No matter, he wouldn't hesitate to sacrifice his body for the sake of more power.

He was the Beacon, after all.

Cackling with glee, SmibSmob grabbed another glass from the now-messy cabinet and searched for the bottle of Spitfire. That was the easiest it had ever felt to conjure the spark. Perhaps Mariah really did strengthen him, and that was something worth celebrating.

However, after several minutes of searching for the elusive bottle, SmibSmob came to a realization: the General still had it.

"Beardless dwarf," SmibSmob cursed, quite Nalgene-like, his spirits lowering. How was he supposed to practice without the exceptionally flammable liquid?

But then, SmibSmob had another thought: why did he need the Spitfire? He was the Beacon, and so he couldn't rely on dousing all his enemies in alcohol before igniting them. Mariah had kindled his flame, and he knew he was strong enough to create fire without the crutch.

SmibSmob studied the room, looking for something to incinerate, and his eyes rested on one of the chairs that Kraalek claimed to win from someone or something. The gnome remembered the General's first demonstration to him in this basement, and he soared with confidence. A simple firebolt to burn the chair, how difficult could it be?

So, SmibSmob raised his hand, and envisioned what he required: a small orb of fire, not larger than his palm, that he could wield and throw at the chair. He closed his eyes and looked deep within the gaping void for his Inner Fire. This would be the largest display of magic he had ever attempted — at least after he lost his dark powers. Back then it all just seemed so easy ...

SmibSmob shook the thoughts away and concentrated. His goal was clear in his mind, and he felt the cosmic energy bending to his commands. Energy began to reverberate through him, and he knew he had done it! Yes, let the whole fucking world burn!

SmibSmob howled with glee and opened his eyes.

NOW *BURN*!

The energy condensed, and then, in a brilliant display of magical prowess, a small, insignificant spark appeared in his palm, before fizzling away almost immediately.

SmibSmob was astounded — he had felt the magic so keenly, and that was all he could muster? Another worthless mote of fire? At least he managed to summon it in the air this time, rather than in the glass of Spitfire. He assumed it was progress, but it felt like two steps backwards. The counterattack was *tomorrow*, and he needed to be ready.

No matter, perhaps it was a fluke. He was still warming up. Yes, that was it. A warmup. Now that he had passed that pathetic trail round, his next attempt would be glorious. It had to be. And so, he closed his eyes, repeating the ritual and guiding the universal flow of energy to create what he so desired.

Another surge of electric power, another shout, and he opened his eyes.

Once more, he could produce nothing more than a faltering speck of orange.

No matter, performance issues happened with everyone, he was sure. He told himself it wouldn't be like this next time. Mariah had kindled his powers, and that had to count for something.

But his following twelve attempts all procured identical results. No matter how much he concentrated, or how furiously hot his powers felt, he could never manage more than the singular, fleeting spark.

The chair still stood unblemished, taunting him for his weakness.

Grumbling in frustration, he kicked it, but *damn* it was heavy, and he barely managed to move it a hair's-width across the floor. And now his toe was throbbing in pain. Perhaps this is why gnomes usually weren't warriors.

Temporarily defeated, he turned and sat in the chair. Reaching up, he felt his hat upon his head, and pulled it off, studying it. His gift from Mariah. Supposedly a relic he used to battle evil with. How worthless. All it was good for was manifesting bread, rope, and simple weapons. And last he checked, a loaf of sourdough would hardly be enough to defeat the Shadow. The darkness was ravenous, obviously, but apparently it preferred the taste of living flesh over freshly-baked bread.

SmibSmob threw his hat on the ground and thought of Mariah. Where was she? And who was she looking for? He needed her *now*. He was kindled, sure, but how did he tap into that power? He prayed for help.

Please, Mariah, I reckon you can't hear me, but if you can, I need your strength. Help me defeat the Shadow.

He waited patiently for three minutes but never received a response. He snorted, maybe she was dead, and that was why she couldn't answer his prayers, but he dismissed the absurd thought as quickly as it had revealed itself. Mariah was strong, and he was positive that there was nothing that the Shadow could conjure that could bring her to her knees, let alone kill her.

Another three minutes passed, and he stood from the chair, grabbing his hat from the floor and replacing it on his head. She gave it to him for a reason, even if he couldn't see why, so he would respect the gift. Besides, it would be difficult for him to train while he was moping about in a chair all day.

And so, SmibSmob continued this cycle for the remainder of the day and into the night. He would imagine the fireball, feel the cosmic power, and then suffer a dysfunctional performance. Not once did he ever manage to conjure more than the singular spark. At some point during his tedious training, he found himself wandering over to the workstation covered in gemstones, but he didn't dare touch it. Currently, the General seemed to be tampering with a green gemstone and had carved several transparently-thin sheets from the stone. By the end of the day, his body was wracked with hunger and exhaustion — even though his attempts were pathetic, they still required significant energy.

Foiled, frustrated, and flabbergasted, SmibSmob escorted himself out of the basement. He didn't bother to clean it. Kraalek had never returned. Now at the top of the stairs, he was surprised that he was able to open the trapdoor without the General there, but he supposed it would be very insensitive of the man to lock him in the dank underground.

A *Resurgence of Hope*

Now, back in the city, SmibSmob saw that night had fallen, and the streets were full of their trademark fireflies. He shuffled through the streets randomly, completely absorbed in his dreary thoughts, and didn't even bother to glance at the beautiful bugs. Eventually, a group of Sparks found him in some back alley and escorted him back to the bar.

Kraalek wasn't there, either.

SmibSmob collapsed into bed, hoping that Mariah would visit him again tonight, and praise him for being oh-so strong and powerful. The counterattack was just several hours away, and he couldn't feel worse about his decision to participate. But Mariah had commanded it, and he *wanted* to unleash his revenge upon the Shadow, so he wouldn't back down now. Perhaps tomorrow his powers will miraculously unlock within him.

SmibSmob didn't dream that night.

◆　　◆　　◆

SmibSmob stood before the Torch, the other companions by his side. They were all equipped with shiny new weapons and armor, ready for the assault. All living members of the Torch, except for Kraalek, were present. Nalgene was grumbling something pointless to him, but SmibSmob ignored it. He was much too preoccupied thinking about his journey into the Shadow as the Beacon. In fact, that was precisely what the Torch was discussing:

"General Cardmaster sent word that you would be participating in the mission to Fisherbay," Agmund, the great bear, said to SmibSmob.

The gnome glanced up at the hulking man, and as always, he felt as if he were about to be squashed like a bug. But he didn't let his insignificant feelings hold him back.

"That is correct. I am the Beacon, and so I shall go."

"Such miraculous resolve!" Don exclaimed.

"And why should you participate, it will be very dangerous," said Saber, feigning concern. Remarkably, it was all too easy. Her problems would soon all be over, and she could hardly contain her glee.

"Because Mariah came to me and decreed it so, and because I want to, as the Beacon."

"The blessed Oracle has returned!" Don exclaimed.

"I do miss her little chats with us," Andromeda said.

"Eh, that fiery woman be back?"

"Fire lady friend!"

"How nice of her to only visit you," Margaret commented.

"Indeed, is that what she said?" Saber continued, ignoring the rattlings of the companions. "Then I say it shall be so. What say you, Torchhead?"

Agmund stared at SmibSmob, contemplating the decision. After the death of so many other Beacons, was he willing to risk it once more?

"Worry not, I will keep him safe," Saber purred to Agmund, placing his hand on his arm. That seemed to do the trick, because he nodded. These weak men were so easy to control.

"So be it. You will accompany the force into the darkness. May your light defeat the Shadow, our Beacon."

SmibSmob smiled and respectfully bowed his head. He was still brooding about the events of the previous night, but he couldn't allow his failures to restrain him from his destiny. This would be the day the Light struck back against the Shadow.

"Splendid, now that we have that cleared up, shall we be off?" Sylven said, suddenly appearing by the door. He was balancing his blue dagger on this finger. "Companions and fellow Generals, if you may?"

"Hold, General Quickfoot, we are missing General Cardmaster."

"No doubt he got distracted at the brothel last night," Sylven sighed. "How irresponsible. And just before our grand day, as well."

SmibSmob shuffled from foot to foot and gave a despondent glance at the most beautiful Saber. She was truly so enchanting and commanding ... No. Kraalek was supposed to ask her to dinner, so what happened? But the woman was immovable and unreadable.

Just then, Commander Estar entered the room carrying a very intoxicated Kraalek. The sly man was in shambles, his hood was drawn, and he couldn't even stand without support. The General tried to say something, but only a groan and a grumble escaped his mouth.

"Hail, Torch," the Commander began. "I pardon the intrusion, but I found General Cardmaster quite incapacitated at a bar on the south side of the city. I understand that today he is supposed to be leading the army into the Shadow."

SmibSmob stared at his mentor in horror. Just what *happened* over dinner? Maybe it was a bad case of food poisoning? There was no way he was that irresponsible to inebriate himself to such an extent last night. SmibSmob had seen the focused, intense side of the man, and he refused to believe that one sour dinner would reduce the man to this withering state.

But the visible evidence was difficult to dispute, as well.

SmibSmob glanced at the alluring Saber once more and found some relief that she appeared just as shocked as he. The only difference was her surprise was in elation, while his surprise was in horror, but he didn't know or recognize that.

"Serves that slimy bastard right," Nalgene whispered beside SmibSmob.

"You're beginning to look like him," Margaret said, elbowing Ro in the arm. The draconian made no comment, other than to rub his head.

"Thank you, Commander Estar. Your interruption is excused."

"And it seems I was spot on in my guess," Sylven chuckled. "Very, very naughty of him."

"The Light cannot tolerate such brash conflicts of faith!"

"What are we to do about this, Torchhead? We cannot in good conscience allow him to lead our armies in this state," Saber said.

SmibSmob rushed forward, reaching for the drunk General. But, somehow, while still being supported by the Commander, Kraalek expertly and dexterously deflected the gnome's advances. SmibSmob tried to get a clean look at his mentor's face, but it was always just out of view underneath the man's crimson cowl.

"Leave him be, me brother," Nalgene said, grabbing his brother's arm to pull him back. SmibSmob fought out of his brother's grip.

"Don't touch me."

It sounded harsh as soon as he said it, and the pained look that washed over Nalgene's face hit SmibSmob like the thrust of a spear, but he didn't regret his words. Kraalek was supposed to be here for him today to train and support him in the Shadow. At least, that was how he had envisioned it.

But perhaps Nalgene was right. Mariah said that it was *he* that the Shadow feared, not Kraalek. Perhaps he didn't need him on this venture. He *was* the Beacon.

"You are correct, General Umbra," Agmund began. "This is disgraceful. We cannot compromise the mission by sending him in this state. In fact, with the winged monster still roaming in the darkness, perhaps we shouldn't even have the mission at all."

"No!" both SmibSmob and Saber shouted at the same time.

"But we have the Beacon now," Sylven said. "I'm sure he can fight off any enormous flying undead that comes our way. Besides, I worked so hard on this idea, I would hate for it to go to waste."

"Quickfoot is correct," Saber continued, composing herself. Just like that, her plans would have dissolved into nothing. She *must* solve the problem. The mission had to continue.

"The Light has faith in the Beacon!"

"I'm glad they're always so unified in their opinions," Margaret said. Andromeda snickered in response.

"Let us go," SmibSmob said. "For the will of Mariah, and the will of the Beacon."

"A most noble proclamation!"

"Plus, the army is already at Forthold," Sylven said. "All we need to do is lead it out of the gates — er — hole."

"Me brother, it be dangerous out there. Ye didn't be seein' the beastie …"

SmibSmob ignored the miserable mewls of Nalgene. He had no time, or desire, to play pathetic little brother at the moment — or ever again, for that matter. It was time he fully embraced his role and his destiny. He would burn the Shadow from this land.

"What do you reckon, Torchhead? Will you allow us this mission?" Saber asked innocently.

Agmund was silent for a long time as he studied the room. Would this one, singular mission result in the doom of the Flame? Or would it be a glorious strike against the Shadow to be remembered in the history books? Would this be the turning point in the endless war for survival?

Perhaps he just needed to take a leap of faith.

"So be it. The mission shall continue."

SmibSmob smiled in glee as he stared at the hulking man. Suddenly, he no longer felt as if he was about to be crushed like a bug.

"Splendid," said Sylven, already leaving the room. "Let's be off, shall we?"

"General Umbra, accompany General Quickfoot, the Beacon, and the companions to Forthold. The soldiers have already amassed; they just need their leaders. Commander Estar, dispose of

General Cardmaster where you found him. General Lighthammer, return to your previous postings. The Torch is dismissed. May we all survive to reignite its flame."

The giant man walked out of the room, followed quickly by General Lighthammer. SmibSmob gave a final glance at his mentor as the Commander pulled him away. The gnome was certain he saw Kraalek give him a wink, but it was difficult to tell under the man's cowl. He figured he was imagining things.

SmibSmob exited the room with the other companions. They were saying stuff amongst themselves, but he didn't pay attention. He was much too preoccupied with the burden — nay, gift — that Mariah bestowed upon him. He would help lead the charge against the Shadow. The darkness would know fear.

They met Sylven in the main atrium, where he was holding an orange gemstone. SmibSmob's stomach churned at the sight. Teleportation wasn't friendly for little gnomes. But he would persevere, as the Beacon.

"Come now, everyone put their hands on me."

The companions obeyed, but Saber, who was also with them, did not.

"Saber?" Sylven asked, prompting her to join the fun.

"I must grab my equipment from my lodgings. I will meet you at Forthold."

"Hm, you're as irresponsible as that drunkard, it seems. Suit yourself."

"Perhaps."

Sylven began his chant, and fire engulfed the companions. As the flames burned his body away, SmibSmob couldn't help but stare at the beautiful and wonderful Saber. His eyes traced her curves but eventually rested on her crooked smile.

For some reason, that smile just didn't seem so beautiful to the gnome.

And then they were gone.

*C*hapter 11

The Shadowfriend stood diligently in the city square. He was thin, as most Shadowfriends were, due to the long, starving nights. He had a mushroom of curly black hair and an unkempt beard. He didn't know what the city used to be named; all he knew was that it was once the trading capital of Cilia. And that the Flame — his old brothers, sisters, and home — was soon marching to destroy it. Next to him stood ranks of other Shadowfriends, similarly tempted by the prospect of survival. But was this dreary half-life even survival?

He wasn't so sure.

An army of cultists surrounded the Shadowfriends, eyeing them with disgust. At least *their* ancestors had the wisdom to side with the Shadow upon its conception, rather than fruitlessly try to resist its hunger. There were also many Deathspeakers — more than the Shadowfriend had ever seen before — lurking about in the shadows between the buildings, staring at them with their purple eyes, and a host of undead, ranging from the humble zombie to the fearsome dreadknight, patrolling the streets. This city was the home of one of the Dreadrings, a node of power for the Shadow, and so it was to be protected at all costs.

The Shadowfriend could feel the Dreadring's presence. It was like a looming demon lurking just over his shoulder. The city was *dark*, impossibly so, as the abyssal edifice gnawed at the light. He never actually saw the thing, as it was located deeper in the city, but he had no desire to. The Shadowfriend was tempted to light a torch, but he knew the creatures in the dark wouldn't hesitate to kill him for it. Instead, he strained his eyes to see the dimly illuminated silhouettes around him. At least the sun was up, or so he thought, offering a meager sampling of gray light. Why did he choose this life?

He was sure he knew his answer.

Suddenly, in front of him in the center of the square, the air itself appeared to collapse *inward*, distorting around a singularity. Then there was a *pop*, and the most beautiful woman he had ever seen appeared before his eyes, holding a stack of papers. Immediately, he recognized her: General Saber Umbra. But here, in the Shadow, she had a different name: the Sister of Sin. And she was here, to talk to *him*. It was an unprecedented moment in his life. Perhaps his betrayal was worth it. If he could impress the Sister, that would guarantee his place in the new world.

As soon as she appeared, the cultists and Deathspeakers surged forward, eager to be in her presence, but they didn't dare get too close. Sister was known to be ruthless.

"Great and powerful Sister," one of the Deathspeakers began in its thin, snake-like voice, but it stopped as Saber turned and glared at it. Normally, she would have decimated the creature for daring to speak to her, but she was feeling much too ecstatic today. Charitable, even, so she let the miserable thing live. For now.

"I don't need to remind you about what is transpiring tomorrow," Saber began, her voice ringing loud and clear across the city. "The Flame will soon be at our door, the Beacon at its head, and it will be the day we claim victory for the Shadow."

A Resurgence of Hope

A cacophony of hideous hollers and ghastly groans filled the air. The Shadowfriend found himself joining the rallying call. *Today* was the day he had been waiting for. This was why he turned his back from the Light. So that he could secure victory for the Shadow and claim a spot for himself in the new world. For his survival. For his glory. And for his new family.

"I will personally ensure the death of the Beacon. But as for all you other fine and ... wonderful creatures, the Beacon has a select group of friends. These people are very special to him. I expect you to kill them all. They are a greater threat than you can ever know."

Another chorus of discordant cries followed her proclamation.

Saber began to distribute the papers in her hand. As the Shadowfriend received his, his fingers, for just the briefest of moments, brushed hers, and he felt his cold, broken heart beat once more.

"These are your targets. Shall you kill any of them, you will be ... handsomely rewarded. Tomorrow will be the last day the Flame ever feels hope. And it will be the first day the Shadow knows true victory. At last, our problems will be solved."

Yet another barrage of chants and hoots filled the air.

"Additionally, the army carries with it supply carts. I expect them to be destroyed. Let them know hunger and fear before the end."

A final voracious cry followed her orders.

"Do not fail me now."

The Shadowfriend imagined that the Sister was staring directly at him as she said those last words. She was beautiful. She was powerful. She was terrifying. And she would know how valiantly he would fight for the Shadow. Besides, he could only dream what the promised rewards were ... This is why he turned his back from the Light. For more than just his survival — it was for his *life*. When the Shadow destroyed his town, he knew there was no hope in fighting it. As the old adage goes: if you can't defeat it, join it.

Saber disappeared, leaving the city square. The Shadowfriend looked down at the paper in his hand. In it there was a list of names and descriptions for who needed to die, all written in an elegant, flowing script. He assumed it was the Sister's handwriting, and his heart fluttered once more.

He would do this for her. He would do this for the new world. He would do this for himself. He would do this for his new family.

He scanned the list, digesting it slowly. There was a gnome, two orcs, a feline, and lastly, a gray-scaled draconian.

They would know hunger and fear before the end.

♦   ♦   ♦

The fire extinguished, and Ro found himself back in Forthold. In the three days it has been since he last saw the place, the Sparks certainly tidied up the place, clearing out rubble, rebuilding outposts, and washing the blood away. The collapsed section of the wall was still missing, however, not that he was particularly surprised by that. It would take more than just three days to repair that devastation.

As the last flickers of flame faded in the air, the signature sick feeling washed over his stomach like a literal punch in the gut. He resisted the urge to upheave last night's dinner — with dinner meaning the alcohol stash he had inhaled — which didn't help much with the headache he was brewing. Who knew draconians could get hungover? Although, to his credit and in his memory, he had never indulged in the liquid courage enough to inebriate himself. But now, he realized that ale had its perks. Hardiness for long distance travel just wasn't one of them.

A Resurgence of Hope

As Ro battled through the nausea, he couldn't help but envy General Cardmaster. The man was a disaster, no doubt, but Ro wished he could be tearing up the bars with the man instead of here. Now there was a man that had no problems or regrets in his life — or that is what Ro thought.

An image of Roan and Dain being devoured at the Shadowfront flickered through his mind, followed quickly by an image of the burning bodies of Johnson and Denver — or maybe it was Roan and Denver and Johnson and Dain? Ro, on the other hand, was being suffocated by his regrets.

A final image of Fasto's face appeared in his mind, the orc simply standing by and watching as Roan and Johnson — Johnson and Denver? — succumbed to the claws of the undead.

Speaking of the devil, Ro's brooding thoughts were interrupted by Fasto's words:

"Fasto brother coming?"

Shaking his head, burying the violent tendencies, and once more cursing his headache, Ro glanced up to see the rest of the companions walking towards the fallen wall. Only Fasto remained to wait for his family. The orc held his hand outstretched towards Ro.

"Yeah, yeah," mumbled Ro, joining the others. He didn't take the orc's hand.

"I warned you to stay away from the ale last night," Margaret quipped, her voice oozing with "*I told you so*". "Aren't you just the victim of your own actions?"

Ro shrugged and did his best to put a strong — and not hungover — face on. He was supposed to be the noble leader, after all, although it seemed SmibSmob, being the Beacon and all that something, was shadowing him in that regard.

"I do most appreciate your kind and compassionate words, Margaret," Ro began, watching Margaret roll her eyes at his eloquent words, "but I assure that my stature is grand and ready."

"Ye be an idiot, Ro," Nalgene said, uncharacteristically shuffling away from his brother to join the others.

"But at least you're *our* idiot," Andromeda said, suddenly appearing beside Ro. The draconian almost screamed in surprise, but he held himself together. Howling in fright wouldn't be very noble of him.

Ro opened his mouth to shoot a retort, but another flash of Deckard and Richard — or was it Doan and Cain? — flashed through his mind, sobering his joyous mood. So instead, he just grunted.

The companions, following General Quickfoot, passed through the rubble of the great, stone wall. On the other side, the army of the Flame welcomed them. Hundreds of Sparks spread across the battlefield, forming four files, each with five ranks. Each rank was a squadron of twelve soldiers spearheaded by a Captain. Two Commanders — Commander Ecker and Commander Oldgate — each controlled half of the army. Flametouchers were dispersed evenly throughout the legion, ready to aid a wounded warrior or unleash fiery hell upon the undead. Additionally, each file had its own supply cart, filled with food and water to last in the Shadow. The carts were pulled by horses and were covered to protect the valuable stash from environmental hazards. Finally, at the head of it all, was General Quickfoot, the Beacon, and the other companions.

Sylven raised one of the horns to his mouth and his voice echoed across the army, ordering them to prepare to march. He gave a grand speech, no doubt, and while it didn't have the same effect as Roark's, the soldiers were excited, nonetheless. This was the first counterattack by the Flame. Perhaps there was hope yet.

But Ro was only half listening, still fighting against the urge to vomit. Why couldn't they just teleport directly to the Dreadring, snuff it out, and teleport away? It would save everyone a lot of walking. He was certain they gave him some half-baked answer at the Torch, but unfortunately, he couldn't remember much of what they said.

A Resurgence of Hope

As the General finished his speech, there was a disturbance in the back of the army as General Saber, having just arrived, marched to join the others at the front. As she passed, Sparks ogled her seductive form, and Ro couldn't help but join. The taste of her pale thighs ... The rosy color of her plump lips ...

He shook his head, trying to clear the lustful thoughts, but in his current state, hungover and dour, he didn't have the strength.

"Greetings, Quickfoot," she said when she arrived. Her eyes scanned the rest of the companions, only to land upon the Beacon. She couldn't wait to watch him squirm. "Are we ready to march?"

As Sylven was filling Saber in on the attack plan and troop arrangement, Ro allowed himself to study the woman once more. While she still wore her trademark silver boots and black cloak, at her side was now a vicious looking longsword. It had a black blade and silver hilt. Its pommel was shaped like a skull, and two obsidian gemstones glittered in its eyes. For a moment, he thought it was a very strange weapon for a General of the Flame to wield, but he was quickly distracted by her appearance once more. Saber caught him staring and shot him an alluring wink. Ro almost melted.

His thoughts were interrupted by an elbow from Margaret. Her elbows were becoming quite the regular occasion for him. "Careful, you might start drooling," she said.

Ro grunted, wiped his mouth, and peeled his eyes off the General. "I was just examining the General's equipment to ensure that it was secure and ready for our impending conflict."

"Mhm. I'm sure. Keep using more fancy words and I might believe you."

With that, the army began its trek into the Shadow towards the ruined city of Fisherbay. Marching briskly — and they most certainly were — it would take them until tomorrow afternoon to reach the city. Perfect, that would give Ro plenty of time to recover from last night's escapades. Although, it was a shame none of the supply carts had any alcohol ...

As they marched to the northwest between the mountains, Ro, along with Nalgene, Fasto, and Margaret, found themselves drifting back to join the ranks of Sparks behind them. Andromeda and SmibSmob remained in the lead with the Generals. With every step, another image of the burning bodies of Richard and Doan — why couldn't he remember their names clearly? It felt as if his brain was full of fog — flashed across his vision. While the names temporarily eluded him, their faces were clear. He felt the nausea bubble in his stomach, and the bile crawling up his throat. His nose filled with the smell of their burning flesh. The acid spilled from his throat, and he had to cover his mouth to prevent hurling on the spot.

Beside him, two Sparks noticed his obvious discomfort, and they reached out to console him. Ro felt a tugging on his arm, and he turned to regard the Sparks.

"You doing alright there, lad?" said the man, a cheery-eyed man with a bushy beard.

"Aye, you're not looking too hot," said the other, this one a woman with a thin face. Her eyes traced up and down his body. "Well, you are looking hot, just not well …"

"So, you're into the scales now, are you?" the man said, giving the girl a playful nudge.

"No, of course not! Well, maybe a little," she replied, blushing. "Especially if those scales are of the leader of the heroes. You are part of the new group of heroes, aren't you?"

Ro stared at the woman, digesting her words and praying that the roiling in his stomach would cease. However, in his brilliant state, the only words he could spurt out were:

"You're a girl?"

The woman reeled back, surprised by the question, but she quickly recovered. Ro wasn't the first one to ask her this.

"Yes, I am."

"At least you'd hope so!" the man butted in.

"It seems you're quite charming and observant for a hero," she continued. She held out her hand to him. "Name's Daina."

"And my name's Croak," the man followed, also holding his hand out to Ro.

Ro stared at the outstretched hands and all he could see was the faces of Johnson and Denver — ah! So that was their names! — staring back at him. The nausea, and the charred smell, washed over him once more.

"Fasto find new friends!" Fasto said, interrupting the merry meeting. Ro withheld a violent snap at the orc. Fasto wouldn't need new friends if he had just saved the others ...

"What's wrong, oh-noble leader? I thought you'd be licking their boots by now," Margaret said, pulling Fasto away from the two Sparks.

"Er ... well ... good to see a fellow Spark still burning bright," he managed to choke out. No, he couldn't allow himself to get attached to two new Sparks. Why was it always two? And why did one of their names always begin with the letter 'D'? He already vowed to protect the other pairs and look where that got them. Devoured and burned. And what could he do about it? Nothing, except try to forget his failures as a leader and protector.

"Me name's Nalgene," Nalgene said, taking the Sparks' hands. "I don't be knowin' why Ro — that'd be his name — is actin' all funny, but I can talk with ye's while we walk."

"Splendid," Daina beamed. "Although I really was hoping to talk to him ..."

"You really do have something for the scales now, don't you?" Croak, well, croaked.

"I just heard so many brave things about him — and all of you, for that matter."

"Did you hear that, Ro? 'Brave things'. Probably about how many bottles of liquor you could handle."

Ro grunted at Margaret's comment and slowed his march, falling deeper into the ranks. Margaret had a sense that she pushed it too far, but the draconian was being deplorable. She wanted to look to him as a leader, and Daina had a point, but ...

"Aye, what things did ye be hearin' about me?" Ro heard Nalgene say. Daina responded with something flattering, no doubt, but Ro wasn't listening anymore. The images of the other Sparks, those he almost considered his friends, were still fresh. How long would it take for them to fade? How long would he have to carry this burden?

He felt another flash of envy for General Cardmaster who no doubt was back inside another bar.

How did it come to this? Was it the helplessness against that winged monster? Was it watching those he vowed to protect die, even against his best efforts? Or was he just not the great and noble leader that he thought? He was so proud to protect the others, yet all it did was result in their deaths.

The march continued through the afternoon and into the evening. Several other Sparks tried to talk to him, but he always shied away. He couldn't get attached, not again. It was too painful.

As the evening fell, a group of undead assaulted the army. It was a zombie giant accompanied by a swarm of lesser fiends. They rushed in from the right flank, charging straight at one of the supply wagons. Immediately, orders filled the air, and the army surged to protect it. They could not afford to lose their supplies. All manners of fiery spells barraged the undead host, incinerating the majority of them on the spot. The giant tried to stomp out the lives of several soldiers, but Commander Ecker was there, and he easily crippled the behemoth. Ro, along with the others, simply watched the spectacle. It was an almost embarrassing effort from the Shadow. However, in their distraction, they didn't notice the small group of Shadowfriends emerging on the opposite flank.

◆　　◆　　◆

A Resurgence of Hope

The Shadowfriend, along with three others that he didn't know the names of, unearthed themselves from the small burrow they had dug in the ground. He heard the orders and shouts of General Quickfoot. He knew General Umbra — no, the Sister — was right there by the elvish man's side. But he couldn't allow himself to get distracted now.

As they emerged from the ground, they slithered towards the army. The majority of the Sparks were watching the show across the way, and so they didn't even notice when the Shadowfriends, dressed in identical armor as their Flame counterparts, infiltrated their ranks.

"Is that the best the Shadow got?" the Shadowfriend heard one of his associates say to a Spark.

"Heh, this is nothing we can't handle," the man replied, not suspecting a thing.

The Shadowfriend's other two companions similarly distracted the surrounding soldiers as he approached the supply wagon. He studied the surrounding people for anyone that matched the description of the list, but to no avail. They must be located somewhere else in the masses. He felt his axe banging against his thigh, and he thumbed at the pack of torches strapped to his hip. He would only get one chance. He was ordered to give the army hunger and fear, and so he would obey.

This was for his survival. For his spot in the new world, and the family he would have in it. As the old adage goes: if you can't defeat it, join it.

As he approached the wagons, one of the Captains stopped him.

"What do you think you're doing?"

The Shadowfriend showed the man his final trick granted by the Deathspeaker: a bundle of supposed rations, identical to the ones inside the wagon. Of course, it wasn't really rations. But the appearance was uncanny and convincing enough.

"This fell out of the wagon," he said, trying to keep his voice steady. "I'm just going to put it back. We can't afford to lose any food; we need to be spick and spanner for the battle tomorrow." He was always nervous when dealing with Sparks. Could they tell he was a traitor? Could they feel the cold where his Inner Fire once was? But this wasn't his first mission, and he was determined to make a new life for himself. After the promised rebirth that would follow the Shadow.

At least, that is what he was told.

"Very well, but make haste, we must be alert for more undead."

The Shadowfriend nodded, then climbed aboard the supply wagon. The horses pulling it were exceptionally trained and didn't spook at the calamity on the other side of the army. That was perfect, as it would make his associates' jobs easier. Once inside, the Shadowfriend examined the contents of the wagon. A large pile of rations was stacked high inside crates, and several barrels of water were lined beside them. He knew he didn't have much time, only seconds before someone got suspicious.

That was all the time he needed.

He grabbed his axe, and with several swift strikes, cut gouges in the bottoms of the water barrels. Immediately, the water began to spill out and through the floorboards, saturating the ground below the wagon. It was dark enough that nobody would notice. Then, he grabbed the bundle of torches and waited for his cue. He only had seconds before someone got suspicious.

One of the horses shrieked in pain as his companions slit its throat. And then another. Shouts of "Shadowfriends" filled the air, and the Shadowfriend heard the sounds of drawn steel.

That was his cue.

Immediately, he lit the bundle of torches and cast it onto the food. Luckily enough, the dry food was readily flammable, and soon the entire pile was engulfed in flames. Not bothering to admire his work, the Shadowfriend bolted out of the wagon. He looked around, and he saw two of his associates locked in combat with several Sparks, including the Captain that had questioned him. The third was already dead on the ground. He knew the other two would be soon to follow. He wouldn't mourn them. After all, he didn't even know their names.

The Shadowfriend played into the coup, shouting about traitors amongst their ranks. Then the wagon caught ablaze, and as the nearby Sparks cried in alarm, he took his opportunity to scamper off into the darkness. Back to where he belonged.

This was for his survival.

◆   ◆   ◆

Ro heard the shouts from the other flank and turned just in time to see the supply cart ignite. And what could they do to stop it? They all had flame powers. Only Nalgene could wield water, and it was much too late. The supplies were destroyed. Ro imaged the bodies of Johnson and Denver in that inferno. Coughing, he joined the Generals in the lead.

The army quickly disposed of the remaining undead. The incident report filtered through the ranks. One of the supply carts was destroyed, its horses killed, water emptied, and food reduced to ashes. Not a single Spark was killed — from either conflict. The only casualties were the three Shadowfriends responsible for the sabotage. It was a calculated attack. Much too calculated, in fact, for anyone's comfort. Somehow, the Shadow knew exactly the structure of the army and how to exploit it. While the loss wasn't very impactful — each soldier would just have slightly reduced rations — the impact on morale was more substantial. Additionally, the Sparks would find little rest as they were posted to watch the remaining supply carts. They could not afford any more losses.

However, under the direction and guidance of General Saber, they were urged to continue the mission. She wouldn't let some minor setbacks jeopardize their chance of striking back at the Shadow! General Quickfoot agreed, and so the march continued.

During the night and through the following morning, their journey was largely uneventful. There were several more attacks from the undead, of course, but they were quickly warded off. The remaining supply wagons all remained intact, and only four Sparks died during these events, much to the discontent of Saber. She was hoping for more "hunger and fear" to be instilled within the troops. The dead Sparks were given a brisk, yet still ceremonial, incendiary send-off. This did not help Ro's traumatic nausea, although his headache had now dissipated. There was no sign of the winged beast.

As they drew closer to the ruined city, and consequently the Dreadring within it, the air grew dark and heavy. A black spiral enveloped the horizon, and there was no doubt what it was: the symbol of their death. But they marched on. Despite the gray sun now high in the sky, its light was cold and distant. In fact, several Sparks were ordered to light torches for better visibility.

After several more hours of walking, they finally reached the sprawling city. Towering skeletons of buildings stretched high in the sky like bony fingers, reaching for salvation. Debris cluttered the main gateway, and bricks littered the surrounding landscape. To the east, a vast lake — the same one that the companions journeyed around while still in the Shadow — stretched as far as the eye could see, which wasn't far in the suffocating dark. By now, nearly half of the army was wielding torches. There wasn't a single undead in sight.

"No doubt slinking in their holes," Ro heard Sylven mutter to himself. "All the more fun when we drag them out."

The General lifted a horn and began to billow out orders, commanding formations, final distributions of rations, and equipment inspections. Once they entered the city, there would be no leaving until either they destroyed the Dreadring or died. And they didn't even know what exactly the Dreadring was, let alone how to destroy it. That didn't do much for troop morale, either. However, despite the grumbles, the soldiers obliged. It was their duty for the Light, and they wouldn't let this opportunity go to waste. For Saber, there wasn't nearly enough distress around her. Her Shadow worms had terribly disappointed her.

Just then, a scout approached them from the northeast. No matter, she had other plans.

"Good to see a fellow Spark still burning bright," the scout said, hailing the troupe. The Sparks eyed him warily, cautious about Shadowfriends, but General Umbra was quick to alleviate their suspicions by welcoming the scout.

"Ah, I'm so glad you're still alive. Do you bring news?" she said.

The scout's eyes seemed to rest on her for far too long, but eventually he either found the courage, or the permission, to speak.

"I bring dire news. A Mistress has been spotted in the north, towards the lost Moonshard. If she arrives, it could mean doom to your entire expedition."

Saber pretended to ponder the news for a moment. Of course, it was exactly what she commanded him to say. It was delightful how easily these weak men did succumb to her will.

"A Mistress, you say?" Sylven asked, jumping into the conversation. "What do you say, kitty, want to tango with another one?"

Andromeda flicked her tail nervously but otherwise didn't respond.

"No, Quickfoot, I think it would be best if you remained here," Saber said. "This counterattack was your brilliant idea, and it would be a shame if you didn't see it through. Besides, you need more time to recover from your last encounter. We both know they are no meager foe."

Sylven's eyes twinkled as he stared at Saber, absorbing her words. "You're right, Saber. I shall remain here. Besides, there's still plenty of fun to be had in the city."

"How far away is the Mistress?" Saber asked the scout.

"Not two hours from here, at the edge of the forest. She is nearing as we speak."

"Then we shall make haste. A Mistress is too dangerous to allow to interfere with the attack! Quickfoot, I shall go and dispose of the vile creature while you storm Fisherbay."

"Sounds like a splendid idea!"

"And I shall take the Beacon with me."

That brought a pause to the conversation.

"You want me to go?" SmibSmob stammered.

"Indeed, that would be most dangerous for our savior."

"Eh, what did she be sayin'?"

"You heard the Beacon at the Torch: Mariah blessed his presence to be here. Perhaps this is what the Oracle foresaw. What better way to strike fear into the heart of the Shadow than to have the Beacon defeat one of its very own servants?"

"I can do this," SmibSmob said to himself more than anyone else. Nalgene tried to support his brother, but the gnome just waved him off.

"This seems dangerous, and it was not part of the original mission," Sylven said, uncertain.

"Take a leap of faith, Quickfoot. You will let me take the Beacon."

Sylven smiled at that. The sneaky woman using his own phrases against him. Plus, the way she said her last sentence made him feel quite compelled to listen … But, either way, she was right. They couldn't allow the Mistress to flank them from behind while they were occupied in the city. As the late Roark would say: "the wisest strategy would be to neutralize the threat".

"So be it, leap I shall. But the Beacon shall not go alone. We must have … fail-safes. Commander Ecker, as well as several of our esteemed heroes, shall accompany you in this journey."

Saber clicked her tongue in annoyance. "So be it."

"Fasto go with family!" Fasto shouted, volunteering himself.

"Perfect," Sylven replied. "Margaret — that is your name, yes? — join your fellow orc with Saber. Additionally, Nalgene, perhaps you can go, as well, being his brother and all."

Margaret rolled her eyes in annoyance. "So be it."

Nalgene stared long and hard at SmibSmob, hoping and praying for his brother to give him any sign of acknowledgement. But his brother — no, the Beacon — was absorbed with Saber, who now stood by him.

"I think I'd be best stayin' here," Nalgene finally said, much to the surprise of all. "Me power's better on large hordes, ye see."

"Then it shall just be Saber, the Beacon, Rodrick, Fasto, and Margaret. Be sneaky and quick, Saber, you know how dangerous a Mistress is. If it proves too dangerous a foe, you must escape to the Light with the Beacon. Even if we all die here, in Fisherbay, the Beacon must survive."

"Of course, Quickfoot," Saber purred. Although, if she had her way and her solution, the Beacon would never be seeing the Light again.

Saber turned to the scout and dismissed him, then gathered her small troop. Commander Ecker appeared, a giant steel maul in his hands. Fasto had his white bow, and Margaret her demonic arm, as well as the new plate mail.

"Are you ready, Beacon?" Saber said, placing her hand on SmibSmob's shoulder.

"I am."

With that, they were off, traveling to the north to find and defeat the Mistress, followed by a rallying cry from the soldiers. Or so everyone thought that was what they were to do. Saber knew the truth of it, and she couldn't be more thrilled. It was just so easy with Ashyla out of the way. They would go to that forest in the north, and there, the Beacon would meet his doom.

Nobody could see it in the dark, but Saber wore a most wicked smile.

"You didn't want to go with SmibSmob?" Ro asked Nalgene.

"Ah, he can be takin' care o' himself," the gnome said, clearly deflecting his true thoughts. "He be strong, like he used to be, I suppose."

Once again, Ro reminded himself to ask Nalgene about his supposed regained memories.

"Are you ready to hunt?" Sylven said, joining them and interrupting Ro's thoughts.

"Mmm, I most certainly am," Andromeda purred. She was eager to test this new halberd on some real flesh.

"Let's begin the assault, for the glory and vengeance of the Light," Ro began, feeling a noble speech bubbling deep within him. "The dark and unforgiving Shadow shall have its talons removed today, and our light will pierce its heart, and our fire will burn its flesh …"

An image of Johnson and Denver's burning corpse filled his mind, and he trailed off. It was difficult to give speeches when your pride and nobility only resulted in people's deaths. The bile tickled his throat again. Where was the alcohol? He just wanted to forget …

"Splendid," Sylven applauded. "What he said."

◆　　◆　　◆

The Shadowfriend darted across the street, his eyes already searching for his next victim. Blood covered his hands — Spark blood — and he felt no remorse. It was either their survival or his, and he knew which option he preferred.

Around him, the city was raging with battle. Explosions and fiery pillars illuminated the area, painting the desolate buildings in a fierce, orange glow. Screams filled the air, both from the undead legions and from the living soldiers battling against them. A horde of hobbling undead creatures swarmed the streets, with cultists and the occasional Deathspeaker dotting their ranks. Already the cobblestone lanes were covered in thick, black blood. But that didn't stop the Shadowfriend. War gave little thought to the emotions of its victims.

A group of cloaked cultists passed by him, led by a Deathspeaker, and he followed them into the fray. In his hand he clenched a wicked and twisted dagger, and it was ready to feast. They came upon a pair of Sparks struggling against a three-armed zombie, and they didn't waste the opportunity. The cultists grabbed at the poor soldiers, and then, without missing a beat, the Deathspeaker placed his hands upon their chests and unleashed two vile lances of shadow into them. They died before they could even scream.

The group moved on, eager for more prey. But then there was an explosion, and the cultists were blasted into charred pieces of flesh. Good riddance, the Shadowfriend had no love for the cloaked figures. But the Deathspeaker persevered. Its black cloak was smoldering and torn, revealing the wrinkly, gray skin underneath. Its purple eyes glowed, and it raised its hands. A dark, swirling orb formed between its palms, and with a snake-like hiss, it lobbed the projectile into the battle, no doubt killing another unfortunate soul.

The Shadowfriend was reminded why he never crossed the necromantic fiends.

There were more explosions, more screams, and more blood. After a time, it all faded into one, continuous blur. At some point, he was separated from the Deathspeaker, only to rejoin with it some time later. Or maybe it was a different Deathspeaker? The bastards all looked identical. At another point, several Sparks were urging him onwards, confusing him for their ally. He quickly slit their throats. After that, he was struck in the arm with a firebolt, but he didn't let the pain stop him. Or his survival. Or his place in the new world.

This is why he fought.

The Shadowfriend felt a cold wash over him, and he turned to see a dreadknight approaching. To him, the cold was merely physical, and it didn't have the soul-numbing effect as it did for the opposing Sparks. He supposed that that was one perk for sacrificing his Inner Fire. The armored behemoth marched steadily forward, crushing and hacking at any lesser undead in its path. Barrages of fiery spells rained down upon it, but it was hardly affected. It was the true titan of the Shadow.

But it was not infallible. That the Shadowfriend knew.

A broad man with a striking white mustache appeared before the dreadknight, swinging a flaming glaive down upon its neck. Of course, the dreadknight deflected the blow, and so the two combatants were locked in mortal combat. It was not a place the Shadowfriend had any desire to be. To be near it would risk being caught in collateral damage, and if it was defeated … he had no hope against the mustached man.

So, the Shadowfriend left, sneaking through a fallen building and appearing on an adjacent street. As he climbed out of the rubble, a Spark — a young male with a patchy beard and a soft face — was there to meet him. The man's eyes widened as the Shadowfriend appeared, and he began to reach for his sword. The Shadowfriend saw the fear and uncertainty in his eyes. He saw the shake of the man's hand. In another life, perhaps before his Severance, he would have felt pity for the man. Why was one so young forced to war? It was brutally unfair.

But this was not another life, and so the Shadowfriend struck with his dagger. His eyes locked on the Spark's as his dagger cut the man's throat. He felt the blood ooze down the blade, covering his hand. It was warm. And it was not the first blood he had felt today. The Spark looked surprised as he fell to the ground. Too bad for him, surprises are a good way to die. So, the Shadowfriend flicked his dagger, throwing off the blood, and stepped over the fresh corpse. Soon, it would blend in with the rest of them, just another body in the annals of time.

As he stepped forward, a bright flash filled his vision, and he looked up to see a gray draconian blasting a skeleton away with a devastating breath attack. The Shadowfriend's breath caught in his throat. He watched the draconian's sword swing in a wide arc, decapitating a nearby zombie. The draconian glanced over at him, then down to the corpse at his feet, then to the dagger in his hand, and then finally back to lock eyes. So, this was one of the Beacon's friends. The Shadowfriend recognized the description from the list he was given.

A crooked smile crossed his mouth. With this singular kill, it would cement him his spot in the new world. With just one more kill, he was promised his eternal survival. One final kill, and his new family would know their days of peace.

He approached the draconian.

♦   ♦   ♦

Ro watched the man — undoubtedly a Shadowfriend — approach him. In the man's hand was a wicked dagger, caked in drying blood. A vile smile was on the man's face as he stalked towards him.

Ro clenched his sword and his shield, bracing himself for the coming bout. He opened his mouth to blast the man with a blast of lightning, but something held him back. The man was evil, no doubt, but in his eyes, Ro saw purpose. And not just a dark purpose, but a real, honest purpose. This man was fighting for something he believed in, just like Ro.

Or just like Ro thought he was. In truth, he wasn't sure what he was fighting for anymore. He knew he didn't want the Shadow to win, but other than that? His friends? Maybe, but they would probably die like the others. Like Roan and Dain. Like Johnson and Denver. In fact, he didn't even know where the others were in this bleak cityscape. Probably fighting valiantly against the darkness. But potentially dead.

And he was supposed to be their leader.

And so, Ro didn't kill the man with his breath. There was already too much death around him. Rotting undead soldiers he had no hesitations with. But a living, breathing, feeling, thinking, and believing man? The nausea once again bubbled in his stomach as he pictured the burning flesh of those two poor Sparks.

The Shadowfriend was upon him, and without so much of a word, he swung his dagger at Ro. Ro easily deflected the strike with his shield. The man was slow, sloppy, and weak. It should have been a decisive victory. As the man's arm was forced wide, Ro had a clean strike to the man's chest. It would be a certain kill. He raised his arm, ready to attack, but the man's eyes brought him pause. The flames and screams around him disappeared as he studied the Shadowfriend's gaze, leaving only the burning bile in his stomach.

And so, he didn't strike.

The Shadowfriend regained his momentum, brought the dagger to bear, and plunged it at Ro's chest. The draconian, slow and sluggish, by all accounts of the Shadowfriend, should have died, but he had managed to twist away, causing the blade to stick into his shoulder instead of his heart. No matter, one more strike would guarantee the Shadowfriend's survival. The blade easily pierced the draconian's light armor, and blood oozed once more over the blade and Shadowfriend's hand. It, too, was warm.

Ro gasped in pain as the blade tore through his muscles. He vomited and fell to one knee. The Shadowfriend retracted the blade, grabbed his neck, and leaned in close. Ro felt the man's lips brush against his ear.

"Thank you," he heard the Shadowfriend whisper.

The Shadowfriend's blade was pointed at his neck, and Ro knew it was the end for him. Good, now he could join and apologize to the lost Sparks he vowed to protect. He was a bad friend and a worse leader. He was so proud to bear the weight, but all it did was result in people's deaths. As the Shadowfriend's dagger plunged for his throat, all he could wonder about was why the man had thanked him.

Suddenly, there was a *pop* of fire. A hand grabbed the Shadowfriend's wrist, preventing the fatal plunge. The tip of a blue dagger protruded from the Shadowfriend's throat, spraying Ro with a gargle of blood, before disappearing. Then, the man was unceremoniously thrown to the ground, leaving only a concerned looking Sylven standing before Ro.

"Boy, am I going to have to train you too?" the General asked, holding his hand, now covered in the Shadowfriend's blood, out for Ro. "And that kitty of yours even said you were a good fighter and that you have a good heart."

Ro blinked his eyes, trying to puzzle through the events. He glanced down at the corpse of the Shadowfriend. That man was fighting for a cause. A cause that he had believed in. And now he was dead. Just like the rest of them.

Sighing, Sylven pulled Ro to his feet, not bothering to wait for the draconian to take his hand. They were still in a battle, after all. They didn't have time to pansy around.

As Ro returned to his feet, he clutched at his shoulder, the pain finally fully catching up with him.

"Looks like you put your shield to good use," Sylven said. "Come, let me bring you to a Flametoucher."

Ro nodded absently and followed the General. But his thoughts were elsewhere, and he glanced back at the dead Shadowfriend.

"Why do they turn to the Shadow?"

"Hmm?" the General responded while dismantling several approaching undead. He didn't pin this draconian as the philosophical type, but people are so full of surprises.

"It's just ... Do you think they believe in what they're fighting for? They're people, just like us."

"Ah, I see." Sylven appeared in front of Ro, both of his hands upon the draconian's shoulders. The gesture greatly pained Ro, but he didn't pull away. "Do you feel bad for that man's death?"

Ro shrugged.

"Don't. He's dead. That's that. And you would have been dead instead, had I not seen your bumbling attempt at a duel."

"But he's ... a person. He thanked me."

"What? So?"

"It's just ... he seemed like he was fighting *for* something."

"Aren't we all?

Ro shrugged again.

Sylven sighed. "Everyone is fighting for something. Some fight to protect their family. Others fight for glory. Many people fight simply so they don't die. In battle, the reason never matters. At the end of every duel is someone's death. And who's to say whose cause is right? Not me. Not you. Not anyone. But fight we must, and fight we will, because at the end of the day, we all believe in our own reason. What his reason was, I don't care. He is no longer part of the Light, and so that is enough for me."

"Why do you fight, General?"

"Listening isn't your strong suit, is it?"

Ro shrugged for a third time, and Sylven sighed once more.

"Look, Lighthammer is much better at these sorts of talks. Once we return, you can quibble about ... verisimilitude, or whatever word you want to call it, with him. But to do that, you need to *not* die. Can you do that, at least?"

At last, Ro nodded. If he couldn't fight to protect others, at least he could fight to protect himself.

"Good. Now, to the Flametoucher."

With that, the pair was off. Around them, the battle raged on, Shadow and Light clashing against each other. They met many undead on their way to a Flametoucher, and while Ro attempted to battle them off, it was really the General doing the majority of the heavy lifting. But eventually they did reach the Flametoucher, and Ro's shoulder was mended, not that it made him feel much better.

After that, Sylven bellowed more orders into one of the horns, and a host of Sparks, including Commander Oldgate, gathered around them. The General gave a rallying speech, and together, as a unit, they plunged into the heart of the city.

Fire. Explosions. Screams. Death. It was just a singular span of empty motion for Ro. His nausea had passed, and so, whenever a Shadowfriend crossed his path, this time he didn't hesitate to strike — with either sword or lightning breath. For his survival — or whatever arbitrary reason he told himself. But he excluded none from his blade. He struck down zombies, skeletons, and cloaked cultists alike. He felt as if he were back fighting in that prison so long ago.

Several wraiths had materialized around the group, killing Sparks with their frosty claws. But they, too, succumbed to the whirlwind of the Commander and General. Orbs of shadow assaulted the platoon from the buildings, killing even more Sparks. But, despite their dwindling numbers, they pushed on. This was the *only* chance they would get, and so they would not waste it. They could not.

And that was their reason.

To Ro, the battle felt like an eternity. The seconds blended into minutes blended into an hour. He was hardly cognizant of his surroundings. At some point, Andromeda and Nalgene, accompanied by the remaining few Sparks, reunited with them. The undead legion was endless, but against all odds, somehow, they were making progress. The swirling darkness of the Dreadring was nearly tangible. Ro thought that if he opened his mouth, he would be able to bite it.

But, of course, it would not be that easy. The Shadow would consume all.

Two icy-blue eyes illuminated the darkness in front of them, and the dreadknight stepped forward, its greatsword scraping against the cobblestone street. The cold washed over Ro, and now he really *did* feel as if he were back in the prison: helpless and hopeless. And, for some reason, he knew that there wouldn't be the Goddess to save them.

Sylven shouted an order, and the remaining Sparks surrounded the armored titan. Together, they unleashed a storm of firebolts against it, but they fizzled before reaching the behemoth's impenetrable armor. Something was sapping away their magical power. Commander Oldgate rushed forward, his glaive lit and swinging for the dreadknight's head. Andromeda appeared on the fiend's shoulders, her halberd desperately hacking away. A swirling orb of water crashed into its chest, knocking it back a step. Ro just stood there, helpless and contemplating death.

At the end of the barrage, the dreadknight was hardly affected. Its greatsword slashed, deflecting Oldgate's strike, and then it punched, its heavy first cracking into the Commander's chest and driving him back several steps. There was a fierce cry, and several Sparks, realizing that their spells were useless, bravely charged at the dreadknight, weapons drawn.

Its sword slashed again, drawing a thin line of frost in the air, and one of the Sparks, the woman that tried to befriend Ro earlier, fell to the ground, severed in two. Another slash, and her partner, the man with the bushy beard, died as well. And all Ro did was watch. He didn't even remember their names. And he certainly didn't notice them joining the group. But there they were, both dead. He wondered what they were fighting for. Certainly, it was for a more substantial reason than not dying. But he didn't even bother to ask them. He isolated himself so that he wouldn't feel guilty when others died, and now he felt even more guilty.

In those brief moments, Sylven's words echoed in his head, and he actually *listened*. Those two Sparks had a reason that they believed in, but the Shadow didn't care. All it cared about was that they were still living, and so it ended them. And Ro hated that with every fiber of his being. He may have failed as a leader, but he would be damned if he failed as a living, breathing soul.

He suddenly remembered *why* he was fighting. It wasn't so he could survive. And it wasn't for the glory and honor of being a leader. No. If he died, he would accept that wholeheartedly. He was fighting so that *others* didn't have to. For their dreams and their hopes. And he didn't need to be a leader for that.

A savage growl escaped Ro's lips, and he charged at the dreadknight. He was angrier at himself than anything, but it was enough of a catalyst for now. He figured he would work through it over a bottle of liquor when — if — he returned, but for now, he needed to fight. As he neared the dreadknight, he felt the cold biting at his life, but he didn't slow. He opened his mouth, and felt the natural, magical essence of the universe coalesce to his will. The cosmic energy formed a bolt of lightning, and it shot from his jaw, blasting the armored figure with electricity. Another ball of water crashed into it, sliding it back several steps. The dreadknight's sword slashed again, ending the life of another Spark, but Ro didn't slow.

He was next to it now, and he cut with his longsword, as powerful as he could muster, into the beast's knee, hoping and praying that it would collapse. It didn't. But Ro did capture its attention. The blue eyes focused on Ro, and he stared defiantly back. Fear crept under his scales, but he didn't let it control him. Not now, when the lives of the Sparks were on the line.

Commander Oldgate's glaive crashed into the dreadknight's head, throwing it off balance. Then, General Sylven was there, and his blue dagger was able to cut through its armor. The dreadknight swatted at Ro with his fist, but he deflected the blow with his shield. Its greatsword struck, but Andromeda appeared on its arm, pulling its strike off target. The remaining Sparks fruitlessly unleashed more fire upon it, hoping and praying for its doom.

Flashes of orange light filled Ro's vision, and he unleashed another blast of lightning at the dreadknight. Oldgate's glaive struck again and again, denting the demon's armor, and Sylven dashed this way and that, slashing impossibly quickly at the weak points between the plates. More water, more fire, and the dreadknight stumbled off balance.

But it wasn't done just yet. Its fist cracked into the Commander's face, throwing him to the ground. Then, it grabbed Andromeda from its body and flung her to the dirt, and she howled in pain. Three more Sparks died from its sword. But Ro would not back down. Damn it, he would drink later, but right now he had never felt more sober.

"Nalgene!" he roared, sheathing his sword and grabbing his shield with two hands. He stood in front of the dreadknight, as if challenging it to a duel, staring into its gaze. He hoped the gnome would understand.

Ro was not disappointed. A fierce torrent of water crashed into the dreadknight's head, and with that, he rushed at the devil. His legs burned as he drove his shield and shoulder into its armored chest. His body stiffened and weakened under its deathly aura, but he did not stop. It staggered back, but it did not topple. Ro felt its fist pummel his head, and stars filled his vision, but he just kept moving forward. Then Andromeda was there once more, attaching herself to its arm. Sylven slashed its other hand, severing fingers and causing it to drop its sword. And finally, the Commander, recovering from his blow, was there too, grappling the dreadknight's legs. Roaring in fury, Ro pushed with one final surge of energy, and the dreadknight fell to the ground, landing upon the ground with a metallic *clang*. Without wasting a moment, Sylven was there, and plunged his dagger into the dreadknight's face. The icy eyes went dark.

Ro fell on top of the dreadknight, and, using his shield like a hammer, began to bash its head. Of course, it didn't do much, but *damn* was it satisfying. Together, they had conquered the unbreakable soldier of the Shadow. Now Ro knew this was different than their fight in the prison. They didn't need some divine protection to save them from their dooms — they could save themselves. They were powerful.

Then why did everyone around him keep dying? Ro shook his head. He would ponder the thought later over some ale.

There was no time to celebrate their victory. The Dreadring was still waiting at the center of the city, a dark heart at the core of a decaying mass of rubble and stone. Ro found his sword, Nalgene healed the group as best he could, the Sparks rallied, and they were off. The darkness was suffocating now, and they cast fire into the darkness for visibility as much as defense. More cultists, wraiths, and other undead appeared from the abyss, killing more Sparks and trying to halt their progress. But they did not stop. Several Deathspeakers also appeared, but upon seeing the demise of the dreadknight, quickly retreated into undiscoverable holes.

More minutes passed — or maybe it was an hour, it was difficult to tell — but at long last they reached the nucleus of the Dreadring. It was tucked against the side of a towering clock tower on the coast of the great lake. Exhaustion, caused by both the Dreadring and the battle, bore down on the group — even the infallible General — but they had made it. Hunger and fear be damned. The Commander, three Captains, twenty Sparks, and Nalgene formed an arc around the nexus, protecting the General, Andromeda, and Ro as they approached the central node of the Dreadring from the oncoming undead. They wouldn't hold for long, with their arms already sluggish and weary, but they had to give them as much time as possible to try to destroy the Dreadring.

If it was even possible.

Ro did his best to ignore the sounds of battle raging behind him as he approached the core, Sylven and Andromeda at his side. Sylven's dagger was humming with potential energy, and it cast a blue light around them, allowing them to see what was before them. And it was not what they expected.

At the heart of the swirling and suffocating darkness was a flower. A black, twisted, and rotting flower, but a flower, nonetheless. And it was surviving in the midst of all the death. As Ro stared at the curious vegetation, he felt as if his very strength were being absorbed into it. The nausea returned.

"What is it?" he stammered.

"I don't know," the General replied.

They were now just several steps in front of the flower. If it was not for Sylven's glowing dagger, it would have seemed as if they were surrounded by an infinite blackness, so thick was the tangible darkness. Even with the glowing, they could barely realize each other, or the flower in the black. The sounds of battle had completely disappeared behind them, although whether from the vexing magic of the place or because the rest of the Sparks had died, they couldn't tell.

"Let's cut the flower, shall we?" said Andromeda.

"That seems such a shame to decimate a wonderful piece of nature," Ro replied, slipping back into some of his noble eloquence. "It's like this is the only piece of joy left in this heart of Shadow."

Sylven shrugged. "Even so, we need to destroy this Dreadring. Flower or not, we cut it. What's the worst that could happen?"

But just as he was about to slash at it with his dagger, an ooze began to excrete from the flower, like black honey leaking from a rotten hive. They took a step back, and the slime began to take shape. It started as a hand, and then an arm, covered with onyx black armor, and it began to pull itself from the gunge. A shoulder materialized, and then a head.

A Resurgence of Hope

The head had curled and short black hair, brown skin, and a wicked smile. Two, infernal red eyes burned locked on to the General. The trio took another step back, fear washing over them. The being spoke in a discordant voice:

"Normally, we would wait longer before returning, but when we saw you here, we just had to continue our fun, *General.*"

Sylven's eyes widened as he realized what was manifesting: the Mistress that he had supposedly killed. Andromeda had the same realization and was already trembling in fear. She tried to fade into the darkness, but terror held her paralyzed. They had barely survived against it before, and they knew a brawl against it now could only mean certain death.

"It's not dead?" Andromeda whispered faintly.

"Fuck," was all the General said before pointing his dagger at the reforming Mistress. A brilliant beam of light erupted from its tip, engulfing the Mistress and the flower.

As the flower disintegrated, it released a huge shockwave swept through the city, flattening the trio onto their backs. The last thing Ro heard was an ungodly roaring sound, like that of a great wind. The last thing he saw was a blinding nova of white light, enveloping everything around him. And the last thing he felt was a searing burn across his scales.

Daniel *Whitman*

*C*hapter 12

Fasto trailed behind Margaret, his eyes dutifully scanning the surrounding land for any sign of the supposed Mistress. Whatever that was. He wasn't sure, but he knew it sounded dangerous. And danger meant his family and friends would be in trouble, and he refused to allow that. He would protect and save them. He would ensure the Mistress was swiftly defeated so that they could all return to Firelight and enjoy their next, hearty meal. After all, he defeated the giant winged monster, so how difficult could some Mistress be compared to that?

In front of Margaret was Saber, Commander Ecker, and SmibSmob. They had been walking due north for an hour, but there was no sign of the Mistress. There were several minor skirmishes with a few lowly undead, but the encounters were over in seconds due to the efforts of the Commander, Fasto, and Margaret. The Beacon and the General did not partake in these squabbles. Besides that, the land was barren, desolate, and gray. However, if there was consolation — aside from the fact that they didn't have to fight the Mistress — it was that the world grew brighter as they wandered farther from the Dreadring. No longer was it a gloomy and suffocating black. Instead, it was a slightly less gloomy and not-quite-so suffocating dark gray. A wonderful improvement, in Fasto's opinion.

As they traveled, they hardly spoke a word between each other. They had to remain stealthy in order to surprise the Mistress. It wouldn't be much use yammering and giving away their position. So, battling against his desire to speak with his friends and family, Fasto held his tongue. To distract himself from speaking, he dug notches into his bow using one of his fingernails.

SmibSmob, however, was growing impatient. He needed something to *burn*, and the silence wasn't helping his fiery fever. He wasn't having much luck — as in any luck — producing anything more substantial than a feeble spark, so, despite the precedent set by the group, he decided to break the silent march.

"So, uh … what exactly is a Mistress?" he asked. "I reckon it would be good information to have before we meet and fight it."

Fasto's ears perked up at this question. The gnome made a great point. Any information was good information for the orc if it meant he could protect his family better. Perhaps a Mistress had a shiny weak spot like the winged beast. Fasto knew he would be able to pierce it with one of his arrows. Maybe he'd even make a big-boom arrow again.

"Well," Commander Ecker began, scratching his goatee, "we don't exactly be knowin' what them things are, if I'm bein' honest."

"Great. Isn't that helpful," Margaret said, rolling her eyes. As long as she could punch it, she supposed that was good enough for her. Why was she sent on this mission again? No doubt Ro and Andromeda were knee-deep in blood and filth by now. She licked her lips thinking about it. She had to satiate her damn arm somehow.

"If we want to be goin' off what the Oracle has told us, then thems be the commanders of the Shadow. They tell it when and where and why and how to strike out as uses. And, if we want to be goin' off what we as the Flame have discovered, then thems be the devils of the Shadow. They tell it who and what to kill."

"I don't mean to be the obvious one, but that doesn't sound very encouraging."

"You said it, SmibSmob," Margaret said.

"Fasto encourage! We kill Mistress lady!"

"Now, that's more encouraging," Margaret sighed.

"Do you know anything about them, General Umbra?" SmibSmob asked Saber.

Saber pondered the question for a moment. She knew more about them than she would ever want to admit. But, of course, if she told them the truth, it would compromise her position. And she wasn't quite ready to do that yet, not until they were deep in the forest where nobody would ever discover their rotting, mutilated bodies. How could she explain away the fact that she was there when the Mistresses were first created? Or when the *Shadow* was first created? She shivered at the haunting memory. Human women weren't known to live for more than sixty years, let alone over two-hundred, or even over a thousand! Once again, she thanked herself that she wasn't one of those worthless creatures. If there was one good thing that *he* granted her, it was that he didn't create her as one of *them*.

"It is as Ecker said," she began, feigning careful contemplation. It was so delectable and easy to lie to these filthy rats. "They control the Shadow, telling it where and when to strike. And they are not a foe to be taken lightly ..."

She trailed off dramatically, then stopped walking. Perturbed, the rest of the group halted, as well. Saber turned and placed her hand on SmibSmob's shoulder, forcing him to look into her eyes.

"It will take all of your strength to defeat this foe, Beacon, but together, with the others, I know we can overcome such an obstacle. For the light of the Flame."

SmibSmob nodded along with her words. Of course, the General was correct. Why would he have any reason to doubt her?

While it was splendid that his friend SmibSmob now fully understood the complex inner workings of the Mistress, that still left Fasto with one, critical question:

"Where Fasto shoot?"

Margaret snorted. "Good one. Very important."

"Well, I'd be shootin' thems dead straight in the chest, if I was a bettin' man," the Commander answered, chuckling. "That's your best chance to hit."

Fasto gave a salute to the man and forced the information into his brain. Chest. Shoot. Best. Roger that. Fasto understood clearly. And he wouldn't miss his shot. However, just to be sure he wouldn't forget when the crucial time came, using his fingernail, he began to indent a stick-figure diagram of a lady with a target on her chest into his bow. If he had time, he would have drawn it out in the dirt beneath their feet, but as they were still walking, he was afraid he wouldn't have time to complete his illustration. It would have to wait for when he returned to the city. All Sparks would soon know the weakness of the Mistresses. According to Fasto, that is.

Now that the group was all caught up on the mysteries of the Mistresses, they continued walking towards the distant forest. Silently. As they marched, the sky grew brighter still, and the faint gray orb of the sun could be seen faintly through the smog and the haze. The light was cold, but it was light, nonetheless.

After another hour, the group finally came to the edge of the forest. They had slowed their march as they neared as they needed to be diligent for any sign of their quarry. Of course, there was no sign, and that brought a sense of relief to them. Perhaps the scout was wrong? Fasto, with his brilliant tracking skills, still saw nothing more than shriveled grass and dirt around them.

"I'm not thinkin' that this Mistress is here," the Commander said, his eyes scanning the surroundings fruitlessly. "Perhaps wes should be headin' back to support the others at Fisherbay. The information the scout gaves us is old, the Mistress could be anywhere."

"Does that mean walking two hours back for nothing?" Margaret whined.

"No, Ecker, we cannot abandon our mission just yet," Saber said, her voice unwavering. She would *not* let the doubts of some lowly human ruin her plan. "Yes, this is where the scout reported seeing the Mistress, and yes, in the time it took us to travel, it no doubt moved. However, it is still our job to find it and eradicate it. We cannot let it, along with the undead that surround it, flank the Sparks at Fisherbay. Do you want to be the reason for their deaths, Commander?"

The Commander grumbled and scratched his goatee. "I'm hearin' you, General Umbra. Of course, I will listen to your orders, I just thought I would be givin' my thoughts, that's all."

"I agree with General Umbra," SmibSmob said, his voice nearly a shout. Fasto thought it was strange to be so loud, when they were all in such close proximity, but he just assumed his friend was nervous. "We must find the Mistress. I reckon there was a reason why Mariah urged me on this attack, and this must be it."

Saber had to restrain herself from cackling with glee. There most certainly *was* a reason, and this most certainly *was* it. Just as soon as they were deep enough in the woods …

"Fasto follow friend!" Fasto needed to stay by SmibSmob's side and offer comfort to ease the gnome's nerves. That was what a good friend would do.

"So, how do we be trackin' this thing down, General?" the Commander asked.

For once, Saber wished she could create illusionary sensations like the wretched Ashyla. Then, she could bestow upon the group a vision of the Mistress, but instead she had to use her words. Luckily for her, her words were remarkably powerful.

She turned to the noble and righteous Beacon — noble and righteous were such disgusting words — and once more placed her hands on his small, pathetic shoulders. Her hands began to squeeze.

"I think that we should let the Beacon guide us now," Saber said.

SmibSmob squirmed uncomfortably under her grasp, but he couldn't wiggle free. Who knew Generals of the Flame held such raw physical strength? He supposed he shouldn't be surprised; they were no amateurs, after all.

"Well, I don't mean to be the obvious one, but —"

He was interrupted by the words of the General:

"You feel it, don't you?" she cooed at him. "Tell them you feel it in the woods. It's lurking among the trees."

SmibSmob visibly relaxed, and Fasto took that to mean his nerves were escaping him. The General was a very friendly woman, that much was clear. Perhaps, if Fasto was lucky, he could tag along on more adventures with her. Plus, he did just love staring at her as she walked …

"I feel it in the woods," SmibSmob echoed softly. "That is where we must go. That is where I — we — will defeat it."

"Splendid, so no walking back for nothing?"

"Fasto follow friend!"

"As you says, Beacon," the Commander replied, bowing respectfully to his hero. If both Mariah and General Umbra had faith in this little gnome from the Shadow, then he would too. "Into the woods we go."

"Indeed," Saber said, releasing the gnome. "Lead the way, little Beacon." It was difficult to keep the excitement from her voice now. Her problem was almost solved.

The group entered the forest. The trees were twisted and dead, much like the original forest that the companions had been placed in after their escape from the prison. The branches were sharp and crooked, and it seemed that they were reaching out to grab the group's clothes. The Commander, Margaret, and SmibSmob watched the wooden sentinels warily, a slight tinge of fear in their steps. Saber, of course, was not affected by the eerie nature of the forest. And Fasto … well, Fasto had never felt more at home.

As the companions trudged deeper into the woods, Fasto began to feel a tickle at the back of his thoughts. He felt a weight lift from his mind, and a deep sense of relaxation washed over him. Distant images began to dance across his vision, but he couldn't decipher if they were real or not, so he tried swatting them away, which garnered a strange look from Margaret.

"You alright there, pal?" she asked, slowing to walk beside him.

"I feel fantastic," Fasto replied. This stopped Margaret dead in her tracks.

"You mean, 'Fasto fantastic', right?"

Fasto turned and looked at his fellow orc, quite puzzled. Yes, his name was Fasto, he was sure of that, but why would he say it like that? The tickle in his brain became a sharp spear, burning into his mind as if it were attempting to break through an impenetrable barrier. It felt like someone was twisting a hot iron into his skull. His vision grew blurry for just a moment, and he stumbled on his feet before quickly recovering.

"Ah, no? I mean that I — and yes, I am Fasto — feel fantastic."

"So, you can talk? Normally, I mean? It's just — I mean I never thought you were dumb, that would just be insensitive, but — you know …"

Fasto's brow furrowed as he studied Margaret. No, he clearly did not know what she was rambling about.

"Don't I always talk normally? I'm not sure I — Fasto — am following."

"Well — you see — yes? Uh …"

"Youses good back there?" the Commander called back from up ahead, interrupting their jovial conversation. "Let's not be losin' each other in these woods. Hurry up!"

"Coming!" Fasto called, but not too loudly. They were still tracking the Mistress, and it wouldn't do much good to alert it to their presence. Although, he figured it already knew they were coming anyway, judging by the numerous undead stalkers watching them between the trees. He held out his hand to Margaret. "Come, my friend, let's find this Mistress."

"Ah — ber — uh — yeah," she stammered, cautiously approaching him. Who was this man and what did he do with the bumbling Fasto? He did say "friend" this time, which was a relief, but the sentence was still much too structured. Was it a doppelganger? If so, when did they switch? In the majority of her memories — granted she still couldn't recall many of them — he was always a dolt. The only time she could remember him nearly speaking normally was in the forest just after the prison, but she wasn't paying enough attention to really care. She figured she just imagined it. High stress and all that. There was also that time traveling with the two Sparks before the Shadowfront, but he was barely more coherent than usual, so it didn't really count. Other than that, ever since they met at the prison, Fasto was just, well … that guy. And she didn't have a problem with that, of course. Not anymore.

The hot iron in his mind twisted once more, and this time Fasto fell to one knee. Shit, what was wrong with him? Why did he feel so fantastic right now? Clearly whatever was affecting him was *not* fantastic. He wiped his brow, which was beginning to sweat, and looked up to see Margaret before him.

"Are you okay?" she asked, alarmed, and reached out to take his hand and help him back to his feet.

As soon as her hand touched his, the pain in his head roared to a staggering magnitude, and the barrier in his mind cracked.

◆   ◆   ◆

A Resurgence of Hope

The orc trailed his friend through the woods, tracking down the last remaining member of the opposing force. His friend was also an orc, and she was miraculous at devastating their foes with her mighty punches. He did feel remorse about her arm, however. No one should have to live with a burden like that. He hoped that soon she would realize that she had the power to be rid of it forever.

Together, they weaved between the trees. The foliage and brush provided them with adequate cover as they trailed their quarry, which wasn't difficult, given the dotted blood trail leading them along. But they couldn't allow any to escape, else they could warn the garrison of the incoming attack, which would be less than ideal. The keep between the mountains was an imposing structure, and it would not fall easily.

The orc, however, had no doubt that they would have it secured by the end of the week. With minimal casualties, nonetheless. A bold strategy demanded a bold team. And bold they were.

The orc knew these woods like the back of his hand. He had memorized a detailed map of the region specifically for this outing, and he had ensured to give a thorough debriefing of it to his squadron, as well. Of course, he and his friend had left the others far behind, allowing them ample time to rest and recover before the next phase of the mission. They, however, did not need such rest. Between them, they had not but four scratches to show for injuries in the prior battle.

The orc relished every opportunity to foray in the woods of the land. It reminded him of his childhood — just this time with more blood and killing — which soothed his mind and made him feel at peace in the chaotic, war-torn world. His parents never wanted him to venture into the woods, which was strange for orcish culture, but being born in his stature meant that he had to spend more time at fancy dinners, speech lessons, and ballroom dances than mucking about with the roots. The food was delectable, no doubt, but it always left him yearning for something more ... wild.

As they moved, the blood trail became more distinct, with the splotches growing larger and more frequent. Their target was slowing down. While tracking people was slightly different than tracking the stags he was used to while hunting, his feline friend, who was currently infiltrating the fortress, had taught him the nuances of it. And so, upon seeing the signs, the orc knew the chase was over.

His friend disappeared through a bush, and he dove in right behind her. They found themselves in a small, quaint clearing, and the bright sun shone brightly through the canopy. It was a beautiful day for a run. In the center of the clearing, supporting himself against a large rock, was their target. It was just a man, wearing simple leather armor and wielding a chipped longsword. Blood oozed from the man's side, saturating the grass beneath his feet. The orc never enjoyed killing people, but it was a necessary evil of the war that had been raging for almost one-hundred years. As he studied the man, he wondered why he was fighting, and what drove him to the side of darkness.

The female orc rushed into the clearing, an icy mass already forming around her fist. The orc supposed he never would get the chance to ask the man. His friend was always so eager with the punching.

Just then, the orc spotted a shadow moving among the trees. There was another person! He saw the glint of light catch on the tip of an arrow aiming directly at his friend. Immediately, in one, fluid motion, he nocked an arrow, brought his bow to bear, exhaled his breath to steady his aim, and released. There was a blinding flash of light as his arrow lasered towards the assailant in the trees. A muffled grunt of pain met his ears, and then a thudding sound as the body hit the floor. No longer did he see the tip of the arrow. The orc smirked. He wasn't known as the Deadshot for nothing.

A Resurgence of Hope

Meanwhile, his friend, not even reacting to the flash of light behind her, had flattened their target's head against the rock. It was a gruesome sight, and much too barbaric for the orc's comfort, but he knew she had her reasons. In the brief moments they spoke about her early years, he could understand her pain. No one deserved to be tortured like that, especially not at such a young age. And it was the opposing side that had committed such vile atrocities to her, so perhaps that justified it.

His friend turned and walked towards him, shaking the blood and bone fragments from her black fist. She asked him about the arrow, and he told her not to worry. He would always protect his friends. He would always protect her, most of all. There were few orcs on their side of the conflict, so they had to stick together. And stick together they did.

Just then, there was a flash of rainbow light behind them in the trees. Turning, they saw a man approaching them from the bracken, and they saluted him as he drew closer. It was their commander and the leading authority of their people. The man had long, shaggy hair and a ridiculously bushy mustache. His flowing, blue cape got snagged on several twigs, and the man yanked it free, miraculously, without tearing a hole in the fabric. The man gave them a smile, and said something, but the orc found that he couldn't understand the words. A dark haze fell over his vision, and his legs grew weak. It felt as if a hot iron was twisting into his mind. He glanced up at that strange man, who was talking with his friend. He saw a marvelous hammer of silver and gold in the man's hand ...

◆　　◆　　◆

Fasto heard the muffled sound of some words, but he couldn't decipher what they were. Then he felt someone shaking his body, and he slowly opened his eyes. The haziness faded, and he realized he was staring up at the gray, desolate sky. There was another orc — Margaret — beside him. So, that was why he was shaking.

He heard the muffled words again, and he rolled over, trying to lift himself to his feet. The ground wasn't very comfortable. What happened? Was he attacked by the Mistress? He didn't know what the scope of their powers were, but could they possibly inflict a coma on an unsuspecting victim?

Fasto staggered to his feet, using a nearby tree to support himself. He blinked, clearing away the last remaining fog, and studied his surroundings. He saw Margaret, SmibSmob, the Commander, and the exquisite and charming General Umbra. His eyes rested on her shapely, pale legs for longer than he would ever care to admit. However, in his study, one thing became clear: they were all safe.

"Fasto, are you alright? It's not smart to black-out randomly," Margaret said, brushing the dirt from his armor. "You might smash your head on the ground and bleed out. Not very ideal."

Fasto chuckled at this comment. Margaret always did have such a way with words. "I'm fine," he said. "Although Fasto — I — appreciate the concern."

"Are you sure?" the Commander asked. "We don't be wantin' yous to fall again."

"Wait, you're talking?" SmibSmob asked, approaching Fasto with wide eyes.

"Yes, I am sure. And yes, I am? Why is everyone so surprised by me — Fasto — talking? Last I checked, I wasn't mute."

"Well, no, I reckon you're right, but ..."

"I'm glad you're alright, Fasto," Saber said. In her hands was his stained, white bow, and she held it out for him. He must have dropped it during his little incident. He graciously accepted the gift and cherished the moment when his fingers brushed hers. As they did, he looked into her eyes and was surprised to see the faintest sign of alarm. She tried to hide it, but he could see it anyway. He shrugged, figuring that she was just concerned about him.

"Thank you," he said, smiling at the beautiful General, and feeling the refreshing touch of the wooden bow in his palm.

In reply, Saber retracted her arm and turned away. She was, in fact, slightly alarmed by this development. If he was once again speaking eloquently, then that might mean he was beginning to remember. And if he could remember … well, her position would certainly be compromised. However, her alarm quickly passed when she saw the trademark enchanted look that all men — and even some women — ogled her with while she was nearby. No, he didn't remember anything. And besides, even if he did, she could just accelerate her plans. Ideally, she would like to be deeper in the woods, but, if it came down to it, here would be as good a place to begin the slaughter as any.

"What happened?" Fasto asked, rubbing a minor bump on his head. "Was this caused by the Mistress?"

"Fear not," Saber answered, pulling SmibSmob along beside her and walking deeper into the woods. "It seems you must have stumbled upon a root and hit your head. Accidents happen, but let's be more careful next time. Trust me, if the Mistress had caused it, it would have been much more violent."

Fasto nodded, then silently scolded himself for being so clumsy.

"Wells, that'll be settlin' that," the Commander said, trailing after the General and Beacon.

Margaret appeared beside Fasto and shook her head. "You didn't trip on anything."

Fasto looked at her quizzically. "Then what happened?"

"I was hoping you'd know." Margaret gave him a gentle punch on the arm with her normal fist. "Maybe the fear is starting to catch up to you finally."

"Hm, I sincerely doubt that, but if that's your theory, who am I to dispute."

"Although I'm not sure why Saber would say you tripped …"

Saber heard the two orcs mumbling between each other and decided that that was quite enough talking for the event. If they began conversing too greatly, perhaps some memory of the bastard orc's would come dislodged, and she wanted nothing to jeopardize her plan.

"That's enough talking," she commanded them, turning to shoot them a friendly glare. "The Mistress might be close; we best not alert it to our presence. From now on, we travel lightly and in silence. If you need to communicate, use hand signals."

Margaret opened her mouth to reply, but caught herself, and gave a thumbs-up to the General. As much as she wanted to explore this newly renovated Fasto, it was difficult to dispute Saber's logic. From what she was told of the Mistress, caution was required, and they needed every advantage they could get to defeat it.

Fasto gave a salute to the General and gestured to Margaret to tail behind him as he began following the others deeper into the woods. His mind relaxed, and he no longer felt the searing pain thrusting at the back of his head. And while the trees were mangled and grotesque, he still felt a sense of weightlessness and relief. As he had mentioned to his friend, he did, indeed, feel quite fantastic.

Just then, there was a white eruption of light from the distance behind them. Several seconds after that, a hefty gust of wind rushed through the trees, causing the skeletal branches to sway. Fasto turned to study the source, but he couldn't see anything. However, judging by the direction, it may have been from Fisherbay. His heart sank into his stomach, and he hoped that it wasn't from the city.

Commander Ecker waved his hands in alarm in an attempt to communicate with the group. Of course, while Fasto couldn't understand the obscure and vague hand symbols, he could guess well enough what they meant.

"What the fuck was that?" Margaret asked, ignoring the flailing Commander and already breaking the no-talking rule.

"Do you think it was from Fisherbay?" SmibSmob asked, his voice weak. The gnome rubbed his hands together nervously.

"I don't know," Saber said, also confused. It was true, she had absolutely no idea what that flash of light was. Never before in the history of the Shadow had such an event occurred. And that frightened her. The only other times she could recall such an outburst of power was during the Fall of the Moon, and that was when a great conduit of creative power was irrecoverably destroyed. Did that mean …? Shit, this was not good — for the Shadow, at least. But she knew the wretched darkness would endure. As for her current plan, well, as long as they continued in the woods, it would hardly affect anything.

"But let us not get distracted. We cannot know what the cause of that was, or even if it came from Fisherbay. The Shadow is a mysterious force, and these are unprecedented times. Our plan doesn't change. We must assume the best for our allies, find the Mistress, and eradicate it."

"Yes, I agree." SmibSmob said, steeling his resolve. Mariah had sent him here for a reason.

"But …" Fasto began, still concerned about the flash, but the General interrupted him.

"You will trust me on this."

"Of course," Fasto heard himself say, although he didn't even mean to. She was just so commanding and beautiful and … He shook his head. Of course, she was a General, he would trust her judgement.

"Come now, the Beacon knows we are nearing the Mistress," Saber continued, not even bothering to verify that fact with SmibSmob. But apparently, she didn't need to, as he dutifully nodded right along. "Once more, if you need to communicate, use hand signals. Let us solve this problem for our friends."

With that, she went through the trees towards the heart of the forest, SmibSmob in tow. The Commander followed shortly after, and then Fasto and Margaret took up pursuit.

"No talking again?" Margaret whispered to Fasto. "She really does make things enjoyable."

Fasto smiled and gave her a gentle punch in reply. At least he was enjoying this.

The group delved deeper into the ominous woods, following Saber's lead. Just a little longer and no one would ever find their bodies … Several undead watched them progress through the trees, but they all maintained their distance. They wouldn't dare attack Saber, at least not at the moment. And so, the group eyed the undead stalkers cautiously but otherwise paid them no attention. If stealth was the priority, then slaughtering undead with a flourish of bright arrows, flaming strikes, and icy punches wouldn't help keep a low profile.

Then, Fasto, now at the helm of the group with the General and Beacon, heard a disturbance in the trees. Immediately, he held his arms out, urging them to stop. They obliged and allowed him his scan of the area. Saber was wary about what he might find — there wasn't actually supposed to be a Mistress — but, if there was, then it would help her slaughter all the same. Although, she was certain whatever the ugly orc noticed was not a Mistress.

Fasto studied each tree, attempting to determine the source of the noise. No, it wasn't that one. Or the small grouping to his left. He heard the shuffling sound again and noticed the faintest flicker of crimson peeking out from behind a thick trunk.

There. That was the Mistress.

Slowly, deliberately, he drew his bow and nocked an arrow. He didn't spend the time to forge a new one. If he had his shot, just this one simple arrow would be enough. He brought the bow up before him, and his eyes noticed a small indent in the shape of a woman on his bow. It had a target on her chest. Yes, he knew where to shoot: dead center at the tree, just about where he estimated the

Mistress's heart to be. As that is where he was told to aim. And that is where he etched into his weapon. Dead center. He pulled the string back, and exhaled his breath, steadying his hands. One shot to secure their victory at Fisherbay.

The arrow released, whizzing off in a brilliant ray of light. His aim was certain, and the arrow pierced directly through the decaying trunk, spraying splinters and shards in all directions, before streaking off in the distance beyond. There was no scream or shout or reaction of any kind, other than a thin, crimson-robed figure scrambling out from behind the tree at the very last moment to avoid being skewered.

The figure brushed off its clothes, straightened its cowl, and gave an exaggerated bow before standing straight and facing them.

"Why, you nearly killed me," Kraalek said, feigning distress. "That certainly is not a very polite way to say 'hello'."

"Kraalek!?" Saber and SmibSmob exclaimed together.

"I'm sorry?" Fasto muttered, lowering his bow.

"Oh, great," Margaret mumbled. "I'd rather it be a Mistress at this point."

"What are you doin' here, General Cardmaster?" Commander Ecker asked, saluting the skinny man in return.

"Yes, have you decided to relieve yourself of the taverns, Cardmaster?" Saber hissed, quite annoyed and frustrated at this sudden development. But, while this was a deep wrinkle in her plan, she didn't survive this long without the ability to adapt.

Kraalek looked up at Saber, and suddenly his visage was stern and intense. No longer was he the bumbling, drunk fool.

"I suppose I have," he began, his stack of metallic cards appearing in his hands. He began to shuffle them through his fingers. "In fact, I was never drunk at all."

"Am I supposed to be impressed, Cardmaster?" Saber replied, her voice oozing with menace. "Go to Fisherbay, I'm sure they need you there. That was the original plan, after all."

"And was this part of the original plan, Saber?"

"The Torchhead gave us his blessing to pursue more, if needed. Tracking a Mistress seemed a worthy task to guarantee our victory here today."

"And is that what you're doing, Saber, pursuing a Mistress? We both know there isn't a Mistress here, isn't that right?"

"What is he saying, General Umbra?" SmibSmob asked Saber, looking up at her with two miserably beady eyes. How Saber wanted to gouge them from his skull. And she would, all too soon. "Mariah told me to come. This *must* be the reason why: to kill a Mistress and prove my strength."

"He does love talking in riddles," Margaret grumbled. But while she was grumbling, her firsts were tense. She was ready to fight.

"It seems the Mistress relocated on our way here, Cardmaster," Saber continued, her voice returning to a steady calm. Perhaps there was no need to fear. "But if you say that there is no Mistress about, then we shall return to Fisherbay."

Her gaze grew intense and bored into Kraalek's eyes. "Leave now. We will follow shortly once we have secured the area."

Kraalek nodded and began to turn around. But, at the last moment, he stopped himself, shook his head, and turned back to face Saber. His gaze was no less intense now.

"Now, that is quite the nifty ability you have, Saber. I should suspect no less from one of the Demigods."

Saber's eyes were open in shock. He resisted her charm? This was a most unfortunate deviation from her plan. It seemed she had one more new problem to solve.

"Demigod?" SmibSmob asked. Saber almost struck the Beacon on the spot. That repugnant gnome was just full of stupid questions.

"Shall you tell them, or should I?"

Saber paused for a moment before answering, allotting her time to regain her composure. So, the game was almost up. She figured someone would put the pieces together eventually, but for it to be this abhorrent man, it made her unbelievably furious.

"So, it seems you have been drinking. I have no idea what you're speaking of. We both know the only Demigod remaining is Mariah."

Fasto nocked an arrow in his bow. Whatever was happening, he didn't like it. He needed to be ready. There was no doubt someone would be getting shot by the end of this debate.

"And so, that is what I thought, as well. But you see, I've never seen you eat anything. And you've refused my every attempt to treat you to a splendid dinner."

"And why would I want to dine with you? I seek no personal relationship."

"It's interesting, because how would you survive if you've never eaten, isn't that right? Unless you weren't like us. But alas, perhaps you feast when stray eyes aren't watching. Embarrassment and all that. However, despite your lack of proper nutrition, I've never actually seen you use a gem-call."

Saber said nothing. SmibSmob was frantically looking between the two Generals, searching desperately for answers. The others, Fasto included, were just as bewildered. It was most likely a safe bet to just allow the two Generals to work this over — whatever this was — before getting involved.

"You know, our good friend Beacon here told me something quite interesting the other day about the companions. He said that one day, during their journey in the Shadow, Mariah came to them with a warning. She said: 'beware Sab'. Now, who do we think she was referencing?"

Saber still said nothing. So, there was another time when Mariah had escaped Calitha without her knowledge. This was an unfortunate piece of information that would have been critical to know. If she knew of Mariah's warning, she would have ensured that her untimely end occurred much sooner. Even so, she was surprised the companions didn't catch on. It seemed they too were vulnerable to her presence.

"The pieces began to reveal themselves. From that strange occurrence with the Captain in Calinad to your mysterious and semi-frequent disappearances. But the final stone that caved the donkey's legs is what I found in a book. It mentioned you, Saber Umbra, one of the Demigods of old, and your part to play at the beginning of the Shadow. It's a pity you didn't have the foresight to change your name."

"WHAT!?" Margaret and SmibSmob exclaimed in unison. The gnome began to back away from Saber.

"I don't likes where this is going," the Commander stammered, grabbing his maul from his back. The head began to flicker with hints of flame.

Fasto said nothing but began to aim his bow at the woman. The pieces were fitting together. And Saber's lack of defense certainly did not help her cause. One shot, directly through the chest.

"However, despite that, I *still* doubted what I found," Kraalek continued, "because I wanted to believe that I was wrong. So, I followed you for a night, watching you from the darkness of your halls. Unfortunately for me, you were squeaky clean that night. So, I relieved myself from leading this counterattack to give myself another opportunity to observe. And that's when I saw you with that scout, commanding him to give his oh-so crucial report."

"What are you saying, General?" the Commander pried, but Kraalek continued. Saber remained motionless, her eyes never leaving Kraalek's face.

"Suddenly, it became so clear to me. Ever since you joined the Torch — seemingly randomly and out of nowhere after the disappearance of Mariah — the Flame has been *losing*. No doubt, it is because of *you* and that seductive little charm of yours. You danced around, whispering poison in our ears. Say, Demigods were rumored to be formed from the emotions of the races, I wonder what yours is?"

A *R*esurgence of *H*ope

And even still, Saber remained silent, taking the accusations without reaction.

"And so, that brings me to my question: what are you doing with the prophesied Beacon in the middle of the woods so far from where the main force of the Flame is stationed? I was eager to settle this quandary, so I waited and watched, always just ahead of your little group here, until alas, I made my grand entrance."

"Mariah sent me ..." SmibSmob said weakly. "This was my task ... As the Beacon ..."

Saber snorted and then began to howl hysterically in laughter at the absurdity of the situation. If only that bitch Ashyla hadn't played her worthless game, this would all be over. She wouldn't have to stand here and be ridiculed by some lesser being.

"Pathetic insect, drawn to flame," she cackled, turning her glare over to the Beacon. "I always did hate Mariah. She didn't send you. *I* wanted you here, little slug."

SmibSmob's jaw was opened in shock, and the only word he could force out was: "Why?"

"She means to kill you, SmibSmob," Kraalek answered for Saber. "Listen, oh wonderful and beautiful General Umbra. Release the Beacon, his friends, and the Commander into my control, and I'll let you leave. I'm sure neither of us desires a fight."

"Hm, don't we now?"

"Be reasonable. If I wanted to fight, I would have simply attacked you from hiding. I just wanted to negotiate. We will go our way, and you can slink back to whatever dark abyss you crawled from. The entire Flame will know of your treachery, and shall you ever be found within the Light again, there will be consequences."

Kraalek's cards disappeared from his hands, and he reached into one of his many pouches, pulling out his signature brown die. Without breaking eye contact with Saber, he tossed it to the ground beneath her feet, where it landed on one of its identical, blank faces.

"You've lost, isn't that right?"

Saber stared at the man long and hard, not making a single move. Not taking a single breath. Just perfectly still.

The clearing was silent, waiting for the tension to snap. There was not a breeze blowing nor the passing groan of an undead. Fasto could feel his heart thumping in his chest. His bow was aimed directly at Saber's chest. One wrong move and she would feel its sting. SmibSmob looked horrified and stood petrified, his eyes glued to Saber. The Commander had circled over to stand beside Kraalek and was ready for a brawl. While he knew of the man's alcoholic antics, he also knew the man was blazingly brilliant, and so, he would stand by his side in this moment of uncertainty. Finally, there was Margaret, who had flakes of ice swirling around her first. She just wanted to punch something — anything — and if it was the snarky Saber, all the better for it.

Finally, after several minutes of brooding, Saber stomped on the die, flattening it into the ground with her silver boot.

"Fuck it, I'll kill you too."

Without missing a beat, she turned and stared Fasto in the eyes. Just as he was about to release his arrow, he was transfixed by her alluring gaze. He wanted to shoot her, but he found that he simply could not. She was just so beautiful …

"Kill Margaret," Fasto heard her command him. Complying, he turned and pointed his bow at Margaret, his friend.

Next, Saber looked the Commander in the eyes. "Kill Kraalek."

"Yes, misses," he replied before swinging his flaming maul down upon Kraalek's head without hesitation. Shouting in alarm, there was a *pop* of fire beneath Kraalek's feet, and the nimble man darted to the side, just avoiding the fatal blow and scampering to safety. But the Commander pursued.

"Run, SmibSmob!" Kraalek shouted while avoiding his assailant, his metallic deck once more in his hands. "You must survive! For the fate of the Flame!"

SmibSmob nodded and readied himself to flee, but then Saber was in front of him.

"Stay put, little worm," Saber said to the gnome, and, despite his best efforts, he listened. Terror paled his face, but he had no choice. Saber's beauty and words compelled him, and what hope did he have to resist the power of a Demigod? Saber drew her silver longsword, and the black gemstones embedded in its hilt refracted menacingly with the fiery light from the Commander's weapon. The gems were like the eyes of a devil. "I'll deal with you personally."

Margaret turned to face Fasto, her mouth opened in shock. The situation had devolved into madness, and it seemed she was the only sane person remaining.

"Fasto?" she asked, raising her hands helplessly. She knew she couldn't reach him in time. "What are you doing? Why don't you put the bow down? Can't you see we need to kill *her*?"

Fasto snarled, and pulled the bowstring back, glanced at the diagram on his bow, and aimed for the center of Margaret's chest. He knew where he needed to shoot. It felt wrong to aim the bow at her, but it felt even worse to disobey the stunning Saber. She was beautiful. And she was putting her faith and trust in *him*. At that moment, Fasto felt as if he would die for Saber. He didn't want to accept that fact, but he knew it to be true.

So, he aimed his bow at Margaret. Aiming for the kill. It was a sure shot. And Fasto never missed a shot.

"Fucking shit, why? Snap out of it! You're my friend!"

"I — Fasto — am sorry," he said, exhaling his breath to steady his aim.

He released the arrow, and the beam of light streaked towards her heart.

It was a sure shot.

Daniel Whitman

*C*hapter 13

Margaret saw the flash of radiant light as Fasto released his arrow. Time seemed to slow for her as she watched the white arrow streak towards her. She just couldn't understand. Why was he doing this? Why was he fighting *her*? Clearly, that shady-ass Saber was playing tricks with his mind. He did apologize, after all, but apologizing was hardly consolation for killing your friend. It just didn't make any sense. But despite her troubled mind, one thing was clear to her at this moment: she either had to move, or she would die.

And she really wasn't thrilled about the second option.

Tensing every muscle in her body, she twisted her torso, attempting to avoid Fasto's arrow. In that goal, she was hardly successful. But at least she didn't die. Sometimes it's acceptable to fail if it means you can keep living. She almost wanted to laugh at the thought. What a pretentious time to be insightful. Of everything that she could be thinking at this moment, she was dreaming about back-alley philosophy? Wow, she never liked pretentious people. She also never liked being shot at by her friends.

Margaret felt a ripping pain exploding as the arrow pierced her heavy armor and into her shoulder, followed by even more pain as the arrow completely penetrated and whisked off in the distance behind her. It was cold. Or maybe it was hot? Fuck, it did hurt, and she wasn't confused about that. It really fucking hurt. Her arm fell to her side, smacking against her hip with a hollow *thud*. She felt a scream escape her lips, and then she felt the blood ooze down her crippled arm.

The blood. *Her* blood.

Margaret's eyes locked onto the orc standing before her. He was readying another arrow, no doubt this time aiming to finish the job. She saw him pull the string back.

From her peripherals, she saw flashes of orange fire, and heard the frantic sounds of a voice, but she paid them no heed. All that mattered was the orc before her. And her warm, flowing blood.

Her black arm was now pulsing wildly, drumming uncontrollably in her ears. Hell, if there was any consolation prize, it was that the fucker shot the wrong arm. A smile widened over Margaret's face, and all thoughts fled from her mind, leaving but one goal before her:

The bastard orc.

Just before her opponent could release his second arrow, Margaret waved her black arm before her. A thick, cragged wall of ice thrust from the ground under the orc's feet, causing him to wobble and lose balance. Perfect, that was the only opening she needed to kill the miserable creature.

Her arm pulsed, and all she could see was the orc's ugly face with his jutting jaw.

Without missing a beat, Margaret dashed towards her foe, an icy axe forming in her hand. Howling in rage, she swung it down on the unbalanced orc, expecting and hoping for a glorious, gruesome kill, but he was more dexterous than she gave him credit for.

The ugly cretin rolled to the side, just barely avoiding the fatal blow. As he did, he scooped up a fistful of dirt from the ground. It was a trick he had learned from an old Shadowfriend.

Both of Margaret's arms screamed in agony, one from the pain and the other from the demonic fury. She towered over her quarry as he scrambled in the dirt, struggling to avoid her devastating attack. Perfect, she wouldn't miss the next one. Yanking her axe free from the ground, she charged at her assailant, once more eager to taste his blood. But then there was a fistful of dirt in her eyes, and she lost sight of her foe. The dirt filled her nose and her mouth, causing her to cough in an attempt to recover from the dirty trick. Wiping her eyes, she knew she didn't have much time. She saw a glimpse of stained white wood from the corner of her vision.

The bastard orc.

Roaring, Margaret slammed her demonic fist into the ground, feeling the cosmic energy envelop her. She knew what she wanted, but she didn't really care where. As long as it impaled that fucking brute. He needed to bleed so she could lather herself in his thick blood.

Margaret felt the magic succumb to her will and released it into the earth. Dozens of thick, frozen spikes sprouted from the ground, stabbing randomly and wildly at anything near her. She didn't aim. She didn't need to. Why waste precious time trying to meticulously control the location of creation when you could just create spikes everywhere? She felt it was much more flavorful that way.

Margaret heard a soft groan of pain, and the smell of fresh blood filled her nostrils. Not her blood, of course, but *his*. Her vision regained, her eyes locked onto her foe, who was recovering from an unfortunate incident regarding an ice shard in his calf. Margaret licked her lips. Soon, she would taste flesh.

Roaring once more, she charged at the orc, bashing through the icy skewers of her own creation and sending glistening fragments gliding through the air. She didn't care. All she cared about was throttling the person that had dared wound her. There were more orange flashes of light, and more disgruntled words from elsewhere in the battle, but, as before, she paid them no mind. And why would she? Everything else was just so insignificant compared to the frenzy in her body.

Her arm screamed and pulsed and raged and burned. The coward must die.

Just before Margaret could strangle the orc with her black fist, he managed to wiggle free from his impalement. A rush of fresh, red blood released from his leg, coating the nearby ice in a slick coating of crimson paint. That was always Margaret's favorite color. Her fist swung in a wide arc, desperately trying to connect, but the orc slipped backwards, half from the ice under his feet and half from his own reflexes. However, while she didn't manage to successfully hit her target, her fist clipped his white bow, sending it spiraling out of his hands to land somewhere in the forest. Perfect, now she wouldn't need to worry about any more unwanted punctures.

The bastard orc.

Her fist swung again, now aiming at his head, but he managed to duck. Margaret felt his body press up against hers, his hip thrusting into her side, and then she was in the air. She couldn't understand it, but there she was. It was like she was flying. What a remarkable feeling. Such a thrill. She felt her opponent's broad back against her chest, and if her weak arm wasn't so damaged, she would've grappled him on the spot. But, alas, it was useless, and so she was ass-up in the air. Fucking injuries, what good were they, anyway?

Then Margaret felt a *thud* as she slammed into the icy ground. Her breath blasted from her lungs, and she felt a *popping* sensation in her back. Fuck, that couldn't be healthy. Her damaged shoulder screamed in protest as a shard of ice — or maybe it was a rock — dented her armor and dug the hard metal into her mangled flesh. Pain wracked her mind, and she felt a new river of warm, delectable blood flow down her arm and across her body.

Now, she was ravenous. Her demonic arm howled in hunger, eager to tear away at her opponent's flesh.

The orc was standing over her, an arrow in each of his hands. If Maragret knew any better, and if she was in the appropriate mental headspace to care, she would've almost thought that he looked remorseful. But, of course, she was not, and so she didn't notice. Or care. All she wanted was to feel the delightful tearing as her fangs punctured his weak flesh, and the warm gush of thick blood down her throat.

The orc stabbed down at her with one of the arrows, aiming at her face. By pure instinctual reaction, she caught the orc's wrist with her black hand. There, they paused for just a brief moment, locking eyes, but he was too corrupt, and she was too infuriated to make amends. It would be to the death, exactly how she enjoyed it. Margaret felt her arm pulse, and with a surge of unnatural strength, she threw the bitch to the ground next to her, where he collided with the ground. Now it was his turn to have the air blasted from his lungs, and for the ice — or stones — to grind into his back. The orc's head whipped backwards as his body met the dirt, cracking his skull against the earth. A slight hint of blood trickled from the back of his head, filling her nostrils with a reinvigorated stench of iron. It was mouth-wateringly scrumptious. While she was no healer, Margaret knew that the bleeding couldn't be healthy, but she didn't take the time to pity him. Such a shame … for him. For her, it was a gift. He dared draw her blood, so he deserved the worst. Now, it was her time to drink.

The bastard orc.

Without missing a beat, Margaret rolled over, mounting the man and sitting on his stomach to prevent him from escaping. She squeezed her knees, crushing his ribs and latching on firmly. The orc looked up at her, snarling and spitting. What an ugly face.

Margaret's black fist collided with his jaw, cracking his head back into the unforgiving dirt. She felt a splatter of blood across her knuckles as she flattened his nose, and she relished the enjoyment. Her foe tried to bring his hands up to defend himself, but Margaret didn't relent. Summoning an icy gauntlet around her fist, she pummeled him again, tearing the flesh away from his forearms and drawing even more sweet, sweet blood. He deserved to die.

The orc's arms dropped from his face, instead grabbing at her hips and attempting to throw her off. It was truly pathetic. Plus, the first thing she was taught about fighting was to always keep her hands up. She wasn't particularly gifted at listening to that lesson, but it was noteworthy, nonetheless. It was a shame that her opponent didn't have the same training.

Her black arm pulsed with glee.

Her fist collided with his face again, drawing a deep gash across his cheek. One of his eyes was now swollen shut. His bottom lip was torn and ragged. His nose was crumpled and bloody. The orc's hands fell to his sides, and he lay there defenseless, taking her beating with deplorable acceptance. Another punch cracked into his face, twisting his head to the side. Margaret's fist was saturated in a juicy layer of crimson blood now, and she took a brief moment to lick some of the spoils from her palm.

It was delicious.

But still, the fucker just laid there. He wasn't even spitting and snarling anymore. He just looked up at her, a pitiable look in his remaining red eye.

Margaret brought her fist up once more, eager to finish the job. The bastard didn't need either eye, as far as she was concerned. Blood dripped from her hand, landing on the orc's chest in a sporadic pattern of splotchy crimson dots. This truly was a form of art.

But, for some reason, she didn't strike. Her black arm pulsed wildly, urging her to continue feeding. And how she wanted to listen. How she wanted to succumb to the temptations. But there was just something about the way the orc — the not-so-bastardly orc — was looking up at her that caused her to pause. Perhaps it was his eye, full of knowledge, experience, and life. Perhaps it was his jutting jaw, now split and shattered. Or perhaps it was that deep down, she recognized the person beneath her.

And that person was her friend.

Her friend that she was about to kill.

What has she done?

Slowly, deliberately, she brought her arm down. It screamed in protest, but she didn't relent. She wouldn't let her demons force her to do the unspeakable. She closed her eyes, desperately fighting against the urges. She was a monster, of that she had no doubt. But she wasn't so much of a monster that she was ready — or willing — to kill one of her close friends. Not anymore, at least.

The pulsing in her arm quieted, and Margaret felt the frenzied rage lift from her mind. Clarity slowly returned, the red haze dissipating. Maybe she didn't need to be a monster every time. Perhaps she could just be, well, Margaret.

It was a strange thought, and an even stranger time to be having such a dramatic revelation, with the death of the Beacon on the line and all that political fuss, but apparently philosophy didn't wait for the time to be convenient. Wow, she never enjoyed philosophy. Punching was so much simpler — as long as she wasn't punching her dear friend.

Margaret's arm finally quieted, releasing her from its now tenuous grasp. Maybe she was imagining it, but she thought that it even looked somewhat lighter, and somehow thinner.

Now returned from her barbaric rage, she looked down at the battered and beaten face of Fasto beneath her. His breath was short and raspy, but his eye never stopped staring, accusing her of all her foul deeds. Her knees relaxed, releasing him from her clench, and the ice around her fist melted away. What has she done?

With her rage gone, her pain returned like a tsunami, rocking her body. She almost vomited. Her shoulder howled with her every breath and movement, threatening to sink her into unconsciousness. Fuck, where was Nalgene when you needed a quick heal? But she persevered. She would not succumb to her agony, for the sake of her dignity and the sake of those around her. She locked gazes with Fasto, who was still motionless beneath her, except for the gentle rising and falling of his chest.

"Why are you doing this? What are you thinking?" she pleaded softly. "Why are you fighting me? What the fuck is wrong with you?"

Fasto moved his lips, but no sound came forth. Margaret sighed.

"You always said you would 'protect friends', so why the fuck are you trying to kill me? What the fuck did that bitch Saber to do you?"

Fasto opened his mouth again, and this time he spoke. Margaret could tell by his voice that he was in great pain — no thanks to her handiwork. What the fuck was *she* thinking?

"I ... am sorry. Come close, I must tell you something ..."

Obliging, Margaret leaned her head close to listen to what he had to say. Maybe he was finally snapping out of it?

Fasto's fist came cracking into the side of her jaw, whipping her head to the side. She felt the inside of her cheek gash against her sharp teeth, and a spray of blood escaped her lips. That fucking lying bastard orc. Immediately, the pulsing in her arm returned, begging and pleading her to fall victim to its cravings once more, but she resisted. *Not* against her friend.

She supposed that answered her question. Fasto was not snapping out of anything.

Beneath her, he began to squirm, twisting and biting and scratching and snarling. Thankfully, her armor defended her against the worst of it, but that isn't what concerned her. A frenzied look burned deep in his wild, bloody eye. He actually was trying to kill her, and she knew he would stop at nothing until the task was complete.

How did it come to this? What the fuck was Saber doing to him?

Behind her, the battle against the Demigod raged on. SmibSmob was backed against a tree, paralyzed by both fear and the command of Saber. In front of him, a desperate protector of the last hope of the Flame, was Kraalek, doing his best to fend off both Saber and the Commander.

The Commander rushed in, his maul swinging for Kraalek's chest. The General didn't move, simply holding his stance and bracing himself. As the mighty weapon connected, instead of crumpling his chest, it went *through* Kraalek as his body became flickering fire, leaving him quite unscathed. The General flicked his wrist, and a metal card spiraled towards the Commander's calf, drawing a wicked slash and dropping him to his knee. It would have to do, for now.

But then, there was also Saber. The Demigod followed behind the Commander, a sadistic smile on her face. A card appeared in Kraalek's hand, and he moved to throw it at her, but, for some reason, for just a moment, he hesitated. A flash of sorrow filled his eyes.

In that moment of hesitation, the Commander reached out with his hand, grabbing Kraalek by the ankle and yanking him off balance. The General stumbled, caught off guard by the attack, before regaining focus and transforming his leg into flame. The Commander, unable to hold onto the formless fire, rose to his feet, preparing his weapon once more.

Then, Saber was there, her sword arcing in for the General's chest. His eyes widened, and there was a *pop* of flame under his feet, launching him sideways and out of range of the Demigod's attack. More cards appeared in his hands, and he flicked them at Saber, this time immune to the lapse of hesitation.

But Saber's sword waved this way and that, deflecting each and every card the General threw her way. She didn't survive this long and *not* become proficient in the blade. While she certainly wasn't the strongest swordsman out of the Demigods of old, her skill was more than proficient for this measly, drunkard General.

"Kill the Beacon," Saber ordered the Commander, taking advantage of the opening. Nodding his head, the Commander charged at the Beacon, his maul high above his head.

"Fuck," Kraalek cursed, watching Ecker approach the defenseless SmibSmob. A singular card appeared in his hand, and it began to glow red with heat.

Meanwhile, Margaret was still struggling to reason with Fasto. She pinned his arms with her legs, but still he squirmed, bit, and spat at her, desperately trying for her life. She heard Saber's words and braved a quick look behind her. The sight wasn't pretty, that was for sure. Three against two, they were simply outmatched. Well, technically it was three on three, but SmibSmob wasn't much help shitting his pants by that tree. So much for being the savior of the Light or whatever the prophecy everyone kept yammering about said. Why didn't Nalgene, Ro, Andromeda, or literally anyone else tag along with them on this side-quest?

Margaret felt Fasto begin to wiggle free from her pin, and so she returned her focus to him. She would just need faith that Kraalek — the slimy drunkard himself — could survive and defend for a few more minutes. As for Fasto, well, she needed to remove him from the fight. One of his arms broke free, and he swatted at her face once more, bruising her cheek and drawing more blood. She really needed to work on her blocking. Her arm pulsed, but she refused to succumb to it. Not now. She didn't need it.

Margaret clamped her hand on Fasto's neck, squeezing the air from his neck. He squirmed and kicked and thrashed and punched, but she didn't relent. She needed to remove him from the fight, and, aside from killing him, she just didn't see any other option. His free hand grabbed at her wrist, desperately attempting to pry it free. And he almost succeeded, but, before he could, she created a thin barrier of ice around her demonic arm, making it impossible for Fasto to have sufficient grip to pull her away.

A Resurgence of Hope

Fasto's eye began to bulge from the lack of oxygen, and his face grew a sickly shade of purple. He wheezed, hacking up more blood that coated her icy hand. But his struggle grew weaker, and his punches less frequent. She needed to remove him from the fight, and to do that, she needed to remove the fight from him.

As Margaret choked out Fasto, she once more looked back at Kraalek, hoping and praying that he was still alive. Her hopes didn't last for more than a few heartbeats.

Kraalek tossed the glowing card onto the ground in front of the Commander. As it hit the ground, the dead grass around it smoked and withered away from the heat. Then, the card began to billow with flames, sending sparks arcing through the air like a great firework. The flames took shape, condensing into the form of a great animal. Four, bulging legs manifesting in the fire, followed by a muscular and sleek back. There was a long tail tipped with a tuft of fiery fur, and finally, a majestic mane crowning the savage head of a lion. Unleashing a fiery — yet somehow guttural — roar, the lion pounced upon the Commander, dragging him to the ground and searing his skin from the heat.

Somewhat satisfied, the General turned back to Saber, who was quickly closing the distance. He brought his hand up, and a pillar of fire erupted beneath her feet, engulfing the canopies of the surrounding trees. But the Demigod was too quick, and rolled to the side, just managing to avoid incineration. She didn't survive this long by being slow, either.

The Commander, recovering from the initial surprise of being tackled by a lion formed by fire, rose to his feet and swung his maul, matching the animal blow for blow and expertly defending himself. Of course, he knew of Kraalek's ability — his so-called "Heart of the Cards", as the General named it — and he knew that a lion was quite tame compared to what other creative creatures the General could manifest. But to manifest anything larger could bring danger to the cowering Beacon, and so, the General was handicapped with what he could summon. All the better for the Commander, and for Saber.

The lion bit at the Commander, but with a flash of fire under his boots he darted to the side, avoiding the attack. Just for the hell of it, he swung down with his maul on the animal's back. As expected, the result was less than exceptional, and the lion wasn't harmed at all — fire wasn't known to be susceptible to blunt attacks, after all. But Ecker didn't mind, he knew he couldn't actually kill the beast. All he had to do was kill the Beacon. So, he rushed past the lion, bringing his hand before him and preparing to launch a fireball upon the pathetic gnome.

Kraalek also readied his hands, preparing to blast Saber with a devastating fireball of his own. A conflux of flame appeared in his palms, flickering with destructive anticipation. He wished he could unleash more potent magic, but the collateral damage would most certainly either injure SmibSmob or cause a league-wide forest fire, and that was just not a risk he was willing to take. At least not now. The Beacon had to survive. And so, he was quite limited in his scope. The smaller spells were still quite dangerous, of course, but much less … flashy than what he was used to. If only he could draw Saber and the Commander away from the Beacon, then he would have a chance to obliterate them both, but alas, he was having no such luck. Instead, he just had to defeat Saber while handicapped.

As the Demigod appeared from behind the tree she was using for cover, Kraalek raised his hands to release his spell, but as his eyes fell upon Saber — or rather his dead wife that Saber was impersonating — he hesitated once more. Shit, the Demigod had no shortage of foul tricks. Of course, he knew it wasn't actually his dead wife, but to bring himself to cause her harm … the amount of drinking that would ensue in order for him to forgive himself might kill him instead.

The flaming lion pounced on the Commander, bringing him to the ground and distracting him from the Beacon. Of course, SmibSmob made no move to defend himself, simply sitting there with wide eyes of fear, but that was why Kraalek needed to defend him so valiantly. The Commander felt his skin blister and bubble under the heat of the lion. He felt his eyes dry and throat parch, and he knew he had to escape. With another *pop*, he forced himself out from under the animal and to his feet. His body howled in pain, but the order in his mind was still crystal clear: "kill the Beacon." And to do that, he had to get past this damn lion. His maul appeared before him, and he approached the flaming beast. Perhaps he could kill it. So, ignoring his wounds, he engaged with the beast.

In Kraalek's moment of hesitation, Saber closed the distance, her sword swinging. Startled, Kraalek extinguished his fireball, darted back, and instead opted to send a humble firebolt at the Demigod. Of course, she avoided it effortlessly.

"What's wrong, Kraalek?" Saber taunted, running at Kraalek. "And here I thought you were supposed to be the most powerful spellcaster in the Flame."

Kraalek flicked some cards her way — which she also deflected — but otherwise made no verbal response. He knew she was trying to get into his head, and in a way, it was working. But to banter mid-battle would bring nothing but distractions, and he needed all the focus he could muster to maintain his flaming lion while defending both himself and the Beacon from Saber.

The Demigod was now too close. It would be impossible to avoid all of her attacks. Damn, was she frustratingly quick. Frantically, Kraalek shoved one of his hands into a pouch, digging for something to use. Saber reached out for him with her free hand, and he tried to dash away, but she caught a hold of his arm at the last second. Stumbling, he quickly turned his body to flame, causing her hand to pass right through him, before successfully darting several strides away.

Kraalek braved a quick glance at the Commander, who was still locked in battle against the lion, then over to Margaret, who was still choking out Fasto, and then over to the Beacon, who hadn't moved from that lone tree. Kraalek was lucky enough to have grabbed the gnome and placed him by the tree at the beginning of the skirmish, but now it was more of a liability than anything. He would need to finish things quickly. He gave up on his search through his pouches and instead decided that more cards would be best. One appeared between his fingers. If only he had more time to prepare for this encounter — he really was betting on a peaceful negotiation — and if only he knew the precise capabilities of Saber. Also, it didn't help that he left his more experimental gemstones in his lab. Damn, maybe he should stop drinking.

During Kraalek's quick surveillance of the battlefield, Saber once more closed the distance. She was frustratingly quick, after all.

"Getting distracted, darling?" she teased.

Alarmed, Kraalek whipped his head back and began to dash away. But as he did, he hesitated, stumbling on the ground, and once again his eyes grew wide with sorrow.

"Delilah?"

Saber's sword thrusted for his gut, and Kraalek immediately knew his error. How many times would he succumb to that same dirty trick? His wife was *dead*.

But what was the danger? It was just a sword, after all, and he would simply turn his body to flame, rendering the attack useless. Of course, he would rather keep dodging, as immolating his body required great concentration, and he was already concentrating on maintaining the flaming lion, but he was never as quick as Sylven — and certainly not as speedy as the holy-man Don himself. So, self-immolation would have to do.

As Saber's sword plunged towards Kraalek's gut, his body turned to flames in anticipation, expecting a harmless attack. Saber smirked. It was such a shame he couldn't truly comprehend what he was facing. Miserable men and their miserable egos always thought of themselves as superior. It was their great undoing, and it was why Saber took such great pleasure in their deaths.

A Resurgence of Hope

The sword harmlessly penetrated Kraalek, passing through the flames that were his stomach. But, despite his incorporeal form, the General's eyes widened, and he screamed in pain, although he wasn't quite sure why.

While Kraalek's body wasn't physically harmed due to his fiery body, the weapon cut through so much more than just flesh and bone. A wrenching tear ripped through his soul as Saber's sword passed through him. It felt as if his very heartstrings were being severed by the blade, and as if his every hope and dream was being smothered by an overwhelming sorrow. As he screamed, he lost concentration on both his immolation and his fiery lion. His physical body reformed around the blade, and this time it *was* physically cutting through his flesh and bone. Blood oozed from his stomach as Saber retracted the weapon, and she lorded over the wounded General. Oh, for ten years she imagined what this gangly man's screams would sound like, and it was so much more beautiful than she anticipated.

Margaret heard the General's scream and saw him fall to his knees, and she knew her time was up. She growled in frustration. Recently, at the Shadowfront with the winged monster and now here, with Saber, she felt as if she was just a simple bystander, destined to stand and watch as the great Generals battled against the greatest agents of the Shadow. First with Roark and now with Kraalek, what use was she, sitting atop her friend and choking him out? It was exceedingly annoying, and she knew she had to make a change. She was destined to fight, not to watch, and so that was exactly what she was going to do.

Beneath her, Fasto had finally stopped struggling, so she shot to her feet, not bothering to ensure that he was actually unconscious. She didn't have time to check. Kraalek needed her help, and she could watch no more. Saber was just twenty lunges away, and Margaret began to run directly at her. The Demigod noticed her approach and gave a courteous smile, flicking the blood from her silver sword. Margaret didn't slow. She would have preferred it if Saber didn't notice her charge, but what difference would it have made? Stealth was for bitches, anyway.

Kraalek gasped for breath, fighting against the pain in his stomach. He had to persevere for the sake of the Beacon. The Beacon! He whipped his head around to see the Commander not two strides from SmibSmob, his flaming maul held high above his head. The fiery lion had dissipated, and so, the Commander was free to complete the task bestowed upon him by the most beautiful and alluring Saber.

Kraalek would only have one shot, and he couldn't afford to miss. He supposed he would have to ask for pardon from Agmund later. His wrist flicked, sending the metallic card in his hand whistling through the air, spinning edge over edge. It curved this way and that as it went, but Kraalek's aim was true.

A victorious roar escaped the Commander's mouth, but it was cut short as Kraalek's card severed his throat. Immediately, blood began to fountain from his neck and down his throat, filling his lungs. The Beacon was so close, yet he couldn't finish Saber's orders. He knew that she would be disappointed, and he was ashamed of that. Ecker's vision went hazy then black, and he felt himself stumble, only to land hard on the ground. He coughed and wheezed, causing bubbles of blood to pop in his mouth and on his slit throat. His maul fell from his hands, extinguished. The last thought he had before death was of the most gorgeous Saber.

As Kraalek released the card, he grabbed an orange gemstone from one of his pouches. At least he always knew where he kept his stash of these. He needed to escape, to somehow gather reinforcements before Saber killed the Beacon. He didn't know how or where, but it was worth a shot. He wouldn't stop fighting, not now. He felt his connection to the gemstone, manipulating the very cosmic energy and space around him to teleport him far from the forest.

Saber swatted the gemstone from his hands, sending it tumbling into the twisted bracken of the forest. Then her sword flashed, creating another gash — both physically, spiritually, and emotionally — on the General. Next, just for the sheer pleasure of it, she kicked him in the face and took great glee in watching his limp body plummet to the ground. As she did, she saw the dead body of the Commander in front of the Beacon. Such a shame, but she most certainly wouldn't mourn that loss.

Margaret watched Kraalek fall. Of two things Margaret was certain: this Saber was brutal and was an absolute bitch. Only several seconds had passed, and she was now only five leaps from that whore of a woman Saber. A spear of ice appeared in her hand, and with a growl, she hurled it at the Demigod, hoping to impale the slut directly through the chest. That was where Fasto was supposed to shoot a Mistress, so perhaps it would also do the trick for a Demigod.

Saber's eyes locked back on Margaret, and with barely any effort, she avoided the projectile. She even had the gall to laugh at her. No matter, Margaret preferred to do things close up. Closing the remaining distance, she summoned another frosty axe in her hand and swung it down at Saber. The Demigod nimbly stepped to the side, avoiding the blow, and so Margaret swung again, this time horizontally. Saber's sword flashed, severing the frozen weapon.

Fucking shit. No matter, Margaret preferred to do things hand-to-hand.

Margaret swung her black first in a wicked hook, hoping to shatter Saber's jaw and annihilate that condescending smirk of hers. The Demigod didn't even bother to avoid it this time, and so Margaret knew it would be a direct hit.

But then, Saber's hand shot up, *catching* Margaret's punch and holding her motionless as surely as if she had attempted to punch an iron wall. Holy shit, was this bastard woman strong. Why did Demigods have to be so fucking powerful? Margaret felt the bones in her hand grind as Saber squeezed her hand, and the pulsing thrummed to life. This time, perhaps, she would succumb to the demonic urges. Saber most definitely was not her friend.

But before Margaret could go berserk, Saber slashed her stomach with her sword, drawing a thick line of blood. Margaret felt the physical pain, but it was nothing compared to the cut in her soul. It was numbing, blazing, freezing, and all sorts of other "-ings", and, most importantly, it fucking *hurt*. The closest comparison she could make would be the freezing aura of the winged abomination or a dreadknight, but this was much more concentrated and direct. She wanted to unleash the demonic powers of her arm, but, suddenly, she just felt so disconnected from it. A barbaric battle cry escaped her mouth, and she locked eyes on the Demigod.

No matter, Margaret would do things the old-fashioned way.

Margaret began to swing wildly with her black fist, hoping and praying to anybody or anything that was listening that one of her strikes would connect. But none of them did. Shit, if only her other arm wasn't out of commission. She felt the blood oozing down her shoulder and now oozing from the fresh wound on her stomach. Her jaw was sore from Fasto's punches, but she didn't stop screaming or fighting. She couldn't watch any longer.

Another punch, and Saber deftly stepped to the side.

Another swing, and Saber effortlessly deflected it with her hand.

For Margaret, it was unbearably frustrating. For Saber, it was most exhilarating playing with her food.

Another strike, and this time Saber didn't even bother to avoid or block it. However, just as Margaret was swinging in, suddenly it wasn't Saber in front of her, but *Ro*.

Shocked, Margaret pulled her punch, not wanting to injure another friend today. Ro? Why Ro? What the hell was he doing here? And where was … oh shit. Before her eyes, Ro disappeared, leaving only a cackling Saber in his place.

Before Margaret could fully comprehend what had transpired, she felt Saber's sword enter her gut. There was more raw physical pain coupled with all the "-ing" pains, and it drove her to her knees. Fucking bitch motherfucker rat-ass Demigod. The pulsing raged, but it was so distant and quiet. Even if she wanted to, she just couldn't bring herself to join in its foreboding melody.

Margaret looked up at Saber, hatred in her eyes. Saber looked down at her victim, ecstatic at the results. Not only would the Beacon die today, but also one of the Commanders, one of the Generals, *and* two of the gnome's friends? All of her problems were truly resolving themselves in the most beautiful and enjoyable ways. It was such a shame that Ashyla was too blind to see how easily everything could be resolved. Oh well, she didn't need the Goddess anymore. Perhaps, when they released Ashyla, she would finally be grateful for everything Saber had accomplished. For everything she had secured. For everything she had conquered.

Margaret spat at Saber and felt some sense of satisfaction in watching the Demigod wipe her spittle from her face. If only it was her fist on the woman's face. She brought one leg up, preparing to bring herself to her feet, but before she could, two muscular arms wrapped around her body, pulling her down to the muck in defeat. She really should have double checked if Fasto was unconscious.

Fasto wrapped his arms around her and squeezed, wracking her body with furious pain. She tried to roll, tried to escape, but he was too strong.

"Fasto, what the fuck is wrong with you?" she howled, vainly trying to release him from Saber's spell. Of course, it was futile. "Let me go, you fucking moron! It's her we need to kill!"

Saber stepped forward and placed her silver boot on Margaret's chest.

"Oh, isn't he just a glorious little mutt?" she taunted, aiming her sword at Margaret's chest.

"What the fuck did you do to him?"

"Me?" Saber gasped, feigning innocence. "I did nothing but suggest a different course of action for him. Don't blame the ugly fellow, it's not his fault he was weak enough to listen."

Margaret whipped her head back, desperately trying to escape Fasto's grip, but she was unsuccessful.

"Fasto, get the fuck off of me!"

Margaret focused on her arm, imagining what sort of icy creation would save her from this mess. She felt the universal energy condense and cool around her, but then Saber stabbed her black shoulder with her sword, and, coupled with the freezing and blazing and numbing pains, she felt her connection with the cosmic energy sever. Her demonic arm went limp, and the pulsing stopped, leaving nothing but a hopeless silence in its wake. There was no more ice, no more power, and no more hope.

Margaret's scream was a string of unintelligible curses and sounds.

"That wasn't very polite," Saber said, turning away and walking towards Kraalek, who was now squirming on the ground in an attempt to stand. "Now, why don't you be a good mutt like your friend and shut the fuck up to watch my victory. I'm sure you would enjoy the spectacle of me relieving the Beacon of his miserable intestines."

"FUCK YOU!" Margaret howled at Saber's back and spit once more. Her phlegm landed short, much to her frustration. She was still struggling and fighting and kicking and twisting, but Fasto was too strong, and she was much too injured for it to do any good.

Saber paused and turned back.

"Fasto, you fucking rat, I believe I told you to kill her."

"Yes, you're right. I — Fasto — will kill her."

"Aren't you just delightfully obedient?"

Margaret felt one of Fasto's arms press against her throat and felt the other one bracing the back of her head. His muscles tensed as he began to squeeze, slowly and painfully suffocating her. The pressure on her windpipe was immense, and she began to cough uncontrollably, sending a rain of red flecks into the still air. She tried to tuck her chin in a last attempt to save herself, but Fasto grabbed her hair and forced her head back, revealing her vulnerable throat.

Her kicking grew weaker and less frequent, and soon she didn't even have the strength to struggle. She couldn't move her arms, couldn't bite him, and couldn't stop her death. It was strange, knowing that she was soon to die, and knowing that she could do nothing else to stop it. All the fighting in the world didn't matter — sometimes the opponent was just too powerful.

"Fasto, please ..." she croaked, hoping that maybe this time he would finally snap out of it and listen. He didn't.

The pressure in Margaret's head grew to unbearable levels as her blood was trapped in her brain. She felt herself grow dizzy, and her vision began to flicker black. As unconsciousness grabbed her, the last thing she saw was Saber dragging a limp Kraalek by the hair over towards SmibSmob, who was still cowering against a tree.

"Fasto ..."

And all went silent and black.

Chapter 14

Time seemed like a blur for SmibSmob. The events of the battle merged together into a single macabre charade of blood, fire, and death. He watched Kraalek get stabbed and kicked in the face. He watched Margaret get strangled by Fasto. He watched as Commander Ecker battled a fiery lion before his ultimate doom. It was one continuous and sickening mirage. It had to be. This couldn't be happening. Yet he knew it was.

So much for being the hero Mariah had told him he would be. Although from what Saber had said, maybe it wasn't even really Mariah that urged him on this ridiculous quest.

SmibSmob's back was still against the tree where Kraalek had placed him at the beginning of the battle, and he was unable to move, escape, or even aid the efforts of his friends. Try as he might — and damn it he did try — he just couldn't bring himself to disobey the command of that beautiful Saber.

Stay put, little worm.

In his heart, he knew that she was somehow controlling his actions. Hell, at that moment, she wasn't even beautiful anymore.

But his mind and body argued otherwise, and so, he sat there, like a little worm, staying put and watching the world unravel around him. It was one thing knowing you were about to die, it was another thing entirely to watch it coming and know you could do nothing to stop it. So much for being the Beacon, whatever that was worth.

Now, he just wished that he could see his brother one last time before the end.

As the events of the battle concluded, SmibSmob blankly stared at the corpse of the Commander lying just out of reach, face down in a pool of thick blood. That man was trying to kill him, he kept telling himself, but it didn't make him feel any better about it. Just fifteen minutes ago they were walking through the woods as comrades and allies and now, the man was murdered. By Kraalek. The General killed the Commander. Of course, SmibSmob knew it was to protect him, but it was still murder, nonetheless. Murder of another living soldier. The gnome felt the nausea bubble in his stomach, and he belched on the dead grass beside him.

"Aw, feeling sick, are we? And here I thought the Beacon would be of a stronger stomach."

SmibSmob glanced up, snapping out of his haze, to see Saber strutting towards him, dragging a coughing Kraalek by the hair behind her. Her hideously tantalizing thighs glistened with sweat, and her rosy lips seemed so scrumptious as she berated him. Maybe he was truly a worm. And a despicable one, at that. What hero would sit and do nothing but snivel and cower while others tried to protect him? He knew his brother wouldn't. Damn, he really wished he could be with Nalgene right now.

"I wish I could've killed you two-hundred years ago, maggot," Saber taunted, her seductive eyes boring holes into SmibSmob. He hated that he enjoyed her gaze. He reckoned that something seriously ill was happening in his brain.

"But ... I don't mean to be the obvious one, but I'm not that old."

Saber laughed a most sadistically melodious chortle, which didn't aid the sinking feeling in his chest, or give clarity to his confusion. However, after everything strange that he had been told by Mariah and Kraalek, as well as his puzzling lack of memories, he wasn't so quick to dismiss her statement. Perhaps she really did try to kill him that long ago. Maybe Nalgene would know.

How he missed his brother right now. He wished he had taken the opportunity to spend time with him those nights in Firelight, because, right now, he didn't think he would ever spend a night with him again.

Saber dropped Kraalek disgracefully on the ground, then kneeled down beside him and grabbed his bloody head with both hands.

"Be a good boy and watch me play with my toy," she told the General, locking eyes with him. Slowly, he began to nod in agreement.

"Yes, Delilah ..." he mumbled softly.

Satisfied, Saber released him, stood, and turned back to SmibSmob. The General remained kneeled on the ground, staring absentmindedly at the gnome, not making a single move to aid his proclaimed Beacon. It was too easy with these weak and insignificant people.

SmibSmob screamed and berated himself in his thoughts, urging himself to run. Any ideas of using his powers to retaliate against the woman were far dismissed. He knew he was pathetic and weak. Mariah had betrayed him. But his eyes were locked on the gorgeous Saber, and so, his body didn't respond to his pleas to flee.

"Are you going to kill me now?" he asked, unable to keep the solemn undertone of defeat from his voice.

Saber paused and feigned to ponder it for a moment, tapping her finger on those voluptuous lips.

"Don't you sound just absolutely fucking miserable."

To SmibSmob, that was music to his ears. Yes, there was something seriously ill with his mind at the moment, and it was all due to that woman — no, that Demigod — in front of him.

"No, I won't kill you quite yet," Saber continued. "After all my efforts, it would be such a disappointment to kill you like this. What's the joy in just slaughtering a sick puppy? Best let it imagine that it could survive, first."

SmibSmob felt even smaller than he did when standing before the gargantuan Agmund. His eyes flickered to her boots, and he imagined getting squished under those silver heels. Why did he take masochistic pleasure at the thought?

Saber's eyes locked onto his, and he found that he couldn't look away. He was lost in those swirling, blue depths. The same way he was lost when she ordered him to stay put like a little worm.

"Fight me, you disgusting Beacon, and prove to everyone else that you're just another fucking fraud in a long line of hopeless pretenders."

Something stirred within SmibSmob, and suddenly, despite his survival instinct pleading otherwise, he no longer wished to flee the battle. Nay, he itched to *fight*. His beautifully menacing Saber had ordered it so, and so he would stop at nothing to follow through with that command. Nothing except his soon to come death.

Shakily, SmibSmob rose to his feet, studying Saber up and down her shapely body. From her smooth legs to her flowing hair to her plump lips ... No! He was the Beacon. He couldn't allow these deranged distractions. He wasn't fighting because she told him to, he was fighting because he wanted to. He wanted to burn the Shadow because of what it put him — and his brother — through. And now it was painfully obvious to him that Saber was with the Shadow.

She needed to feel the burn.

Snarling, SmibSmob brought his hands before him, his palms facing the approaching Saber.

"Remarkable. You look awfully menacing."

SmibSmob ignored the taunt and closed his eyes. He knew what he needed. It was the same thing as he had attempted to cast upon the chair in Kraalek's basement: a fireball. He closed his eyes, mentally picturing the bead of flame in his palm, and urged the cosmic energy to bend to his will. It was true, he never succeeded in casting the spell during his self-imposed practice. But that was then, and this was now. Now, the lives of the General and his friends depended on his abilities. Now, he had truly internalized himself as the Beacon. No, Mariah *had* sent him here for a reason, he had to believe it. And this must have been the reason. To burn the entire fucking world of Shadow to the ground.

SmibSmob felt the now-familiar connection to his Inner Fire and felt the universal strands of magic warp to his will. The picture of the fireball glowed bright in his mind, and his palms grew warm and sweaty. This was it! Damn what Saber said, it was her that would be dying this day.

The conflux of blazing energy was ready.

Screaming, SmibSmob opened his eyes and cast the roaring fireball at Saber, expecting and hoping for a quick, yet still painful, incineration. Damn the Demigod and her wicked ways, he was fighting for himself now.

But there was no roaring fireball. Only a feeble spark that fizzled away after traveling a mere finger's-width from his hand. SmibSmob felt the weight of failure buckle his knees and hollow his stomach. He was no more use in a fight than a mote of dust. He had failed once again as the Beacon and as a friend.

Then, Saber was there, towering over him like a ravenous wolf over an injured rabbit. She swung her arm, brutally backhanding the gnome across the face and sending him spinning to the ground. Yes, she was going to enjoy this, even more so than she did with that hag Mariah.

"You're fucking pathetic."

SmibSmob coughed away the blood flecking in his mouth and scrambled away from the terrifyingly stunning Saber. He was pathetic. He was a failure.

An image of Nalgene flashed through his mind.

No! He would still fight! If there was even a shred of a sliver of hope to see his brother again to make amends, he would stop at nothing to seize it. Fuck being the Beacon, he needed to be a brother right now. He felt a burning rage in his stomach, and he turned to glare at Saber, who was calmly walking towards him.

She needed to feel the burn.

"Hmm, that's quite the terrifying look," she cackled. "I'm almost scared. Are you finally going to make this enjoyable, you fucking fraud of a hero?"

SmibSmob said nothing in reply but rose to his feet and squared his shoulders towards her. If he didn't have the strength to cast a fiery spell at her, perhaps he could just create one *on* her instead. Just like he did with those glasses of Spitfire by creating the spark inside them. Only this time, the spark would need to be much bigger.

He closed his eyes again, digging deeper and deeper for his Inner Fire. He could feel it, and he knew it was there, but he needed to truly tap into its fiery potential. He imagined Saber engulfed in a ball of fire. For some sick reason, the image was beautiful to him. This would be for his allies. This would be for the Commander. This would be for Fasto and Margaret. This would be for Kraalek. This would be for Nalgene.

He felt the burn. He felt the rage. He felt the hate. This *had* to be it. She *needed* to feel the burn. Little worm he would be no more.

The cosmic energy surrounded him, flowing through him and towards Saber. He opened his eyes, once more unleashing a most furious howl. The magic obeyed his command, coagulating into a singular, screaming-hot sphere of fire to engulf the Demigod. SmibSmob knew the heat would sear the flesh from her bones.

SmibSmob knew the fire would torch her remains to nothing but black ash. And he was glad for it. Hell, he was ecstatic for it. This would be Saber's doom.

Except there was no screaming-hot sphere of fire. Only a paltry spark that appeared on her tunic, merely singing several strands of the fabric before she casually brushed it off of herself, sending it tumbling into the dirt where it quickly dissipated.

SmibSmob felt as if he were just stabbed in the gut. He wanted to puke again. What was the point of having all of this rage and hatred if it couldn't manifest itself into anything more dangerous than a blade of grass in the wind? What was the point of having all of this resolve about fighting for his allies, his friends, and his brother if it didn't carry through to the moments when it mattered most?

Saber was in front of him again, gloating over his dejected self. She grabbed his face with her hand, lifting him into the air to stare at him directly in his eyes. He squirmed and kicked and grabbed at her fingers, but she didn't budge.

"Of all the Beacons that I've killed, you are, by far, the most worthless fucking one of them all."

With that, Saber threw him into a nearby tree. SmibSmob hit the tree horizontally, his spine wrapping around the trunk with a sickening *crack* of bones. His body ignited with pain, and his breath was blasted from his lungs. Coughing, wheezing, and crying, he fell to the cold, unforgiving earth, kicking up a cloud of gray dust. Was this what it was like to die?

SmibSmob heard the gentle *thumps* of Saber's boots as she approached him. He heard the march of death.

Slowly, painfully, he looked up to see his entrancing abuser. It was too late, he didn't have time to crawl away, she was already atop him. She held out her sword, placing its blade under his chin, and used it to lift his head higher, exposing his pale neck. For the last moments of life, he wouldn't forget that gleefully infernal look in Saber's eyes.

Her sword flashed. This was to be his death. His neck would soon look like Commander Ecker's: severed, bloody, and torn.

Except Saber didn't slash his throat. Instead, she made two deliberate cuts across his chest in the shape of a cross, identical to what she had done to Mariah and Ashyla. It was the symbol of the Beacon. It was the symbol of his doom.

SmibSmob gasped in pain and felt the blood begin to bubble beneath his sliced cloak. He moved his hand to stanch the flow, but Saber's sword flashed again, creating a deep gash across the back of his hands and nearly severing his fingers. Another mewl of pain escaped his lips.

"Your piteous cries are so delectable."

Then, Saber chambered her leg and kicked him square across the face, sending him spinning to the ground. SmibSmob felt a *crunch* in his mouth, and spat a broken tooth onto the ground, along with an unhealthy spray of blood. That ravishing woman was certainly enjoying her time with him. He wanted to cry. He wanted to quit. He wanted to escape.

Most of all, he wanted to see his brother.

But he could do none of those things now. Saber's words echoed in his mind, forcing him to continue the tortuous ordeal:

Fight me, you disgusting Beacon.

And so, despite every nerve in his body protesting against it, he had no choice but to continue fighting. Her words were seduction. Her words were power. And he was just another victim in the long line of broken souls.

Growling, SmibSmob planted his hands on the ground and pushed himself up onto his shaky feet. Now standing, he glared at the bitch, imagining what her curvaceous body would look like engulfed in a swathe of searing flames.

He closed his eyes, felt the connection with his Inner Fire, summoned the cosmic energy of creation, and once more unleashed it upon the approaching Demigod.

Once more, there was nothing more than a feeble, harmless spark.

Once more, Saber cackled and mocked him, sinking his soul and spirit ever lower into the dark abyss.

Her sword flashed, slicing his unbruised cheek and drawing a line of red. Impotently, he swung his fists at her in a desperate attempt at retaliation. The first several strikes, she simply avoided. But after that, having grown tired of watching his doddering swats, Saber caught his wrist.

How her fingers squeezed, pressing into his flesh like a steel vice. SmibSmob squirmed and kicked and thrashed as best he could, but his best was no more dangerous than a flailing fish caught out of water.

Smiling that seductively evil smirk, Saber twisted her hand, snapping SmibSmob's wrist. The *crunching* and grinding sound of his bones was unmistakable, and the agony was unparalleled. At this point, SmibSmob couldn't even register the scream that escaped his mouth.

For the first time since Mariah had cured him, SmibSmob wished he still had his shadowy powers. With them, he knew he would be able to hold equal footing against the Demigod — or at least that is what he thought. With them, he could simply absorb the life from his surroundings to rejuvenate himself and mend his wounds. But now, broken and alone, he was forced to endure.

Still holding the worthless gnome, Saber stabbed her sword through his foot, impaling it onto the ground. Another soundless cry rang out from the Beacon's mouth, and he instinctively bent down to grab his injured foot with his good hand. As he did, she let go of his arm and thrust a knee into his face, shattering his nose and sending him sprawling backwards. As he fell, his foot slipped back with him, pulling itself through the blade of the sword and slicing itself cleanly in half between the toes. Saber relished the amount of blood pooling the ground.

This was so much more enjoyable than what she did with Mariah.

SmibSmob lay on the ground, quivering in terror. Everything hurt so much that he could feel no more pain. His body was numb, and he was slowly descending into shock. Why wouldn't she just kill him? He wished she did, for the sake of ending his misery. Everything was a lie. He was no hero. He was no Beacon. He was just another shitty gnome under the boot of a shittier world. At this point, he was ready to impale himself on Saber's sword just to be merciful to himself.

But of course, he did not. If he did, then all hope of seeing his friends or his brother again would vanish. If he did, he would disobey Saber's orders, and his mind, body, and soul wouldn't permit that. Her magic was simply too strong. Therefore, against all odds, he did as he was bidden, like the good little mutt that he was, and stood once more to fight.

Another surge of cosmic energy, another lamentable spark.

Another kick to his gut, keeling him over and emptying the contents of his stomach. His throat burned from the acid of his bile, and his eyes grew hazy and black. Fuck whatever magical charm Saber had placed on him, he knew his body wouldn't be able to handle much more torment. He had physical limits, and she had already pushed him way beyond the breaking point.

Saber chuckled at how quickly the gnome — the Beacon of prophecy — had succumbed to despair. At least Mariah had resisted for longer.

SmibSmob felt Saber clench his throat, lifting him into the air. His gaze locked onto her sapphire eyes, and he whimpered. He didn't even bother struggling to escape her grasp.

"What's wrong, pathetic slug? Done fighting already?"

SmibSmob didn't move, but his whimpering didn't cease.

"Poor baby. Cry for me now."

And so, he did. He didn't want to — oh, how he didn't want to — but his body was beyond his control. Therefore, despite his thoughts protesting vehemently — at this point his protests weren't very resolute — he was forced to give Saber the satisfaction of watching him break. He felt the tears well up in his eyes and spill down his face. He felt the phlegm choke up his throat.

"Good boy. If only the Flame could see you now, so broken and pitiful. Perhaps I'll send them your shattered body as a parting gift just so they could see how fucking misguided their faith in you was."

SmibSmob felt the snot running down his broken nose and the drool oozing from his cracked lips, coating Saber's delicate hand. This, she did not appreciate.

"Fucking disgusting animal," she snarled, tossing his limp body into another tree.

SmibSmob felt his body wrap around the trunk, but he didn't register the pain. He felt his body slam into the ground, but he didn't notice the crack of his ribs. There he lay, flitting between life and death, praying for any kind of miracle and thinking of Nalgene. Where was Mariah? Perhaps she would appear and save him once more.

He would never know how illusionary that hope was.

"Stand up and fight me again, you fucking cretin. I'm far from done with you."

SmibSmob, against all logic, reason, and physical limitations, somehow rose back to his feet under her indomitable will. She was before him, that sadistic grin still plastered across her attractive face. She flicked her sword, scattering the blood — his blood — from its silver blade, and once more began her slow and solemn march towards him.

SmibSmob, using his unbroken hand, wiped the tears and mucus from his face, resolving to die with at least some dignity. However, he didn't even bother casting a spell at her again. He knew that it would be worthless. How was he supposed to fight? By compulsion, he was forced to, but she never specified exactly how he needed to fight. But what could he do?

His gaze darted to Kraalek, hoping that perhaps the General had another clever trick up his sleeve, but Kraalek was still kneeling on the ground in the exact location where Saber had left him, his hollow, unblinking eyes staring back at the gnome. He would find no hope in the General.

His gaze darted to Fasto, hoping that perhaps the orc had snapped out of his murderous trance, but Fasto was still on the ground, grappling with a now-still Margaret, his red eye watching the conflict with apathetic disinterest. He would find no hope in the orc.

So, what could he do? Saber's boots *thumped* softly on the ground as she stalked towards her prey. This was his death. This was his doom.

"I told you to *fight*."

Nodding mindlessly, SmibSmob reached up and grabbed his pointed hat from his head with his healthy hand. It was remarkable that it had remained there throughout the entire fight, but perhaps that was just the miracle he had hoped for. Holding it before his eyes, he studied the mysterious folds. He swore he still saw clumps of stale mashed potatoes within the creases. The hat was truly an enigma to him, blessing him with fortunate gifts whenever he desired. He almost felt guilty, as this was the gift bestowed upon him by Mariah, and ever since he had learned to channel his Inner Fire, even if weakly, he hadn't even given the hat any thought — aside to belittle it in Kraalek's basement.

So, against all odds, holding the hat against his body with his elbow, he put his good hand into the hat, feeling for something — anything — to save him from his demise. In the past, it always seemed to conjure exactly what he needed for the scenario, excluding the bread it had manifested during the initial bout with Captain Osann. Whether it was a rope in the mountain pass or a golden dagger for a friend, the hat had provided.

Now this time it would have to do the same. What choice did SmibSmob have? He needed to fight, and this was his only option now. Besides, no matter what the hat summoned, he knew he was still going to die, so what did it matter?

SmibSmob closed his eyes and concentrated. Suddenly, he felt a great influx of cosmic energy — greater than he had ever noticed before — concentrating inside his hat. He felt his Inner Fire roar to life, more intensely than he had ever noticed before. He felt as if the very *essence* of the universe was coagulating into the hat, flowing in as a rushing river under his guidance. And by manipulating the cosmic energy enough, maybe, just maybe, he could even create something.

Suddenly, it all became clear to the gnome.

SmibSmob had always assumed that the magic of his hat was distinct from his lost shadow powers. He had always assumed that it was different from his new flame powers. But now, he realized the error of his theory. They were all the same. All of his magic was united under a singular banner: creation. It was *him* that was creating the shadowy tendrils. It was *him* that was creating the feeble sparks. And it was *him* that was creating the gifts within the hat, not the artifact itself.

With this revelation, he willed into existence something within his hat that could save him from the oncoming slaughter from Saber. He didn't care precisely what it was, but as he channeled the magic, the image of Saber's naked body incinerating in a billowing ball of fire burned into his mind.

SmibSmob felt his fingers brush up against something smooth.

Smiling for the first time since his beating began, SmibSmob pulled his creation from his hat. It was a dark, crimson glass in the shape of a demon's head with an open mouth and two ruby eyes. It was a bottle of Spitfire.

Immediately SmibSmob's hopes plummeted. Maybe he should have been slightly more specific about what he was trying to create. Now his one and only chance was squandered, and his death secured.

Saber's steps grew louder. She was not but ten steps away.

"Oh, so you're trying to take after that deplorable Kraalek and drink your problems away?"

SmibSmob writhed and roiled with rage and frustration. The majority of it was cast at himself for being so fucking pathetic and weak and arrogant and delusion. But some of that was also cast at Saber. For her insistent taunting and her humiliation of him and his friends. But most of all, it was because she would be the reason he never saw Nalgene again.

She needed to feel the burn.

Shouting with all his might — which wasn't very mighty at the moment — he threw the bottle of Spitfire at Saber. It twirled through the air directly towards her chest. Snickering, Saber slashed her sword, shattering the bottle mid-air and dousing herself in alcohol.

"I'm sure your dear puppy Kraalek would berate you for the waste of alcohol. It's a shame you won't be around to hear his words. Now you die, fucking rat."

SmibSmob digested her words, unable to dispute them. Yes, the General would no doubt give him a spectacular lashing for wasting the alcohol. He had learned that the liquor certainly was not cheap to acquire, so any spill would cost him dearly.

But there was one other thing that Kraalek had taught him about Spitfire.

SmibSmob felt for his Inner Fire, channeling the cosmic energy and bending it to his will. His goal was the same as before: a spark to cast upon Saber. However, this time, with his new understanding of magic, his confidence wasn't misguided.

An orange spark appeared on Saber's chest, nearly the size of SmibSmob's fist. This time, his magic wasn't so feeble. Oscillating tendrils of flame licked the alcohol smothering her body.

And it truly was exceptionally flammable.

Saber exploded in a brilliant ball of green and orange fire, illuminating the first and unleashing a blazing wave of heat through the air. SmibSmob heard her agonizing scream and smiled. SmibSmob smelled the stench of her scorching flesh and nearly laughed. She was indeed feeling the burn.

Suddenly, he felt as if a great weight was lifted from his shoulders. The illness in his mind dissipated. No longer did he find her unnaturally beautiful. In fact, he found her utterly repulsive. And no longer did he have his detrimental compulsion to fight the Demigod. He was free. Her charm was lifted.

As with all alcohol, the fire burned quickly and hot. In a matter of moments, the flames engulfing Saber disappeared, leaving her standing in their wake. Gone was the smooth, pale skin, replaced with blistered and red splotches of flesh. Gone was the long, flowing black hair, replaced with a twisted knot of ashen strands. Her cloak was similarly tattered and ruined, disintegrated by the infernal fires.

But her eyes remained locked on SmibSmob, shooting venomous daggers at the gnome. This was turning into a much greater problem than she bargained for. The game was up. There would be no slow, tortuous death for the Beacon, much to her disappointment. No, she would end this here and now. One final slash of her blade and she would be free of the filth of this world.

"You fucking BITCH!" Saber howled, stepping towards SmibSmob. It was time to solve this unfortunate problem.

SmibSmob stepped back, his euphoria quickly dissipating. How was she not dead? What could he do against her now? Frantic, he shoved his hand back into his hat, desperately trying to conjure something to save him. He felt the magic answer his beckoning, but it was too late. He was too slow. And Saber would be upon him. As he was retreating, his foot caught on the root of a tree, and he fell to the ground, landing hard on his back. His hat fell to the ground. Now in the dirt, he looked up to watch Saber's approach. This was his doom.

Suddenly, Kraalek appeared in front of him, shielding him from Saber. One of the General's hands cupped his bleeding stomach while the other held a card.

"Get the fuck out of my way," Saber snarled.

"Not this time, pretty."

The card in Kraalek's hand began to glow orange with heat and he flicked his wrist, sending it spinning towards the Demigod. This time, she wasn't so quick to deflect it, and it ripped through her flesh, slicing and cauterizing at the same time. She gritted her teeth and groaned but didn't allow herself to howl in pain again.

Several more cards quickly followed suit, these ones not glowing. She managed to deter several of the projectiles, but several more passed her defenses, creating more gashes and lines of blood.

"I said, get the fuck out of my way, worm!"

Saber took a step forward.

But then, Fasto was also there, his face beaten, swollen, and with one eye still shut, but his hands were raised, ready to brawl.

"You'll go no farther. I will kill you if you try."

Saber laughed, but she didn't take another step. Then, Kraalek raised his hand, and an orange orb of flames appeared in his palm. This time, he wasn't worried about catching SmibSmob in the collateral.

"I'm the most powerful spellcaster in the Flame, isn't that right?"

Saber's eyes darted between SmibSmob's two defendants, panic slowly settling in. At the moment, she was hurt, weak, and slow. Most likely she could still defeat these two doddering morons, but then again, there was a chance she could not. One more fireball and she knew she would be ash, and she heard no bluff in Kraalek's voice. So much for solving her problems today.

"Your time will come, Kraalek. You can't protect the Beacon forever."

With those words, Saber began waving her arms before herself. Kraalek yelped in alarm, casting his spell towards the Demigod as Fasto charged at her. Thankfully, the General's spell was much quicker than the orc's legs, so it reached its target first.

A Resurgence of Hope

A blinding cone of fire engulfed Saber's position and extended fifty strides beyond her, instantly incinerating tree, bush, and grass alike. The wash of heat dwarfed SmibSmob's meager Spitfire spectacle, and they were forced to close their eyes to prevent permanent damage.

But it was too late. Just before Kraalek's spell collided with Saber, she disappeared, teleporting away and leaving the forest far, far behind.

"NO!" Kraalek raged. "That fucking bitch got —" Before he could finish his sentence, he collapsed forward, landing face down on the dirt. Fasto rushed to the fallen man, but he was unable to catch him in time. Instead, he just patted the fallen man's back.

"General!" SmibSmob cried, grabbing his hat and crawling forward to kneel beside Kraalek. A pool of blood was underneath the man's body from the wound on his stomach. "No, no, no, no! Stay with me!"

Without thinking, he placed his good hand upon Kraalek's back. He knew that Flametouchers had the ability to heal others, as did Nalgene. But how did they actually do it? He realized he never gave it much thought. But he had to try. Reaching down, he activated his Inner Fire, then tried to picture what he might create to save the General. Maybe he would create the flesh inside the gash to mend the wound? That seemed like a good enough idea to him. Fire flowed from his palm, washing over the fallen General. Fasto, alarmed, took a step back, but did not stop SmibSmob's magic.

SmibSmob felt the magic doing … something, and he hoped it was healing the man. If anything, he could clearly see that the fire wasn't burning Kraalek. So, he continued for as long as he could. But his energy was almost already spent. As he cast his spell, all of the pain descended upon him like a swarm of vultures, picking and gnawing at his body. His sliced foot. His broken wrist. His shattered ribs. His crumpled nose. His gashed chest.

SmibSmob's connection with his Inner Fire severed, and he felt himself falling backwards and backwards and backwards … His vision grew hazy, and it seemed to be bright and dark at the same time. He no longer knew where he was or even who he was. All he knew was the hurt. And he just kept falling and falling and fading and fading and falling and hurting and fading ...

Suddenly, a surge of warmth embraced his body, The gnome felt his strength somewhat return through the flames, and the most life-threatening wounds disappeared from his achy body.

SmibSmob's eyes flew open to see that Kraalek was now kneeled over him and was returning the favor.

"I'm no Flametoucher," the General said, "but I've managed to pick up one or two of their tricks."

"You're alive!" SmibSmob cried, sitting up in joy.

"Yes, yes. It'll take more than just some shabby stab wound to kill me, isn't that right?"

SmibSmob nodded and hugged the man, who reluctantly returned the embrace. It seemed the General was absolutely right in that regard. Thankfully.

"What about the others? I don't mean to be the obvious one, but ...

"Ah, right you are, my good gnome. Let me see what I can do."

Kraalek healed Fasto next, and then had the orc carry over the limp body of Margaret. Her face was pale, and a devilish bruise covered her neck from Fasto's strangulation. The orc was deeply ashamed by his actions, but he was wise enough to recognize that he really didn't have much of a choice. There was just no way he could wiggle out of Saber's charm.

Kraalek placed his hands on Margaret's chest and cast his healing flames. As he did, he had Fasto fetch the body of the fallen Commander and place it next to Margaret. Kraalek worked his sorcery for several minutes without any success, but right before he was about to surrender his hope, Margaret's eyes opened, and she gave a weak cough.

"Hey, what the hell happened ..."

A Resurgence of Hope

"You're alive!" Fasto shouted, holding Margaret's face in his hands. However, upon seeing Fasto's face, Margaret's gaze grew harsh, and she tried to escape.

"Get the fuck away from me ..."

"No, it's okay," Fasto whispered to her, stroking her cheeks. "Saber is gone. Whatever my sins, I swear to do you no more harm."

"That's what you said when you tried to kill ..." Margaret's voice trailed off, her eyes closed, and her head fell limp. But she was breathing, even if shallowly.

"Like I said, I'm no Flametoucher. Speaking of, that is where we shall go, they will be able to mend your wounds more properly."

"I reckon the rest of the group at Fisherbay still has plenty of Flametouchers that could help us," SmibSmob said as cheerily as he could manage.

Kraalek's eyes bored holes into the gnome at that statement.

"No, we will not be returning to the group. We will travel to Firelight. There, we will find our healers. The Shadow is much too dangerous for you, Beacon. We do not know where Saber went, but if I had to wager an ass and a hare on it, she'll be back to finish the job."

SmibSmob gulped, and he didn't have the heart to dispute that reasoning. Today, he had already brushed death more than enough to last the remainder of his lifetime.

Then, he remembered the bright flash of light emanating in the direction of Fisherbay, and an alarm rang in his thoughts. Nalgene was in the city. What if his brother was inside of that radiant explosion? What if his brother was *dead*? Suddenly, SmibSmob had a sliver of heart to argue with the General.

"There was a flash of light from the city," he began, building his case. "We need to ensure that they're all safe, and that the mission was successful! I don't mean to be the obvious one, but we can't just abandon them to die. My brother —"

"That isn't obvious and yes, you will be abandoning them. Fear not, little Beacon, once I deposit you into Firelight, I will return to Fisherbay to aid the survivors of this 'flash of light', as you called it. Assuming there are any, and I pray for all our sakes that there are."

"You'd have us abandon them?"

"I'd have you abandon them, not me," Kraalek continued, gesturing to the trees now billowing in flames due to his magic. "Plus, the fire is starting to spread, and I've got a feeling it's about to get very uncomfortable in these woods."

"But —"

"No. It's over." Kraalek's voice grew harsh. "I am getting you out of the Shadow whether you give me your blessing or not, Beacon. You cannot stop me. I will bring you to safety. Right now, the Flame needs its savior, and right now, its savior needs proper healing and protection."

SmibSmob opened his mouth to respond, but Kraalek's intense gaze kept him silent. So much for having the heart to debate.

Satisfied that SmibSmob would now remain silent, Kraalek shuffled over to the body of Commander Ecker. He knew what he had done: murder, and there was no amount of healing he could muster to bring the man back to life. But he didn't have a choice. It was either the Commander died, or the Beacon did, and he wouldn't hesitate for a moment to kill Ecker again. But it still brought him no joy. The Commander was a good man and an inspiration for his troops. Now, he would be nothing more than another rotting body in the Shadow.

Kraalek reached into one of his pouches and revealed his token in the symbol of a burning cross. Identical to what Captain Osann did in the Shadow, he laid the medallion upon the Commander's chest, and a dull flame ignited upon it for a brief moment, sending an orange spark billowing through the canopies and into the heavens above. After that, Kraalek closed his eyes and was silent for several heartbeats in a solemn vigil, before rising to his feet and replacing the token in its pouch. He did not bother to incinerate the body.

"Come now, to Firelight." An orange gemstone appeared in his hands. SmibSmob swore Saber swatted it off into the forest, but it seemed the General had a stash of them ready and handy. For some reason, the gnome wasn't surprised by this.

Fasto nodded, picking up Margaret's body and draping it across one of his shoulders. With his other hand, he grabbed the General's arm.

SmibSmob stood still, eyeing the General. Where was Nalgene? He just wanted to see his brother and apologize to him and hug him and tell him everything was now going to be different. Once more, he opened his mouth to plead Kraalek to take him to Fisherbay, but before he could, the General shook his head, denying the motion as if reading the gnome's thoughts.

Grumbling and disheartened, SmibSmob reluctantly placed his hand on Kraalek's arm. Kraalek hesitated a moment, then frantically searched the nearby ground, looking for something. But when he didn't find it, he grumbled to himself and closed his eyes.

Immediately, they were engulfed in a column of fire, and then they were gone.

◆　　◆　　◆

The group appeared in one of the many plazas in Firelight. Immediately, Kraalek ushered them down one of the streets, dragging SmibSmob along by the arm as Fasto followed closely behind carrying Margaret. However, this time, in a very uncharacteristic move, the General didn't take the winding back alleys of the city. Instead, he remained on the main roads, traveling as directly and efficiently as possible. They needed healing, and he needed to return to the Shadow.

After just several minutes of walking, they found themselves in front of a barracks. The soldier at the door didn't hesitate to open the door and allow them passage. As soon as they were inside the building, Kraalek whistled for Flametouchers, and they were quickly swarmed by four of them, two men and two women. The men each had two golden stripes on their cloaks while the women had three.

The healing was bliss. While the General did a sufficient job at mending SmibSmob's wounds in the forest, it just didn't compare to the magical prowess of these masterful Flametouchers. The only person's healing capabilities that rivaled the Flametouchers was Nalgene, and how SmibSmob wished it was his brother caring for him now.

As quickly as it began, the process was over, and the group was rejuvenated, and they prepared to exit the barracks, the General graciously thanking the Flametouchers for their service. They tried to ask him questions about the assault on Fisherbay, but he waved them off. This was no time to banter. Before leaving, the General grabbed one of the Sparks, ordering it to escort Fasto and Margaret to a nearby inn for rest and recovery.

"Rest and recovery?" Margaret asked, taking a menacing step towards Fasto. Her voice turned harsh. "With him?" Fasto's eyes widened, and he retreated backwards with his hands in the air.

"Fasto sorry! Wasn't Fasto!"

Kraalek twirled around to glare at Margaret and opened his mouth to speak, but before he could, Margaret rushed forward and embraced her friend.

"I know. It's okay."

She released the orc, stepped back, and studied him with a piteous look. Fasto just stood there drooling.

Kraalek cleared his throat, then turned back to the door, urging SmibSmob out of the building. "Splendid, may you live happily ever after."

"What about me?" SmibSmob asked Kraalek, but the General ignored him.

With that, they left the barracks, Fasto and Margaret following the Spark down the street. SmibSmob watched them walking away, and he was tempted to chase after them, but Kraalek grabbed his arm and pulled him in the opposite direction. They descended a hill, and he could no longer see his two friends.

"What about me?" SmibSmob repeated, desperately trying to pull his arm out of the General's grip. Why was the man so strong? And why was he walking so quickly? His little gnome feet could barely keep up. "Shouldn't I rest and recover at the inn too? You said the Shadow wasn't safe for me."

"No inn is safe for you, either."

"But —"

"You are quite confrontational today; didn't you fight enough? Help me help you."

"Why does you helping me always mean dragging me through the city?"

The General paused, released SmibSmob, and continued walking, taking a sharp turn down a side lane.

"I suppose you can walk by yourself. Keep up."

So, SmibSmob went, despite his urges to escape the man and chase after his friends. He knew, deep down, that the General was right. And he also knew, deep down, that he was absolutely terrified at the moment. He reckoned that if he saw Saber — or any creature from the Shadow — he would pass away on the spot from fright alone. So, off he went, into the winding alleys of the city with the General, hoping that Nalgene would find him and ease his rattled nerves.

Perhaps this feeling was what Nalgene was grumbling about several days ago. The feeling of powerless mortality after facing an undefeatable horror.

SmibSmob berated himself for ignoring his brother then. When Nalgene needed a shoulder, SmibSmob wasn't there for him.

Now, with the roles reversed, he hoped Nalgene would be there for him.

As always, SmibSmob quickly lost track of where they were in the city. Too many twists and turns. But eventually, the destination became clear. It should have been obvious to the gnome from the beginning, but his mind was too muddled to piece it together.

Kraalek escorted SmibSmob into his decaying shack of a house — if that was even what the General was calling it. Following the usual routine, the General crawled under the central table, activated the hidden mechanism to open the trapdoor, and followed SmibSmob down into the basement. Upon entering, SmibSmob wasn't surprised to see that it was once again magically cleaned, with the shards of glass cleared and the burning alcohol stains washed away. How did Kraalek always find the time to tidy this place?

"You will be safe here," Kraalek said, appearing in the center of the room and offering SmibSmob a chair. "Please, make yourself comfortable."

SmibSmob didn't sit, but that didn't seem to bother the General much. Shrugging, the man darted towards the stairs.

"I'm off to Fisherbay. Let us pray for the good fortunes of those in the battle," Kraalek said before ascending the steps.

"Wait!" SmibSmob cried, chasing after the man. "If — when you find Nalgene, can you bring him here, please? I need to see him."

But he never received a response. Kraalek was already gone, leaving SmibSmob alone in the dungeon of his own making.

Undeterred, SmibSmob raced up the stairs, pushing against the trapdoor to catch the General and relay his message. But as he pushed against the wood, it didn't budge. This time, the door was locked. And now, SmibSmob knew there would be no escaping.

A bubbling rage roiled inside of him. A rage against Saber. A rage against the General. A rage against the oppressive Shadow.

But mostly, it was a rage against himself. When Nalgene needed him most, he turned away, obsessed with his shiny new powers.

Just like he was with his dark abilities. In the end, nothing had changed, and only he was to blame.

"I'm such a beardless dwarf," he said, his voice catching in his throat. Defeated, he trekked down the stairs and studied the room. The chair Kraalek had offered him was still in the center of the basement. Despondent, SmibSmob took a seat. It was remarkably comfortable, but that did not lift his dour spirits. For a brief moment, he thought of incinerating the chair, continuing his unsuccessful practice before the counterattack. He knew he could, with his new understanding of magic. But the thought left a sour taste in his mouth, so instead he just sat in a silent vigil.

Thinking of his brother.

Time seemed like a blur for the gnome. It was exceedingly difficult to determine its passage in a sunless basement. Perhaps he was sitting for an hour, or maybe it was several. Maybe an entire day passed by. He felt numb to the world, as if he was a spectre watching from an outside perspective, powerless to cause a difference. During this time, Saber's words cycled through his head:

I wish I could've killed you two-hundred years ago, maggot.

Prove to everyone else that you're just another fucking fraud in a long line of hopeless pretenders.

Of all the Beacons that I've killed, you are, by far, the most worthless fucking one of them all.

At some point while wallowing in his sorrows, SmibSmob felt his stomach growl. Perhaps some food would cheer him up. Slowly, he pulled his hat from his head, then reached into its folds. Why did he even need the hat, anymore? He knew its secret: nothing. It was just a regular hat. Maybe he just liked the symbol of it. Or maybe it was the last remnant he had of Mariah — along with his now dirty and tattered purple cloak.

He felt his power surge, felt something manifest in his hand, and pulled it out to reveal a delightfully bright fruit. He chuckled to himself; at least it wasn't bread this time. SmibSmob took a bite of the fruit, letting the sweetness envelop his tongue, but the taste quickly passed, turning to ash and gray. That did not improve his dejected mood.

So, SmibSmob dropped the fruit on the floor and watched it roll away under one of the cabinets. He was sure Kraalek would somehow manage to find it and clean it, so he didn't bother chasing after it. His stomach growled again, the lone bite of fruit having hardly satiated his hunger, but he didn't pull anything else from his hat. In fact, he dropped his hat on the ground, then placed his head in his palms.

Suddenly, SmibSmob realized he was crying, and he wasn't entirely sure why. But, this time, at least it wasn't because Saber had commanded him to. He didn't attempt to stop the tears, instead allowing the charade to play out in full. Snot dripped from his nose. Drool dribbled down his chin. Gasps of breath escaped his lungs.

Today was supposed to be his moment — Mariah had ascertained that for him. But, in the end, nothing had changed. Just like before the counterattack, he was alone, in the damn basement, wallowing in his own pity and doubt. Eventually, SmibSmob grew numb to his own bawling, and the tears ceased, leaving him once more alone and afraid in Kraalek's dungeon.

More time passed. Maybe several hours — he didn't know or care anymore. It was all just pointless time for him. But at least he was safe, right? Safe from the Shadow, perhaps, but not safe from himself.

Then, SmibSmob heard a *click,* followed by the creaking of the trapdoor opening. Kraalek's voice echoed through the basement:

"Come, Beacon."

Wiping the crust from his face, SmibSmob stood from the chair, grabbed his hat from the ground, and shuffled towards the stairs. At the top, he saw the General waiting for him. The man's face was unreadable. That only caused SmibSmob's heart to begin thumping in his chest.

"We must go to the Torch."

Nodding, and without much of a choice, SmibSmob obliged, trundling up the stairs. He felt the onset of tears again, but he held them back. Not in front of the General. It was time to become the Beacon once more. Why him? Why was he blessed with such a burden?

He found no answers in his own musings.

SmibSmob exited the basement, and Kraalek closed the trapdoor behind him before guiding the gnome out of the house and down the street. As they walked, SmibSmob asked the man one, simple question:

"Is Nalgene safe?"

Daniel Whitman

Chapter 15

Saber appeared in the middle of a decaying field. To the north was a vast lake, twinkling in the gray light from the twilight sun. To the east was a vast mountain range, wrapping to the south as far as her eyes could see. To the south was a spiraling monolith of black energy, reaching up like an obsidian spire towards the sky far above. It was the true Black Heart of the Shadow, where all the accumulated energy was transferred and stored. Saber imagined that one day, if it grew powerful enough, it might just become tall enough to reach the sun and tear that flaming orb from the cosmos, enveloping the world in a permanent night. Of all places, why did it have to be here? Of course, her choice was logical: to get to the place furthest from the Flame, but the thought still didn't make her comfortable. But the inevitable explosion of fire demanded urgency, and in her haste, she hadn't carefully considered where she might go, except for the one place she knew the bastards could never reach her. Where else would she be safe? With Calitha? No, that bitch was far too aggravating. So, this was where it was to be.

Saber collapsed to her knees, coughing up flecks of blood. Everything was *pain*. Her skin was scorched and peeling, with bubbling blisters covering her exposed flesh. It was agony to move. It was anguish to breathe. Perhaps this is what Ashyla felt — No! She would never bring herself to sympathize with that bitch. It was all that fucking Beacon. What the fuck did he do to her? He was supposed to be weak and repugnant — and he was, up until the point he planted a fucking fireball on her head.

Saber knew she had erred. In her arrogance she didn't realize that the game had concluded. Oh, how she wished she could have continued to toy with that worthless gnome for eternity, trapping him in a perpetual cycle of torment, but it seemed her luck had run dry, and her wish didn't come true. Her problem hadn't been resolved. That fucking Beacon. She should have just killed him from the start. Even despite her folly toying she still would have still killed him if it weren't for that bastard of a drunkard. They were all fucking wriggling worms to her, but sometimes, the insects bit back.

It enraged her. Of course, it was much more satisfying to revel in her victim's suffering, but what did it cost her?

Everything.

Now she was burnt, physically and metaphorically, and her hubris had become her downfall. Her beauty was shattered, and her power was nullified. What a fucking joke. No matter, she was still a Demigod, and she would recover much more swiftly than that fucking cretin of a Beacon. And when she did, she wouldn't make the same mistake again. When she did, her blade would meet his heart before his brain could even realize he was dead. Yes, this was only a delay. Her problems could still be solved. Her domination, her control, and her freedom were still guaranteed.

Saber began to crawl across the ground, moving towards the north. The shriveled grass brushing against her skin sent bolts of pain through her body, but she endured. Perhaps a cleansing swim in the lake would ease her pain. She could attempt to teleport the short distance to the water, but, in her current state, she didn't trust her own precision. She almost laughed at the thought.

Her? Saber? Doubting herself? But she could not deny it. The game had concluded, and in her arrogance she had lost.

Fucking Beacon.

Saber heard the sounds of gentle footsteps behind her. Grunting away the pain, she put on her best "get-the-fuck-away-from-me" facade and stood to face the unfortunate, approaching soul. Best case, it was some trundling undead so that she could unleash her frustrations. Worst case, it was Ashyla, now escaped from her fears and hunting her with an undying vendetta.

Somehow, even worse: it was neither.

Approaching Saber was a silvery-blonde girl with pale skin. The woman's hair was tied in a messy bun, with several long strands swaying in front of her angular face. She wore a simple white dress, which was in harsh contrast to the two black wings extending from her back like the closed curtains before a stage performance. However, the woman's most striking features were that her hands and forearms were nothing but bones, and that her eyes were purely empty voids. Her black hole eyes won't gaze now, but they drew Saber in just the same.

Saber didn't know how to react to the approaching woman. Initially, a rush of panic swept through her, but it was replaced with senses of cautious hope, wavering relief, and, of all things, shallow joy. Joy?

Saber began to trudge towards the strange woman.

"Help me, sister!"

The woman paused, and she simply stared at Saber, her brow furrowed in thought.

"Sister …" the woman said in a monotone, deadpan voice, as if she were merely a recorded message being spoken through the single tone of a dreary instrument. She held onto the word for a moment, chewing on it as if she couldn't quite understand its meaning. "How strange a word."

Those senses of hope, relief, and joy began to slowly fade away.

"You know me, Anabasa."

"The only reason we should be called sisters," Anabasa continued, ignoring Saber's comment, "is that we were created at the same time. Of all the others, *he* decided to forge us together. Does that make us sisters? Perhaps, if that is what you should so desire to call us."

"You must help me!" Saber pressed, waving her arms. "I'm wounded. Those fucking rats in the Flame, look what they did to me!"

"So, I see. And so, I saw." Anabasa began to walk towards Saber once more, her white dress brushing against the ground. Saber was amused to see that the bottom of the dress was stained, torn, and dirtied from Anabasa's careless use of it. At least her sister's clothes didn't defy logic, unlike those of Calitha.

"And how should I help you, Saber?" Anabasa asked, now within arms-length of Saber. Saber was frustrated to see that Anabasa was taller than her. That was never the case.

"I don't know. Do something — anything — so that I, or we, can retaliate against that stain of a Flame. We can do it together."

"You never did come to speak with me. For all this time, not once did you deign to see me ... sister." Anabasa still said the word "sister" as if it were a rock caught in her throat. There was no anger or malice in her voice, just the empty monotone stating facts like a machine.

Saber's hope, relief, and joy were rapidly plummeting now. At this point, she realized that Anabasa wasn't really listening to what she had to say. Additionally, she was mildly surprised that Anabasa was capable of memory and thought, but it was too late now to consider the woman's sorry feelings — if she even had any emotions left. That woman was basically a shell now.

"I'm sorry, it's just … you aren't you anymore." Fuck, bad move, that wasn't how she wanted her words to come out. She berated herself for the carelessness of her response. Why was every single other woman in this damn world impossible to have normal conversations with?

"Yet you just called me sister. Has that not changed?"

"You'll always be my sister, but what Ashyla made you …" Fuck, there she goes again with that stupidly loose tongue of hers. She really just needed to shut the fuck up, escape this questionable situation, heal, and murder the Beacon.

"What did she make me? If I am not myself, then what am I?"

Shit. This truly was not where she wanted the conversation to go. Perhaps if she was in a healthier state, she would be more tactfully eloquent with Anabasa, but all she could feel now was the pain. She wanted it to end. She wanted revenge. Saber's words choked in her throat. She knew what she wanted to say, but she wasn't about to say it — yet. Even Saber knew that wouldn't be wise.

During Saber's silence, Anabasa reached out and grabbed Saber's face with her skeleton hands. Saber felt the raw, harsh edges of bone snagging and tearing at her burnt and peeling skin. She wanted to scream, and she felt tears well in her eyes, but she persevered.

Anabasa's inky orbs drilled holes into Saber's very soul.

"Tell me what I am. I know your thoughts. I've heard what you whisper in the night."

By now, all of Saber's hope, relief, and joy had long fled her mind. At this point, she would rather be dealing with fucking Ashyla. There was a reason why she avoided Anabasa for the last two-hundred years — many reasons, in fact. Why did she choose to teleport here, of all places? And why did her damn sister also have to be here?

Anabasa's bony fingers dug into Saber's flesh.

"What am I?"

Saber could bear the agony no longer. She just wanted this entire charade to be over. She was so exhausted and frustrated. Her tongue slipped.

"You're a fucking monster, that's what! You're disgusting. I hate you and everything you've become. You're not my sister; you're just a vessel for the plagues of this world. Is that what you wanted to hear?"

"We're all monsters. Why do you think we were created?"

"To be slaves," Saber spat without hesitation. She knew the destiny that *he* forged for them all.

Anabasa didn't reply. Instead, she planted one of her hands across Saber's eyes and nose and gripped Saber's chin with the other, peeling open Saber's mouth and bending her head backwards. Undead hands burst from the ground and restrained Saber, their rotting fingers groping at her legs and feet, pinning in her place and preventing any feeble attempts at escape.

"I lost a part of me today," Anabasa said, leaning over Saber. Somehow, she seemed even taller than before. "You will fix that."

Before Saber could digest those words and formulate a reply, a deep, unnatural gurgling sound emanated from Anabasa. Saber desperately struggled against Anabasa's grasp, but it was futile. She couldn't move.

She was trapped with the monster.

Then, a vile, writhing slime regurgitated from Anabasa's mouth and into Saber's. Saber felt as if she were a pathetic bird during morning feeding and she tried to spit the sticky mass out, but it crawled down her throat. Fuck. That couldn't be good. She could feel it wiggling inside her, spreading like a sickly mold on a rotten fruit. Panicking, and with no other option, Saber grabbed her sword and stabbed Anabasa squarely in the chest.

Anabasa didn't move, blink, gasp, or react in any way. Even as her black blood dripped out of the wound and down Saber's blade. Except, it wasn't actually blood leaking from Anabasa's body, it was just more of the Shadow's filthy tar.

Anabasa, who has now finished vomiting, released Saber's head. Black bile dribbled down Anabasa's chin, but the woman didn't care to wipe it. Saber felt the undead binding her legs release her from their grasp, and she took a step away from her sister. For the hell of it, she withdrew her blade before stabbing Anabasa once more.

Just as before, the woman didn't react at all, except to look down at the sword impaling her chest.

Slowly, deliberately, Anabasa walked backwards, leisurely retracting herself from Saber's sword and, once she was free, she turned and began to strut away towards the shadowy monolith of energy without saying another word.

Saber felt a strange, nauseating feeling in her gut, followed by a numbing sensation flowing across her limbs, and she was forced to the ground as a spew of black bile crawled up her throat, out of her mouth, and onto the ground in front of her, where it squirmed in the grass as if it had its own life. She felt a piercing in her mind, as if someone had just thrust a spear through her skull, and it was followed by a diabolical fracturing of her thoughts. This agony was like no other. Damn the Beacon and his pitiful fireball, *this* was true torment. Her stomach roiled, and she was forced to puke more black ooze onto the ground.

By now, Anabasa was already strides away.

Looking up at her sister, with drool and bile hanging from her blistered lips, Saber only knew terror. From the moment of her creation up until her brawl with the Beacon, she never knew horror this profound. Nothing Ashyla had ever said or done instilled such a sickening dread within her. Not even Calitha frightened Saber so thoroughly, and that literally *was* what that ghostly woman embodied.

No, this was different. This was primal.

"WAIT!" Saber desperately howled at her sister's back, hoping, even if vainly, that Anabasa would revert whatever she had done. This was never how it was supposed to go. Today was supposed to be when all of her problems were solved, not multiplied and amplified. *She* was supposed to be in control. She was supposed to be *free*.

Anabasa paused and turned back to look at Saber. There was no life, pity, or regret in her soulless black eyes.

"I am overjoyed that you will join me … sister."

With that, Anabasa once more began walking away, and no matter how much Saber called after her, she didn't look back again.

Defeated, Saber lay on the ground for a long moment. Already, she could no longer feel the pain of her burns. If there was one consolation for what was about to happen, it would be that she would never feel pain again. What a fucking prize. Just peachy.

Her stomach churned, and she unleashed yet another round of devilish ooze onto the grass. Then, against her will, she stood from the ground. It felt as if she were a puppet on a marionettist's strings. While her mind was still lucid, her body was no longer her own. She turned to the southeast. Then, slowly, like an ant infected with a parasitic fungus, she began to march in that direction towards the mountains, urged on by a mysterious and unconquerable force.

How she wanted to stop. How she wanted to scream. How she wanted to fight. But she couldn't. There was nothing she could do to stop what was coming. *She* was supposed to be in control, she was supposed to finally taste freedom after a lifetime of servitude, and now she'll never have control of herself again. Just how many problems could she accrue on this day?

She took another step and deposited another load of vomit on the ground and her feet. She didn't — couldn't — make the effort to wipe them off, instead forced to take yet another step.

That was all she could do now: walk. Always to the southeast. Through mountains and dunes and trees, her journey would continue, forevermore into the awaiting gloom.

A Resurgence of Hope

Until the Shadow claimed her as its own.

◆   ◆   ◆

Nalgene, trudging behind Sylven, Ro, Andromeda, and the remaining handful of surviving Sparks, walked through the ruins of Fisherbay. They had succeeded. They had destroyed the Dreadring in a brilliant nova of light. That explosion ... it was so purifying. It was just raw, unfiltered energy, exactly the stuff that Nalgene had channeled into his crystalline bottle, and exactly what he, along with all others he knew and could remember, used to create stuff with magic. Of course, the explosion also burned like a bitch, but that was nothing that he couldn't heal with his abilities.

As soon as the core of the Dreadring — a black flower, or so he was told, but he thought that sounded absurd — was destroyed, the oppressive weight of the Shadow lifted not only from his own being, granting him back the strength and magical prowess it was sapping from him, but also from the entire surrounding land. Not only that, but all the nearby undead simply lost their will for unlife and returned to being just regular corpses. Thankfully, that saved them the hassle of having to battle back out of the city.

The experience had left them all quite humbled, even the noble and proud Ro, and there was not much conversation among the group. The final thing that the Dreadring, its flower, and its resulting white nova did was remind the group just how little they knew of the world or the Shadow. However, as they finally exited the city to examine the environment around them, their vigor returned.

Above the group, the sky was clear and full of the colors of twilight. To the west, the sun was dancing across the surface of the lake, causing refractions of glittering light to twinkle in the shallow waves. In the sky, faintly burning in the unreachable heavens, were stars.

The Light had returned to reclaim this portion of the corrupted land.

"It's beautiful," Andromeda purred, looking at the stars, and Nalgene couldn't disagree. Despite his still sour mood, even this new hope could breach his grouchy barriers.

However, it wasn't all sunshine and rainbows. The supply carts that were posted outside the city were destroyed, and their horses slaughtered. Corpses, both from the Light and the Shadow littered the ground both inside and outside of the city. While the air was clear and refreshing, the stench of death undercut any comfort they could garner from their victory.

But it was a victory nonetheless, and an unprecedented occasion for the battle across Ansalon.

"Ah, that doesn't look too pleasant," Sylven said, gesturing to a towering smoke column from the north.

"May the Light protect General Umbra, the Beacon, and the others from whatever misfortune might have fallen upon them," Commander Oldgate said in a deep, rumbling voice.

Nalgene's heart dropped. The smoke was emanating from where SmibSmob had wandered off to. Could it be related? If so, what caused it? Was his brother safe? His mood became even more dour, if it was possible. He just felt so frustrated and numb.

"We should not assume anything about what events occurred in the north," Sylven said, consoling the group. "As far as we know, the smoke is completely unrelated to the pursuit of the Mistress."

Ro, Andromeda, the Commander, and surrounding Sparks nodded in agreement. That sounded logical, perhaps it was just some freak wildfire. Nalgene, however, had his own suspicions.

"Now, with our segment of the mission complete, we shall prepare to return to Forthold." Sylven studied the meager number of survivors of his brilliant counterattack, contemplating the best course of action. He would not risk the three-day journey back to Forthold on foot. While the undead were temporarily defeated, that didn't mean that others couldn't find them. And there was still that winged monster, somewhere, waiting in the darkness to feast on more flesh. No, there was only one real option. An orange gemstone appeared in his hand. "Everyone, gather your boots and breeches, we are returning to Forthold."

However, before the Sparks could gather around the General to complete the gem-call, a fiery pillar ignited before them, and when it disappeared, General Kraalek was waiting to greet them.

Now Nalgene's mood had truly reached rock-bottom at the sight of the slimy man.

"Ho, Sylven!" Kraalek hailed, skipping over to his fellow General with relief on his slim face. "I'm thrilled to see you alive, although I fear you might be less thrilled at the news I bring."

Sylven lowered his gemstone and studied Kraalek.

"Is the news that you finally found the bottom of your liquor bottle?"

"No. And although that would be dire news indeed, this is far more severe."

Sylven's jovial attitude fled. If the Cardmaster wasn't willing to banter words about alcoholism, then it was severe indeed.

"Saber betrayed us. She tried to kill the Beacon. Thankfully, I was able to protect him."

Everyone stood in stunned silence at Kraalek's declaration. Nalgene could feel the adrenaline pumping through his veins. Saber? The beautiful woman? Tried to kill his SmibSmob? His adrenaline was followed by the crushing weight of guilt. He should have followed his brother into those woods instead of staying behind where his spells were "more effective". What a bunch of stinky dwarf shit. What the hell was he thinking?

"So, it seems you haven't quite reached the bottom of your liquor yet," Sylven said quite stoically, absorbing the information. "Tell me everything."

Kraalek relayed the events of the Beacon's final stand against the evil Demigod, including Fasto and Margaret's duel, the murder of the Commander, his own failings to protect SmibSmob, and the final, brilliant fireball that defeated Saber. During his recital, no one, not even the witty Sylven, jaded Ro, or grumpy Nalgene, dared to interrupt. At his conclusion, when he was questioned how he deduced that Saber was truly a maleficent villainess in disguise, he revealed the information he had gathered from his brief investigation, as well.

Nalgene's stomach was in his boots. He wanted to vomit; he was so appalled. Both at Saber and at himself. How could he have not foreseen this? Why could he not remember Saber from his past? It seemed he was still missing quite a few memories, despite his recent breakthrough. That blasted slimy woman and that blasted slimy Kraalek, it seemed that SmibSmob was surrounding himself with all of the winners, and Nalgene had done nothing to stop him.

Well actually, when Nalgene wanted to be there for his brother, SmibSmob had pushed him away. While that made Nalgene feel slightly better about himself, it did nothing to alleviate his disgust at the current situation.

"Where are our friends?" Ro asked Kraalek. "Please tell me they're safe."

"Aye, where is me brother?"

Kraalek turned to regard the companions. "Yes, everyone is quite safe now, or so I pray. In fact, now that I know of your fates — thankfully you are all still walking and breathing — I surmise it is past time for a reunion. But, if you would bear with me for just a moment longer, please do enlighten me on the events here in Fisherbay. As you're still alive, does that mean the mission was successful? Did you close the Dreadring?"

Sylven took the liberty in relaying the events leading up to and including the battle in the city. Kraalek was particularly interested in the description of the Dreadring, and of the mysterious flower that blossomed in its heart. Nalgene grunted at the description. Seemed like dwarvish trickery to him. How the hell would a flower survive in the middle of the darkness, and why was some woman crawling out of it?

"Fascinating," was all Kraalek said as Sylven concluded his tale.

"What now?" Sylven asked. "You're the mastermind here, Kraalek. No matter what happened in that forest or with Saber, the men need to return to Forthold and rest." He raised the gemstone at Kraalek, showing the General his intent to leave.

"Of course, of course, but I did just promise our good friends a happy reunion, and I would hate to be called a liar. Say, you bring the soldiers to Forthold while I bring Ro, Andromeda, and Nalgene to Firelight. Then, join me at the Torch. We will have much to discuss."

Sylven shrugged, which Kraalek took to signal agreement. Then, Quickfoot barked some orders at the Sparks, and they gathered around the General. As they did, Ro, Andromeda, and Nalgene joined Kraalek. Sylven's gemstone blazed to life, and he and his band of Sparks disappeared in a great conflagration.

"Ready to see your friends?" Kraalek asked, holding his very own gemstone.

"That sounds splendid," Andromeda said.

"Yeah," Ro mumbled.

"Even me brother?" Nalgene asked.

Kraalek didn't answer Nalgene's question. They all placed their hands upon the scrawny man, and they were engulfed in flames, traveling across the world to the city of Firelight.

◆　　◆　　◆

The group appeared in Firelight. By now, the night life was beginning to fill the streets, and fireflies dotted the air. However, they didn't have time to appreciate the beauty, as Kraalek quickly urged them down the street, pushing past the jolly civilians, and towards a nearby inn. Inside, they found Fasto and Margaret sitting at the bar, enjoying a scrumptious meal of meat and potatoes.

"Go, rest and enjoy the company with your friends," the General says, beckoning them through the door. "The Flame will call upon you soon enough to discuss the events."

Ro and Andromeda eagerly entered the bar, pulling up chairs and swapping smiles with the two orcs. Nalgene, however, wasn't quite so quick to enter.

"Where's me brother?" he asked the General, who was attempting to make a sly getaway. The slimy bastard wouldn't escape today.

Kraalek didn't even turn to regard the gnome.

"He's somewhere safe."

"Eh? That be some horseshit. I know ye can be tellin' —"

Nalgene was interrupted by the frustrating voice of Fasto, who was running over to approach him.

"Gnome friend! Fasto so happy!"

Nalgene turned to defend himself from the grabby hands of the orc, desperately trying to ward off the embraces, but without much success. The orc was quite strong, unfortunately, and Nalgene was just a small gnome. He contemplated blasting the orc with some water, like spraying a mischievous cat away from a valuable vase at the edge of a table, but he didn't. The only abilities he wanted to use on the others — his begrudging friends — were his healing ones.

So, despite Nalgene's grumbles and grunts, Fasto smothered him in an awkward hug before returning to the bar to join the others. When Nalgene finally felt his feet upon the wooden floor once more, he turned to continue his heated debate with the General.

"I be askin' ye again, where's me ..." Nalgene trailed off when he realized the General was long gone. That slimy no-good beardless dwarf of a man. Where was he hiding SmibSmob? Or maybe SmibSmob felt himself too holy — being the bloody Beacon and all — to join his mortal companions at the inn.

Nalgene hated himself for the thought, but he could not shake the possibility. This wouldn't be the first time SmibSmob hadn't joined them for a gathering. No, SmibSmob wouldn't be that selfish, right? But then, Nalgene remembered how his brother had all but ignored him after the battle against the winged avatar of death, and suddenly he remembered just how selfish his brother could be.

No, not his brother. The SmibSmob he knew and adored would never be so egotistical — that was always Nalgene's specialty. But recently, SmibSmob had changed, and not entirely for the better. Nalgene knew it was all because of that slimy Kraalek. That bloody General had corrupted his dear brother with grandiose illusions of spectacle and power. Perhaps it was better that SmibSmob didn't join them at the bar.

Grumbling to himself, Nalgene found a seat beside the others, who were already talking and laughing. He still held some doubt against his revelations, but each day those doubts grew weaker. Maybe SmibSmob did want to see them. Maybe SmibSmob was still his brother.

But he wouldn't put his money on it. Perhaps the meeting at the Torch would tell.

"Bah, Nalgene, why such a glum chum?" Ro asked, smacking Nalgene on the back and interrupting his thoughts. The gnome noted that in the draconian's other hand was a pint of ale. At least there were no vegetables hanging from Ro's mouth — yet. "I was just telling Fasto and Margaret about our heroic endeavor through the vicious and unforgiving city to encounter the cryptically beautiful flower at the heart of that soulless vortex of darkness, death, and destruction. Why don't you help fill in your noble and proud moments of this grand tale?"

Nalgene had to battle another urge to blast one of his friends with a jet of water. "Well, Ro, with yer dumbass words, I think ye be describin' it all just fine."

"Mmm, I have to agree with the gnome. In fact, I think you could be even more verbose. It would be a shame if you forgot *any* detail," Andromeda giggled.

Ro laughed, and continued his tale of remarkable heroics, tragic deaths, and strange magics. Nalgene only half listened, and he only almost interrupted a single time when Ro was describing his "one-on-one" battle against the dreadknight. But he didn't. He supposed it wouldn't hurt for the draconian to have a bit of fun after they all had almost died.

At least then one of them would be in a good mood.

When Ro had finished — and damn did he manage to make that tale lengthy — Fasto and Margaret were certainly intrigued.

"Dreadring poof?"

"That explains that weird ass light we saw. Glad you're all safe."

After that, the orcs took their turn relaying their story. Thankfully, they were far less wordy than Ro, simply saying:

"Evil lady make Fasto fight friend. Evil lady go boom. Evil lady gone."

"Saber's a bitch, that's that. Turns out she's some Demigod that wanted everyone dead. I'm not sure what the hell is wrong with all you men, killing for her and whatnot, but I always knew she had a weird stink to her. Guess that means I'm just wiser than the rest of you — unsurprisingly. Unluckily for you, however, dumbass over here choked me out for half the battle, so I can't really tell you anything else. I'm sure he could, but he's back to ... well ..."

Of course, they both said slightly more words than that, but again Nalgene stopped listening. He was able to discern the gist of the story, anything after that was just fluff in his ears. But as the night wore on, and the rest of the group was merrily laughing and eating and drinking, Nalgene couldn't help but relax. He even joined Ro for a toast and managed to stomach some food. Perhaps it wasn't so bad without his brother. SmibSmob could take care of himself, after all … Right?

Thinking of his brother again immediately crushed the mounting fun within his spirits.

The night was interrupted as a group of Sparks appeared in the door of the inn, calling them to meet with the Torch. Begrudgingly, they followed the soldiers out of the door and into the streets where they made their way towards the brilliant white building. Ro had to be forced to leave his ale behind.

The companions rushed up the marble stairs, past the central fountain, through the main entrance, up the spiral staircase, and finally into the meeting room of the Torch. There, the Generals were waiting for them. Agmund held his head in his hands, Sylven balanced his blue dagger on his fingertip, Don was as unreadable and mechanical as ever, and, finally, Kraalek was riffling his cards through his hands. It was strange seeing two of the chairs empty — one once belonging to Roark and the other where Saber once sat next to the Torchhead. Except the Generals weren't the only ones in the room. SmibSmob was also there, standing behind Kraalek like an obedient lapdog.

Nalgene's anger bubbled at the sight. So SmibSmob couldn't join them earlier, and now he's playing leader with the Torch? Did his brother think he was better than the rest of them? One glimpse of some prophesied power and suddenly he leaves the rest of them in the dirt. SmibSmob noticed his brother's glare and gave a soft smile. This inspired some hope in Nalgene, and he returned the smile.

Perhaps SmibSmob hadn't completely abandoned them — yet.

The Sparks escorting the companions excused themselves and backed out of the room, leaving them alone before the Torch.

Again. They were getting used to this. Agmund raised his head from his hands and stood.

"I have already heard of the events at Fisherbay," the imposing man said, initiating the meeting. "As well as the unfortunate development regarding General Umbra. Companions, do you have any special insights regarding these topics?"

"No, great and heroic Torchhead Giantheart," Ro said, his words slightly slurred. Bastard draconian really was developing a problem.

The rest of them, including Nalgene, all shook their heads. They all saw the same things as Kraalek and Sylven, and in some cases, even less than the two Generals.

"I see," Agmund said, sitting once more. "Then we need not repeat the reports."

That brought another smile to Nalgene's face. He was getting awfully tired of hearing the same stories.

"What a brilliant victory for the Light!" Don exclaimed.

"Yes, very brilliant indeed, but at what cost? What about Gene — Saber?"

"How could I — we — have not foreseen this?" Agmund sighed, his head once more in his hands. How could his doe not have warned him of the brewing trouble?

"She fooled us all, if that is any consolation," Kraalek said.

"This has been a dark time for the Flame," Agmund continued, quite dejected. "The destruction of the Dreadring is a monumental step towards the return of the Light, but we cannot afford to lose hundreds of men, including Commanders and Generals, every time we attempt to retaliate."

"May the Light stand proud even with its noble sacrifices!" Don cried.

"Yes. As for Gener — Saber, we shall hold a vigil tonight to mourn her loss, along with the loss of Commander Ecker and all other Sparks who gave their lives in the assault. While Saber has solidified herself as a traitor, we cannot let the public know of her deception. To do so will cause mass panic and mistrust in the Flame. For all the people will know, she died defending the Beacon from a Mistress. Is that understood?"

"Yes, Torchhead."

"Who doesn't love a little white lie?" Kraalek mused.

"Even the most faithful of the Light can be brought to sin in pressing circumstances," Don said.

"Of course, you have my — and all of my friends' — oaths to fulfill this most noble of charges," Ro said, his words slurred.

"Why are we even here?" Margaret grumbled to herself. "This shit doesn't have anything to do with us." Nalgene had to agree. Couldn't this have just been summarized in a letter? Saber was evil and the Dreadring was destroyed, he got the point.

"Somebody needs to be cuttin' Ro off o' his drinks."

Andromeda snickered. "I find it quite entertaining."

"Good," Agmund said, regaining control of the room. "Now, General Cardmaster, you mentioned you have something to discuss regarding the Beacon."

"Yes, indeed. The Beacon and I have had an intriguing idea."

"Go on."

"Please do, I'm sure this is truly earth-shattering," Sylven remarked.

Kraalek stood from his chair, his cards disappearing, walked behind SmibSmob, and grabbed the gnome by the shoulders. SmibSmob shuffled his feet uncomfortably, and Nalgene scowled. He wasn't sure he would approve of any idea that came out of the slimy man's mouth.

"You said it before, Agmund, this has been a dark time for the Flame. The loss of two Generals, and in quick succession, nonetheless, is truly unprecedented in our history. However, I believe we can fill one of those vacancies."

"I'm listening," Agmund prompted.

"I propose the Beacon be inducted as a General of the Flame."

Nalgene almost choked at the proclamation. However, looking around at the other companions, they didn't seem quite so disturbed by the development. Fasto was even clapping for the gnome.

"I know this is very unorthodox, but these are unorthodox times, isn't that right? And I think — nay, I know — that the little gnome is more than capable of the role. As the Oracle had prophesied, and as she delivered, SmibSmob descended from on high to save this land. It was the *Beacon* that tipped me off to Saber's deception. It was the *Beacon* that delivered the decisive blow against the Demigod. And it is the *Beacon* who is bringing a resurgence of hope for the Light. And while it is tragic that Mairah is still missing, our Beacon, as one of the leading Generals of the Flame, can take her reins and bring peace to the people of the Light. Plus, I can think of no safer place for the Beacon than amongst us."

The room was silent as the other Generals mulled over the proposition. SmibSmob looked as if he were about to puke from all of the intense eyes on him. He was just a little gnome in a very big world; could he really save it?

"A glorious revival for the Light! Like a phoenix of myth, I approve of SmibSmob rising to be the glowing bastion of hope for the Light," Don said.

"Seems reasonable to me," Sylven said. "I have no objections. We have already made so many leaps, what is one more?"

"I, as a hero of Fisherbay, support my dear friend SmibSmob in his remarkable promotion to the highest rank of this good green land," Ro interjected.

"What this dumbass said," Margaret agreed, placing her hand on the draconian's shoulder.

"Yes, splendid," Andromeda purred.

A Resurgence of Hope

Nalgene said nothing. So, this was SmibSmob's grand idea? To become a General and leave his friends and family for the vultures? What a bloody joke. Perhaps his brother really did change, and there would be no saving him now. The SmibSmob he remembered and knew always despised the spotlight, preferring to be the humble hero in the background. But this? This would put nothing but the spotlight on SmibSmob. This was not his brother any longer.

But still, a sliver of hope remained in the gnome. Perhaps it was really all just the slimy Kraalek, pulling his brother like a puppet on strings, but the hope was exceedingly faint.

Finally, it was Agmund's turn to answer. All eyes were on the Torchhead now. He stood from his chair, walked over to SmibSmob, placed one of his massive paws on the gnome's head, kneeled down, and looked directly in the Beacon's eyes. It was almost comical, the size difference, like a pebble beside a mountain.

"Can you do this?" the man asked SmibSmob.

SmibSmob's voice rang clear and resolute:

"Yes."

Agmund smiled. "Then I welcome you to the Torch, Beacon. We shall hold the official ceremony tomorrow morning."

A rowdy cheer from Fasto filled the room, followed by rambunctious applause from Ro.

"Splendid," Margaret said. "I'm still not sure why we had to be here for this, but I'm happy for him. This is a big deal. Probably."

"Does this mean that you're no longer the leader, Ro?" Andromeda teased.

"The best leaders know when to allow their followers to take charge."

"Oh, so you were the best leader? Debatable. I thought the best would be more sober," Margaret said.

"What do you think, Nalgene?" Andromeda said, turning to the gnome and brushing him with her tail. "Aren't you happy for your brother?"

"O' course," Nalgene managed to grunt. He wanted to be proud. He wanted to be happy. He wanted to hug his brother. But he just didn't feel it. If only he could speak to SmibSmob alone, he was sure they could clear up everything. He hoped.

"Companions," Agmund said, turning to the group. "It fills my heart with joy that you support the Beacon so justly. It is good for him to have such fine friends and family in these times. You are dismissed, now go enjoy the night. I hope that you will join us for the vigil tonight, and that you will show your support for the Beacon at the ceremony tomorrow morning. Ever burn bright for the Flame!"

The other companions saluted the Torchhead and left the room. Nalgene remained in place; his eyes locked on his brother. Noticing his gaze, SmibSmob attempted to join him, but he was stopped by an upraised hand from Agmund.

"Not yet, Beacon. You can join their company soon, but for now we must inform you of your new role as a General."

"Uh … right. I see." SmibSmob shot an apologetic look at Nalgene as he was nudged towards one of the empty chairs — Roark's chair. "Let's talk, Nalgene. I want to see you, and I reckon you want to see me too. I've missed you."

Instantly Nalgene's hope was rejuvenated. Perhaps there was still a shard of his brother left!

"Aye, that'd be great."

"Right-o," Kraalek said, appearing before Nalgene and corralling him out of the room. "There shall be plenty of time for reunions soon, isn't that right? Shouldn't take more than an hour. Feel free to wait outside, my good gnome."

"Eh?"

"Oh, give the gnome a break, Kraalek," Sylven sighed.

A Resurgence of Hope

"No, General Cardmaster is correct," Agmund said, dismissing Nalgene in finality. "Go enjoy the night. The Beacon can join you soon."

Grumbling, Nalgene complied and left the room. The door closed behind him. The other companions were already on their way out of the building, laughing and joking, but he didn't chase after them. He would be damned if he was going far. Wait outside the door? He could do that. His brother wanted to talk to him! His brother missed him! He would wait for a thousand hours if it meant he could hug SmibSmob again.

Nalgene patiently waited outside the door. He could hear the muffled sound of the Generals' voices inside, but he couldn't decipher any words. No matter, he was sure their discussion was important, and that it would be over in a timely manner. It had to be.

An hour came and went. The discussion was still ongoing. It was growing late, and Nalgene felt his exhaustion begin to creep in — he hadn't had any real rest since Fisherbay, after all, but he didn't allow himself to succumb to its clutches.

The second hour passed, and still the meeting continued. Nalgene passed the time by twiddling his thumbs, creating little fountains of water in his hands, and counting the number of different Flametouchers running around on the lower level of the building. His eyelids were heavy.

After the third hour, while Nalgene was half asleep sitting on the ground, the voices stopped. Immediately, he awoke to the sound of the General's footsteps. The door opened, and out stepped Agmund, who gave him a nod before walking down the hall. Next was Don, who offered to perform a prayer on Nalgene, but the gnome waved him off. After that came Sylven, who shot Nalgene with a sly wink. The door closed behind Quickfoot as he left.

There was no sign of Kraalek or SmibSmob. No matter, they were certain to be leaving soon. Nalgene had the urge to enter the room, but he patiently held himself back, resting his head on the wall. His brother would come to him. He just knew it. Soon, he felt himself nodding off once again.

After the fourth hour, Nalgene heard some shuffling in the room, and he groggily opened his eyes. Suddenly, there was a flash of orange light from under the door.

Alarmed, and now wide-awake, Nalgene bolted to his feet and opened the door. The room was empty, save for a trickle of smoke wisping from a smolder on the ground.

His brother had left him. Again. Without coming to talk. SmibSmob had *lied*.

Screaming in rage, Nalgene shot a ball of water at the flicker of fire, extinguishing it. Immediately, he heard the *thumping* of boots as half a dozen Sparks rushed into the room to determine the commotion.

"Is everything alright?" they asked, cautiously eyeing Nalgene with their hands on their weapons.

"Aye," was all Nalgene bothered to reply. Fuming, he stormed out of the room, down the stairs, and out of the building. His entire body was shaking as he walked. He didn't even notice the crowds of people gathering. His brother had abandoned him. Again.

Eventually, somehow, Nalgene made it back to the inn, where, coincidentally, the others were just leaving.

"Whaaaat's wrong, buddy-o Nalgene?" Ro asked, obviously plastered.

"Are you coming to the vigil?" Margaret asked him, supporting the draconian with her shoulder. She, too, had a flagon of ale in her hand, presumably in celebration, and she was looking up at Ro with absurd googly eyes. What's the worst thing that could happen after a single drink?

Nalgene just grunted and tried to push past them. Margaret stepped away from Ro, causing the draconian to stumble to the side, and grabbed the gnome with her free arm.

"Are you okay?"

"Aye, just be tired, is all." He struggled in her grip.

"Are you sure?"

"Aye."

"Let him rest, Margaret," Andromeda said, placing her hand on the orc's arm.

"Suit yourself, see you in the morning," Margaret said, releasing Nalgene and returning to Ro.

"Goodnight, friend!" Fasto called.

"Buuuuu-bye, noble and grumpy Nalgene," Ro said, waving at the gnome.

Nalgene wanted to punch Ro in the throat, but he didn't. Instead, he just stood in the doorway and watched as his friends disappeared onto the street. Andromeda gave him a sympathetic flick of her tail as she left.

Alone now, Nalgene trundled into the building, up the stairs, and managed to find an open bedroom. This would be another mourning ritual he wouldn't be watching with his brother. For a third time. In fact, Nalgene wouldn't be watching this one at all.

Instead, the gnome climbed into the bed. He didn't want to move. He didn't want to think. He didn't want to eat. He just wanted to scream. But he didn't.

He really just wanted SmibSmob. This was the second time he was lying in some random bed at an inn, alone and heartbroken. His brother sure knew how to make a tradition of it.

Almost as soon as Nalgene's head hit the pillow, sleep enveloped him in its heavy arms. Nalgene had no dreams that night.

♦　　♦　　♦

Nalgene awoke to the sound of a great commotion occurring outside. There were shouts, cheers, songs, and all manners of percussive instruments feigning for control of the air waves.

Grumbling, Nalgene pulled himself from his bed. What in the bloody hell was going on? It sounded like a ceremony.

The ceremony! SmibSmob's induction ceremony!

Why the hell should he go to that? While his frustration and anger from the previous night had mellowed, it was still very much present, like a predator lurking just below the water for the perfect moment to rear its ugly head.

Shaking his head, Nalgene left his room and went downstairs. The inn was empty, and his friends were already gone. Without anything better to do, he exited the inn, following the sounds of the commotion down the streets and towards the Torch building. There, he found himself at the rear of a roaring crowd. Humans, elves, dwarves, draconians, felines, orcs, and others of all ages created a giant cesspit of celebration. The sounds were almost unbearable to the still sleepy gnome.

The building had been transformed for the festivities, with large, crimson banners adorned with the symbol of a burning cross — the symbol of the Beacon — draping from the roof and flowing in the breeze. Ridiculous golden tassels seemed to be stuck anywhere and everywhere, creating a chaotic and glittery glamour. At the top of the great marble staircase were the Generals. All except SmibSmob, Nalgene couldn't see his brother. He could barely see anything at all, given his short height, but he was far enough away that he had a vantage on the proceedings. Agmund stood at the center of the others, one of the mysterious horns in his hand. He raised his hand towards the sky, and a brilliant ball of fire launched into the air, exploding with a glorious dance of yellow and red flames.

The crowd fell silent. Agmund put the horn on his lips.

"GREETINGS, GOOD PEOPLE OF THE FLAME!"

A roaring cacophony of sound answered his call. Damn, these people were quite excited about this ceremony.

"You all know of the endless battle the Flame wages against the unrelenting Shadow. You all know of the endless death and destruction it has caused, including the loss of our mighty Commanders and Generals, and the disappearance of our beloved Oracle."

The crowd responded with confused whispers. Should they cheer?

"BUT THAT ENDS TODAY! TODAY, A NEW HOPE ARISES FOR THE LIGHT! TODAY, I PRESENT THE NEWEST GENERAL OF THE FLAME, AND MAY HE BRING TERROR TO THE DARKNESS PLAGUING THESE LANDS!"

This time, the crowd cheered. Nalgene didn't join the excitement.

"The great Oracle Mariah promised us a Beacon in this time of black, and today, he has come to fulfil his prophecy. THE SHADOW SHALL FALL. I PRESENT THE HOPE, THE SAVIOR, THE BEACON: GENERAL SMIBSMOB HOPEBRINGER!"

The crowd roared even louder, if it was even possible. But Nalgene didn't notice. His eyes were glued to the makeshift stage where SmibSmob stepped out from behind Agmund, a smile on his face and his hands waving to his new people. The gnome's eyes were scanning the crowd, seemingly looking for something — or someone — but Nalgene didn't notice or care.

So, there was the bastard. There was his brother.

SmibSmob was wearing a new crimson robe and had a golden crown upon his head. His pointed hat and purple cloak were gone. Nalgene thought it revolting. So, instead of spending time with him last night, SmibSmob was off getting decorated by the city's finest clothiers and jewelers?

Nalgene's simmering rage pounced, engulfing him completely. He needed to vomit. He needed to run. He needed to escape. His fucking brother had abandoned him for glory and prestige — exactly what Nalgene was guilty of in the past. A red haze was gnawing at his mind, and he knew that if he succumbed to it here, people would die. Because of him. He would drown them all, just as he did in those battles from his memory. And he would never forgive himself for it.

So, Nalgene ran.

He didn't care where — anywhere was better than at that ceremony. As he left, he heard Agmund speaking again, but he didn't listen to the words. As he darted down the streets, turning left, then right, then left again, the sounds faded behind him. His legs burned, but he didn't stop. He just kept running. Somewhere. Anywhere. The sounds had all but disappeared, and with it, the red rage was also withdrawing. But it didn't dissipate completely.

Nalgene, now out of breath, collapsed on the side of a street. Tears started falling from his eyes, but he wiped them away. He still needed to run; this was not time to cry. But where would he go? Nowhere seemed far enough, at the moment. Panting, he brought himself back to his feet and continued with his aimless exile in the city.

As he walked, his hand eventually found itself in his pocket. When did he put his hand there? His fingers brushed against something, and he pulled it out, turning it before his eyes. It was an orange gemstone. The one Saber had gifted him. Nalgene had forgotten about the trinket.

Nalgene paused and studied the jewel. He needed to escape somewhere where he could clear his head and squash his anger. Perhaps SmibSmob had a valid reason for not seeing him last night. Perhaps SmibSmob really wasn't gone. But Nalgene couldn't consider those thoughts now, not in his current mental state.

He was too afraid that SmibSmob was gone for good.

How could he escape? His eyes didn't leave the orange gem.

Instinctively, Nalgene began to channel his magical energy into the stone. If Sparks could use it to teleport places, so could he, damn it. Where should he go? For some reason, a picture of that far away beach where he tossed away his crystal bottle came to mind, so he settled upon that. There, he could collect himself. He felt the cosmic weave answer his call, intensified by the innate magic of the jewel.

He was angry. He was hurt. He was *afraid*.

Suddenly, a pillar of water sprouted from the ground, submerging Nalgene. When it receded, the gnome was gone, leaving nothing but a wet, empty street.

♦ ♦ ♦

Nalgene felt a slight tugging on his body.

The water cleared, and the gnome found himself in a shadowy forest. A thick mist seeped from the ground, and crooked branches reached for him with razor claws. This most certainly was not the beach he had imagined. Perhaps new trees were planted? No, he couldn't smell the ocean either. No matter, as long as he could relax among the dark trees and suppress his red rage, he could return to Firelight and try to resolve things with his lost brother once and for all — for better or worse.

At least he would try, even if SmibSmob wouldn't. Nalgene wouldn't give up just yet.

Nalgene pocketed the gemstone and began to walk aimlessly through the woods. Every way looked the same, so what difference did it make? As he walked, he focused on his breathing, slowly and deliberately steadying it. Skulking undead followed him at a distance, forever watching, but they didn't attack. Nalgene didn't mind, he figured as long as that winged menace didn't arrive, he was more than powerful enough to handle any and all undead that came his way.

However, just for the hell of it, he decimated some of the wandering creatures with jets of water. It was therapeutic.

Nalgene wasn't sure how long he walked for; it was difficult to determine time passing when everything just looked gray. He spent his time studying the ground, attempting to avoid tripping on the gnarled roots. But he felt his fire cool. He felt clarity return to his troubled mind. Yes, perhaps SmibSmob did have a valid reason for not visiting him. Perhaps his brother wasn't gone. He was afraid he was wrong, but he felt the hope returning. Ironic, given his brother's new title as "Hopebringer". It certainly had a better ring to it than SmibSmob's old one.

Suddenly, illogically and without warning, Nalgene found himself in an open clearing of shriveled grass. He looked up, and his heart dropped. Fear tickled his neck.

Above him was a swirling sky of black, and to the west the peaks of mountains peeked over the trees. Floating in the middle of the clearing was a thin, ghostly woman with short, silver hair and a simple, gray dress. The woman turned to face Nalgene, her head tilted at an unnatural angle. He saw that her eyes were sewn shut, and that she had an oozing gash on her chest.

"What is it that brings you fear, Raging River?"

The terror was paralyzing. He couldn't move. He couldn't run. He couldn't speak. He couldn't blink. Horror and dread caressed his body and mind, leaving him helpless at the mercy of whatever twisted fate awaited. He felt himself getting pulled closer.

Just then, Nalgene realized that he recognized the woman.

The laceration across Calitha's chest began to peel open.

*E*pilogue

Ashyla glanced around the room. It was white. Everything was white. The ceiling, the floor, the walls, all white. It was infuriating. It was puzzling. It was terrifying. Where the hell was she? How the hell did she get in here? There must be a door somewhere, right? But no, it was all white. Perfectly and dementedly monotone. The pristinely flat complexion of her surroundings was threatening to drive her past the brink of insanity — more than she already was. There were no details, no scuffs of dirt, and no visible edges or corners.

Just fucking white.

What the fuck did those insufferable children do to her? How the hell did she get here? It was frightening.

Ashyla walked forward, moving across the empty expanse, hoping desperately to reach any sort of … well, anything. But did she even move? It was difficult to tell when there was no reference from which to measure motion. The only thing that gave her confidence in movement was the friction of her feet across the ground. There was ground, right? She glanced down, and she was truly thrilled by what she saw: more fucking white. For her own mental fortitude, she reached down and placed her palm on the floor. It was smooth, cold, and as awfully uninteresting as it was visually pleasing.

But at least it was something.

Perhaps she would attempt a different way to escape. While she could not see, she could certainly feel. Standing up, she reached her arms out to the side, trying to find the walls of the infernal prison. She found them quickly — too quickly. She couldn't even straighten her arms because the walls were so close. And they were *pushing*, getting closer with every breath.

Just where the hell was she?

She tried to teleport away. Nothing. She tried to resist the collapsing of the walls. Nothing. She could do nothing but wait as the endless nothingness swallowed her whole.

Panicking now, Ashyla tried to dash forward, but her face gracefully met another wall. Of course, she couldn't see it, as it looked identical to everything else in the blinding void, and so her nose found it for her. Painfully. Frustratingly. Terrifyingly.

She was trapped. The walls were closing in on all sides. She could feel the floor rising up and the ceiling lowering down. Into her. Onto her. Crushing. Pushing. Threatening. Maddening.

◆　　◆　　◆

The chains restricting Ashyla, seemingly crafted of white light itself, seared at her skin. They were abhorrently hot. Blazingly so. Just really fucking hot. Like the sun.

That was because she was *inside* the sun, trapped, burning, and helpless.

Every time she tried to squirm, the chains burned and blistered her skin more, causing her to flinch from the agonizing pain, which in turn made the chains burn her more, thus causing more desperate thrashing ... The cycles could last for hours, until the numbness and the defeat settled in, and then she would just lie there, limp and wishing for release. All day. Every day. For hundreds of years, she had smoldered in this blazing prison of a star. She was mutilated by her wounds. She was maddened by her agony. She was enraged by her impotence.

But the burning and the pain and the torture and the physicality of it was not what brought her true despair. No, she could endure the pain. She was the Goddess, eternal and endless ever since It had created her those thousands of years ago. Rather, it was watching her children suffer that brought her the most anguish. And, bound, broken, and powerless, she could do nothing to aid them.

All she could do was watch.

That fucking Sergarious. He was delivered as the God of life, and now all he brought was death. To her children. While his miserable ants roamed free and massacred her one true triumph: her garden.

All she could do was watch.

How many of her children did she have to watch being slaughtered before it would end? Tens? Hundreds? All of them?

She knew it would never end,

She would avenge them, even if it meant the destruction of the very world she once created.

She could always make another, and she would ensure that that fucking demon wasn't around to corrupt it again.

But that was just a dream; a distant, harrowing, future dream that she knew she could never hope to ascertain.

Now, the chains still burned at her skin. Now, she was still strung helplessly in the core of a blazing star.

Now, all she could do was watch.

Far below her, in one of the forests on Ansalon, she watched as the soldiers and mages circled the dragon — her poor child. Its wings were bloodied and torn, and it no longer had the strength to fly and escape. The raiders had made certain of that. Blood oozed from its countless wounds, and large patches of scales were missing from its body, exposing the vulnerable flesh underneath. Large chains with razor spikes appeared in the sky above it, descending upon her child and pinning it to the ground. It struggled against the snare, but every movement caused more gashes in its flesh. Screaming in pain, it opened its mouth to unleash a devastating breath attack, but suddenly its head was submerged in a massive sphere of water, extinguishing any attempt at a flame.

It was drowning.

And all she could do was watch. She tried to call upon her powers to aid it, but they were sealed away. She learned long ago that the only thing she could create now was false images and sensations. What use would a fucking fake butterfly be to her wounded child? No, she could create nothing real, and that included no more children.

Each one that perished, she could never get back.

The soldiers moved in, their weapons hacking at the dragon's legs, coating the foliage below in a thick coat of blood. Just for the sheer amusement of it, the mages cast arcs of lightning into the metal chains ensnaring her child, laughing as the voltage caused the beast to twist and jerk sporadically. It lashed with its tail, but that too was stopped as a mighty blade materialized in the air above it and fell upon the tail, severing it completely and cleanly. How her child tried to scream, but inside that globe of water, only bubbles escaped its maw.

The pitiful charade continued for hours, with the mages and soldiers toying with the defeated beast. They didn't kill for food or defense or survival, no, those days had long ago passed. Now, they killed for sport. They killed for the simple reason that they could. The once proud and mighty dragon, now nothing more than an oversized chew toy for the relentless devils.

In its last breaths, her child looked to the sky. Its eyes locked onto the sun, blinding itself in an attempt to reach its mother. Its helpless and worthless mother. Why wasn't she there to protect it? Why did she let it suffer so? Why did she permit such pain?

Ashyla watched as the life faded from her child's eyes, and guilt wracked her body. The agony never faded, no matter how many of her children she watched being slaughtered. Each one was a fresh wound, and each one drove her closer to the brink of insanity.

She screamed and thrashed, but the chains dug deep into her blistered skin, rejuvenating the arduous pain. So, the cycle would continue, she knew, and there wasn't a single fucking thing she could do to stop it.

All because of the devils and parasites he created in her garden. All because of those wretched Demigods, created and instilled with his revolting power. All because of that bastard God Sergarious.

Now, all she could do was watch.

◆　　◆　　◆

Ashyla opened her eyes to regard the featureless, white expanse surrounding her. What the fuck did those odious traitors do to her? Where the hell was she? She tried to reach out to touch something — anything — in the white void, but there was nothing. Everywhere she looked it was identically and miserably monotone.

It was terrifying.

She took a step — or did she? It was impossible to judge motion when there was no reference to compare it to. But then, she had the sensation that she was falling. What did that feel like exactly? That was difficult for her to rationalize or explain. But it was freeing, and frightening, and wonderful, and awful. She thrashed her arms and legs about, desperately trying to catch something to stop her falling, but, of course, there was nothing but the white.

But maybe she wasn't falling and was rather floating in the nothingness. It would be quite difficult to discern the difference from an active reference frame, she mused, but the thought of endlessly floating with no control brought her no relief from her predicament. Where was she falling? Somewhere — anywhere, perhaps. It was all the same to her.

She closed her eyes, imagining being somewhere — anywhere else. She tried to teleport away. Nothing.

Always nothing.

Her eyes opened, and she resumed her endless fall — or was it a float?

What did it matter anyway?

♦   ♦   ♦

Ashyla stood amidst the endless cosmic ocean of stars. Wherever she looked, the distant lights twinkled with brilliant illumination. Great clouds of celestial dust swathed areas of the cosmos, creating a blanket of illustrious colors across the heavens. It was beautiful. It was breathtaking. But It always was.

Beneath her far below was her garden: Ansalon. And it was not beautiful. No, it was ravaged from centuries of ceaseless war, littering the lands with blood, bodies, and death. Repulsive lifeforms — *his* lifeforms — had spread like a plague on her lands, decimating and devouring at will. She never asked for him to be created; he was thrown upon her like a sack of rice atop a mule, and now she was stuck picking up his pieces — the pieces of her crumbling world.

It was inexcusable.

Turning away from her garden, Ashyla considered the heavenly sea once more. As she watched, the stars and nebulae began to slowly move and coalesce together before her, leaving the rest of space alone in the blackness. As she watched, a shape, formed from the very components of the universe, appeared before her. It was every shape and no shape all at once, constantly morphing and equilibrating at the same time. But she knew what It was, regardless of how It appeared to her meager eyes.

The Creator had decided to bless her with Its presence once more.

A grimace appeared on her lips. How she resented It for what It had done to her. Now, after five-hundred years of her wasting screams at the sky, It had decided to reveal itself to her.

The Creator towered over her, encompassing everything and nothing at the same time. It dwarfed the entire universe — It *was* the entire universe — but yet still somehow resided within it. Ashyla didn't waste her energy trying to comprehend the Creator's mysterious guise. She was angry. And she wanted — nay, needed — It to know.

"Why did you do this?" she asked. As always, It didn't respond, merely existing before her.

"Why did you create *him*? After a thousand years, why create him to obliterate what you birthed me to do?"

No answer. Of course, there was no answer. Why did she expect this to be any different? She never asked for him to be created. For all the nonsense about "good" and "freedom" and "righteous" and "life" that Sergarious spouted, she knew he was only capable of death. The death of everything she knew.

"WHAT THE FUCK DO YOU WANT FROM ME?" she howled, her voice seeming miniscule indeed before the infinite being before her.

The Creator simply looked at her — or did It? It didn't have "eyes" as anything else did — and once more said not a word in response. Ashyla gestured towards her garden.

"IS THIS WHAT YOU WANTED?"

The Creator began to disperse before her very eyes, returning to the endless expanse of nothingness where It came from. Stars returned to their rightful place in the cosmos — wherever that would be — and the clouds of dust once more imbued the void with stripes of color. And It was beautiful.

But Ashyla didn't care to appreciate Its beauty. She cursed and spat and raged, casting mighty bolts of creative energy into the infinite nothing. As expected, it had no effect. It seemed that nothing she did, or nothing that happened, had any effect on the Creator. Her tantrum was as futile as collapsing the universe itself.

But why did It even create her if It was just going to watch and do nothing? Why did It create him? Why did It do anything?

The only thing It did was leave her broken and forsaken in the endless void of Itself.

◆　　◆　　◆

Ashyla was in the white room, on her hands and knees. Where the hell was she? The only sensation that gave her confirmation that there was a floor was the contact of her skin. Everything else, in fact everything at all, was featureless, monotone, and infuriating.

She was screaming, spittle flying from her mouth to land … somewhere. Why was she screaming? She didn't hear anything, and the silence was deafening, but she knew she was screaming. Perhaps the screaming was what kept her sane. Or, more likely, it was just the last strands of lucidity escaping her broken mind.

All she knew was her silent screaming.

That, and the fear harrowing her soul.

◆　　◆　　◆

A Resurgence of Hope

The chains restricting Ashyla, seemingly crafted of white light itself, seared at her skin. They were abhorrently hot. Blazingly so. Just really fucking hot. Like the sun.

That was because she was *inside* the sun, trapped, burning, and helpless.

again.

Every time she tried to squirm, the chains burned and blistered her skin more, causing her to flinch from the agonizing pain, which in turn made the chains burn her more, thus causing more desperate thrashing ... The cycles could last for hours, until the numbness and the defeat settled in, and then she would just lie there, limp and wishing for release. All day. Every day. For hundreds of years, she had smoldered in this blazing prison of a star. She was mutilated by her wounds. She was maddened by her agony. She was enraged by her impotence.

But the burning and the pain and the torture and the physicality of it was not what brought her true despair. No, she could endure the pain. She was the Goddess, eternal and endless ever since It had created her those thousands of years ago. Rather, it was watching her children suffer that brought her the most anguish. And, bound, broken, and powerless, she could do nothing to aid them.

All she could do was watch.

Again.

That fucking Sergarious ... While his miserable ants roamed free and massacred her one triumph: her garden.

All she could do was watch.

How many of her children did she have to watch being slaughtered before it would end? Tens? Hundreds? All of them?

She knew it would never end,

She would avenge them ...

She could always make another, and she would ensure that fucking demon wasn't around to corrupt it again.

But that was just a dream …

Now, the chains still burned at her skin. Now, she was still strung helplessly in the core of a blazing star.

Now, all she could do was watch.

Again.

Far below her, in one of the forests on Ansalon, she watched as the soldiers and mages circled the dragon — her poor child … Blood oozed from its countless wounds … It struggled against the snare … Screaming in pain …

It was drowning.

And all she could do was watch. She tried to call upon her powers …

The soldiers moved in … It lashed with its tail … How her child tried to scream …

AGAIN.

In its last breaths … Its helpless and worthless mother … Ashyla watched as the life faded from her child's eyes … She screamed and thrashed …

Now, all she could do was watch …

AGAIN.

Again? The thought flitted through Ashyla's mind, and she grasped at her, desperately holding on with whatever strength she had left. That's right, it was happening again. She had seen this before. She had experienced this before. She had felt this fear before. This was … again.

Again. What a strange concept. In her mulling over the word, her terror slowly left her body. She regained some semblance of self. Suddenly, she remembered something: what those pretentious children had done to her. She was trapped, by Calitha, in her own sorrows and fears. The chains around her wrists disappeared.

Again! That's right. She *had* experienced all of this before, but not in Calitha's labyrinth. No, she had watched her children slaughtered for hundreds of years, long before Daughter had ever ensnared her with her cheap tricks. And, back then, when it was *real*, that was when Ashyla was afraid. Now, after realizing it was nothing but pathetic charades and faltering illusions, why would she ever cower away? It was all merely manifestations of her own twisted creations. Ashyla wanted to laugh at the absurdity of the situation. Her? Under the fist of Calitha? And fooled by Saber? No, this was not the end for her. This was barely even the beginning. She would escape.

Never again.

♦   ♦   ♦

Ashyla was in the white room once more, except it wasn't as featureless and monotone as she now remembered it to be. Rather, it was collapsing, with cracks snaking through the walls. As she watched, a chunk of white fell away into nothing before her, leaving a gaping crevice for her to walk through. Laughing hysterically, she ran towards the hole, driving against the nothing beneath her feet. For the hell of it, she decided to summon a swarm of butterflies from her palm.

They did not disappear, and she knew elation.

Without hesitating, Ashyla leapt through the rift and into the ethereal void beyond.

♦   ♦   ♦

Ashyla opened her eyes, studying her surroundings. She was lying in an open clearing flanked by twisting trees with a swirling vortex in the sky — Calitha's clearing. She had escaped. Her fears no longer held her bound in inability, and her beautiful form had returned. She smirked.

Truly fascinating.

Floating in the center of the clearing, as usual, was Calitha, with her legs curled beneath her. Slowly, Ashyla rose to her feet and began to approach the woman. As she took her first step, Calitha's head twisted to the side at an unnatural angle, and she turned to regard the approaching Goddess, blood dripping from her ever-shut eyes.

"Has Mother escaped her fears?"

Ashyla merely smiled and continued her determined march towards the traitor.

"I know what it is that brings you fear, Mother," Calitha said, waving her hand at Ashyla. The Goddess felt a slight pull in her body, but, besides that, the motion had no effect. She continued to march.

Calitha uncurled her legs, her feet touching — or maybe passing through — the ground beneath her. She waved her hand again, and this time Ashyla didn't feel anything at all. The Goddess smiled even wider.

"What is it that brings Mother fear?" Calitha mumbled to herself, the tinge of concern in her voice. Was this to be another maniacal tantrum?

Ashyla's voice was venomous as she replied: "You think you know my fear, child?"

Calitha continued to wave her hands, and her efforts continued to have no effect on the fuming Goddess.

"There is nothing Mother can do to actually harm Daughter. Mother is powerless."

"Perhaps." Ashyla never stopped walking. Butterflies appeared around her hand, and this time they didn't wither away. When they cleared, flapping into the surrounding air, Ashyla now held her magnificent sword.

If Calitha's eyes could widen, they surely would have. With panic settling over her, and with her normal abilities rendered inadequate, Calitha had no choice but to imprison Ashyla once more. There were some that could temporarily escape their fears, but they always seemed to succumb to despair with the return of the haunting images.

The world went oppressively silent, and the vortex in the sky bubbled and oozed. Blood dripped from the laceration on Calitha's chest, and the flaps of flesh unfolded, revealing her black eye with its rows of fangs and grotesque tongues.

Ashyla looked right into that eye, unflinching, and continued to walk towards the insolent bastard. Butterflies circled and swarmed the clearing like a field ripe with locusts.

Calitha mumbled to herself, although there was no sound, and she began to frantically float away. Why wasn't the Goddess returning to her horrors? She knew what brought Mother fear, and no one could truly escape their darkest apparitions. Perhaps Mother somehow *knew*, and it was giving her strength. No, that couldn't be it ...

Then, Ashyla was *there*, directly in front of Calitha, emerald eyes gleaming with green fire. With her free hand, she grabbed that revolting eldritch eye and squeezed. The tongues wrapped around her wrist, and the teeth scraped against her flesh, but she didn't relent. A vigorous wind rushed through the clearing, and cracks of lighting flashed all around, igniting trees and filling the air with silent booms. Ashyla still squeezed and twisted. With a burst of thick blood, the eye popped.

Suddenly, the storm above the clearing calmed. Suddenly, all the sound returned. And suddenly, Calitha was screaming. The noise was a mix of the distant howl of a wolf and a sword scraping against armor. And it only made Ashyla smile more.

Still clenching the squirming and pathetic Demigod, Ashyla leaned in close, her lips brushing against Calitha's ear.

"You think you can prey on my terror, my dear Calitha? Is it tragic that with all your infatuation on the subject, you could not recognize one, simple fact? My fears? Look around you, for I am already living them."

Ashyla's sword plunged through Calitha's chest, and the Demigod's scream increased in volume. It was music to the Goddess's ears, and she relished every moment of tormenting the pitiful Daughter.

Calitha's arms wrapped around Ashyla, clawing and scratching, but to no avail. Ashyla was indomitable — immovable. Now, Calitha knew what brought herself fear. She just had to survive, right? In a last effort to parlay, in a final desperate attempt at survival, Calitha blabbered out some words, and regretted them immediately:

"Daughter has him!"

Ashyla's grip loosened slightly. "Him?"

Now, Calitha's mind was scrambling. No, Ashyla couldn't know. Not now, and not ever. But perhaps she had a way to cover up her mistake.

"Daughter has one! Daughter captured one of them!"

Ashyla released the woman's crippled eye, and stepped back, slowly — oh, so slowly — retracting her sword from her chest. She took great delight in watching the red river run from the penetrative wound. Blood dripped from her fingers, dripping on the soft, grassy ground with loud *plop* sounds.

"Daughter has caught one of the companions!"

Ashyla pursed her lips, intrigued, and ran the possibilities through her mind. Was Calitha lying? No, of all her vexing quirks, dishonesty wasn't one of them. This was truly becoming a wonderful day.

"How long has it been?"

Calitha gasped, grasping at her fatal wounds. "Mother was trapped for six months."

Ashyla laughed, her hysteria beginning as a soft chuckle and rising to a throaty bellow. Six months? That was all? Merely a fraction of an instant in her lifetime. The horrors that she had endured — the real ones, and not the facades of the labyrinth — had lasted far, far longer than that. It was absurd. It was hilarious. It was pathetic.

After a long minute, the Goddess managed to bring herself down from mania. With a flap of the butterfly wings, her sword disappeared.

"Where is my child?"

"Mother knows where."

Ashyla shrugged, assuming it to be true. Either way, her baby would be easy enough to find. As long as it wasn't dead, that is.

"Where is Saber?"

"Mistress has Sister," Calitha replied, now coughing red flecks.

"I see … so she finally found the white rabbit. It is a shame that I missed the family reunion, is it not?" In truth, Ashyla thought it was a fitting and poetic end for the insolent woman.

Calitha didn't reply — she was too preoccupied with survival. How truly tragic.

"Perhaps it is time enough that I have a talk with Anabasa," Ashyla said, turning away from Calitha. She began to walk away, but the Demigod's voice brought her pause.

"What will Mother do?"

Ashyla didn't hesitate with her answer. "What it was that I was doing fifty years ago before his escape: reclaiming my world, my self, and my vanquished children with the Shadow."

"Mistress — the Shadow — has never ceased claiming the world."

"Yes, but now I shall return to aid the cleansing, and finish what it is that I began."

"He — Bringer, will stop you."

Ashyla shrugged once more as if it didn't matter. "If he was capable of stopping me, he would have done so already."

Calitha was quiet for a long moment, contemplating her situation. She knew Ashyla was telling the truth. And she also knew that he couldn't stop her. "But what of the other companions?" she finally asked, her voice gurgling with blood.

"What of them?"

"Mother … saved them before."

Ashyla stopped. "Perhaps they shall still have their use, or perhaps not. It matters little now."

The Goddess resumed her walking away. The butterflies whizzing through the air collected themselves and began to swirl around her. Ashyla gave a final glance back at the dying Demigod.

"Enjoy the taste of fear, my dear Calitha, for it shall be plentiful. In fact, I want you to *indulge* in it. Please, have your fun."

With that, Ashyla, along with the inky insects, disappeared, leaving Calitha alone in the clearing. As soon as Ashyla left, the swirling turmoil in the sky returned. Calitha fell to her knees, feeling at her body with her hands, and found that she wasn't quite so dying after all. Her demonic eye was whole and unharmed, and there was no sign of any stab wound. She had survived another fit, but she was nearly broken. She almost gave everything away.

Curling her legs beneath her, Calitha floated into the air, returning to her solemn vigil. Had Mother truly escaped, or was it all an illusion? No, Mother was free, and there wasn't a single thing

Calitha could do about it — not that she wanted to. Mother's fears were beyond her command.

The trapped companion, and her other victims, well … She would relish their horrors. And who knew what tattered souls she would find once she started indulging herself?

◆   ◆   ◆

Ashyla stood on the shores of a great lake, the dark water lapping her feet. Behind her, to the north, was a tall mountain range, looking down upon her with jagged peaks. She was staring emptily across the water, lost in her thoughts. Tears fell from her face, splashing into the waves beneath her. She hardly noticed.

Before her, the water began to bubble, and two hollow eyes appeared just below the surface. Her gaze snapped down to match them. Then, slowly, a large serpentine head crested the water and rested on the sand next to her. It was covered with rotting flesh, and its spear-like teeth could be seen in its skull. Ashyla glanced at the creature next to her and placed her hand upon it. A nurturing hand. A mother's hand.

Then, there was the great sound of flapping wings, followed by a *thud* as the mighty dracolich, now regenerated from its battle at Forthold, landed on her other side. It also lowered its head into the sand. And, as with the sea serpent, she placed her hand upon its majestic brow.

There they rested for a long moment — there was never enough time with her children, and too much of that had been robbed of her already. Together, they were undisturbed and at peace. Except for the tears still raining from Ashyla's eyes. She just couldn't stop, haunted by the vision in her head. She knew what she had to do. She knew what she *wanted* to do. And it was eating her alive. These two were all she had left. But this is what she created her children for, was it not? To destroy and kill? To avenge her garden? She forced them to be the tools of her wrath.

But what mother wants to raise her babies to become murderers, even if it is justified?

She knew that they didn't deserve this fate. They were beautiful and innocent. But it was the fate she was blessing them with — nay, cursing them with — nonetheless.

"I am sorry, my wonderful children, please understand ... You must do this for me."

Together, they both gave a low, rumbling growl as if accepting her apology.

"Soon, you will have more siblings. Soon, you will have a peaceful home. Soon ... I shall make you again, I promise."

Her children *purred* again, softly, and nestled up against her like two oversized kittens. It broke her heart.

But what choice did she have? With their sacrifices and valiance, she would have all the children she could ever want, and nothing — not that bastard Sergarious or his fucking Demigods or his infectious races — would ever disturb them again. But was it worth the cost?

She already knew her answer.

"Soon, my precious babies, we shall have our retribution."

There would be no going back.

Her tears continued to fall.

About the Author

Daniel Whitman is an engineer who, on the side, loves to dabble in the realm of fantasy. He grew up reading fantasy books and playing games such as Dungeons & Dragons, Magic: The Gathering, and Diablo. Now, he is taking this childhood passion and crafting his own stories.

Daniel's passion is for dark fantasy, with a special interest in morally complex characters and heart-wrenching moments. He wrote his first book, *A Land in Shadow*, while he was still in high school. Now, in graduate school, he wrote his second book, and the continuation of the series, *A Resurgence of Hope*. Moving forward, he is determined to continue the adventures of both engineering and writing!